THE TOMB

THE TOMB

THE TOMB

BY

F. PAUL WILSON

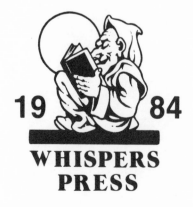

19 84

**WHISPERS
PRESS**

ISBN#: 0-918372-11-9 (Trade edition)
ISBN#: 0-918372-12-7 (Signed edition)

FIRST EDITION

1   2   3   4   5   6   7   8   9   10

Book Design by Stuart David Schiff

ACKNOWLEDGMENTS

Abe's neon sign originally appeared in *The Weapon Shops of Isher* by A.E. van Vogt,© 1951 by A.E. van Vogt. Used here by permission of the author.

Knowingly and unknowingly, the following individuals have aided me in ways large and small during the course of writing this book: Betsy Bang and Molly Garrett Bang *(The Demons of Rajpur),* Richard Collier *(The Great Indian Rebellion),* Larry Collins and Dominique LaPierre *(Freedom at Midnight),* Harlan Ellison (with the last line of "Croatoan"), Ken Follett, L. Neil Smith, Steven Spruill, Al Zuckerman; and most of all, the old-time tellers of Weird Menace/ Yellow Peril Tales.

to my own Vickys: Jennifer and Meggan

THE TOMB

CHAPTER ONE

Thursday, August 2, 198-

1.

Repairman Jack awoke with light in his eyes, white noise in his ears, and an ache in his back.

He had fallen asleep on the couch in the spare bedroom where he kept his Betamax and projection TV. He turned his head toward the set. A nervous tweed pattern buzzed around on the six-foot screen while the air conditioner in the right half of the double window beside it worked full blast to keep the room at seventy.

He got to his feet with a groan and shut off the TV projector. The hiss of white noise stopped. He leaned over and touched his toes, then straightened and rotated his lower spine. His back was killing him. That couch was made for sitting, not sleeping.

He stepped to the Betamax and ejected the tape. He had fallen asleep during the closing credits of the 1931 *Frankenstein,* part one of Repairman Jack's unofficial James Whale Festival.

Poor Henry Frankenstein, he thought, slipping the cassette into its box. *Despite all evidence to the contrary, despite what everyone around him thought, Henry had been sure he was sane.*

Jack located the proper slot in the cassette rack on the wall, shoved *Frankenstein* in and pulled out its neighbor: *Bride of Frankenstein,* part two of his private James Whale Festival.

A glance out the window revealed the usual vista of sandy shore, still blue ocean and supine sunbathers. He was tired of the view.

1

THE TOMB

Especially since some of the bricks had started showing through. It had been three years since he'd had the scene painted on the blank wall facing the windows of this and the other bedroom. Long enough. The beach scene no longer interested him. Perhaps a rain forest mural would be better. With lots of birds and reptiles and animals hiding in the foliage. Yes ... a rain forest. He filed the thought away. He'd have to keep an eye out for someone who could do the job justice.

The phone began ringing in the front room. Who that could be? He'd changed his number a couple of months ago. Only a few people had it. He didn't bother to lift the receiver. The answerphone would take care of that. He heard a click, heard his own voice start his standard salutation:

"Pinocchio Productions ... I'm not in right now, but if you'll—"

A woman's voice broke in over his own, her tone impatient. "Pick up if you're there, Jack. Otherwise I'll call back later."

Gia!

Jack nearly tripped over his own feet in his haste to reach the phone. He turned off the answerphone with one hand and picked up the receiver with the other.

"Gia? That you?"

"Yes, it's me." Her voice was flat, almost resentful.

"God! It's been a long time!" Two months. Forever. He had to sit down. "I'm so glad you called."

"It's not what you think, Jack."

"What do you mean?"

"I'm not calling for myself. If it were up to me I wouldn't be calling at all. But Nellie asked me to."

His jubilation faded, but he kept talking. "Who's Nellie?" He drew a blank on the name.

"Nellie Paton. You must remember Nellie and Grace—the two English ladies?"

"Oh, yeah. How could I forget? They introduced us."

"I've managed to forgive them."

Jack let that go by without comment. "What's the problem?"

"Grace has disappeared. She hasn't been seen since she went to bed Monday night."

He remembered Grace Westphalen: a very prim and proper Englishwoman pushing seventy. Not the eloping sort.

"Have the police—?"

THE TOMB

"Of course. But Nellie wanted me to call you to see if you'd help. So I'm calling."

"Does she want me to come over?"

"Yes. If you will."

"Will you be there?"

She gave an exasperated sigh. "Yes. Are you coming or not?"

"I'm on my way."

"Better wait. The patrolmen who were here said a detective from the department would be coming by this morning."

"Oh." That wasn't good.

"I *thought* that might slow you up."

She didn't have to sound so smug about it. "I'll be there after lunch."

"You know the address?"

"I know it's a yellow townhouse on Sutton Square. There's only one."

"I'll tell her to expect you."

And then she hung up.

Jack tossed the receiver in his hand, cradled it on the answerphone again and flipped the switch to On.

He was going to see Gia today. She had called him. She hadn't been friendly, and she had said she was calling for someone else—but she had called. That was more than she had done since she had walked out. He couldn't help feeling good.

He strolled through his third-floor apartment's front room which served as living room and dining room. He found the room immensely comfortable, but few visitors shared his enthusiasm. His best friend, Abe Grossman, had, in one of his more generous moods, described the room as "claustrophobic." When Abe was feeling grumpy he said it made the Addams Family house look like it had been decorated by Bauhaus.

Old movie posters covered the walls along with bric-a-brac shelves loaded with the "neat stuff" Jack continually picked up in forgotten junk stores during his wanderings through the city. He wound his way through a collection of old Victorian golden oak furniture that left little room for anything else. There was a seven-foot hutch, intricately carved, a fold-out secretary, a sagging, high-backed sofa, a massive claw-foot dining table, two end tables whose legs each ended in a bird's foot clasping a crystal sphere, and his favorite, a big, wing-back chair.

3

THE TOMB

He reached the bathroom and started the hated morning ritual of shaving. As he ran the Trac II over his cheeks and throat he again considered the idea of a beard. He didn't have a bad face. Brown eyes, dark brown hair growing perhaps a little too low on his forehead. A nose neither too big nor too small. He smiled at himself in the mirror. Not an altogether hideous grimace—what they used to call a shit-eating grin. The teeth could have been whiter and straighter, and the lips were on the thin side, but not a bad smile. An inoffensive face. As an added bonus, there was a wiry, well-muscled, five-eleven frame that went along with the face at no extra charge.

So what's not to like?

His smile faltered.

Ask Gia. She seems to think she knows what's not to like.

But all that was going to change starting today.

After a quick shower, he dressed and downed a couple of bowls of Cocoa Puffs, then strapped on his ankle holster and slipped the world's smallest .45, a Semmerling skeleton model LM-4, into it. He knew the holster was going to be hot against his leg, but he never went out unarmed. His peace of mind would compensate for any physical discomfort.

He checked the peephole in the front door, then twisted the central knob, retracting the four bolts at the top, bottom, and both sides. The heat in the third floor hall slammed against him at the threshhold. He was wearing Levi's and a lightweight short-sleeve shirt. He was glad he had skipped the undershirt. Already the humidity in the hall was worming its way into his clothes and oozing over his skin as he headed down to the street.

Jack stood on the front steps for a moment. Sunlight glared sullenly through the haze over the roof of the Museum of Natural History far down the street to his right. The wet air hung motionless above the pavement. He could see it, smell it, taste it—and it looked, smelled, and tasted dirty. Dust, soot, and lint laced with carbon monoxide, with perhaps a hint of rancid butter from the garbage can around the corner in the alley.

Ah! The Upper West Side in August.

He ambled down to the sidewalk and walked west along the row of brownstones that lined his street to the phone booth on the corner. Not a booth, actually; an open chrome and plastic crate on a pedestal. At least it was still in one piece. At regular intervals someone yanked out its receiver, leaving multicolored strands of wire dangling

4

from the socket like nerves from an amputated-limb stump. At other times someone would take the time and effort to jam a small wedge of paper into the coin slot, or the tips of toothpicks into the tiny spaces between the pushbuttons and the facing. He never ceased to be amazed by the strange hobbies of some of his fellow New Yorkers.

He dialed his office number and sounded his beeper into the mouthpiece. A recorded voice—not Jack's—came over the wire with the familiar message:

"This is Repairman Jack. I'm out on a call now, but when you hear the tone, leave your name and number and give me a brief idea of the nature of your problem. I'll get back to you as soon as possible."

There was a tone and then a woman's voice talking about a problem with the timer on her dryer. Another beep and a man was looking for some free information on how to fix a blender. Jack ignored the numbers they gave; he had no intention of calling them back. But how did they get his number? He had restricted his name to the white pages—with an incorrect street address, naturally—to cut down on appliance repair calls, but people managed to find him anyway.

The third and last voice was unique: smooth in tone, the words clipped, rapid, tinged with Britain, but definitely not British. Jack knew a couple of Pakistanis who sounded like that. The man was obviously upset, and stumbled over his words.

"Mr. Jack . . . my mother—my grandmother—was beaten terribly last night. I must speak to you immediately. It is terribly important." He gave his name and a number where he could be reached.

That was one call Jack would return, even though he was going to have to turn the man down. He intended to devote all his time to Gia's problem. And to Gia. This might be his last chance with her.

He punched in the number. The clipped voice answered in the middle of the second ring.

"Mr. Bahkti? This is Repairman Jack. You called my office during the night and—"

Mr. Bahkti was suddenly very guarded. "This is not the same voice on the answering machine."

Sharp, Jack thought. The voice on the machine belonged to Abe Grossman. Jack never used his own voice on the office phone. But most people didn't spot that.

"An old tape," Jack told him.

"Ahhh. Well, then. I must see you immediately, Mr. Jack. It is a

5

matter of the utmost importance. A matter of life and death."

"I don't know, Mr. Bahkti, I—"

"You *must*! There can be no refusal!" A new note had crept in. This was not a man used to being refused. The tone was one that never set well with Jack.

"You don't understand. My time is already taken up with other—"

"Mr. Jack! Are the other matters crucial to a woman's life? Can they not be put aside for even a short while? My ... grandmother was mercilessly beaten on the streets of your city. She needs help that I cannot give her. So I've come to you."

Jack knew what Mr. Bahkti was up to. He thought he was pushing Jack's buttons. Jack mildly resented it, but he was used to it and decided to hear him out anyway.

Bahkti had already launched into his narrative.

"Her car—an American car, I might add—broke down last night. And when she—"

"Save it for later," Jack told him, happy to be the one doing the cutting-off for a change.

"You will meet me at the hospital? She is in St. Clare's—"

"No. Our first meeting will be where I say. I meet all customers on my home turf. No exceptions."

"Very well," Bahkti said with a minimum of grace. "But we must meet very soon. There is so little time."

Jack gave him the address of Julio's Bar two blocks uptown from where he stood. He checked his watch. "It's just shy of ten now. Be there at ten-thirty sharp."

"Half an hour? I don't know if I can be there by then!"

Fine! Jack liked to give customers as little time as possible to prepare for their first meeting.

"Ten-thirty. You've got ten minutes grace. Any later and I'll be gone."

"Ten-thirty," Mr. Bahkti said, and hung up.

That annoyed Jack. He had wanted to hang up first.

He walked north on Columbus Avenue, keeping to the shade on the right. It was opening time for some of the shops, but most had been going strong for hours.

Julio's was open. But then, Julio's rarely closed. Jack knew the first customers wandered in minutes after Julio unlocked at six in the morning. Some were just getting off their shift and stopped by for a beer, a hard-boiled egg, and a soft seat; others stood at the bar and

THE TOMB

downed a quick bracer before starting the day's work. And still others spent the better part of every day in the cool darkness.

"Jacko!" Julio cried from behind the bar. He was standing up but only his head and the top half of his chest were visible.

They didn't shake hands. They knew each other too well and saw each other too often for that. They had been friends for many years, ever since the time Julio began to suspect that his sister Rosa was getting punched around by her husband. It had been a delicate matter. Jack had fixed it for him. Since then the little man had screened Jack's customers. For Julio possessed a talent, a nose, a sixth sense of sorts for spotting members of officialdom. Much of Jack's energy was devoted to avoiding such people; his way of life depended on it. And, too, in Jack's line of work he very often found it necessary to make other people angry in the course of serving a customer's interests. Julio also kept an eye out for angry people.

So far, Julio had never failed him.

"Beer or business?"

"Before noon? What do you think?"

The remark earned Jack a brief dirty look from a sweaty old codger nursing a boilermaker.

Julio came out from behind the bar and followed Jack to a rear booth, drying his hands on a towel as he swaggered along. A daily regime with free weights and gymnastics had earned him thickly muscled arms and shoulders. His hair was wavy and heavily oiled, his skin swarthy, his mustache a pencil line along his upper lip.

"How many and when?"

"One. Ten-thirty." Jack slipped into the last booth and sat with a clear view of the door. The rear exit was two steps away. "Name's Bahkti. Sounds like he's from Pakistan or someplace around there."

"A man of color."

"More color than you, no doubt."

"Gotcha. Coffee?"

"Sure."

Jack thought about seeing Gia later today. A nice thought. They'd meet, they'd touch, and Gia would remember what they'd had, and maybe ... just maybe ... she'd realize that he wasn't such a bad guy after all. He began whistling through his teeth. Julio gave him a strange look as he returned with a coffee pot, a cup, and the morning's *Daily News*.

"How come you're in such a good mood?"

THE TOMB

"Why not?"

"You been a grouch for months now, man."

Jack hadn't realized it had been so obvious. "Personal."

Julio shrugged and poured him a cup of coffee. Jack sipped it black while he waited. He never liked first meetings with a customer. There was always a chance he wasn't a customer but somebody with a score to settle. He got up and checked the exit door to make sure it was unlocked.

Two Con Ed workers came in for a coffee break. They took their coffee clear and golden with a foamy cap, poured into pilsner glasses as they watched the TV over the bar. Phil Donahue was interviewing three transvestite grammar-school teachers; everyone on the screen, including Donahue, had green hair and pumpkin-colored complexions. Julio served the Con Ed men a second round, then came out from behind the bar and took a seat by the door.

Jack glanced at the paper. "Where Are the Winos?" was the headline. The press was getting lots of mileage out of the rapid and mysterious dwindling of the city's derelict population during the past few months.

At ten-thirty-two, Mr. Bahkti came in. No doubt it was him. He wore a white turban and a navy blue Nehru-type tunic. His dark skin seemed to blend into his clothes. For an instant after the door swung shut behind him, all Jack could see was a turban floating in the air at the other end of the dim tavern.

Julio approached him immediately. Words were exchanged and Jack noted the newcomer flinch away as Julio leaned against him. He seemed angry as Julio walked toward Jack with an elaborate shrug.

"He's clean," he said as he came back to Jack's booth. "Clean but weird."

"How do you read him?"

"That's jus' it—I don' read him. He's bottled up real tight. Nothing at all out of that guy. Nothing but creeps."

"What?"

"Something 'bout him gives me the creeps, man. Wouldn't want to get on his wrong side. You better be sure you can make him happy before you take him on."

Jack drummed his fingers on the table. Julio's reaction made him uneasy. The little man was all macho and braggadocio. He must have sensed something pretty unsettling about Mr. Bahkti to have even mentioned it.

THE TOMB

"What'd you do to get him riled up?" Jack asked.

"Nothing special. He just got real ticked off when I gave him my 'accidental frisk.' Didn't like that one bit. Do I send him back, or you wanna take off?"

Jack hesitated, toying with the idea of getting out now. After all, he probably was going to have to turn the man down anyway. But he had agreed to meet him, and the guy had arrived on time.

"Send him back and let's get this over with."

Julio waved Bahkti toward the booth and headed back to his place behind the bar.

Bahkti strolled toward Jack with a smooth, gliding gait that reeked of confidence and self-assurance. He was halfway down the aisle when Jack realized with a start that his left arm was missing at the shoulder. But there was no pinned-up sleeve—the jacket had been tailored without a left sleeve. He was a tall man—six-three, Jack guessed—lean but sturdy. Well into his forties, maybe fifty. The nose was long; he wore a sculptured beard, neatly trimmed to a point at the chin. What could be seen of his mouth was wide and thin-lipped. The whites of his deep walnut eyes almost glowed in the darkness of his face, reminding Jack of John Barrymore in *Svengali*.

He stopped at the edge of the facing banquette and looked down at Jack, taking his measure just as Jack was taking his.

2.

Kusum Bahkti did not like this place called Julio's, stinking as it did of grilled beef and liquor, and peopled with the lower castes. Certainly one of the foulest locations he had had the misfortune to visit in this foul city. He was probably polluting his karma merely by standing here.

And surely this very average-looking mid-thirtyish man sitting before him was not the one he was looking for. He looked like any American's brother, anyone's son, someone you would pass anywhere in this city and never notice. He looked too normal, too ordinary, too everyday to supply the services Kusum had been told about.

If I were home . . .

Yes. If he were home in Bengal, in Calcutta, he would have everything under control. A thousand men would be combing the city for the transgressor. He would be found, and he would wail and

9

curse the hour of his birth before being sent on to another life. But here in America Kusum was reduced to an impotent supplicant standing before this stranger, asking for help. It made him sick.

"Are you the one?" he asked.

"Depends on who you're looking for," the man said.

Kusum noted the difficulty the American was having trying to keep his eyes off his truncated left shoulder.

"He calls himself Repairman Jack."

The man spread his hands. "Here I am."

This couldn't be him. "Perhaps I have made a mistake."

"Perhaps so," said the American. He seemed preoccupied, not the least bit interested in Kusum or what problem he might have.

Kusum turned to go, deciding he was constitutionally incapable of asking the help of a stranger, especially this stranger, then changed his mind. By Kali, he had no choice!

He sat down across the table from Repairman Jack. "I am Kusum Bahkti."

"Jack Nelson." The American proferred his right hand.

Kusum could not bring himself to grasp it, yet he did not want to insult this man. He needed him.

"Mr. Nelson—"

"Jack, please."

"Very well . . . Jack." He was uncomfortable with such informality upon meeting. "Your pardon. I dislike to be touched. An Eastern prejudice."

Jack glanced at his hand, as if inspecting it for dirt.

"I do not wish to offend—"

"Forget it. Who gave you my number?"

"Time is short . . . Jack"—it took conscious effort to use that first name—"and I must insist—"

"I always insist on knowing where the customer came from. Who?"

"Very well: Mr. Burkes at the U.K. Mission to the United Nations." Burkes had answered Kusum's frantic call this morning and had told him how well this Jack fellow had handled a very dangerous and delicate problem for the U.K. Mission during the Falklands crisis.

Jack nodded. "I know Burkes. You with the U.N.?"

Kusum knotted his fist and managed to tolerate the interrogation. "Yes."

"And I suppose you Pakistani delegates are pretty tight with the

THE TOMB

British."

Kusum felt as if he had been slapped in the face. He half-started from his seat. "Do you insult me? I am not one of those Moslem—!" He caught himself. Probably an innocent error. Americans were ignorant of the most basic information. "I am from Bengal, a member of the Indian Delegation. I am a Hindu. Pakistan, which used to be the Punjab region of India, is a Moslem country."

The distinction appeared to be completely lost on Jack.

"Whatever. Most of what I know about India I learned from watching *Gunga Din* about a hundred times. So tell me about your grandmother."

Kusum was momentarily baffled. Wasn't "Gunga Din" a poem? How did one watch a poem? He set his confusion aside.

"Understand," he said, absently brushing at a fly that had taken a liking to his face, "that if this were my own country I would resolve the matter in my own fashion."

"So you told me on the phone. Where is she now."

"In St. Clare's hospital on West Fif—"

"I know where it is. What happened to her?"

"Her car broke down in the early hours of this morning. While her driver went to find a taxicab for her, she foolishly got out of the car. She was assaulted and beaten. If a police car hadn't come by, she would have been killed."

"Happens all the time, I'm afraid."

A callous remark, ostensibly that of a city-dweller saving his pity for personal friends who became victims. But in the eyes Kusum detected a flash of emotion that told him perhaps this man could be reached.

"Yes, much to the shame of your city."

"No one ever gets mugged on the streets of Bombay or Calcutta?"

Kusum shrugged and brushed again at the fly. "What takes place between members of the lower castes is of no importance. In my homeland even the most desperate street hoodlum would think many times before daring to lay a finger on one of my grandmother's caste."

Something in this remark seemed to annoy Jack. "Ain't democracy wonderful," the American said with a sour expression.

Kusum frowned, concealing his desperation. This was not going to work. There seemed to be instinctive antagonism between him and this Repairman Jack.

11

THE TOMB

"I believe I have made a mistake. Mr. Burkes recommended you very highly, but I do not think you are capable of handling this particular task. Your attitude is most disrespectful—"

"What can you expect from a guy who grew up watching Bugs Bunny cartoons?"

"—and you do not appear to have the physical resources to accomplish what I have in mind."

Jack smiled, as if used to this reaction. His elbows were on the table, his hands folded in front of him. Without the slightest hint of warning, his right hand blurred across the table towards Kusum's face. Kusum steeled himself for the blow and prepared to lash out with his feet.

The blow never landed. Jack's hand passed within a millimeter of Kusum's face and snatched the fly out of the air in front of his nose. Jack went to a nearby door and released the insect into the fetid air of a back alley.

Fast, Kusum thought. Extremely fast. And what was even more important: He didn't kill the fly. Perhaps this was the man after all.

3.

Jack returned to his seat and studied the Indian. To his credit, Kusum hadn't flinched. Either his reflexes were extremely slow, or he had something akin to copper wire for nerves. Jack figured Kusum's reflexes to be pretty good.

Score one for each of us, he thought. He wondered how Kusum had lost that arm.

"The point is probably moot," Jack said. "Finding a particular mugger in this city is like poking at a hornets' nest to find the one that bit you. If she saw enough of him to identify a mug shot, she should go to the police and—"

"No police!" Kusum said quickly.

Those were the very two words Jack was waiting to hear. If the police were involved, Jack would not be.

"They may well be successful eventually," Kusum went on, "but they take much too long. This is a matter of the utmost urgency. My grandmother is dying. That is why I've gone outside official channels."

"I don't understand this whole thing."

"Her necklace was stolen. It's a priceless heirloom. She must have

12

THE TOMB

it back."

"But you said she's dying—"

"Before she dies! She must have it back *before* she dies!"

"Impossible. I can't ..." U.N. diplomat or not, the guy was obviously a nut. No use trying to explain how hard it would be just to find the mugger. After that, to learn the name of his fence, find that fence, and then hope that he hadn't already removed whatever precious stones were in the necklace and melted down the settings, was simply beyond the wildest possibility. "It can't be done."

"You must do it! The man must be found. She scratched him across the eyes. There must be a way he can be traced!"

"That's police work."

"The police will take too long! It must be returned tonight!"

"I can't."

"You *must!*"

"The chances against finding that necklace are—"

"Try! *Please!*"

Kusum's voice cracked on that last word, as if he had dragged it kicking and screaming from an unused part of his soul. Jack sensed how much it cost the Indian to say it. Here was an inordinately proud man begging him for help. He was moved.

"All right. I'll do this: Let me talk to your grandmother. Let me see what I've got to work with."

"That will not be necessary."

"Of course it will be necessary. She's the only one who knows what he looks like." Was he trying to keep him away from his grandmother?

Kusum looked uncomfortable. "She's quite distraught. Incoherent. She raves. I do not wish to expose her to a stranger."

Jack said nothing. He merely stared at Kusum and waited. Finally the Indian relented.

"I shall take you there immediately."

Jack allowed Kusum to lead him out the front door. As he left, he waved to Julio who was setting up his infamous sign, Free Lunch: $2.50.

They caught a taxi immediately on Columbus Avenue and headed downtown.

"About my fee," Jack said once they had settled into the back of the cab.

A small, superior smile curled Kusum's thin lips.

13

THE TOMB

"Money? Are you not a defender of the downtrodden, a crusader for justice?"

"Justice doesn't pay the bills. My landlord prefers cash. So do I."

"Ah! A Capitalist!"

If that was supposed to rile Jack, it did not.

"If you don't mind, I prefer to be called a Capitalist Swine or, at the very least, a Capitalist Running-dog. Plain old Capitalist has so little color. I hope Burkes didn't let you think I do this out of the goodness of my heart."

"No. He mentioned your fee for the U.K. Mission. A rather steep one. And in cash."

"I don't take checks or charges, and I don't take physical danger lightly, especially when I could be on the receiving end."

"Then here is my offer . . . Jack: Just for trying, I will pay you in advance half of what the British paid you last year. If you return the necklace to my grandmother before she dies, I will pay you the other half."

This was going to be hard to turn down. The job for the U.K. Mission had involved terrorist threats. It had been complex, time-consuming, and very dicey at times. Normally he would have asked Kusum for only a fraction of that amount. But Kusum seemed quite willing and able to pay the full fee. And if Jack managed to bring that necklace back, it would be a bonafide miracle and he would deserve every penny of it.

"Sounds fair to me," he said without missing a beat. "*If* I take the job."

4.

Jack followed Kusum through the halls of St. Clare's until they came to a private room where a private-duty nurse hovered near the bed. The room was dark—curtains pulled, only a small lamp in a far corner throwing dim light across the bed. The lady in the bed was very old. White hair framed a dark face that was a mass of wrinkles; gnarled hands clutched at the sheet across her chest. Fear filled her eyes. Her ragged breathing and the hum of the blower by the window were the only sounds in the room.

Jack stood at the foot of the bed and felt the familiar tingle of rage spreading through his chest and limbs. With all he had seen, all he had done, he had yet to learn how to keep from taking something like

14

this personally. An old woman, helpless, beaten up. It made him want to break something.

"Ask her what he looked like."

Kusum rattled off something in Indian from beside the head of the bed. The woman replied in kind, slowly, painfully, in a hoarse, rasping voice.

"She says he looked like you, but younger," Kusum said, "and with lighter hair."

"Short or long?"

Another exchange, then: "Short. Very short."

So: it was a young white, either a GI on leave or someone still into the punk look.

"Anything else?"

As the woman replied, she raked the air with clawed fingers.

"His eyes," Kusum said. "She scratched him across his left eye before she was knocked unconscious."

Good for you, Granny.

Jack smiled reassuringly at the old lady, then turned to Kusum. "I'll see you out in the hall." He didn't want to talk in front of the private nurse.

As he stood outside the door, Jack glanced at the nurses' station and thought he saw a familiar face. He walked over for a closer look at the Junoesque blonde—every man's fantasy nurse—writing in a chart. Yes—it was Marta. They had had a thing a few years back in the days before Gia.

She greeted him with a friendly kiss and a hug, and they talked about old times for a while. Then Jack asked her about Mrs. Bahkti.

"Fading fast," Marta said. "She's gotten visibly worse since I came on. She'll probably last out this shift, but I'll be surprised if she's here tomorrow. You know her?"

"I'll be doing some work for her grandson." As with most people Jack knew socially—and there weren't many—Marta was under the impression that he was a "security consultant." He saw Kusum come out into the hall. "There he is now. See you later."

Jack led Kusum to a window at the end of the hall where they were out of earshot of patients and hospital personnel.

"All right," he told him. "I'll give it a try. But I make no promises other than to do my best." Jack had decided he wanted to catch up with this creep.

Kusum exhaled and muttered what sounded like a small prayer.

THE TOMB

"No more can be asked of any man. But if you cannot find the necklace by tomorrow morning, it will be too late. After that, the necklace will be of secondary importance. But I still want you to keep looking for the assailant. And when you find him, I want you to kill him."

Jack tightened inside but smiled and shook his head. This guy thought he was some sort of hit man.

"I don't do that."

Kusum's eyes said he didn't believe him.

"Very well. Instead, you will bring him to me and I will—"

"I will work for you until tomorrow morning," Jack said. "I'll give you my best shot till then. After that, you're on your own."

Anger flitted across Kusum's face. *Not used to having someone say no to you, are you?* Jack thought.

"When will you start?"

"Tonight."

Kusum reached inside his tunic and brought out a thick envelope. "Here is half of the payment. I will wait here with the other half should you return with the necklace tonight."

Feeling more than a twinge of guilt at taking so much money on such a hopeless venture, Jack nevertheless folded the envelope and stuffed it in his left rear pocket.

"I will pay you ten thousand extra if you kill him," Kusum added.

Jack laughed to keep the mood light but shook his head again. "Uh-uh. But one more thing: Don't you think it would help if I knew what the necklace looked like?"

"Of course!" Kusum opened the collar of his tunic to reveal a heavy chain perhaps fifteen inches long. Its links were crescent-shaped, each embossed with strange-looking script. Centered side-by-side on the necklace were two elliptical, bright yellow, topazlike stones with black centers.

Jack held his hand out but Kusum shook his head.

"Every member of my family wears a necklace like this—it is never removed. And so it is very important that my grandmother's be returned to her."

Jack studied the necklace. It disturbed him. He could not say why, but deep in his bowels and along the middle of his back a primitive sensation raised warning. The two stones looked like eyes. The metal was silvery, but not silver.

"What's it made of?"

16

THE TOMB

"Iron."

Jack looked closer. Yes, there was a hint of rust along the edges of a couple of the links.

"Who'd want an iron necklace?"

"A fool who thought it was silver."

Jack nodded. For the first time since talking to Kusum this morning, he felt there might be a slim—very slim—chance of recovering the necklace. A piece of silver jewelry would be fenced by now and either hidden away or melted down into a neat little ingot. But an heirloom like this, with no intrinsic value . . .

"Here is a picture," Kusum said, handing over a polaroid of the necklace. "I have a few friends searching the pawnshops of your city looking for it."

"How long has she got?" he asked.

Kusum slowly closed his collar. His expression was grim.

"Twelve hours, the doctors say. Perhaps fifteen."

Great. Maybe I can find Judge Crater by then, too.

"Where can I reach you?"

"Here. You *will* look for it, won't you?" Kusum's dark brown eyes bored into his. He seemed to be staring at the rear wall of Jack's brain.

"I said I would."

"And I believe you. Bring the necklace to me as soon as you find it."

"Sure. As soon as I find it."

Sure. He walked away wondering why he had agreed to help a stranger when Gia's aunt needed him. Same old story—Jack the sucker.

Damn!

5.

Once back in the darkened hospital room, Kusum returned immediately to the bedside and pulled up a chair. He grasped the withered hand that lay atop the covers and studied it. The skin was cool, dry, papery. There seemed to be no tissue other than bone under the skin. And no strength at all.

A great sadness filled him.

Kusum looked up and saw the plea in her eyes. And the fear. He did his best to hide his own fear.

"Kusum," she said in Bengali, her voice painfully weak. "I'm

17

THE TOMB

dying."

He knew that. And it was tearing him up inside.

"The American will get it back for you," he said softly. "I've been told he's very good."

Burkes had said he was "incredibly good." Kusum hated all Britishers on principle, but had to admit Burkes was no fool. But did it matter what Burkes had said? It was an impossible task. Jack had been honest enough to say so. But Kusum had to try *something*! Even with the foreknowledge of certain failure, he had to try!

He balled his only hand into a fist. Why did this have to happen? And now, of all times? How he despised this country and its empty people! Almost as much as the British. But this Jack was different. He was not a mass of jumbled fragments like his fellow Americans. Kusum had sensed a oneness within him. Repairman Jack did not come cheaply, but the money meant nothing. Only the knowledge that someone was out there searching gave him solace.

"He'll get it back for you," he said, patting the limp hand.

She seemed not to have heard.

"I'm dying," she said.

6.

The money was a nagging pressure against his left buttock as Jack walked the half block west to Tenth Avenue and turned downtown. His hand kept straying back to the pocket; he repeatedly hooked a thumb in and out of it to make sure the envelope was still there. The problem now was what to do with the money. It was times like this that almost made him wish he had a bank account. But the bank folks insisted on a Social Security number from anyone who opened an account.

He sighed to himself. That was one of the major drawbacks of living between the lines. If you didn't have an SSN, you were barred from countless things. You couldn't hold a regular job, couldn't buy or sell stock, couldn't take out a loan, couldn't own a home, couldn't even complete a Blue Shield form. The list went on and on.

His thumb casually hooked in his left rear pocket, Jack stopped in front of a rundown office building. He rented a ten by twelve cubicle here—the smallest he could find. He had never met the agent, nor anyone else connected with the office. He intended to keep it that way.

18

THE TOMB

He took the creaking Otis with the penny-studded floor up to 4 and stepped off. The hall was empty. Jack's office was 412. He walked past the door twice before pulling out the key and quickly letting himself in.

It always smelled the same: dry and dusty. The floors and window-sills were layered with dust. Dust bunnies clogged the corners. An upper corner of the only window was spanned by an abandoned spider web—out of business.

There was no furniture. The dull expanse of floor was broken only by the half dozen or so envelopes that had been shoved through the mail slot, and by a vinyl IBM-typewriter cover and the wires that ran from it to the telephone and electrical outlets in the wall on the right.

Jack picked up the mail. Three were bills, all addressed to Jack Finch in care of this office. The rest belonged to Occupant. He next went over to the typewriter cover and lifted it. The phone and the answerphone beneath appeared to be in good shape. Even as he squatted over it, the machine clicked on and he heard Abe's voice give the familiar salutation in the name of Repairman Jack, followed by a man complaining of an electric dryer that wasn't drying.

He replaced the cover and went back to the door. A quick peek showed two secretaries from the shoe importing firm at the other end of the hall standing by the elevator. Jack waited until the door slid shut after them. He locked his office, then ducked for the stairway. His cheeks puffed with relief as he started down the worn steps. He hated coming here and made a point of doing so at rare, random intervals at odd times of the day. He did not want his face in any way connected with Repairman Jack; but there were bills to be paid, bills that he didn't want delivered to his apartment. And popping into the office at random hours of the day or night seemed safer than having a post office box.

Most likely none of it was necessary. Most likely no one was looking to get even with Repairman Jack. He was always careful to stay far in the background when he fixed things. Only his clients ever saw him.

But there was always a chance. And as long as that chance existed, he made certain he was very hard to find.

Thumb hooked again into that important pocket, Jack moved into the growing lunch hour crush, luxuriating in the anonymity of the crowd. He turned east on Forty-second and strolled up to the brick front post office between Eighth and Ninth Avenues. There he purchased three money orders—two in negligible amounts for the

19

THE TOMB

phone and electric bills, and the third for a figure he considered preposterous considering the square footage of office space he was renting. He signed all three Jack Finch and mailed them off. As he was leaving, it occurred to him that while he had the cash, he might as well pay the rent on his apartment, too. He went back and purchased a fourth money order which he made out to his landlord. This one he signed Jack Berger.

Then it was a short walk past an art deco building to the side of the Port Authority Building, then across Eighth Avenue and he was in Sleazeville, U.S.A.—Times Square and environs. A never-ending freak show that would put Todd Browning to shame. Jack never passed up an opportunity to stroll through the area. He was a people-watcher and nowhere was there such a unique variety of *Homo sapiens low-lificus* as in Times Square.

He walked the next block under an almost continuous canopy of theatre marquees. Exploitation Row—films here were either triple-X sex, kung-fu imports, or psycho-with-a-knife splatter films from what Jack liked to call the Julia Childs slice-and-dice school of movie-making. Stuck in between were hole-in-the-wall porn shops, stairways to "modeling studios" and dance halls, the ubiquitous Nedicks and Orange Julius stands, and sundry stores perpetually on the verge of bankruptcy—or so their window signs claimed. Mingling among the patrons of these venerable establishments were hookers and derelicts of both sexes, plus an incredible array of epicene creatures who had probably looked like boys when they were little.

He crossed Broadway behind the building that had given the Square its name, then turned uptown on Seventh Avenue. Here the porn shops were slightly larger, the movie ticket prices higher, and the fast food of a better grade, such as Steak & Brew and Wienerwald. Set up on tables along the curb were chess and backgammon boards where a couple of guys would play anyone for a buck. Farther down were three-card monte setups on cardboard boxes. Pushcarts sold shish-kebab, Sabarett hot dogs, dried fruits and nuts, giant pretzels, and freshly-squeezed orange juice. The odors mingled in the air with the sounds and sights. All the record stores along Seventh were pushing the latest new wave group, Polio, playing cuts from their debut album onto the sidewalk. Jack stood waiting for the green at Forty-sixth next to a Puerto Rican with a giant cassette box on his shoulder blasting salsa at a volume that would probably cause sterility in most small mammals, while girls wearing tube tops that left their

THE TOMB

midriffs bare and satin gym shorts that left a smooth pink crescent of buttock protruding from each leg hole rollerskated through the traffic with tiny headphones on their ears and Sony Walkmans belted to their waists.

Standing directly in the middle of the flow was a big blind Black with a sign on his chest, a dog at his feet, and a cup in his hand. Jack threw some loose change into the cup as he slipped by. Farther on he passed the 'Frisco Theatre which was once again showing its favorite double feature: *Deep Throat* and *The Devil in Miss Jones.*

There was something about New York that got to Jack. He loved its sleaze, its color, the glory and crassness of its architecture. He couldn't imagine living anywhere else.

Upon reaching the Fifties, he turned east until he came to Municipal Coins. He stopped in front and glanced briefly at the low-priced junk under the red and white We Buy Gold sign in the window—proof sets, Confederate paper and the like—then went in.

Monte spotted him right away.

"Mr. O'Neil! How are you!"

"Fine. Just call me Jack. Remember?"

"Of course!" Monte said, grinning. "Always with the informality." He was short, slight, balding, with scrawny arms and a big nose. A mosquito of a man. "Good to see you again!"

Of course it was good to see him again. Jack knew he was probably Monte's best customer. Their relationship had begun back in the mid-Seventies. Jack had been stashing away his cash earnings for a while and was at a loss as to what to do with it. Abe had told him to buy gold. Krugerrands, specifically. It had been the summer of Seventy-six and gold was selling for $103 an ounce. Jack thought that was ridiculously high but Abe swore it was going to go up. He practically begged Jack to buy some.

It's completely anonymous! Abe had said, saving his most persuasive argument for last. *As anonymous as buying a loaf of bread!*

Jack looked around the shop, remembering his anxiety that first day. He had bought a lot of ten coins, a small part of his savings, but all he dared risk on something like gold. By Christmas it hit $134 an ounce. That was a thirty percent increase in four months. Spurred by the profit, he began buying gold steadily, eventually putting every cent he had into Krugers. He became a welcome face at Municipal Coins.

Then gold really took off, approaching eight times the original value of his first coins. The volatility made him and Abe uneasy so they got out for a while in January of 1980, selling off their holdings in small lots around the city, averaging well over 500 percent profit, none of it recorded anywhere as income. He had bought the coins for cash, and he sold them for cash. He was supposed to report his profits to the IRS, but the IRS didn't know he existed and he didn't want to burden them with the information.

Jack had been in and out of gold since, and was buying it now. He figured the numismatic market was depressed, so he was investing in choice rare coins, too. They might not go up for many years, but he was buying for the long run. For his retirement—if he lived that long.

"I think I have something you'll really like," Monte was saying. "One of the finest Barber Halves I've seen."

"What year?"

"It's a 1901S."

There followed the obligatory haggling over the quality of the strike, bag marks, and the like. When Jack left the store he had the Barber Half and a 1909-proof Barber Quarter carefully wrapped and tucked in his left front pocket with a cylinder of Krugerrands. A hundred or so in cash was in the other front pocket. He was far more relaxed heading back uptown than he had been coming down.

Now he could turn his mind to Gia. He wondered if she'd have Vicky with her. Most likely. He didn't want to arrive empty-handed. He stopped at a card shop and found what he was looking for: a pile of furry little spheres, somewhat smaller than golf balls, each with two slender antennae, flat little feet and big rolling eyes: Wuppets. Vicky loved Wuppets almost as much as she loved oranges. He loved the look on her face when she reached into a pocket and found a present.

He picked out an orange Wuppet and headed for home.

7.

Lunch was a can of Lite beer and a cylinder of Country Style Pringles in the cool of his apartment. He knew he should be up on the roof doing his daily exercises, but he also knew what the temperature would be like up there.

Later, he promised himself. Jack loathed his exercise routine and embraced any excuse to postpone it. He never missed a day, but never passed up an opportunity to put it off.

THE TOMB

While nursing a second Lite, he went to the closet next to the bathroom to stash his two new acquisitions. It was a cedar closet, the air within heavy with the odor of the wood. He pulled a piece of molding loose from the base of a side wall, then slipped free one of the cedar planks above it. Behind the plank lay the bathroom water pipes, each wrapped in insulation. And taped to the insulation like ornaments on a Christmas tree were dozens of rare coins. Jack found empty spots for the latest.

He tapped the board and molding back into place, then stepped back to survey the work. A good hidey-hole. More accessible than a safe deposit box. Better than a wall safe. With burglars using metal detectors these days, they could find a safe in minutes and either crack it or carry it off. But a metal detector here would only confirm that there were pipes behind the bathroom wall.

The only thing Jack had to worry about was fire.

He realized a psychiatrist would have a field day with him, labelling him a paranoid of one sort or another. But Jack had worked out a better explanation: When you lived in a city with one of the highest robbery rates in the world and you worked in a field that tended to get people violently angry with you and you had no FDIC to protect your savings, extreme caution as a daily routine was not a symptom of mental illness; it was necessary for survival.

He was polishing off the second beer when the phone rang. Gia again? He listened to the Pinocchio Enterprises intro, then heard his father's voice begin to leave a message. He picked up and cut in.

"Hi, dad."

"Don't you ever turn that thing off, Jack?"

"The answerphone? I just got in. What's up?"

"Just wanted to remind you about Sunday."

Sunday? What the hell was— "You mean about the tennis match? How could I forget?"

"Wouldn't be the first time."

Jack winced. "I told you, dad. I got tied up with something and couldn't get away."

"Well, I hope it won't happen again." Dad's tone said he couldn't imagine what could be so important in the appliance repair business that could tie up a man for a whole day. "I've got us down for the father-and-son match."

"I'll be there bright and early Sunday morning."

"Good. See you then."

23

THE TOMB

"Looking forward to it."

What a lie, he thought as he hung up. He dreaded seeing his father, even for something so simple as a father-and-son tennis match. Yet he kept on accepting invitations to go back to New Jersey and bask in parental disapproval. It wasn't masochism that kept him coming back, it was duty. And love—love that had lain unexpressed for years. After all, it wasn't dad's fault that he thought of his son as a lazy do-nothing who had squandered an education and was in the process of squandering a life. Dad didn't know what his son really did.

Jack reset the answerphone and changed into a pair of lightweight tan slacks. He wouldn't feel right wearing Levi's on Sutton Square.

He decided to walk. He took Columbus Avenue down to the circle. People were lined up outside the Coliseum there waiting to get into a hot rod show. He walked along Central Park South past the St. Moritz and under the ornate iron awning over the Plaza's park-side entrance, amusing himself by counting Arabs and watching the rich tourists stroll in and out of the status hotels. He continued due east along Fifty-ninth toward the stratospheric rent district.

He was working up a sweat but barely noticed. The prospect of seeing Gia again made him almost giddy.

Images, pieces of the past, flashed through his brain as he walked. Gia's big smile, her eyes, the way her whole face crinkled up when she laughed, the sound of her voice, the feel of her skin . . . all denied him for the past two months.

He remembered his first feelings for her . . . so different. With almost all the other women in his life the most significant part of the relationship for both parties had been in bed. It was different with Gia. He wanted to *know* her. He had only thought about the others when there was nothing better to think about. Gia, on the other hand, had a nasty habit of popping into his thoughts at the most inopportune times. He had wanted to cook with her, eat with her, play tennis with her, see movies with her, listen to music with her, *be* with her. He had found himself wanting to get in his car and drive past her apartment house just to make sure it was still there. He hated to talk on the phone but found himself calling her at the slightest excuse. He was hooked and he loved it.

For nearly a year it had been a treat to wake up every morning knowing he was probably going to see her at some time during the day. So good . . .

Other images crept unbidden to the front. Her face when she

24

found out the truth about him, the hurt, and something worse—fear. The knowledge that Gia could even for an instant think that he would ever harm her, or ever allow harm to come to her, was the deepest hurt of all. Nothing he had said or tried to say had worked to change her mind.

Now he had another chance. He wasn't going to blow it.

8.

"He's late, isn't he, mom?"

Gia DiLauro kept both hands on her daughter's shoulders as they stood at the window in the front parlor and watched the street. Vicky was fairly trembling with excitement.

"Not quite. Almost, but not quite."

"I hope he doesn't forget."

"He won't. I'm sure he won't." *Although I wish he would.*

Two months ago she had walked out on Jack. She was adjusting. Sometimes she could go through a whole day without thinking about him. She had picked up where she had left off. There was even someone new creeping into her life.

Why couldn't the past ever stay out of sight where it belonged? Take her ex-husband, for instance. After their divorce she had wanted to cut all ties with the Westphalen family, even going so far as to change her name back to the one she had been born with. But Richard's aunts had made that impossible. They adored Vicky and used every imaginable pretext to lure Gia and her daughter over to Sutton Square. Gia had resisted at first, but their genuine affection for Vicky, their insistent pleas, and the fact that they had no illusions about their nephew—"a bounder and a cad!" as Nellie was wont to describe him after her third glass of sherry—finally changed her mind. Number Eight Sutton Square had become a second home of sorts. The aunts had even gone so far as to have a swing set and a wooden playhouse installed in the tiny backyard just for Vicky.

So when Nellie had called in a panic after Grace had been discovered missing on Tuesday morning, Gia had come right over. And had been here ever since.

Grace Westphalen. Such a sweet old lady. Gia couldn't imagine anyone wanting to harm her, and no ransom demand had been made. So where was she? Gia was frightened and mystified by the disappearance and she ached for Nellie whom she knew was suffering terribly behind her stoical front. It had only been out of love for Nellie and her deep concern for Grace that she had agreed to call Jack this morning. Not that Jack would be much help. From what she had learned of him, she could safely say that this was not his sort of job. But Nellie was desperate and it was the least Gia could do to ease her mind.

Gia told herself she was standing here at the window to keep Vicky company—the poor child had been watching for an hour already—yet there was an undeniable sense of anticipation rising inside her. It wasn't love. It couldn't be love.

What was it, then?

Probably just a residue of feeling, like a smear on a window that hadn't been properly wiped after spring cleaning. What else could she expect? It had only been two months since the breakup and her feelings for Jack until then had been intense, as if compensating for all that had been missing from her aborted marriage. *Jack is the one,* she had told herself. *The forever one.* She didn't want to think about that awful afternoon. She had held the memory off all day, but now, with Jack due any minute, it all rushed back at her . . .

* * *

She was cleaning his apartment. A friendly gesture. He refused to hire a cleaning lady and usually did it himself. But to Gia's mind, Jack's household methods left much to be desired, so she decided to surprise him by giving the place a thorough going-over. She wanted to do something for him. He was always doing little things for her, yet he was so self-contained that she found it difficult to reciprocate. So she "borrowed" an extra key to his apartment and sneaked in after lunch one day when she knew he was out.

She knew Jack as a gentle eccentric who worked at odd intervals and odd hours as a security consultant—whatever that was—and lived in a three-room apartment stuffed with such an odd assortment of junk and hideous old furniture that she had attacks of vertigo the first few times she visited him. He was crazy about movies—old movies, new movies, good movies, awful movies. He was the only man she had ever known who did not have a bank or credit card. He had such an aversion to signing his name that he didn't even have a checking account. He paid cash for everything.

The cleaning chores went smoothly until she found the loose panel at the rear of the base of the old oak secretary. She had been polishing the secretary with lemon oil to bring up the grain and make the wood glow. Jack loved oak and she was learning to love it, too—it had such character. The panel swung out as she was storing away some of his latest "neat stuff"—an original red and green Little Orphan Annie Ovaltine shake-up mug and an official Tom Corbett Space Cadet badge.

Something gleamed in the darkness behind the panel. Curious, she reached in and touched cool, oiled metal. She pulled the object out and started in surprise at its weight and malignant blue color. A pistol.

Well, lots of people in the city had guns. For protection. Nothing unusual about that.

She glanced back into the opening. There were other gleaming things within. She began to pull them out. She fought the sick feeling that intensified in the pit of her stomach as each gun was delivered from the hiding place, telling herself that Jack was probably just a collector. After all, no two of the dozen or so guns were alike. But what about the rest of the contents: the boxes of bullets, the daggers, brass knuckles and other deadly-looking things she had never seen before? Among the weapons were three passports, an equal number of drivers licenses, and sundry other forms of identification, all with different names.

Her insides knotted as she sat and stared at the collection. She tried to tell herself they were things he needed for his work as a security consultant, but deep inside she knew that much of what lay before her was illegal. Even if he had permits for all the guns, there was no way the passports and licenses could be legal.

Gia was still sitting there when he came back in from one of his mysterious errands. A guilty look ran over his face when he saw what she had found.

"Who are you?" she said, leaning away as he knelt beside her.

"I'm Jack. You know me."

"Do I? I'm not even sure your name's Jack any more." She could feel the terror growing within her. Her voice rose an octave. "Who are you and what do you do with all this?"

He gave her some garbled story about being a repairman of sorts who "fixes things." For a fee he finds stolen property or helps people get even when the police and the courts and all the various proper channels for redress have failed them.

THE TOMB

"But all these guns and knives and things . . . they're for hurting people!"

He nodded. "Sometimes it comes down to that."

She had visions of him shooting someone, stabbing him, clubbing him to death. If someone else had told her this about the man she loved, she would have laughed and walked away. But the weapons lay in front of her. And Jack was telling her himself!

"Then you're nothing but a hired thug!"

He reddened. "I work on my own terms—exclusively. And I don't do anything to anybody that they haven't already done to someone else. I was going to tell you when I thought—"

"But you *hurt* people!"

"Sometimes."

This was becoming a nightmare! "What kind of thing is that to spend your life doing?"

"It's what I do. More than that, it's what I am."

"Do you enjoy it when you hurt people?"

He looked away. And that was answer enough. It was like one of his knives thrust into her heart.

"Are the police after you?"

"No," he said with a certain amount of pride. "They don't even know I exist. Neither does the state of New York nor the IRS nor the entire U.S. government."

Gia rose to her feet and hugged herself. She suddenly felt cold. She didn't want to ask this question, but she had to.

"What about killing? Have you ever killed someone?"

"Gia . . ." he rose and stepped toward her but she backed away.

"Answer me, Jack! Have you ever killed someone?"

"It's happened. But that doesn't mean I make my living at it."

She thought she was going to be sick. The man she loved was a murderer! "But you've *killed!*"

"Only when there was no other way. Only when I had to."

"You mean, only when they were going to kill you? Kill or be killed?" *Please say yes. Please!*

He looked away again. "Sort of."

The world seemed to come apart at the seams. With hysteria clutching at her, Gia began running. She ran for the door, ran down the stairs, ran for a cab that took her home where she huddled in a corner of her apartment listening to the phone ring and ring and ring. She took it off the hook when Vicky came home from school and had

28

THE TOMB

barely spoken to Jack since.

* * *

"Come away from the window now. I'll tell you when he arrives."

"No, mommy! I want to see him!"

"All right, but when he gets here, I don't want you running around and making a fuss. Just say hello to him nice and politely, then go out back to the playhouse. Understand?"

"Is that him?" Vicky started bouncing up and down on her toes. "Is that him?"

Gia looked, then laughed and pulled on her daughter's pigtails. "Not even close."

Gia walked away from the window, then came back, resigned to standing and watching behind Vicky. Jack appeared to occupy a blind spot in Vicky's unusually incisive assessment of people. But then, Jack had fooled Gia, too.

Jack fooled everyone, it seemed.

9.

If Jack had his choice of any locale in Manhattan in which to live, he'd choose Sutton Square, the half block of ultrahigh-priced real estate standing at the eastern tip of Fifty-eighth Street off Sutton Place, dead-ending at a low stone wall overlooking a sunken brick terrace with an unobstructed view of the East River. No high-rises, condos, or office buildings there, just neat four-story townhouses standing flush to the sidewalk, all brick-fronted, some with the brick bare, others painted pastel colors. Wooden shutters flanked the windows and the recessed front doors. Some of them even had back yards. A neighborhood of Bentleys and Rolls Royces, liveried chauffeurs and white-uniformed nannies. And two blocks to the north, looming over it all like some towering guardian, stood the graceful, surprisingly delicate-looking span of the Queensboro Bridge.

He remembered the place well. He had been here before. Last year when he had been doing that job for the U.K. Mission, he had met Gia's aunts. They had invited him to a small gathering at their home. He hadn't wanted to go but Burkes had talked him into it. The evening had changed his life. He had met Gia.

He heard a child's voice shouting as he crossed Sutton Place.

29

THE TOMB

"Jack-Jack-Jack!"

Dark braids flying and arms outstretched, a little slip of a girl with wide blue eyes and a missing front tooth came dashing out the front door and down the sidewalk. She leaped into the air with the reckless abandon of a seven-year old who had not the slightest doubt she would be caught and lifted and swung around.

Which is exactly what Jack did. Then he hugged her against his chest as she clamped her spindly arms around his neck.

"Where you been, Jack?" she said into his ear. "Where you been all this time?"

Jack's answer was blocked by a lump in his throat the size of an apple. Shocked by the intensity of feeling welling up in him, he could only squeeze her tighter. *Vicky!* All the time he had spent missing Gia, never realizing how much he had missed the little one. For the better part of a year he and Gia had been together, Jack had seen Vicky almost every day, becoming a prime focus of her boundless store of affection. Losing Vicky had contributed much more than he had ever imagined to the emptiness inside him these past two months.

Love you, little girl.

He had not truly known how much until this very instant.

Over Vicky's shoulder he could see Gia standing in the doorway of the house, her face grim. He spun away to hide the tears that had sprung into his eyes.

"You're squeezing me awful tight, Jack."

He put her down. "Yeah. Sorry, Vicks." He cleared his throat, pulled himself together, then grasped her hand and walked up to the front door and Gia.

She looked good. Hell, she looked great in that light blue T-shirt and jeans. Short blond hair—to call it blond was to say the sun was sort of bright: It gleamed, it glowed. Blue eyes like winter sky after all the snow clouds have blown east. A strong, full mouth with a wide smile. High shoulders, high breasts, fair skin with high coloring along the cheeks. He still found it almost impossible to believe she was Italian.

10.

Gia controlled her anger. She had told Vicky not to make a fuss, but at the first sight of Jack crossing the street she had been out the door and on her way before Gia could stop her. She wanted to

30

punish Vicky for disobeying her, yet knew she wouldn't. Vicky loved Jack.

He looked the same as ever. His brown hair was a little longer and he looked as if he had lost a few pounds since she last saw him, but no major differences. Still the same incredible vitality, making the very air around him seem to throb with life, the same feline grace to his movements, the same warm brown eyes, the same lopsided smile. The smile looked forced at the moment, and his face was flushed. He looked hot.

"Hello," Jack said as he reached the top step. His voice was husky.

He leaned his face toward her. She wanted to pull away but affected sublime indifference instead. She would be cool. She would be detached. He no longer meant anything to her. She accepted a peck on the cheek.

"Come in," she said, doing her best to sound businesslike. She felt she succeeded. But the brush of his lips against her cheek stirred old unwanted feelings and she knew her face was coloring. Damn him! She turned away. "Aunt Nellie's waiting."

"You're looking well," he said, standing there and staring at her. Vicky's hand was still clasped in his own.

"Thank you. So are you." She had never felt this way before, but now that she knew the truth about Jack, the sight of him holding hands with her little girl made her skin crawl. She had to get Vicky away from him. "Honey, why don't you go outside and play in your playhouse while Jack and I and Aunt Nellie talk about grown-up things."

"No," she said. "I want to stay with Jack!"

Gia started to speak, but Jack raised a hand.

"First thing we do," he said to Vicky as he guided her into the foyer, "is close the door behind us. This may be a ritzy neighborhood, but they still haven't got around to air-conditioning the street." He shut the door, then squatted in front of her. "Listen, Vicks. Your mother's right. We've got some grown-up stuff to discuss and we've got to get down to business. But I'll let you know as soon as we're through."

"Can I show you the playhouse?"

"Sure."

"Neat! And Ms. Jelliroll wants to meet you. I told her all about you."

"Great. I want to meet her, too. But first—" he pointed to the breast pocket of his shirt— "see what's in there."

Vicky reached in and pulled out an orange ball of fur. "A Wuppet!" she screeched. "Oh, *ex!*"

She kissed him and ran toward the back.

"Who or what is Ms. Jelliroll?" he asked Gia as he rose to his feet.

"A new doll," Gia said as brusquely as she could manage. "Jack, I . . . I want you to stay away from her."

Gia saw his eyes then and knew that she had cut him deeply. But his mouth smiled.

"I haven't molested a child all week."

"That's not what I mean—"

"I'm a bad influence, right?"

"We've been through this before and I don't want to get going on it again. Vickie was very attached to you. She's just getting used to not having you around anymore, and now you come back and I don't want her to think things are going back to the way they were."

"I'm not the one who walked out."

"Doesn't matter. The result was the same. She was hurt."

"So was I."

"Jack," she sighed, feeling very tired, "this is a pointless conversation."

"Not to me. Gia, I'm crazy about that kid. There was a time when I had hopes of being her father."

The sound of her own laugh was harsh and bitter in her ears. "Forget it! Her real father hasn't been heard from in a year and you wouldn't be much of an improvement. Vicky needs a real person for a father. Someone who lives in the real world. Someone with a last name—do you even remember your last name? The one you were christened with? Jack, you . . . you don't even exist."

He reached out and touched her arm.

"As real as you."

"You know what I mean!" Gia said, pulling away. The words poured out of her. "What kind of a father could you be to anybody? And what kind of a husband?"

She was being hard on him, she knew, but he deserved it.

Jack's face tightened. "Very well, Ms. DiLauro. Shall we get down to business. After all, I didn't invite myself over."

"Neither did I. It was Nellie's idea. I was just the messenger. 'Get that friend of yours, that Jack fellow, to help.' I tried to tell her you were no longer a friend but she insisted. She remembered that you worked with Mr. Burkes last year."

"That's when we met."

"And the long string of deceptions began. Mr. Burkes called you 'a consultant,' 'a troubleshooter.' "

Jack made a sour face. "But you came up with a better job description, didn't you: 'thug.' "

It jolted Gia to hear the pain in Jack's voice as he said the word. Yes, she had called him that the last time she had seen him. She had hurt him then and had been glad of it. But she wasn't glad now to know he was still bleeding from it.

She turned away. "Nellie is waiting."

11.

With a mixture of pain and resentment roiling through him, Jack followed Gia down the hallway. For months he had nurtured a faint hope that someday soon he would make her understand. As of now he knew with leaden certainty that that would never happen. She had been a warm, passionate woman who had loved him, and unwittingly he had turned her to ice.

He studied the walnut paneling, the portraits on the walls, anything to keep from watching her as she walked ahead of him. Then they were through a pair of sliding doors and into the library. The dark paneling continued in from the hall, and there was lots of dark furniture: overstuffed velvet chairs with antimacassars on the arms, Persian rugs on the floor, impressionist paintings on the walls, a Sony Trinitron in the corner. It looked lived-in.

He had met Gia in this room.

Aunt Nellie sat lost in a recliner by the cold fireplace. A chubby, white-haired woman in her late sixties in a long dark dress adorned with a small diamond brooch and a short string of pearls. A woman used to wealth and comfortable with it. At first glance she appeared depressed and shrunken, as if she were in mourning, or preparing for it. But as they entered she pumped herself up and arranged her face into a pleasant expression, putting on a smile that wiped away a good many of her years.

"Mr. Jeffers," she said, rising. Her accent was thickly British. Not Lynn Redgrave-British; more like a reedy Robert Morley. "So good of you to come."

"Good to see you again, Mrs. Payton. But just call me Jack."

THE TOMB

"Only if you call me Nellie. Would you care for some tea?"

"Iced, if you don't mind."

"Not at all." She rang a little bell on the end table next to her and a uniformed maid appeared. "Three iced teas, Eunice." The maid nodded and left. An uncomfortable silence followed in which Nellie seemed to be lost in thought.

"How can I help you, Nellie?"

"What?" She looked startled. "Oh, I'm terribly sorry. I was just thinking about my sister, Grace. As I'm sure Gia told you, she's been gone for three days now .... disappeared between Monday night and Tuesday"—she pronounced it Chewsday—"morning. The police have come and gone and find no evidence of foul play, and there's been no demand for ransom. She is merely listed as a missing person, but I'm quite certain something has happened to her. I shan't rest until I find her."

Jack's heart went out to her, and he wanted to help, but . . .

"I don't do missing-person's work as a rule."

"Yes, Gia did say something about this not being in your line"—Jack glanced over to Gia but she avoided his gaze—"but I'm at my wits' end. The police are no help. I'm sure that if we were back home we'd have more cooperation from Scotland Yard than we've had from the New York Police. They simply aren't taking Grace's disappearance seriously. I knew you and Gia were close and remembered Eddie Burkes mentioning last year that your assistance had proven invaluable at the Mission. Never would tell me what he needed you for, but he certainly seemed enthusiastic."

Jack was seriously considering placing a call to "Eddie"—hard as it was to imagine someone calling the U.K. Mission's security chief "Eddie"—and telling him to button his lip. Jack always appreciated referrals, and it was nice to know he had made such an impression on the man, but Burkes was getting just a little bit too free with his name.

"I'm flattered by your confidence, but—"

"Whatever your usual fee is, I dare say I'll gladly pay it."

"It's a question of expertise rather than money. I just don't think I'm the right man for the job."

"You're a detective, aren't you?"

"Sort of." That was a lie. He wasn't any sort of detective; he was a repairman. He could feel Gia staring at him. "The problem is, I'm not licensed as a detective, so I can't have any contact with the police. They mustn't know I'm involved in any way. They wouldn't ap-

34

THE TOMB

prove."

Nellie's face brightened. "Then you'll help?"

The hope in her expression pushed the words to his lips.

"I'll do what I can. And as far as payment goes, let's make it contingent on success. If I don't get anywhere, there'll be no fee."

"But your time is surely worth something, dear fellow!"

"I agree, but looking for Vicky's Aunt Grace is a special case."

Nellie nodded. "Then you may consider yourself hired on your terms."

Jack forced a smile. He didn't expect much success in finding Grace, but he'd give it his best shot. If nothing else, the job would keep him in contact with Gia. He wasn't quitting yet.

The iced tea arrived and Jack sipped it appreciatively. Not a Lipton or Nestea mix, but freshly-brewed from an English blend.

"Tell me about your sister," he said when the maid had left.

Nellie leaned back and spoke in a low voice, rambling now and again, but keeping fairly close to hard facts. A picture slowly emerged. Unlike Nellie, the missing Grace Westphalen had never married. After Nellie's husband was killed in the Battle of Britain, the two sisters, each with one-third of the Westphalen fortune, emigrated to the States. Except for brief trips back home, both had lived on Manhattan's East Side ever since. And both were still loyal to the Queen. Never in all those years had the thought of becoming U.S. citizens ever crossed their minds. They very naturally fell in with the small British community in Manhattan consisting mostly of well-heeled expatriates and people connected with the British Consulate and the United Kingdom's Mission to the United Nations—"a colony within the Colonies," as they liked to call themselves—and enjoyed an active social life and huddled with their countrymen during the Falkland Islands' crisis. They rarely saw Americans. It was almost as if living in London.

Grace Westphalen was sixty-nine—two years older than Nellie. A woman of many acquaintances but few real friends. Her sister had always been her best friend. No eccentricities. Certainly no enemies.

"When did you last see Grace?" Jack asked.

"Monday night. I finished watching Johnny Carson, and when I looked in to say good night, she was propped up in bed reading. That was the last time I saw her." Nellie's lower lip trembled for an instant, then she got control of it. "Perhaps the last time I'll ever see her."

Jack looked to Gia. "No signs of foul play?"

THE TOMB

"I didn't get here until late Tuesday," Gia said with a shrug. "But I do know the police couldn't figure out how Grace got out without tripping the alarm."

"You've got the place wired?" he asked Nellie.

"Wired? Oh, you mean the burglar system. Yes. And it was set—at least for downstairs. We've had so many false alarms over the years, however, that we had the upper floors disconnected."

"What do you mean, 'false alarms'? "

"Well, sometimes we'd forget and get up at night to open a window. The racket is terrifying. So now when we set the system, only the downstairs doors and windows are activated."

"Which means Grace couldn't have left by the downstairs doors or windows without tripping an alarm ..." A thought struck him. "Wait—all these systems have delays so you can arm it and get out the door without setting it off. That must have been what she did. She just walked out."

"But her key to the system is still upstairs on her dresser. And all her clothes are in her closets."

"May I see?"

"By all means, do come and look," Nellie said, rising. They all trooped upstairs.

Jack found the small, frilly-feminine bedroom nauseating. Everything seemed to be pink or have a lace ruffle, or both.

The pair of French doors at the far end of the room claimed his attention immediately. He opened them and found himself on a card-table-sized balcony rimmed with a waist-high wrought iron railing, overlooking the backyard. A good dozen feet below was a rose garden. In a shady corner sat the playhouse Vicky had mentioned; it looked far too heavy to have been dragged under the window, and would have flattened all the rose bushes if it had. Anyone wanting to climb up here had to bring a ladder with him or be one hell of a jumper.

"The police find any marks in the dirt down there?"

Nellie shook her head. "They thought someone might have used a ladder, but there was no sign. The ground is so hard and dry with no rain—"

Eunice the maid appeared at the door. "Telephone, mum."

Nellie excused herself and left Jack and Gia alone in the room.

"A locked-room mystery," he said. "I feel like Sherlock Holmes."

He got down on his knees and examined the carpet for specks of

36

dirt, but found none. He looked under the bed; only a pair of slippers there.

"What are you doing?"

"Looking for clues. I'm supposed to be a detective, remember?"

"I don't think a woman's disappearance is anything to joke about," Gia said, the frost returning to her words now that Nellie was out of earshot.

"I'm not joking, nor am I taking it lightly. But you've got to admit the whole thing has the air of a British drawing-room mystery about it. I mean, either Aunt Grace had an extra alarm key made and ran off into the night in her nightie—a pink and frilly one, I'll bet—or she jumped off her little balcony here in that same nightie, or someone climbed up the wall, knocked her out, and carried her off without a sound. None of them seem too plausible."

Gia appeared to be listening intently. That was something at least.

He went over to the dressing table and glanced at the perfume bottles. There were dozens of them; some names were familiar, most were not. He wandered into the private bathroom and was there confronted by another array of bottles: Metamucil, Phillips' Milk of Magnesia, Haley's M-O, Pericolace, Surfak, Ex-Lax and more. One bottle stood off to the side. Jack picked it up. It was clear glass, with a thick green fluid inside. The cap was the metal twist-off type, enameled white. All it needed was a Smirnoff label and it could have been an airline vodka bottle.

"Know what this is?"

"Ask Nellie."

Jack screwed off the cap and sniffed. At least he was sure of one thing: it wasn't perfume. The smell was heavily herbal, and not particularly pleasant.

As Nellie returned, she appeared to be finding it increasingly difficult to hide her anxiety. "That was the police. I rang up the detective in charge a while ago and he just told me that they have nothing new on Grace."

Jack handed her the bottle.

"What's this?"

Nellie looked it over, momentarily puzzled, then her face brightened.

"Oh, yes. Grace picked this up Monday. I'm not sure where, but she said it was a new product being test-marketed, and this was a free sample."

THE TOMB

"But what's it for?"

"It's a physic."

"Pardon?"

"A physic. A cathartic. A laxative. Grace was very concerned—obsessed, you might say—with regulating her bowels. She's had that sort of problem all her life."

Jack took the bottle back. Something about an unlabeled bottle amid all the brand names intrigued him.

"May I keep this?"

"Certainly."

Jack looked around for a while longer, for appearances more than anything else. He didn't have the faintest idea how he was even going to begin looking for Grace Westphalen.

"Please remember to do two things," he told Nellie as he started downstairs. "Keep me informed of any leads the police turn up, and don't breathe a word of my involvement to the police."

"Very well. But where are you going to start?"

He smiled—reassuringly, he hoped. "I've already started. I'll have to do some thinking and then start looking." He fingered the bottle in his pocket. Something about it . . .

They left Nellie on the second floor, standing and gazing into her sister's empty room. Vicky came running in from the kitchen as Jack reached the bottom step. She held an orange section in her outstretched hand.

"Do the orange mouth! Do the orange mouth!"

He laughed, delighted that she remembered. "Sure!" He shoved the section into his mouth and clamped his teeth behind the skin. Then he gave Vicky a big orange grin. She clapped and laughed.

"Isn't Jack funny, mom? Isn't he the *funniest?*"

"He's a riot, Vicky."

Jack pulled the orange slice from his mouth. "Where's that doll you wanted to introduce me to?"

Vicky slapped the side of her head dramatically, "Ms. Jelliroll! She's out back. I'll go—"

"Jack doesn't have time, honey," Gia said from behind him. "Maybe next trip, okay?"

Vicky smiled and Jack noticed that a second tooth was starting to fill the gap left by her missing milk tooth.

"Okay. You coming back soon, Jack?"

"Real soon, Vicks."

THE TOMB

He hoisted her onto his hip and carried her to the front door where he put her down and kissed her.

"See ya." He glanced up at Gia. "You, too."

She pulled Vicky back against the front of her jeans. "Yeah."

As Jack went down the front steps, he thought the door slammed with unnecessary force.

12.

Vicky pulled Gia to the window and together they watched Jack stroll out of sight.

"He's going to find Aunt Grace, isn't he?"

"He says he's going to try."

"He'll do it."

"Please don't get your hopes up, honey," she said, kneeling behind Vicky and enfolding her in her arms. "We may never find her."

She felt Vicky stiffen and wished she hadn't said it—wished she hadn't thought it. Grace *had* to be alive and well.

"Jack'll find her. Jack can do anything."

"No, Vicky. He can't. He really can't." Gia was torn between wanting Jack to fail, and wanting Grace returned to her home; between wanting to see Jack humbled in Vicky's eyes, and the urge to protect her daughter from the pain of disillusionment.

"Why don't you love him anymore, mommy?"

The question took Gia by surprise. "Who said I ever did?"

"You did," Vicky said, turning and facing her mother. Her guileless blue eyes looked straight into Gia's. "Don't you remember?"

"Well, maybe I did a little, but not anymore." *It's true. I don't love him anymore. Never did. Not really.*

"Why not?"

"Sometimes things don't work out."

"Like with you and daddy?"

"Ummm ..." During the two and a half years she and Richard had been divorced, Gia had read every magazine article she could find on explaining the breakup of a marriage to a small child. There were all sorts of pat answers to give, answers that were satisfying when the father was still around for birthdays and holidays and weekends. But what to say to a child whose father had not only skipped town, but had left the continent before she was five? How to

39

tell a child that her daddy doesn't give a damn about her? Maybe Vicky knew. Maybe that's why she was so infatuated with Jack, who never passed up an opportunity to give her a hug or slip her a little present, who talked to her and treated her like a real person.

"Do you love Carl?" Vicky said with a sour face. Apparently she had given up on an answer to her previous question and was trying a new one.

"No. We haven't known each other that long."

"He's yucky."

"He's really very nice. You just have to get to know him."

"Yucks, mom. Yuck-o."

Gia laughed and pulled on Vicky's pigtails. Carl acted like any man unfamiliar with children. He was uncomfortable with Vicky; when he wasn't stiff, he was condescending. He had been unable to break the ice, but he was trying.

Carl was an account exec at BBD&O. Bright, witty, sophisticated. A civilized man. Not like Jack. Not at all like Jack. They had met at the agency when she had delivered some art for one of his accounts. Phone calls, flowers, dinners had followed. Something was developing. Certainly not love yet, but a nice relationship. Carl was what they called a "good catch." Gia didn't like to think of a man that way; it made her feel predatory, and she wasn't hunting. Richard and Jack, the only two men in the last ten years of her life, both had deeply disappointed her. So she was keeping Carl at arm's length for now.

Yet . . . there were certain things to be considered. With Richard out of touch for over a year now, money was a constant problem. Gia didn't want alimony, but some child support now and then would help. Richard had sent a few checks after running back to England—drawn in British pounds just to make things more difficult for her. Not that he had any financial problems—he controlled one-third of the Westphalen fortune. He was most definitely what those who evaluated such things would consider a "good catch." But as she had found out soon after their marriage, Richard had a long history of impulsive and irresponsible behavior. He had disappeared late last year. No one knew where he had gone, but no one was worried. It wasn't the first time he had decided on a whim to take off without a word to anyone.

And so Gia did the best she could. Good freelance work for a commercial artist was hard to find on a steady basis, but she managed. Carl was seeing to it that she got assignments from his accounts, and she appreciated that, though it worried her. She didn't want any of her decisions about their relationship to be influenced by economics.

But she needed those jobs. Freelance work was the only way she could be a breadwinner and a mother and father to Vicky—and do it right. She wanted to be home when Vicky got in from school. She wanted Vicky to know that even if her father had deserted her, her mother would always be there. But it wasn't easy.

Money-money-money.

It always came down to money. There was nothing in particular she wanted desperately to buy, nothing she really needed that more money could get for her. She simply wanted enough money so she could stop worrying about it all the time. Her day-to-day life would be enormously simplified by hitting the state lottery or having some rich uncle pass on and leave her fifty thousand or so. But there were no rich uncles waiting in the wings, and Gia didn't have enough left over at the end of the week for lottery tickets. She was going to have to make it on her own.

She was not so naive as to think that *every* problem could be solved by money—look at Nellie, lonely and miserable now, unable to buy back her sister despite all her riches—but a windfall would certainly let Gia sleep better at night.

All of which reminded Gia that her rent was due. The bill had been waiting for her when she had stopped back at the apartment yesterday. Staying here and keeping Nellie company was a pleasant change of scenery; it was posh, cool, comfortable. But it was keeping her from her work. Two assignments had deadlines coming up, and she needed those checks. Paying the rent now was going to drop her account to the danger level, but it had to be done.

Might as well find the checkbook and get it over with.

"Why don't you go out to the playhouse," she told Vicky.

"It's dull out there, mom."

"I know. But they bought it 'specially for you, so why don't you give it another try today. I'll come out and play with you in a few minutes. Got to take care of some business first."

Vicky brightened. "Okay! We'll play Ms. Jelliroll. You can be Mr. Grape-grabber."

"Sure." Whatever would Vicky do without her Ms. Jelliroll doll?

Gia watched her race toward the rear of the house. Vicky loved to visit her aunts' house, but she got lonely after a while. It was natural.

THE TOMB

There was no one her age around here; all her friends were back at the apartment house.

She went upstairs to the guest bedroom on the third floor where she and Vicky had spent the last two nights. Maybe she could get some work done. She missed her art setup back in her apartment, but she had brought a large sketch pad and she had to get going on the Burger-Meister place mat.

Burger-Meister was a McDonald's clone and a new client for Carl. The company had been regional in the south but was preparing to go national in a big way. They had the usual assortment of burgers, including their own answer to the Big Mac: the vaguely fascist-sounding Meister Burger. But what set them apart was their desserts. They put a lot of effort into offering a wide array of pastries—eclairs, napoleons, cream puffs and the like.

Gia's assignment was to come up with the art for a paper place mat to line the trays patrons used to carry food to the tables. The copy-writer had decided the place mat should extoll and catalog all the quick and wonderful services Burger-Meister offered. The art direc-tor had blocked it out: around the edges would be scenes of children laughing, running, swinging and sliding in the mini-playground, cars full of happy people going through the drive-thru, children celebrat-ing birthdays in the special party room, all revolving around that jolly, official-looking fellow, Mr. Burger-Meister, in the center.

Something about this approach struck Gia as wrong. There were missed opportunities here. This was for a place mat. That meant the person looking at it was already in the Burger-Meister and had already ordered a meal. There was no further need for a come-on. Why not tempt them with some of the goodies on the dessert list? Show them pictures of sundaes and cookies and eclairs and cream puffs. Get the kids howling for dessert. It was a good idea, and it excited her.

You're a rat, Gia. Ten years ago this never would have crossed your mind. And if it had you'd have been horrified.

But she was not that same girl from Ottumwa who had arrived in the Big City fresh out of art school and looking for work. Since then she had been married to a crumb and in love with a killer.

She began sketching desserts.

After an hour of work, she took a break. Now that she was rolling on the Burger-Meister job, she didn't feel too bad about paying the rent. She pulled the checkbook out of her purse but could not find the bill. It had been on the dresser this morning and now it was gone.

Gia went to the top of the stairs and called down.

"Eunice! Did you see an envelope on my dresser this morning?"

"No, mum," came the faint reply.

That left only one possibility.

13.

Nellie overheard the exchange between Gia and Eunice.

Here it comes, she thought, knowing that Gia would explode when she learned what Nellie had done with the rent bill. A lovely girl, that Gia, but so hot-tempered. And so proud, unwilling to accept any financial aid, no matter how often it was offered. A most impractical attitude. And yet ... if Gia had welcomed handouts, Nellie knew she would not be so anxious to offer them. Gia's resistance to charity was like a red flag waving in Nellie's face—it only made her more determined to find ways of helping her out.

Preparing herself for the storm, Nellie stepped out onto the landing below Gia.

"*I* saw it."

"What happened to it?"

"I paid it."

Gia's jaw dropped. "You *what?*"

Nellie twisted her hands in a show of anxiety. "Don't think I was snooping, dearie. I simply went in to make sure that Eunice was taking proper care of you, and I saw it sitting on the bureau. I was paying a few of my own bills this morning and so I just paid yours, too."

Gia hurried down the stairs, pounding her hand on the bannister as she approached.

"Nellie, you had no right!"

Nellie stood her ground. "Rubbish! I can spend my money any way I please."

"The least you could have done was ask me first!"

"True," Nellie said, trying her best to look contrite, "but as you know, I'm an old woman and frightfully forgetful."

The statement had the desired effect: Gia's frown wavered, fighting against a smile, then she broke into a laugh. "You're about as forgetful as a computer!"

"Ah, dearie," Nellie said, drawing to Gia's side and putting an arm around her waist, "I know I've taken you away from your work by asking you to stay with me, and that puts a strain on your finances. But I so love having you and Victoria here."

And I need you here, she thought. *I couldn't bear to stay alone with only Eunice for company. I would surely go mad with grief and worry.*

"Especially Victoria—I dare say she's the only decent thing that nephew of mine has ever done in his entire life. She's such a dear; I can't quite believe Richard had anything to do with her."

"Well, he doesn't have much to do with her any more. And if I have my way, he'll never have anything to do with her again."

Too much talk of her nephew Richard made Nellie uncomfortable. The man was a lout, a blot on the Westphalen name.

"Just as well. By the way, I never told you, but last year I had my will changed to leave Victoria most of my holdings when I go."

"Nellie—!"

Nellie had expected objections and was ready for them: "She's a Westphalen—the last of the Westphalens unless Richard remarries and fathers another child, which I gravely doubt—and I want her to have a part of the Westphalen fortune, curse and all."

"Curse?"

How did that slip out? She hadn't wanted to mention that. "Only joking, love."

Gia seemed to have a sudden weak spell. She leaned against Nellie.

"Nellie, I don't know what to say except I hope it's a long, long time before we see any of it."

"So do I! But until then, please don't begrudge me the pleasure of helping out once in a while. I have so much money and so few pleasures left in life. You and Victoria are two of them. Anything I can do to lighten your load—"

"I'm not a charity case, Nellie."

"I heartily agree. You're family"—she directed a stern expression at Gia—"even if you did go back to your maiden name. And as your aunt by marriage I claim the right to help out once in a while. Now that's the last I want to hear of it!"

So saying, she kissed Gia on the cheek and marched back into her bedroom. As soon as the door closed behind her, however, she felt her brave front crack. She stumbled across the room and sank onto the bed. She found it so much easier to bear the pain of Grace's disappearance in the company of others—pretending to be composed and in control actually made her feel so. But when there was no one around to play-act for, she fell apart.

Oh, Grace, Grace, Grace. Where can you be? And how long can I live without you?

Her sister had been Nellie's best friend ever since they had fled to America during the war. Her purse-lipped smile, her tittering laugh, the pleasure she took in their daily sherry before dinner, even her infuriating obsession with the regularity of her bowels; Nellie missed them all.

Despite all her foibles and uppity ways, she's a dear soul and I need her back.

The thought of living on without Grace suddenly overwhelmed Nellie and she began to cry, quiet sobs that no one else would hear. She couldn't let any of them—especially dear little Victoria—see her cry.

14.

Jack didn't feel like walking back across town, so he took a cab. The driver made a couple of tries at small talk about the Mets but the terse, grunted replies from the back seat soon shut him up. Jack could not remember another time in his life when he had felt so low—not even after his mother's death. He needed to talk to someone, and it wasn't a cabbie.

He had the hack drop him off at a little mom-and-pop on the corner west of his apartment: Nick's Nook, an unappetizing place with New York City's grime permanently imbedded in the plate glass windows. Some of that grime seemed to have filtered through the glass and onto the grocery display items behind it. Faded dummy boxes of Tide, Cheerios, Gaines•burgers and such had been there for years and would probably remain there for many more. Both Nick and his store needed a good scrubbing. His prices would shame an Exxon executive, but the Nook was handy, and baked goods were delivered fresh daily—at least he said they were.

Jack picked up an Entenmann's crumb cake that didn't look too dusty, checked the fresh date on the side and found it was good till next week.

"Going over to Abe's, eh?" Nick said. He had three chins, one little one supported by two big ones, all in need of a shave.

"Yeah. Thought I'd bring the junky his fix."

THE TOMB

"Tell him I said 'lo.'"

"Right."

He walked over to Amsterdam Avenue and then down to the Isher Sports Shop. Here he knew he'd find Abe Grossman, friend and confidant for almost as long as he had been Repairman Jack. In fact, Abe was one of the reasons Jack had moved into this neighborhood. Abe was the ultimate pessimist. No matter how dark things looked, Abe's outlook was darker. He could make a drowning man feel lucky.

Jack glanced through the window. A fiftyish man was alone inside, sitting on a stool behind the cash register, reading a paperback.

The store was too small for its stock. Bicycles hung from the ceiling; fishing rods, tennis raquets, and basketball hoops littered the walls while narrow aisles wound between pressing-benches, hockey nets, scuba masks, soccer balls, and countless other weekend-making items hidden under or behind each other. Inventory was an annual nightmare.

"No customers?" Jack asked to the accompaniment of the bell that chimed when the door opened.

Abe peered over the half moons of his reading glasses. "None. And the census won't be changed by your arrival, I'm sure."

"*Au contraire.* I come with goodies in hand and money in pocket."

"Did you—?" Abe peered over the counter at the white box with the blue lettering. "You did! Crumb? Bring it over here."

Just then a big burly fellow in a dirty sleeveless undershirt stuck his head in the door. "I need a box of twelve-gauge double-O. Y'got any?"

Abe removed his glasses and gave the man a withering stare.

"You will note, sir, that the sign outside says 'Sporting Goods.' Killing is not a sport!"

The man looked at Abe as if he had just turned green, and went away.

For a big man, Abe Grossman showed he could move quickly when he wanted to. He carried an easy 200 pounds packed into a five-eight frame. His graying hair had receded back to the top of his head. His clothes never varied: black pants, short-sleeve white shirt, shiny black tie. The tie and shirt were a sort of scratch-and-sniff catalog of the food he had eaten that day. As Abe rounded the end of the counter, Jack spotted scrambled egg, mustard, and what could be either catsup or spaghetti sauce.

"You really know how to hurt a guy," he said, breaking off a piece of cake and biting heartily. "You know I'm on a diet." Powdered sugar speckled his tie as he spoke.

"Yeah. I noticed."

"S'true. It's my own special diet. Absolutely no carbohydrates—except for Entenmann's cake. That's a free food. All other portions have to be measured, but Entenmann's is *ad lib.*" He took another big bite and spoke around it. Crumb cake always made him manic. "Did I tell you I added a codicil to my will? I've decided that after I'm cremated I want my ashes buried in an Entenmann's box. Or if I'm not cremated, it should be a white, glass-topped coffin with blue lettering on the side." He held up the cake box. "Just like this. Either way, I want to be interred on a grassy slope overlooking the Entenmann's plant in Bay Shore."

Jack tried to smile but it must have been a poor attempt. Abe stopped in mid-chew.

"What's eating up your *guderim?*"

"Saw Gia today."

"Nu?"

"It's over. Really over."

"You didn't know that?"

"I knew it but I didn't believe it." Jack forced himself to ask a question he wasn't sure he wanted answered. "Am I crazy, Abe? Is there something wrong in my head for wanting to live this way? Is my pilot light flickering and I don't know it?"

Without taking his eyes from Jack's face, Abe put down his piece of cake and made a halfhearted attempt to brush off his front. He succeeded only in smearing the sugar specks on his tie into large white blotches.

"What did she *do* to you?"

"Opened my eyes, maybe. Sometimes it takes an outsider to make you see yourself as you really are."

"And you see what?"

Jack took a deep breath. "A crazy man. A violent crazy man."

"That's what *her* eyes see. But what does she know? Does she know about Mr. Canelli? Does she know about your mother? Does she know how you got to be Repairman Jack?"

"Nope. Didn't wait to hear."

"There! You see? She *knows* nothing! She under*stands* nothing! And she's closed her mind to you, so who wants someone like that?"

"Me!"

THE TOMB

"Well," Abe said, rubbing a hand across his forehead and leaving a white smear, "that I can't argue with." He glared at Jack. "How old are you?"

Jack had to think a second. He always felt stupid when he had to remember his age.

"Uhh ... thirty-four."

"Thirty-four. Surely you've been ditched before?"

"Abe ... I can't remember ever feeling about anyone the way I feel about Gia. And she's afraid of me!"

"Fear of the unknown. She doesn't know you, so she's afraid of you. I know all about you. Am I afraid?"

"Aren't you? Ever?"

"Never!" He trotted back behind the counter and picked up a copy of the *New York Post*. Rifling through the pages he said, "Look—a five-year old beaten to death by his mother's boyfriend! A guy with a straight razor slashed eight people in Times Square last night and then disappears into a subway! A headless, handless torso is found in a West Side hotel room! As a hit-and-run victim lays bleeding in the street, people run up to him, rob him, and then leave him there. I should be afraid of *you*?"

Jack shrugged, unconvinced. None of this would bring Gia back; it was what he was that had driven her away. He decided he wanted to do his business here and go home.

"I need something."

"What?"

"A slapper. Lead and leather."

Abe nodded. "Ten ounces do?"

"Sure."

Abe locked the front door and hung the Back in a Few Minutes sign facing out through the glass. He passed Jack and led him toward the back where they stepped into a closet and closed the door after them. A push swung the rear wall of the closet away from them. Abe hit a light switch and they started down a worn stone stairway. As they moved, a neon sign flickered to life:

Fine Weapons
The Right to Buy Weapons Is the
Right to Be Free

Jack had often asked Abe why he had placed a neon sign where advertising would do no good; Abe unfailingly replied that every good weapons shop should have such a sign.

48

THE TOMB

"When you get right down to it, Jack," Abe was saying, "what I think of you or what Gia thinks of you isn't going to matter much in the long run. Because there isn't going to be a long run. Everything's falling apart. You know that. There's not much time left before civilization collapses completely. It's going to start soon. The banks'll start to go any day now. These people who think they're savings are insured by the FDIC? Have they got a rude awakening coming! Just wait till the first couple of banks go under and they find out the FDIC only has enough to cover a *pupik*'s worth of the deposits it's supposed to be insuring. Then you'll see panic, my boy. That's when the government will crank up the printing presses to full speed to cover those deposits and we'll have runaway inflation on our hands. I tell you ..."

Jack cut him off. He knew the routine by heart.

"You've been telling me for ten years, Abe! Economic ruin has been around the corner for a decade now. Where is it?"

"Coming, Jack. Coming. I'm glad my daughter's full-grown and disinclined toward marriage and a family. I shudder at the thought of a child or a grandchild growing up in the coming time."

Jack thought of Vicky. "Full of good cheer as usual, aren't you? You're the only man I know who lights up a room when he leaves."

"Very funny. I'm only trying to open your eyes so you can take steps to protect yourself."

"And what about you? You've got a bomb shelter somewhere in the sticks full of freeze-dried food?"

Abe shook his head. "Nah. I'll take my chances here. I'm not built for a postholocaust lifestyle. And I'm too old to learn."

He flipped another wall switch at the bottom of the steps, bringing the ceiling lights to life.

The basement was as crowded as the upstairs, only there was no sporting equipment down here. The walls and floors were covered with every one-man weapon imaginable. There were switchblades, clubs, swords, brass knuckles, and a full array of firearms from derringers to bazookas.

Abe went over to a cardboard box and rummaged through it.

"You want a slapper or the braided kind."

"Braided."

Abe tossed him something in a Zip-lok bag. Jack removed it and hefted it in his hand. The sap, sometimes called a blackjack, was made of thin strips of leather woven around a lead weight; the weave tightened and tapered down to a firm handle that ended in a looped thong for the wrist. Jack fitted it on and tried a few short swings. The flexibility allowed him to get his wrist into the motion, a feature that might come in handy at close quarters.

He stood looking at the sap.

This was the sort of thing that had frightened Gia off. He swung it once more, harder, striking the edge of a wooden shipping crate. There was a loud crack; splinters flew.

"This'll do fine. How much?"

"Ten."

Jack reached into his pocket. "Used to be eight."

"That was years ago. One of these should last you a lifetime."

"I lose things." He handed over a ten-dollar bill and put the sap into his pocket.

"Need anything else while we're down here?"

Jack ran a mental inventory of his weapons and ammunition. "No. I'm pretty well set."

"Good. Then let's go upstairs and we'll have some cake and talk. You look like you need some talk."

"Thanks, Abe," Jack said, leading the way upstairs, "but I've got some errands to run before dark, so I'll take a rain check."

"You hold things in too much. I've told you that before. We're supposed to be friends. So talk it out. You don't trust me anymore?"

"I trust you like crazy. It's just ..."

"What?"

"I'll see you, Abe."

15.

It was after six when Jack got back to the apartment. With all the shades pulled, the front room was dark. It matched his mood.

He had checked in with his office; there had been no calls of any importance waiting for him. The answerphone here had no messages waiting.

He had a two-wheel, wire shopping-cart with him, and in it a paper bag full of old clothing—woman's clothing. He leaned the cart in a corner, then went to his bedroom. His wallet, loose cash, and the new sap went on top of his dresser, then he stripped down and got into a T-shirt and shorts. Time for his workout. He didn't want to—he felt emotionally and physically spent—but this was the only thing in his daily routine he had promised himself he would never let slide. His life depended on it.

He locked his apartment and jogged up the stairs.

The sun had done its worst and was on its way down the sky, but the roof remained an inferno. Its black surface would hold the day's heat long into the night. Jack looked west into the haze that was reddening the lowering sun. On a clear day you could see New Jersey over there. If you wanted to. Someone had once told him that if you died in sin your soul went to New Jersey.

The roof was crowded. Not with people, with things. There was Appleton's tomato patch in the southeast corner; he had carried the topsoil up bag by fifty-pound bag. Harry Bok had a huge CB antenna in the northeast corner. Centrally located was the diesel generator everybody had pitched in to buy after the July, '77 blackout; clustered against its north side like suckling piglets against their mama were a dozen two-gallon cans of number-one oil. And above it all, waving proudly from its slim two-inch pole, was Neil the Anarchist's black flag.

Jack went over to the small wooden platform he had built for himself and did some stretching exercises, then went into his routine. He did his push-ups and sit-ups, jumped rope, practiced his tai kwon do kicks and chops, always moving, never stopping, until his body was slick with sweat and his hair hung in limp wet strands about his face and neck.

He spun at footsteps behind him.

"Hey, Jack."

"Oh, Neil. Hi. Must be about that time."

"Right you are."

Neil went over to the pole and reverently lowered his black flag. He folded it neatly, tucked it under his arm, and headed for the steps, waving as he went. Jack leaned against the generator and shook his head. Odd for a man who despised all rules to be so punctual, yet you could set your watch by the comings and goings of Neil the Anarchist.

Back in the apartment, Jack stuck six frozen egg rolls in the microwave and programmed it to heat them while he took a quick shower. With his hair still wet, he opened a jar of duck sauce and a can of Shasta diet cola, and sat down in the kitchen.

The apartment felt empty. It hadn't seemed that way this morning, but it was too quiet now. He moved everything into the TV room. The big screen lit up in the middle of a comfy domestic scene with a

51

husband, a wife, two kids and a dog. It reminded him of Sunday afternoons when Gia would bring Vicky over and he would hook up the Atari and teach the little girl how to zap asteroids and space invaders. He remembered watching Gia putter about the apartment; he had liked the way she moved, so efficient and bustling. She moved like a person who got things done. He found that immensely appealing.

He couldn't say the same about the homey show that filled the screen now. He quickly flipped around the dial and across the cable. There was everything from news to reruns to a bunch of couples two-stepping around hip-to-hip as a parade of Changs and Engs dancing to a country fiddler.

Definitely Betamax time. Time for part two of Repairman Jack's unofficial James Whale Festival. The triumph of Whale's directorial career was ready to run: *Bride of Frankenstein.*

16.

"You think I'm mad. Perhaps I am. But listen, Henry Frankenstein. While you were digging in your graves, piecing together dead tiss-yoos, I, my dear pupil, went for my material to the source of life ..."

Earnest Thesiger as Dr. Praetorius—the greatest performance of his career—was lecturing his former student. The movie was only half over, but it was time to go. He'd pick up where he left off before bedtime. Too bad. He loved this movie. Especially the score—Franz Waxman's best ever. Who'd have thought that later on in his career, the creator of such a majestic, stirring piece would wind up doing the incidental music for turkeys like *Return to Peyton Place.* Some people never get the recognition they deserve.

He pulled on a T-shirt with "The Byrds" written on the front; next came the shoulder holster with the little Semmerling under his left arm; a loose short-sleeved shirt went over that, followed by a pair of cut-off jeans, and sneakers—no socks. By the time he had everything loaded in his mini-shopping-cart and was ready to go, darkness had settled on the city.

He walked down Amsterdam Avenue to where Bahkti's grandmother had been attacked last night, found a deserted alley, and slipped into the shadows. He hadn't wanted to leave his apartment house in drag—his neighbors already considered him more than a little odd—and this was as good a dressing room as any place else.

First he took off his outer shirt. Then he reached into the bag and pulled out the dress—good quality but out of fashion and in need of ironing. That went over the T-shirt and shoulder holster, followed by a gray wig, then black shoes with no heels. He didn't want to look like a shopping-bag lady; a derelict had nothing to attract the man Jack was after. He wanted a look of faded dignity. New Yorkers see women like this all the time, in their late fifties on up toward eighty. They're all the same. They trudge along, humped over not so much from a softening of the vertebrae as from the weight of life itself, their center of gravity thrust way forward, usually looking down, or if the head is raised, never looking anyone in the eye. The key word with them is *alone.* They make irresistible targets.

And Jack was going to be one of them tonight. As an added inducement, he slipped a good quality paste diamond ring onto the fourth finger of his left hand. He couldn't let anyone get a close look at him, but he was sure the type of man he was searching for would spot the gleam from that ring a good two blocks away. And as a back-up attraction: a fat roll of bills, mostly singles, tight against his skin under one of the straps of his shoulder holster.

Jack put his sneakers and the sap into the paper bag in the upper basket of the little shopping cart. He checked himself in a store window: he'd never make it as a transvestite. Then he began a slow course along the sidewalk, dragging the cart behind him.

Time to go to work.

17.

Gia found herself thinking of Jack and resented it. She was sitting across a tiny dinner table from Carl, a handsome, urbane, witty, intelligent man who professed to be quite taken with her. They were in an expensive little restaurant below street level on the Upper East Side. The decor was spare and clean, the wine white, dry, cold, the cuisine nouvelle. Jack should have been miles from her thoughts, and yet he was here, slouched across the table between them.

She kept remembering the sound of his voice on the answerphone this morning . . . "Pinocchio Productions. I'm out at the moment" . . . triggering other memories further in the past . . .

Like the time she had asked him why his answerphone always started off with "Pinocchio Productions" when there was no such company. Sure there is, he had said, jumping up and spinning around. Look: no strings. She hadn't understood all the implications at the time.

And then to learn that among the "neat stuff" he had been picking up in secondhand stores was a whole collection of Vernon Grant art. She found out about that the day he gave Vicky a copy of *Flibbity Gibbit*. Gia had become familiar with Grant's commercial work during her art school days—he was the creator of Kellogg's Snap, Crackle, and Pop—and she had even swiped from him now and again when an assignment called for something elfin. She felt she had found a truly kindred spirit upon discovering that Jack was a fan of Vernon Grant. And Vicky ... Vicky treasured *Flibbity Gibbit* and had made "Wowie-kee-flowie!" her favorite expression.

She straightened herself in her chair. *Out, damned Jack! Out, I say!* She had to start answering Carl in something more than monosyllables.

She told him her idea about changing the thrust of the Burger-Meister place mats from services to desserts. He was effusive in his praise, saying she should be a copywriter as well as an artist. That launched him onto the subject of the new campaign for his biggest client, Wee Folk Children's Clothes. There was work in it for Gia and perhaps even a modeling gig for Vicky.

Poor Carl ... he tried so hard to hit it off with Vicky tonight. As usual, he had failed miserably. Some people never learn how to talk to kids. They turn the volume up and enunciate with extra care, as if talking to a partially-deaf immigrant. They sound as if they're reading lines somebody else wrote for them, or as if what they're saying is really for the benefit of other adults listening and not just for the child. Kids sense that and turn off.

But Vicky hadn't been turned off this afternoon. Jack knew how to talk to her. When he spoke it was to Vicky and to no one else. There was instant rapport between those two. Perhaps because there was a lot of little boy in Jack, a part of him that had never grown up. But if Jack was a little boy, he was a dangerous little boy. He—

Why did he keep creeping back into her thoughts? Jack is the past. Carl is the future. Concentrate on Carl!

She drained her wine and stared at Carl. Good old Carl. Gia held her glass out for more wine. She wanted *lots* of wine tonight.

THE TOMB

18.

His eye was killing him.

He sat hunched in the dark recess of the doorway, glowering at the street. He'd probably have to spend the whole night here unless something came along soon.

The waiting was the worst part, man. The waiting and the hiding. Word was probably out among the pigs to be on the lookout for a guy with a scratched eye. Which meant he couldn't hit the street and go looking, and he hadn't been in town long enough to find someone to crash with. So he had to sit here and wait for something to come to him.

All because of that rotten bitch.

He fingered the gauze patch taped over his left eye and winced at the shock of pain elicited by even the gentlest touch. *Bitch!* She damn near gouged his eye out last night. But he showed her. Fucking-ay right. Bounced her around good after that. And later on, in this very same doorway, when he'd gone through her wallet and found a grand total of seventeen bucks, and had seen that the necklace was nothing but junk, he'd been tempted to go back and do a tap dance on her head, but figured the pigs would've found her by then.

And then to top it all off, he'd had to spend most of the bread on eye patches and ointment. He was worse off now than when he'd rolled the bitch.

He hoped she was hurting now ... hurting real good. He knew he was.

Should never have come East, man. He'd had to get out of Detroit fast after getting carried away with a pry bar on that guy changing a tire out by the interstate. Easier to get lost here than someplace like, say, Saginaw, but he didn't know anybody.

He leaned back and watched the street with his good eye. Some weird-looking old lady was hobbling by on shoes that looked too small for her, pulling a shopping basket behind her. Not much there. He passed her over as not worth the trouble of a closer look.

19.

Who am I kidding? Jack thought. He had been trudging up and down every west side street in the area for hours now. His back was killing him from walking hunched over. If the mugger had stayed in the neighborhood, Jack would have passed him by now.

Damn the heat and damn the dress and most of all damn the

55

goddamn wig. I'll never find this guy.

But it wasn't only the futility of tonight's quest that was getting to him. The afternoon had hit him hard.

Jack prided himself on being a man of few illusions. He believed there was a balance to life and he based that belief on Jack's Law of Social Dynamics: For every action there must be an equal and opposite reaction. The reaction wasn't necessarily automatic or inevitable; life wasn't like thermodynamics. Sometimes the reaction had to be helped along. That was where Repairman Jack came into the picture. He was in the business of making some of those reactions happen. He liked to think of himself as a sort of catalyst.

Jack knew he was a violent man. He made no excuses for that. He had come to terms with it. He had hoped Gia could eventually come to understand it.

When Gia had left him he'd convinced himself that it was all a big misunderstanding, that all he needed was a chance to talk to her and everything would be straightened out, that it was just her Italian pig-headedness keeping them apart. Well, he had had his chance this afternoon and it was obvious there was no hope of a common ground with Gia. She wanted no part of him.

He frightened her.

That was the hardest part to accept. He had scared her off. Not by wronging her or betraying her, but simply by letting her know the truth ... by letting her know what Repairman Jack fixed, and how he went about his work, and what tools he used.

One of them was wrong. Until this afternoon it had been easy to believe that it was Gia. Not so easy tonight. He believed in Gia, believed in her sensitivity, her perceptiveness. And she found him repugnant.

A soul-numbing lethargy seeped through him.

What if she's right? What if I am nothing more than a high-priced hoodlum who's rationalized his way into believing he's one of the good guys?

Jack shook himself. Self-doubt was a stranger to him. He wasn't sure how to fight back. And he had to fight it. He wouldn't change the way he lived; doubted he could if he wished to. He had spent too long on the outside to find his way back in again—

Something about the guy sitting in the doorway he just passed ... something about that face in the shadows that his unconscious had spotted in passing but had not yet sent up to his forebrain. Something . . .

Jack let go of the shopping basket handle. It clattered to the sidewalk. As he bent to pick it up, he glanced back at the doorway.

The guy was young with short blond hair—and had a white gauze patch over his left eye. Jack felt his heart increase its tempo. This was almost too good to be true. Yet there he was, keeping back in the shadows, doubtlessly well aware that his patch marked him. It *had* to be him. If not, it was one hell of a coincidence. Jack had to be sure.

He picked up the cart and stood still for a moment, deciding his next move. Patch had noticed him, but seemed indifferent. Jack would have to change that.

With a cry of delight, he bent and pretended to pick something out from under the wheel of the cart. As he straightened, he turned his back to the street—but remained in full view of Patch whom he pretended not to see—and dug inside the top of his dress. He removed the roll of bills, made sure Patch got a good look at its thickness, then pretended to wrap a new bill around it. He stuffed it back in his ersatz bra, and continued on his way.

About a hundred feet on, he stopped to adjust a shoe and took advantage of the moment to sneak a look behind: Patch was out of the shadows and following him down the street.

Good. Now to arrange a rendezvous.

He removed the sap from the paper bag and slipped his wrist through the thong, then went on until he came to an alley. Without an apparent care in the world, he turned into it and let the darkness swallow him.

Jack had moved maybe two-dozen feet down the littered path when he heard the sound he knew would come: quick, stealthy footsteps approaching from the rear. When the sound was almost upon him, he lurched to the left and flattened his back against the wall. A dark form hurtled by and fell sprawling over the cart.

Amid the clatter of metal and muttered curses, the figure scrambled to its feet and faced him. Jack felt truly alive now, revelling in the pulses of excitement crackling like bolts of lightning through his nervous system, anticipating one of the fringe benefits of his work— giving a punk like this a taste of his own medicine.

Patch seemed hesitant. Unless he was very stupid, he must have realized that his prey had moved a bit too fast for an old lady. Jack did not want to spook him, so he made no move. He simply crouched against the alley wall and let out a high-pitched howl that would have put Una O'Connor to shame.

Patch jumped and glanced up and down the alley.

"Hey! Shut up!"

Jack screamed again.

"Shut the fuck up!"

But Jack only crouched lower, gripped the handle of the sap tighter, and screamed once more.

"Awright, bitch!" Patch said through his teeth as he charged forward. "You asked for it." There was anticipation in his voice. Jack could tell he liked beating up people who couldn't fight back. As Patch loomed over him with raised fists, Jack straightened to his full height, bringing his left hand up from the floor. He caught Patch across the face with a hard, stinging, open-palmed slap that rocked him back on his heels.

Jack knew what would follow, so he was moving to his right even as he swung. Sure enough, as soon as Patch regained his balance, he started for the street. He had just made a big mistake and he knew it. Probably thought he had picked an undercover cop to roll. As he darted by on his way to freedom, Jack stepped in and swung the sap at Patch's skull. Not a hard swing—a flick of the wrist, really—but it connected with a satisfying *thunk*. Patch's body went slack but not before his reflexes had jerked him away from Jack. His momentum carried him head first into the far wall. He settled to the floor of the alley with a sigh.

Jack shucked off the wig and dress and got back into his sneakers, then he went over and nudged Patch with his foot. He groaned and rolled over. He appeared dazed, so Jack reached out with his free hand and shook him by the shoulder. Without warning, Patch's right arm whipped around, slashing at Jack with the four-inch blade protruding from his fist. Jack grabbed the wrist with one hand and poked at a spot behind Patch's left ear, just below the mastoid. Patch grunted with pain; as Jack applied more and more pressure, he began flopping around like a fish on a hook. Finally he dropped the knife. As Jack relaxed his hold, Patch made a leap to retrieve the knife. Jack had half expected this. The sap still hung from his wrist by its thong. He grabbed it and smashed it across the back of Patch's hand, putting all of his wrist and a good deal of his forearm behind the blow. The crunch of bone was followed by a scream of pain.

"You broke it!" He rolled onto his belly and then back onto his side. "I'll have your ass for this, pig!" He moaned and whined and swore incoherently, all the while cradling his injured hand.

"Pig?" Jack said in his softest voice. "No such luck, friend. This is personal."

The moaning stopped. Patch peered through the darkness with his good eye, a worried look on his face. As he placed his good hand against the wall to prop himself up, Jack raised the sap for another blow.

"No fair, man!" He quickly withdrew the hand and lay down again. "No *fair!*"

"Fair?" Jack laughed as nastily as he could. "Were you going to be fair to the old lady you thought you had trapped here? No rules in this alley, friend. Just you and me. And I'm here to *get* you."

He saw Patch's eye widen; his tone echoed the fear in his face.

"Look, man. I don't know what's goin' down here, but you got the wrong guy. I only came in from Michigan last week."

"Not interested in last week, friend. Just last night . . . the old lady you rolled."

"Hey, I didn't roll no old lady! No way!" Patch flinched and whimpered as Jack raised the sap menacingly. "I swear to God, man! I swear!"

Jack had to admit the guy was good. Very convincing. "I'll help your memory a little: Her car broke down; she wore a heavy necklace that looked like silver and had two yellow stones in the middle; and she used her fingernails on your eye." As he saw comprehension begin to dawn in Patch's eye, he felt his anger climbing towards the danger point. "She wasn't in the hospital yesterday, but she is today. And you put her there. She may kick off any time. And if she does, it's your fault."

"No, wait, man! Listen—"

He grabbed Patch by the hair at the top of his head and rapped his skull against the brick wall. "*You* listen! I want the necklace. Where'd you fence it?"

"Fence it? That piece of shit? I threw it away!"

"Where?"

"I don't know!"

"Remember!" Jack rapped Patch's head against the wall again for emphasis.

He kept seeing that frail old lady fading into the hospital bed, barely able to speak because of the beating she had received at this creep's hands. A dark place was opening up inside him. *Careful! Control!* He needed Patch conscious.

"Alright! Lemme think!"

Jack managed a slow, deep breath. Then another.

"Think. You've got thirty seconds."

It didn't take that long.

"I thought it was silver. But when I got it under a light I saw it wasn't."

"You want me to believe you didn't even try to get a few bucks for it?"

"I . . . I didn't like it."

Jack hesitated, not sure of how to take that.

"What's that supposed to mean?"

"I didn't like it, man. Something about it didn't feel right. I just threw it in some bushes."

"No bushes around here."

Patch flinched. "Are too! Two blocks down!"

Jack yanked him to his feet. "Show me."

Patch was right. Between West End and Twelfth Avenues, where Fifty-eighth Street slopes down toward the Hudson River, was a small clump of privit hedge, the kind Jack had spent many a Saturday morning as a kid trimming in front of his parent's home in Jersey. With Patch lying face down on the pavement by his feet, Jack reached into the bushes. A little rummaging around among the gum wrappers, used tissues, decaying leaves, and other less easily identifiable refuse produced the necklace.

Jack looked at it as it gleamed dully in the glow from a nearby streetlight. *I've done it! Goddamnit, I've done it!*

He hefted it in his palm. Heavy. Had to be uncomfortable to wear. Why did Kusum want it back so badly? As he held it in his hand he began to understand what Patch had said to him about it not feeling right. It *didn't* feel right. He found it hard to describe the sensation more clearly than that.

Crazy! he thought. *This thing's nothing more than sculptured iron and a couple of topazlike stones.*

Yet he could barely resist the primitive urge to hurl the necklace across the street and run the other way.

"You gonna let me go now?" Patch said, rising to his feet. His left hand was a dusky, mottled blue now, swollen to nearly twice its normal size. He cradled it gingerly against his chest.

Jack held up the necklace. "This is what you beat up an old lady

60

for?'' he said in a low voice, feeling the rage pushing toward the surface. "She's all busted up in a hospital bed now because you wanted to rip this off, and then you threw it away."

"Look, man!" Patch said, pointing his good hand at Jack. "You've got it wrong—"

Jack saw the hand gesturing in the air two feet in front of him and the rage within him suddenly exploded outward. Without warning, he swung the sap hard against Patch's right hand. As before, there was a crunch and a howl of pain.

As Patch sank to his knees, moaning, Jack walked past him back toward West End Avenue.

"Let's see you roll an old lady now, tough guy."

The darkness within him began to retreat. Without looking back, he began walking toward the more populated sections of town. The necklace tingled uncomfortably against the inside of his palm.

He wasn't far from the hospital. He broke into a run. He wanted to be rid of the necklace as soon as possible.

20.

The end was near.

Kusum had sent the private duty nurse out into the hall and now stood alone at the head of the bed holding the withered hand in his. Anger had receded, as had frustration and bitterness. Not gone, simply tucked away out of sight until they would be needed. They had been moved aside to leave a void within him.

The futility of it all. All those years of life cancelled out by a moment of viciousness.

He could not dredge up a shred of hope for seeing the necklace returned before the end. No one could find it in time, not even the highly-recommended Repairman Jack. If it was in her karma to die without the necklace, then Kusum would have to accept it. At least he had the satisfaction of knowing he had done everything in his power to retrieve it.

A knock at the door. The private duty nurse stuck her head in. "Mr. Bahkti?"

He repressed the urge to scream at her. It would feel so good to scream at someone.

"I told you I wished to be alone in here."

"I know. But there's a man out here. He insisted I give you this."

THE TOMB

She held out her hand. "Said you were expecting it."

Kusum stepped toward the door. He could not imagine . . .

Something dangled from her hand. It looked like—it wasn't possible!

He snatched the necklace from her fingers.

It's true! It's real! He found it! Kusum wanted to sing out his joy, to dance with the startled nurse. Instead, he pushed her out the door and rushed to the bedside. The clasp was broken, so he wrapped the necklace about the throat of the nearly-lifeless form there.

"It's all right now!" he whispered in their native tongue. "You're going to be all right!"

He stepped out into the hall and saw the private duty nurse.

"Where is he?"

She pointed down the hall. "At the nursing station. He's not even supposed to be on the floor, but he was very insistent."

I'm sure he was. Kusum pointed toward the room. "See to her." Then he hurried down the hall.

He found Jack, dressed in ragged shorts and mismatched shirts— he had seen better dressed stall attendants at the Calcutta bazaar— leaning against the counter at the nursing station, arguing with a burly head nurse who turned to Kusum as he approached.

"Mr. Bahkti, you are allowed on the floor because of your grandmother's critical condition. But that doesn't mean you can have your friends wandering in and out at all hours of the night!"

Kusum barely looked at her. "We will be but a minute. Go on about your business."

He turned to Jack who looked hot and tired and sweaty. *Oh, for two arms to properly embrace this man, even though he probably smells like everyone else in this country of beef eaters. Certainly an extraordinary man. Thank Kali for extraordinary men, no matter what their race or dietary habits.*

"I assume I made it in time?" Jack said.

"Yes. Just in time. She will be well now."

The American's brow furrowed. "It's going to patch her up?"

"No, of course not. But knowing it has been returned will help her up here." He tapped his forefinger against his temple. "For here is where all healing resides."

"Sure," Jack said, his expression hiding none of his skepticism. "Anything you say."

"I suppose you wish the rest of your fee."

62

THE TOMB

Jack nodded. "Sounds good to me."

He pulled the thick envelope out of his tunic and thrust it at Jack. Despite his prior conviction of the utter futility of his ever seeing the stolen necklace again, Kusum had kept the packet with him as a gesture of hope and of faith in the goddess he prayed to. "I wish it were more. I don't know how to thank you enough. Words cannot express how much—"

"It's okay," Jack said quickly. Kusum's outpouring of gratitude seemed to embarrass him.

Kusum, too, was taken aback by the intensity of the emotions within him. He had completely given up hope. He had asked this man, a stranger, to perform an impossible task, and it had been done! He detested emotional displays, but his customary control over his feelings had slipped since the nurse placed the necklace in his hand.

"Where did you find it?"

"I found the guy who stole it and convinced him to take me to it."

Kusum felt his fist clench and the muscles at the back of his neck bunch involuntarily. "Did you kill him as I asked?"

Jack shook his head. "Nope. Told you I wouldn't. But he won't be punching out old ladies for some time. In fact, he should be showing up in the emergency room here pretty soon to get something for the pain in his hands. Don't worry. He's been paid back in kind. I fixed it."

Kusum nodded silently, hiding the storm of hatred raging across his mind. Mere pain was not enough, however—not nearly enough! The man responsible here must pay with his life!

"Very well, Mr. Jack. My . . . family and I owe you a debt of gratitude. If there is ever anything you need that is in my power to secure for you, any goal that is in my power to achieve, you have merely to ask. All efforts within the realm of human possibility"—he could not repress a smile here—"and perhaps even beyond, will be expended on your behalf."

"Thank you," Jack said with a smile and a slight bow. "I hope that won't be necessary. I think I'll be heading home now."

"Yes. You look tired." But as Kusum studied him, he sensed more than mere physical fatigue. There was an inner pain that hadn't been present this morning . . . a spiritual exhaustion. Was something fragmenting this man? He hoped not. That would be tragic. He wished he could ask, but did not feel he had the right. "Rest well."

He watched until the American had been swallowed by the

elevator, then he returned to the room. The private duty nurse met him at the door.

"She seems to be rallying, Mr. Bahkti! Respirations are deeper, and her blood pressure's up!"

"Excellent!" Nearly twenty-four hours of constant tension began to unravel within him. She would live. He was sure of it now. "Have you a safety pin?"

The nurse looked at him quizzically but went to her purse on the window sill and produced one. Kusum took it and used it as a clasp for the necklace, then turned to the nurse.

"This necklace is not to be removed for any reason whatsoever. Is that clear?"

The nurse nodded timidly. "Yes, sir. Quite clear."

"I will be elsewhere in the hospital for a while," he said, starting for the door. "If you should need me, have me paged."

Kusum took the elevator down to the first floor and followed signs to the emergency room. He had learned that this was the only hospital serving the midtown West Side of Manhattan. Jack had said that he had injured the mugger's hands. If he should seek medical care, it would be here.

He took a seat in the waiting area of the emergency department. It was crowded. People of all sizes and colors brushed against him on their way in and out of the examining rooms, back and forth to the receptionist counter. He found the odors and the company distasteful, but intended to wait a few hours here. He was vaguely aware of the attention he drew but was used to it. A one-armed man dressing as he did in the company of westerners soon became immune to curious stares. He ignored them. They were not worthy of his concern.

It was less than half an hour before an injured man entered and grabbed Kusum's attention. His left eye was patched and both his hands were swollen to twice their normal size.

This was the one! There could be no doubt. Kusum barely restrained himself from leaping up and attacking the man. He seethed as he sat and watched a secretary in the reception booth begin to help him fill out the standard questionaire his useless hands could not. A man who broke people with his hands had had his hands broken. Kusum relished the poetry of it.

He walked over and stood next to the man. As he leaned against the counter, looking as if he wished to ask the secretary a question, he glanced down at the form. "Daniels, Ronald, 359 W. 53rd St." Kusum stared at Ronald Daniels, who was too intent on hurrying the completion of the form to notice him. Between answers to the secretary's questions, he whined about the pain in his hands. When asked about the circumstances of the injury, he said a jack had slipped while he had been changing a tire and his car had fallen on him.

Smiling, Kusum went back to his seat and waited. He saw Ronald Daniels led into an examining room, saw him wheeled out to x-ray in a chair, and then back to the examining room. There was a long wait, and then Ronald Daniels was wheeled out again, this time with casts from the middle of his fingers up to his elbows. And all the while there was not a single moment when he was not complaining of pain.

Another stroll over to the reception booth and Kusum learned that Mr. Daniels was being admitted overnight for observation. Kusum hid his annoyance. That would complicate matters. He had been hoping to catch up with him outside and deal with him personally. But there was another way to settle his score with Ronald Daniels.

He returned to the private room and received a very favorable update from the amazed nurse.

"She's doing wonderfully—even spoke to me a moment ago! Such spirit!"

"Thank you for your help, Miss Wiles," Kusum said. "I don't think we'll be requiring your services any longer."

"But—"

"Have no fear: You shall be paid for the entire eight-hour shift." He went to the window sill, took her purse and handed it to her. "You've done a wonderful job. Thank you."

Ignoring her confused protests, he guided her out the door and into the hall. As soon as he was sure she would not be returning out of some misguided sense of duty to her patient, he went to the bedside phone and dialed hospital information.

"I'd like to know the room number of a patient," he said when operator picked up. "His name is Ronald Daniels. He was just admitted through the emergency room."

There was a pause, then: "Ronald Daniels is in 547C, North Wing."

Kusum hung up and leaned back in the chair. How to go about this? He had seen where the doctors' lounge was located. Perhaps he could find a set of whites or a scrub suit in there. Dressed in those and without his turban, he would be able to move about the hospital more freely.

As he considered his options, he pulled a tiny glass vial from his pocket and removed the stopper. He sniffed the familiar herbal odor of the green liquid within, then resealed it.

Mr. Ronald Daniels was in pain. He had suffered for his transgression. But not enough. No, not nearly enough.

21.

"Help me!"

Ron had just been drifting off into sleep. *Goddamn that old bastard!* Every time he started to fall asleep, the old fart yelled.

Just my luck to get stuck in ward with three geezers. He elbowed the call button. Where was that fucking nurse? He needed a shot.

The pain was a living thing, grinding Ron's hands in its teeth and gnawing his arms all the way up to the shoulders. All he wanted to do was sleep. But the pain kept him awake. The pain and the oldest of his three ancient roommates, the one over by the window, the one the nurses called Tommy. Every so often, in between his foghorn snores, he'd let out a yell that would rattle the windows.

Ron hit the call button again with his elbow. Because both his arms were resting in slings suspended from an overhead bar, the nurses had fastened the button to one of the side rails. He had asked them repeatedly for another pain shot, but they kept giving him the same old line over and over: "Sorry, Mr. Daniels, but the doctor left orders for a shot every four hours and no more. You'll have to wait."

Mr. Daniels. He could almost smile at that. His real name was Ronald Daniel Symes. Ron to his friends. He'd given the receptionist a phony name, a phony address, and told them his Blue Cross/Blue Shield card was at home in his wallet. And when they'd wanted to send him home, he'd told them how he lived alone and had no one to feed him or even help him open his apartment door. They'd bought it all. So now he had a place to stay, three meals a day, air conditioning, and when it was all over, he'd skip out and they could take their bill and shove it.

Everything would be great if it weren't for the pain.

"Help me!"

The pain and Tommy.

He hit the button again. Four hours *had* to be up! He needed that

THE TOMB

shot!

The door to the room swung open and someone came in. It wasn't a nurse. It was a guy. But he was dressed in white. Maybe a male nurse. Great! All he needed now was some faggot trying to give him a bed bath in the middle of the night.

But the guy only leaned over the bed and held out one of those tiny plastic medicine cups. Half an inch of colored liquid was inside.

"What's this?"

"For the pain." The guy was dark and had some sort of accent.

"I want a shot, clown!"

"Not time yet for a shot. This will hold you until then."

"It better!"

Ron let him tip the cup up to his lips. It was funny tasting stuff. As he swallowed it, he noticed the guy's left arm was missing. He pulled his head away.

"And listen," he said, feeling a sudden urge to throw his weight around—after all, he was a patient here. "Tell them out there I don't want no more cripples coming in here."

In the darkness, Ron thought he detected a smile on the face above him.

"Certainly, Mr. Daniels. I shall see to it that your next attendant is quite sound of limb."

"Good. Now take off, geek."

"Very well."

Ron decided he liked being a patient. He could give orders and people had to listen. And why not? He was sick and—

"Help me!"

If only he could order Tommy to stop.

The junk the geek had given him didn't seem to be helping his pain. Only thing to do was try to sleep. He thought about that bastard cop who'd busted up his hands tonight. He said it was private, but Ron knew a pig when he saw one. He swore he'd find that sadist bastard even if he had to hang around every precinct house in New York until winter. And then Ron would follow him home. He wouldn't get back at him directly—Ron had a bad feeling about that guy and didn't want to be around if he ever got *really* mad. But maybe he had a wife and kids ...

Ron lay there in a half doze for a good forty-five minutes planning what he'd do to get even with the pig. He was just tipping over the edge into a deep sleep, falling ... finally falling ...

THE TOMB

"Help me!"

Ron jerked violently in the bed, pulling his right arm out of the suspensory sling and knocking it against the side rail. A firey blast of pain shot up to his shoulder. Tears squeezed out of his eyes as breath hissed noisily through his bared teeth.

When the pain subsided to a more tolerable level, he knew what he had to do.

That old fucker, Tommy, had to go.

Ron pulled his left arm out of its sling, then eased himself over the side rail. The floor was cold. He lifted his pillow between his two casts and padded over to Tommy's bed. All he had to do was lay it over the old guy's face and lean on it. A few minutes of that and poof, no more snores, no more yells, no more Tommy.

He saw something move outside the window as he passed by it. He looked closer. It was a shadow, like somebody's head and shoulders. A *big* somebody.

But this was the fifth floor!

He had to be hallucinating. That stuff in the cup must have been stronger than he thought. He bent closer to the window for a better look. What he saw there held him transfixed for a long, agonal heartbeat. It was a face out of a nightmare, worse than all his nightmares combined. And those glowing yellow eyes . . .

A scream started in his throat as he reflexively lurched backward. But before it could reach his lips, a taloned, three-fingered hand smashed through the double pane and clamped savagely, unerringly, around his throat. Ron felt incredible pressure against his windpipe, crushing it closed against his cervical spine with an explosive crunch. The rough flesh against the skin of his throat was cool and damp, almost slimy, with a rotten stench arising from it. He caught a glimpse of smooth dark skin stretched over a long, lean, muscular arm leading out through the shattered glass to . . . what? He arched his back and clawed at the imprisoning fingers, but they were like a steel collar around his neck. As he struggled vainly for air, his vision blurred. And then, with a smooth, almost casual motion, he felt himself yanked bodily through the window, felt the rest of the glass shatter with his passage, the shards either falling away or raking savagely at his flesh. He had one soul-numbing, moon-limned glimpse of his attacker before his vision was mercifully extinguished by his oxygen-starved brain.

And back in the room, after that final instant of crashing noise, all

68

THE TOMB

was quiet again. Two of the remaining patients, deep in Dalmane dreams, stirred in their beds and turned over. Tommy, the closest to the window, shouted "Help me!" and then went back to snoring.

CHAPTER TWO

Bharangpur, West Bengal, India
Wednesday, June 24, 1857

1.

It's all gone wrong. Every bleeding thing gone wrong!
Captain Sir Albert Westphalen of the Bengal European Fusiliers
stood in the shade of an awning between two market stalls and sipped
cool water from a jug freshly drawn from a well. It was a glorious relief
to be shielded from direct attack by the Indian sun, but there was no
escaping the glare. It bounced off the sand in the street, off the white
stucco walls of the buildings, even off the pale hides of those nasty
hump-backed bulls roaming freely through the marketplace. The
glare drove the heat through his eyes to the very center of his brain.
He dearly wished he could pour the contents of the jug over his head
and let the water trickle down the length of his body.

But no. He was a gentleman in the uniform of Her Majesty's army
and surrounded by heathens. He couldn't do anything so undig-
nified. So he stood here in the shade, his high-domed pith helmet
square upon his head, his buff uniform smelly and sopping in the
. armpits and buttoned up tight at the throat, and pretended the heat
didn't bother him. He ignored the sweat soaking the thin hair under
his helmet, oozing down over his face, clinging to the dark mustache
he had so carefully trimmed and waxed this morning, gathering in
drops at his chin to fall off onto his tunic.

Oh, for a breeze. Or better still, rain. But neither was due for
another month. He had heard that when the summer monsoon

71

THE TOMB

started blowing from the southwest in July there would be plenty of rain. Until then, he and his men would have to fry.

It could be worse.

He could have been sent with the others to retake Meerut and Delhi from the rebels ... forced marches along the Ganges basin in full uniform and kit, rushing to face hordes of crazed sepoys waving their bloody talwars and shouting "Din! Din! Din!"

He shuddered. Not for me, thank you very much.

Luckily, the rebellion had not spread this far east, at least not to any appreciable extent. That was fine with Westphalen. He intended to stay as far away from the pandies as he could. He knew from regimental records that there was a total of 20,000 British troops on the subcontinent. What if all of India's untold millions decided to rise up and end the British raj? It was a recurrent nightmare. There would be no more raj.

And no more East India Company. Which, Westphalen knew, was the real reason the army was here—to protect "John Company's" interests. He had sworn to fight for the Crown and he was willing—up to a point—to do that, but he'd be damned if he was going to die fighting for a bunch of tea traders. After all, he was a gentleman and had only accepted a commission out here to forestall the financial catastrophe threatening his estate. And perhaps to make some contacts during his term of service. He had arranged for a purely administrative job: No danger. All part of a simple plan to allow him time to find a way to recoup his considerable gambling losses—one might say incredible losses for a man just forty years of age—and then go home and straighten out his debts. He grimaced at the enormous amount of money he had squandered since his father had died and the baronetcy had passed to him.

But his luck had run true here on the far side of the world—it stayed bad. There had been years of peace in India before he had come—a little trouble here and there, but nothing serious. The raj had seemed totally secure. But now he knew that dissension and discontent among the native recruits had been bubbling beneath the surface, waiting, it seemed, for his arrival. He had been here not even a year, and what happened? The sepoys go on a rampage!

It wasn't fair.

But it could have been worse, Albert, old boy, he told himself for the thousandth time that day. It could be worse.

And it most certainly could be far better. Better to be back in

THE TOMB

Calcutta at Fort William. Not much cooler, but closer to the sea there. If India explodes, it's just a hop and a skip to a boat on the Hoogly River and then off to the safety of the Bay of Bengal.

He took another sip and leaned his back against the wall. It wasn't an officerly posture, but he really didn't give a bloody damn at this point. His office was like a freshly-stoked furnace. The only sane thing to do was to stay here under the awning with a water jug until the sun got lower in the sky. Three o'clock now. It should be cooling down soon.

He waved his hand through the air around his face. If he ever got out of India alive, the one thing he would remember more vividly than the heat and humidity were the flies. They were everywhere, encrusting everything in the marketplace—the pineapples, the oranges, the lemons, the piles of rice—all were covered with black dots that moved and flew and hovered, and lit again. Bold, arrogant flies that landed on your face and darted away just before you could slap them.

That incessant buzz—was it shoppers busy haggling with the merchants, or was it hordes of flies?

The smell of hot bread wafted by his nose. The couple in the stall across the alley to his left sold *chupatties*, little disks of unleavened bread that were a dietary staple of everyone in India, rich and poor alike. He remembered trying them on a couple of occasions and finding them tasteless. For the last hour the woman had been leaning over a dung fire cooking an endless stream of *chupatties* on flat iron plates. The temperature of the air around that fire had to be 130 degrees.

How do these people stand it?

He closed his eyes and wished for a world free of heat, drought, avaricious creditors, senior officers, and rebellious sepoys. He kept them closed, enjoying the relative darkness behind the lids. It would be nice to spend the rest of the day like this, just leaning here and—

It wasn't a sound that snapped his eyes open; it was the lack of it. The street had gone utterly silent. As he straightened from the wall, he could see the shoppers who had been busy inspecting goods and haggling over prices now disappearing into alleys and side streets and doorways—no rush, no panic, but moving with deliberate swiftness, as if they had all suddenly remembered somewhere else they had to be.

Only the merchants remained . . . the merchants and their flies.

THE TOMB

Wary and uneasy, Westphalen gripped the handle of the sabre slung at his left hip. He had been trained in its use but had never actually had to defend himself with it. He hoped he wouldn't have to now.

He sensed movement off to his left and turned.

A squat little toad of a man swathed in the orange dhoti of a holy man was leading a train of six mules on a leisurely course down the middle of the street.

Westphalen allowed himself to relax. Just a *svamin* or holy man of some sort. There was always one or another of them about.

As he watched, the priest veered to the far side of the street and stopped his mules before a cheese stand. He did not move from his place at the head of the train, did not even look left or right. He simply stood and waited. The cheese maker quickly gathered up some of his biggest blocks and wheels and brought them out to the little man who inclined his head a few degrees after an instant's glance at the offering. The merchant put these in a sack tied to the back of one of the mules, then retreated to the rear of his stall.

Not a rupee had changed hands.

Westphalen watched with growing amazement.

Next stop was on Westphalen's side of the street, the chupatty stall next door. The husband brought a basketful out for inspection. Another nod, and these too were deposited on the back of a mule.

Again, no money changed hands—and no questions about quality. Westphalen had never seen anything like it since his arrival in India. These merchants would haggle with their mothers over the price of breakfast.

He could imagine only one thing that could wring such cooperation from them: fear.

The priest moved on without stopping at the water stand.

"Something wrong with your water?" Westphalen said to the vendor squatting on the ground beside him. He spoke in English. He saw no reason to learn an Indian tongue and had never tried. There were fourteen major languages on this God-forsaken subcontinent and something like 250 dialects. An absurd situation. What few words he had picked up had been through osmosis rather than conscious effort. After all, it was the natives' responsibility to learn to understand him. And most of them did, especially the merchants.

"The temple has its own water," the vendor said without looking up.

THE TOMB

"Which temple is that?"

Westphalen wanted to know what the priest held over these merchants' heads to make them so compliant. It was information that might prove useful in the future.

"The Temple-in-the-Hills."

"I didn't know there was a temple in the hills."

This time the water vendor raised his turbanned head and stared at him. The dark eyes held a disbelieving look, as if to say, *How could you not know?*

"And to which one of your heathen gods is this particular temple dedicated?" His words seemed to echo in the surrounding silence.

The water vendor whispered, "Kali, The Black Goddess."

Oh, yes. He had heard that name before. She was supposedly popular in the Bengal region. These Hindus had more gods than you could shake a stick at. A strange religion, Hinduism. He had heard that it had little or no dogma, no founder, and no leader. Really— what kind of a religion was that?

"I thought her big temple was down near Calcutta, at Dakshinesvar."

"There are many temples to Kali," the water vendor said. "But none like the Temple-in-the-Hills."

"Really? And what's so special about this one?"

"Rakoshi."

"What's that?"

But the water vendor lowered his head and refused to respond any further. It was as if he thought he had said too much already.

Six weeks ago, Westphalen would not have tolerated such insolence. But six weeks ago a rebellion by the sepoys had been unthinkable.

He took a final sip of the water, tossed a coin into the silent vendor's lap, and stepped out into the full ferocity of the sun. The air out in the open was like a blast from a burning house. He felt the dust that perpetually overhung the street mix with the beads of perspiration on his face, leaving coated with a fine layer of salty mud.

He followed the *svamin* through the rest of the marketplace, watching the chosen merchants donate the best of their wares without a grumble or a whimper, as if glad of the opportunity. Westphalen tracked him through most of Bharangpur, along its widest thoroughfares, down its narrowest alleys. And everywhere the priest and his mule train went, the people faded away at his approach and reappeared in his wake.

Finally, as the sun was drifting down the western sky, the priest came to the north gate.

Now we've got him, Westphalen thought.

All pack animals were to be inspected for contraband before allowed exit from Bharangpur or any other garrisoned town. The fact that there was no known rebel activity anywhere in Bengal did not matter; it was a general order and as such had to be enforced.

Westphalen watched from a distance of about two hundred yards. He would wait until the lone British sentry had begun the inspection, then he would stroll over as if on a routine patrol of the gate and learn a little more about this *svamin* and his temple in the hills.

He saw the priest stop at the gate and speak to a sentry with an Enfield casually slung across his back. They seemed like old friends. After a few moments, without inspection or detention, the priest resumed his path through the gate—but not before Westphalen had seen him press something into the sentry's palm. It was a flash of movement. If Westphalen had blinked he would have missed it.

The priest and his mules were beyond the wall and on their way toward the hills in the northwest by the time Westphalen reached the gate.

"Give me your rifle, soldier!"

The sentry saluted, then shrugged the Enfield off his shoulder and handed it to Westphalen without question. Westphalen knew him. His name was MacDougal, an enlisted man—young, red-faced, hard-fighting, hard-drinking, like most of his fellow Bengal European Fusiliers. In his three weeks as commander of the Bharangpur garrison, Westphalen had come to think of him as a good soldier.

"I'm placing you under arrest for dereliction of duty!"

MacDougal blanched. "Sir, I—"

"And for taking a bribe!"

"I tried to give it back to 'im, sir!"

Westphalen laughed. This soldier must think him blind as well as stupid!

"Of course you did! Just like you gave his mules a thorough inspection."

"Old Jaggernath's only bringing supplies to the temple, sir. I've been here two years, captain, and 'e's come by every month, like clockwork, every new moon. Only brings food out to the hills, 'e does, sir."

THE TOMB

"He must be inspected like everybody else."

MacDougal glanced after the retreating mule train. "Jaggernath said they don't like their food touched, sir. Only by their own kind."

"Well, isn't that a pity! And I suppose you let him pass uninspected out of the goodness of your heart?" Westphalen was steadily growing angrier at this soldier's insolence. "Empty your pockets and let's see how many pieces of silver it took to get you to betray your fellow soldiers."

Color suddenly flooded back into MacDougal's face. "I'd never betray me mates!"

For some reason, Westphalen believed him. But he couldn't drop the matter now.

"Empty your pockets!"

MacDougal emptied only one: from his right-hand pocket he withdrew a small, rough stone, clear, dull red in color.

Westphalen withheld a gasp.

"Give it to me."

He held it up to the light of the setting sun. He had seen his share of uncut stones as he had gradually turned the family valuables into cash to appease his more insistent creditors. This was an uncut ruby. A tiny thing, but polished up it could bring an easy hundred pounds. His hand trembled. If this is what the priest gave to a sentry as a casual reward for leaving his temple's food untouched . . .

"Where is this temple?"

"Don't know, sir." MacDougal was watching him eagerly, probably looking for a way out of dereliction charges. "And I've never been able to find out. The locals don't know and don't seem to want to know. The Temple-in-the-Hills is supposed to be full of jewels but guarded by demons."

Westphalen grunted. More heathen rubbish. But the stone in his hand was genuine enough. And the casual manner in which it had been given to MacDougal indicated that there could be many more where that came from. With the utmost reluctance, he handed the ruby back to MacDougal. He would play for bigger stakes. And to do so he had to appear completely unconcerned about money.

"I guess no harm has been done. Sell that for what you can and divide it up between the men. And divide it equally, hear?"

MacDougal appeared about to faint with surprise and relief, but he managed a sharp salute. "Yes, sir!"

Westphalen tossed the Enfield back at him and walked away,

knowing that in MacDougal's eyes he was the fairest, most generous commanding officer he had ever known. Westphalen wanted the enlisted man to feel that way. He had use for MacDougal, and for any other soldier who had been in Bharangpur for a few years.

Westphalen had decided to find this Temple-in-the-Hills. It might well hold the answer to all his financial problems.

CHAPTER THREE

Manhattan
Friday, August 3, 198-

1.

Jack awoke shortly before ten feeling exhausted.

He had come home jubilant after last night's success, but the glow had faded quickly. The apartment had had that empty feel to it. Worse: *he* felt empty. He had quickly downed two Lites, hid the second half of his fee behind the cedar plank, then crawled into bed. After a couple of hours of sleep, however, he had found himself wide awake for no good reason. An hour of twisting around in his sheets did no good, so he gave up and watched the end of *Bride of Frankenstein.* As the dinky little Universal plane went around the world and said "The End," he had dozed off again for another couple of hours of fitful slumber.

He now pushed himself out of bed and took a wake-up shower. For breakfast he finished off the Cocoa Puffs and started on a box of Sugar Pops. As he shaved he saw that the thermometer outside his bedroom window read 89°—in the shade. He dressed accordingly in slacks and a short-sleeve shirt, then sat by the phone. He had two calls to make: one to Gia, and one to the hospital. He decided to save Gia for last.

The hospital switchboard told him that the phone had been disconnected in the room number he gave them; there was no longer a Mrs. Bahkti listed as a patient. His heart sank. *Damn!* Even though he had spoken to the old lady for only a few minutes, the news of her passing hurt. So senseless. At least he had been able to get the necklace back to her before she packed it in. He told the operator to connect him with the nursing desk on the old lady's floor. Soon he was talking to Marta.

"When did Mrs. Bahkti die?"

"Far as I know, she didn't."

A flash of hope: "Transferred to another floor?"

"No. It happened during the change of shift. The grandson and granddaughter—"

"Granddaughter?"

"You wouldn't like her Jack—she's not a blond. Anyway, they came to the desk at shift change this morning while we were all taking report and thanked us for the concern we'd shown their grandmother. Said they'd take care of her from now on. Then they walked out. When we went to check on her, she was gone."

Jack took the phone away from his ear and scowled at it before replying.

"How'd they get her out? She sure as hell couldn't walk!"

He could almost feel Marta shrug at the other end of the line. "Beats me. But they tell me the guy with one arm was acting real strange toward the end of the shift, wouldn't let anyone in to see her for the last few hours."

"Why'd they let him get away with that?" For no good reason, Jack was angry, feeling like a protective relative. "That old lady needed all the help she could get. You can't let someone interfere like that, even if he is the grandson! You should have called security and had them—"

"Cool it, Jack." Marta said with an authoritative snap to her tone. "I wasn't here then."

"Yeah. Right. Sorry. It's just that—"

"Besides, from what they tell me, this place was a zoo last night after a patient on Five North climbed out a window. Security was all tied up over there. Really weird! This guy with casts on both hands breaks through his room window and somehow gets down the wall and runs away.

Jack felt his spine straighten involuntarily. "Casts? On both hands?"

"Yeah. Came in through the E.R. last night with comminuted fractures. Nobody can see how he climbed down the wall, especially since he must of got cut up pretty bad going through the window. But he wasn't splattered on the pavement, so he must have made it."

"Why the window? Was he under arrest or something?"

"That's the really weird thing. He could have walked out the front door if he wanted to. Anyhow, we all figure the grandkids snuck old Mrs. Bahkti out during all the commotion."

THE TOMB

"What'd the guy who went through the window look like? Did he have a patch on his left eye?" Jack held his breath as he waited for the answer.

"I haven't the faintest, Jack. Did you know the guy? I could find out his name for you."

"Thanks, Marta, but that won't help. Never mind."

After saying good-bye, he cradled the receiver and sat staring at the floor. In his mind's eye he was watching Kusum steal into a hospital room, grab a young man with a gauze patch over his left eye and casts on both arms, and hurl him through a window. But Jack couldn't buy it. He knew Kusum would have liked to do just that, but he couldn't see a one-armed man being capable of it. Especially not while he was busy spiriting his grandmother out of the hospital.

Irritably, he shook off the images and concentrated on his other problem: the disappearance of Grace Westphalen. He had nothing to go on but the unlabeled bottle of herbal fluid, and had only a vague gut suspicion that it was somehow involved. He didn't trust hunches, but he decided to follow this one up for lack of anything better.

He picked up the bottle from where he had left it on the oak hutch last night and unscrewed the cap. The odor was unfamiliar, but definitely herbal. He placed a drop on a fingertip and tasted it. Not bad. Only thing to do was to have it analyzed and see where it came from. Maybe by some far out chance there was a connection to whatever happened to Grace.

He picked up the phone again, intending to call Gia, then put it down. He couldn't bear to hear the ice in her voice. Not yet. There was something else he should do first: Call that crazy one-armed Indian and find out what he had done with the old lady. He dialed the number Kusum had left on the office answerphone yesterday.

A woman answered, her voice was soft, unaccented, almost liquid. She told him Kusum was out.

"When will he be back?"

"This evening. Is ... is this Jack?"

"Uh, yes." He was startled and puzzled. "How did you know?"

Her laugh was musical. "Kusum said you'd probably be calling. I'm Kolabati, his sister. I was just going to call your office. I want to meet you, Repairman Jack."

"And I want to know where your grandmother is!"

"On her way to India," she said lightly, "where she will be cared for by our own doctors."

Jack was relieved but still annoyed. "That could have been arranged without sneaking her out the back door or whatever it was you did."

"Of course. But you do not know my brother. He always does things *his* way. Just like you, from what he tells me. I like that in a man. When can we meet?"

Something in her voice caused his concern for the grandmother to fade into the background. She was, after all, under medical care ...

"Are you staying in the States long?" he asked, temporizing. He had a rule that once he was through with a job, he was through. But he had an urge to see what sort of face went with that incredible voice. And come to think of it, this woman wasn't actually a customer—her brother was.

Jack, you should have been a lawyer.

"I live in Washington, D.C. I rushed up as soon as I heard about grandmother. Do you know where the Waldorf is?"

"Heard of it."

"Why don't we meet in the Peacock Room at six?"

I do believe I'm being asked out for a date. Well, why not?

"Sure. How'll I know you?"

"I'll be wearing white."

"See you at six."

He hung up, wondering at his reckless mood. Blind dates were not his style at all.

But now for the hard part: a call to Gia. He dialed Nellie's number. After precisely two rings, Eunice answered with "Payton residence," and called Gia to the phone at Jack's request. He waited with a curious mixture of dread and anticipation.

"Hello?" Her voice was cool, businesslike.

"How'd things go last night?"

"That's none of your business, Jack!" she said with an immediate flare of anger. "What right have you got to pry into—"

"Hey!" he said. "I just want to know if there's been any ransom note or phone calls or any word from Grace! What the hell's the matter with you?"

"Oh ... sorry. Nothing. No word at all. Nellie's really down. Got any good news I can tell her?"

"Afraid not."

"Are you doing anything?"

"Yeah."

"What?"

"Detective stuff. You know, tracing clues, following up leads. That kind of thing."

Gia made no reply. Her silence was eloquent enough. And she was right; wisecracks were out of place.

"I don't have much to go on, Gia, but I'll be doing whatever can be done."

"I don't suppose we can ask for more than that," she said finally, her voice as cool as ever.

"How about lunch today?"

"No, Jack."

"A late dinner, then?"

"Jack . . ." The pause here was long; it ended with a sigh. "Let's just keep this businesslike, okay? Just business. Nothing has changed. Any lunches you want to have, you have them with Nellie. Maybe I'll come along, but don't count on it. *Capisce?*"

"Yeah." He had an urge to rip the phone out of the wall and hurl it out the nearest window. But he made himself sit there, say a polite good-bye, hang up, and place the phone gently on the table, right where it belonged.

He forcefully removed Gia from his thoughts. He had things to do.

2.

Gia put the phone down and leaned against the wall. She had almost made a fool out of herself a moment ago when Jack had asked her how things had gone last night. She'd suddenly had a vision of Jack trailing her and Carl to the restaurant and from the restaurant to Carl's place.

They had made love for the first time last night. She hadn't wanted their relationship to get that far this soon. She had promised herself to take this one slow, to refuse to rush or to be rushed. After all, look what had happened with Jack. But last night she had changed her mind. Tension had been building up in her all day since seeing Jack, building until she had felt it was going to strangle her. She had needed someone. And Carl was there. And he wanted her very much.

In the past she had gently refused his invitations back to his apartment. But last night she had agreed. Everything had been right. The view of the city from his windows had been breath-taking, the brandy smooth and burning in her throat, the lighting in his bedroom so soft it had made her bare skin glow when he had undressed her, making her feel beautiful.

Carl was a good lover, a patient, skilled, gentle, considerate lover.

But nothing happened last night. She had faked an orgasm in time with his. She didn't like herself for that, but it had seemed like the right thing to do at the time. Carl had done everything right. It wasn't his fault she hadn't even come close to the release she needed.

It was all Jack's fault.

Seeing him again had got her so uptight she couldn't have enjoyed Carl last night if he had been the greatest lover in all the world! And he was certainly a better lover than Jack!

No ... that wasn't true. Jack had been good. Very good. There had been times when they had spent the whole night—

Nellie's front doorbell rang. Since Gia was passing by, she answered it. It was a messenger from Carl to pick up the artwork she had told him about last night. And there was something for her: a bouquet of mums and roses. She handed the messenger the artwork and opened the enclosed card as soon as the door was closed. "I'll call you tonight." A nice touch. Carl didn't miss a trick. Too bad—

"What lovely flowers!"

Gia snapped alert at the sound of Nellie's voice.

"Yes, aren't they. From Carl. That was Jack on the phone, by the way. He wanted to know if there'd been any word."

"Has he learned anything?"

Gia shook her head, pitying the almost childish eagerness in the old woman's face. "He'll let us know as soon as he does."

"Something awful has happened, I just know it."

"You know nothing of the kind," Gia said, putting her arm around Nellie's shoulders. "This is probably all a big misunderstanding."

"I hope so. I really do." She looked up at Gia. "Would you do me a favor, dear? Call the Mission and send them my regrets. I won't be attending the reception tomorrow night."

"You should go."

"No. It would be unseemly."

"Don't be silly. Grace would want you to go. And besides, you need a change of scenery. You haven't left this house all week."

"What if she calls?"

"Eunice is here to relay any messages."

"But to go out and have a good time—"

"I thought you told me you never had a good time at these affairs."

Nellie smiled, and that was good to see. "True ... very true. Well, I rather suppose you're right. Perhaps I *should* go. But only on one condition."

84

THE TOMB

"What's that?"

"You go with me."

Gia was startled at the request. The last thing in the world she wanted to do on a Saturday night was stand around in a room full of U.N. diplomats.

"No. Really. I couldn't—"

"Of course you can!"

"But Vicky is—"

"Eunice will be here."

Gia racked her brain for excuses. There had to be a way out of this.

"I've nothing to wear."

"We'll go out and buy you something."

"Out of the question!"

Nellie pulled a handkerchief out of a pocket and dabbed her lips. "Then I shan't be going either."

Gia did her best to glare angrily at Nellie, but only managed to hold the expression for a few seconds, then she broke into a smile.

"All right, you old blackmailer—!"

"I resent being called old."

"—I'll go with you, but I'll find something of my own to wear."

"You'll come with me tomorrow afternoon and put a dress on my account. If you're to accompany me, you must have the proper clothes. And that's all I shall say on the matter. We shall leave after lunch."

With that, she turned and bustled away toward the library. Gia was filled with a mixture of affection and annoyance. Once again she had been outflanked by the old lady from London.

3.

Jack walked in the main entrance of the Waldorf at six precisely and went up the steps to the bustling lobby. It had been a hectic day but he had managed to get here on time.

He had arranged for analysis of the contents of the bottle he had found in Grace's room, then had gone down to the streets and looked up every shady character he knew—and he knew more than he cared to count. There was no talk anywhere about anybody snatching a rich old lady. By late afternoon he was drenched with sweat and feeling gritty all over. He had showered, shaved, dressed and cabbed over to Park Avenue.

Jack had never had a reason to go to the Waldorf before so he didn't know what to expect from this Peacock Room where Kolabati wanted to meet him. To be safe, he had invested in a lightweight cream-colored suit and a pinkish shirt and paisley tie to go with it—at least the salesman said they went with it. He thought at first he might be over-doing it, then figured it would be hard to overdress for the Waldorf. From his brief conversation with Kolabati he sensed she would be dressed to the nines.

Jack absorbed the sights and sounds of the lobby as he walked through it. All races, all nationalities, all ages, shapes, and sizes milled or sat about. To his left, behind a low railing and an arch, people sat drinking at small tables. He walked over and saw a little oval sign that read "Peacock Room."

He glanced around. If the Waldorf Lobby were a sidewalk, the Peacock Room would be a sidewalk cafe, an air-conditioned model *sans* flies and fumes. He didn't see anyone at the outer tables who fit his image of Kolabati. He studied the clientele. Everyone looked well-heeled and at ease. Jack felt very much out of his element here. This was not his scene. He felt exposed standing here. Maybe this was a mistake—

"A table, sir?"

A middle-aged *maitre d'hotel* was at his shoulder, looking at him expectantly. His accent was French with perhaps a *soupcon* of Brooklyn.

"I think so. I'm not sure. I'm supposed to meet someone. She's in a white dress and—"

The man's eyes lit up. "She is here! Come!"

Jack followed him into the rear section, wondering how this man could be so sure he had the right party. They passed a series of alcoves, each with a sofa and stuffed chairs around a cocktail table, like tiny living rooms all in a row. There were paintings on the wall, adding to the warm, comfortable atmosphere. They turned into a wing and were approaching its end when Jack saw her.

He knew then why there had been no hesitation on the part of the *maitre d'hotel*, why there could be no mistake. This was The-Woman-in-the-White-Dress. She might as well have been the only woman in the room.

She sat alone on a divan against the rear wall, her shoes off, her legs drawn up sideways under her as if she were sitting at home listening to music—classical music, or maybe a raga. A wine glass half full of faintly amber liquid swirled gently in her hand. There was a strong family resemblance to Kusum, but Kolabati was younger, late twenties,

86

perhaps. She had bright, dark, wide-set, almond-shaped eyes, wide cheek bones, a fine nose dimpled over the flare of the left nostril where perhaps it had been pierced to set a jewel, and smooth, flawless, mocha-colored skin. Her hair too was dark, almost black, parted in the middle and curled at the side around her ears and the nape of her neck. Old fashioned but curiously just right for her. She had a full lower lip, colored a deep glossy red. And all that was dark about her was made darker by the whiteness of her dress.

The necklace was the clincher, though. Had Jack the slightest doubt about her identity, the silvery iron necklace with the two yellow stones laid it immediately to rest.

She extended her hand from where she was seated on the couch. "It's good to see you, Jack." Her voice was rich and dark, like her; and her smile, so white and even, was breath-taking. She leaned forward, her breasts swelling against the thin fabric of her dress as it shaped itself around the minute nipple-bulge centered on each. She did not seem to have the slightest doubt as to who he was.

"Ms. Bahkti," he said, taking her hand. Her nails, like her lips, were a deep red, her dusky skin soft and smooth as polished ivory. His mind seemed to go blank. He really should say something more. "Glad to see you haven't lost your necklace." That sounded good, didn't it?

"Oh, no. Mine stays right where it is!" She released his hand and patted the cushion next to her. "Come. Sit. We've much to talk about."

Close up, her eyes were wise and knowing, as if she had absorbed all the wonders of her race and its timeless culture.

The *maitre d'hotel* did not call a waiter but stood by quietly as Jack took his place beside Kolabati. It was possible that he was a very patient man, but Jack noticed that his eyes never left Kolabati.

"May I get m'seur something to drink?" he said when Jack was settled.

Jack looked at Kolabati's glass. "What's that?"

"Kir."

He wanted a beer, but this was the Waldorf. "I'll have one of those."

She laughed. "Don't be silly! Bring him a beer. They have Bass Ale here."

"I'm not much for ale. But I'll take a Beck's Light if you've got it." At least he'd be drinking imported beer. What he really wanted was a Rolling Rock.

"Very good." The *maitre d'hotel* finally went away.

"How'd you know I like beer?" The confidence with which she had

THE TOMB

said it made him uneasy.

"A lucky guess. I was sure you wouldn't like kir." She studied him. "So ... you're the man who retrieved the necklace. It was a seemingly impossible task, yet you did it. I owe you a debt of undying gratitude."

"It was only a necklace."

"A very important necklace."

"Maybe, but it's not as if I saved her life or anything."

"Perhaps you did. Perhaps return of the necklace gave her the strength and the hope to go on living. It was very important to her. Our whole family wears them—every one of us. We're never without it."

"Never?"

"Never."

Full of eccentricities, these Bahktis.

The Beck's arrived, delivered by the *maitre d'hotel* himself, who poured the first glassful, lingered a moment, then wandered off with obvious reluctance.

"You realize, don't you," Kolabati said as Jack quaffed a few ounces of his beer, "that you have made two lifelong friends in the past 24 hours: my brother and myself."

"What about your grandmother?"

Kolabati blinked. "Her, too, of course. Do not take our gratitude lightly, Jack. Not mine. And especially not my brother's—Kusum never forgets a favor or a slight."

"Just what does your brother do at the U.N.?" It was small talk. Jack really wanted to know all about Kolabati, but didn't want to appear too interested.

"I'm not sure. A minor post." She must have noticed Jack's puzzled frown. "Yes, I know—he doesn't seem to be a man who'd be satisfied with any sort of minor post. Believe me, he isn't. Back home his name is known in every province."

"Why?"

"He is the leader of a new Hindu fundamentalist movement. He and many others believe that India and Hinduism have become too Westernized. He wants to return to the old ways. He's been picking up a surprising number of followers over the years and developing considerable political clout."

"Sounds like the Moral Majority over here. What is he—the Jerry Falwell of India?"

Kolabati's expression became grim. "Perhaps more. His singleness of purpose can be frightening at times. Some fear he may become the

THE TOMB

Ayatolla Khomeini of India. That's why everyone was shocked early last year when he suddenly requested diplomatic assignment at the London Embassy. It was granted immediately—no doubt the government was delighted to have him out of the country. Recently he was transferred here to the U.N.—again at his request. I'm sure his followers and adversaries back home are mystified, but I know my brother. I'll bet he's getting enough international experience under his belt so he can go home and become a credible candidate for a major political office. But enough of Kusum ...''

Jack felt Kolabati's hand against his chest, pushing him back against the cushions.

"Get comfortable now," she said, her dark eyes boring into him, "and tell me all about yourself. I want to know everything, especially how you came to be Repairman Jack."

Jack took another swallow of beer and forced himself to pause. He had a sudden urge to tell her everything, to open up his whole past to her. It frightened him. He never opened up to anyone except Abe. Why Kolabati? Perhaps it was because she already knew something about him; perhaps because she was so effusive in her gratitude for achieving the "impossible" and returning her grandmother's necklace. Telling all was out of the question, but pieces of the truth wouldn't hurt. The question was: what to tell, what to edit?

"It just sort of happened."

"There had to be a first time. Start there. Tell me about it."

He settled into the cushions, adjusting his position until the lump of the holstered Mauser .380 sat comfortably in the small of his back, and began telling her about Mr. Canelli, his first fix-it customer.

4.

Summer was drawing to a close. He was 17, still living in Johnson, New Jersey, a small, semirural town in Burlington County. His father was working as a C.P.A. then, and his mother was still alive. His brother was in the New Jersey State College of Medicine and his sister was in Rutgers prelaw.

On the corner down the street from his house lived Mr. Vito Canelli, a retired widower. From the time the ground thawed until the time it froze again, he worked in his yard. Especially on his lawn. He seeded and fertilized every couple of weeks, watered it daily. Mr. Canelli had the greenest lawn in the county. It was usually flawless. The only times it

89

THE TOMB

wasn't was when someone cut the corner turning right off 541 onto Jack's street. The first few times were probably accidents, but then some of the more vandalism-prone kids in the area started making a habit of it. Driving across "the old wop's" lawn became a Friday and Saturday night ritual. Finally, old Mr. Canelli put up a three-foot white picket fence and that seemed to put an end to it. Or so he thought.

It was early. Jack was walking up to the highway towing the family Toro behind him. For the past few summers he had made his money doing gardening chores and cutting grass around town. He liked the work and liked even better the fact that he could adjust his hours almost any way he wished.

When he came into view of Mr. Canelli's yard he stopped and gaped.

The picket fence was down—smashed and scattered all over the lawn in countless white splinters. The small flowering ornamental trees that blossomed in varied colors each spring—dwarf crabapples, dogwoods—had been broken off a foot above the ground. Yews and junipers were flattened and ground into the dirt. The plaster pink flamingos that everybody laughed about were shattered and crushed to powder. And the lawn ... there weren't just tire tracks across it, there were long, wide gouges up to six inches deep. Whoever had done it hadn't been satisfied with simply driving across the lawn and flattening some grass; they had skidded and slewed their car or cars around until the entire yard had been ripped to pieces.

As Jack approached for a closer look, he saw a figure standing at the corner of the house looking out at the ruins. It was Mr. Canelli. His shoulders were slumped and quaking. Sunlight glistened off the tears on his cheeks. Jack knew little about Mr. Canelli. He was a quiet man who bothered no one. He had no wife, no children or grandchildren around. All he had was his yard: his hobby, his work of art, the focus of what was left of his life. Jack knew from his own small-time landscaping jobs around town how much sweat was invested in a yard like that. No man should have to see that kind of effort wantonly destroyed. No man that age should be reduced to standing in his own yard and crying.

Mr. Canelli's helplessness unleashed something inside Jack. He had lost his temper before, but the rage he felt within him at that moment bordered on insanity. His jaw was clamped so tightly his teeth ached; his entire body trembled as his muscles bunched into knots. He had a good idea of who had done it and could confirm his suspicions with little difficulty. He had to fight off a wild urge to find them and run the Toro over their faces a few times.

THE TOMB

Reason won out. No sense landing himself in jail while they got to play the roles of unfortunate victims.

There was another way. It leaped full-blown into Jack's head as he stood there.

He walked over to Mr. Canelli and said, "I can fix it for you."

The old man blotted his face with a handkerchief and glared at him. "Fix it. Why? So you an' your friends can destroy it again?"

"I'll fix it so it never happens again."

Mr. Canelli looked at him a long time without speaking, then said, "Come inside. You tell me how."

Jack didn't give him all the details, just a list of the materials he would need. He added fifty dollars for labor. Mr. Canelli agreed but said he'd hold the fifty until he saw results. They shook hands and had a small glass of barolo to seal the deal.

Jack began the following day. He brought three dozen small spreading yews and planted them three and a half feet apart along the perimeter of the corner lot while Mr. Canelli started restorative work on his lawn. They talked while they worked. Jack learned that the damage had been done by a smallish, low-riding, light-colored car and a dark van. Mr. Canelli hadn't been able to get the license plate numbers. He had called the police, but the vandals were long gone by the time one of the local cops came by. The police had been called before, but the incidents were so random and, until now, of such little consequence, that they hadn't taken the complaints too seriously.

The next step was to secure three dozen four-foot lengths of six-inch pipe and hide them in Mr. Canelli's garage. They used a posthole digger to open a three-foot hole directly behind each yew. Late one night, Jack and Mr. Canelli mixed up a couple of bags of cement in the garage and filled each of the four-foot iron pipes. Three days later, again under cover of darkness, the cement-filled pipes were inserted into the holes behind the yews and the dirt packed tight around them. Each bush now had twelve to fifteen inches of makeshift lolly column hidden within its branches.

The white picket fence was rebuilt around the yard and Mr. Canelli continued to work at getting his lawn back into shape. The only thing left for Jack to do was sit back and wait.

It took a while. August ended. Labor Day passed, school began again. By the third week of September, Mr. Canelli had the yard graded again. The new grass had sprouted and was filling in nicely.

And that, apparently, was what they had been waiting for.

THE TOMB

The sounds of sirens awoke Jack at 1:30 A.M. on a Sunday morning. Red lights were flashing up at the corner by Mr. Canelli's house. Jack pulled on his jeans and ran to the scene.

Two first-aid rigs were pulling away as he approached the top of the block. Straight ahead a black van lay on its side by the curb. The smell of gasoline filled the air. In the wash of light from a street lamp overheard, he saw that the undercarriage was damaged beyond repair: The left front lower control arm was torn loose; the floor pan was ripped open exposing a bent drive shaft; the differential was knocked out of line, and the gas tank was leaking. A fire truck stood by, readying to hose down the area.

He walked on to the front of Mr. Canelli's house where a yellow Camaro was stopped nose-on to the yard. The windshield was spider-webbed with cracks and steam plumed around the edges of the sprung hood. A quick glance under the hood revealed a ruptured radiator, bent front axle, and cracked engine block.

Mr. Canelli stood on his front steps. He waved Jack over and stuck a fifty dollar bill into his hand.

Jack stood beside him and watched until both vehicles were towed away, until the street had been hosed down, until the fire truck and police cars were gone. He was bursting inside. He felt he could leap off the steps and fly around the yard if he wished. He could not remember ever feeling so good. Nothing smokable, ingestible, or injectable would ever give him a high like this.

He was hooked.

5.

One hour, three beers and two kirs later, it dawned upon Jack that he had told much more than he had intended. He had gone on from Mr. Canelli to describe some of his more interesting fix-it jobs. Kolabati seemed to enjoy them all, especially the ones where he had taken special pains to make the punishment fit the crime.

A combination of factors had loosened his tongue. First of all was a feeling of privacy. He and Kolabati seemed to have the far end of this wing of the Peacock Room to themselves. There were dozens of conversations going on in the wing, blending into a susurrant undertone that wound around them, masking their own words and making them indistinguishable from the rest. but most of all, there was Kolabati, so interested, so intent upon what he had to say that he kept talking, saying

92

more than he wished, saying anything to keep that fascinated look in her eyes. He talked to her as he had talked to no one else he could remember—except perhaps Abe. Abe had learned about him over a period of years and had seen much of it happen. Kolabati was getting a big helping in one sitting.

Throughout his narrative, Jack watched for her reaction, fearing she might turn away like Gia had. But Kolabati was obviously not like Gia. Her eyes fairly glowed with enthusiasm and ... admiration.

It was, however, time to shut up. He had said enough. They sat for a quiet moment, toying with their empty glasses. Jack was about to ask her if she wanted a refill when she turned to him.

"You don't pay taxes, do you."

The statement startled him. Uneasy, he wondered how she knew.

"Why do you say that?"

"I sense you are a self-made outcast. Am I right?"

" 'Self-made outcast.' I like that."

"Liking it is not the same as answering the question."

"I consider myself a sort of sovereign state. I don't recognize other governments within my borders."

"But you've exiled yourself from more than the government. You live and work completely outside society. Why?"

"I'm not an intellectual. I can't give you a carefully reasoned man-ifesto. It's just the way I want to live."

Her eyes bored into him. "I don't accept that. Something cut you off. What was it?"

This woman was uncanny! It was as if she could look into his mind and read all his secrets. Yes—there had been an incident that had caused him to withdraw from the rest of "civilized" society. But he couldn't tell her about it. He felt at ease with Kolabati, but wasn't about to confess to murder.

"I'd rather not say."

She studied him. "Are your parents alive?"

Jack felt his insides tighten. "Only my father."

"I see. Did your mother die of natural causes?"

She can read minds! That's the only explanation!

"No. And I don't want to say any more."

"Very well. But however you came to be what you are, I'm sure it was by honorable means."

Her confidence in him simultaneously warmed and discomfitted him. He wanted to change the subject.

93

THE TOMB

"Hungry?"

"Famished!"

"Any place in particular you'd like to go? There are some Indian restaurant—"

Her eyebrows arched. "If I were Chinese, would you offer me egg rolls? Am I dressed in a sari?"

No. That clinging white dress looked like it came straight from a designer's shop in Paris.

"French, then?"

"I lived in France a while. Please: I live in America now. I want American food."

"Well, I like to eat where I can relax."

"I want to go to Beefsteak Charlie's."

Jack burst out laughing. "There's one near where I live! I go there all the time! Mainly because when it comes to food, I tend to be impressed more by quantity than by quality."

"Good. Then you know the way?"

He half rose, then sat down again. "Wait a minute. They serve ribs there. Indians don't eat pork, do they?"

"No. You're thinking of Pakistanis. They're Moslems and Moslems don't eat pork. I'm Hindu. We don't eat beef."

"Then why Beefsteak—?"

"I hear they have a good salad bar, with lots of shrimp. And 'all the beer, wine, or sangria you can drink.'"

"Then let's go," Jack said, rising and presenting his arm.

She slipped into her shoes and was up and close beside him in a single liquid motion. Jack threw a ten and a twenty on the table and started to walk away.

"No receipt?" Kolabati asked with a sly smile. "I'm sure you can make tonight deductible."

"I use the short form."

She laughed. A delightful sound.

On their way toward the front of the Peacock Room, Jack was very much aware of the warm pressure of Kolabati's hand on the inside of his arm and around his biceps, just as he was aware of the veiled attention they drew from all sides as they passed.

From the Peacock Room in the Waldorf on Park Avenue to Beefsteak Charlie's on the West Side—culture shock. But Kolabati moved from one stratum to the other as easily as she moved from garnish to garnish at the crowded salad bar where the attention she attracted was much

94

THE TOMB

more openly admiring than at the Waldorf. She seemed infinitely adaptable, and Jack found that fascinating. In fact, he found everything about her fascinating.

He had begun probing her past during the cab ride uptown, learning that she and her brother were from a wealthy family in the Bengal region of India, that Kusum had lost his arm as a boy in a train wreck that had killed both of their parents, after which they had been raised by the grandmother Jack had met the night before. That explained their devotion to her. Kolabati was currently teaching in Washington at the Georgetown University School of Linguistics and now and again consulting for the School of Foreign Service.

Jack watched her eat the cold shrimp piled before her. Her fingers were nimble, her movements delicate but sure as she peeled the carapaces, dipped the pink bodies in either cocktail sauce or the little plate of Russian dressing she had brought to the table, then popped them into her mouth. She ate with a gusto he found exciting. It was rare these days to find a woman who so relished a big meal. He was sick to death of talk about calories and pounds and waistlines. Calorie-counting was for during the week. When he was out to eat with a woman, he wanted to see her relish the food as much as he did. It became a shared vice. It linked them in the sin of enjoying a full belly and reveling in the tasting, chewing, swallowing, and washing down that led up to it. They became partners in crime. It was erotic as all hell.

The meal was over.

Kolabati leaned back in her chair and stared at him. Between them lay the remains of a number of salads, two steak bones, an empty pitcher of sangria for her, an empty beer pitcher for him, and the casings of at least a hundred shrimp.

"We have met the enemy," Jack said, "and he is in us. Just as well you don't like steak, though. They were on the tough side."

"Oh, I like steak. It's just that beef is supposed to be bad for your karma."

As she spoke her hand crept across the table and found his. Her touch was electrifying—a shock literally ran up his arm. Jack swallowed and tried to keep the conversation going. No point in letting her see how she was getting to him.

"Karma. There's a word you hear an awful lot. What's it mean, really? It's like fate, isn't it?"

Kolabati's eyebrows drew together. "Not exactly. It's not easy to explain. It starts with the idea of the transmigration of the soul—what we call the *atman*—and how it undergoes many successive incarnations or lives."

"Reincarnation." Jack had heard of that—Bridey Murphy and all.

Kolabati turned his hand over and began lightly running her fingernails over his palm. Gooseflesh sprang up all over his body.

"Right," she said. "Karma is the burden of good or evil your *atman* carries with it from one life to the next. It's not fate, because you are free to determine how much good or evil you do in each of your lives, but then again, the weight of good or evil in your karma determines the kind of life you will be born into—high born or low born."

"And that goes on forever?" He wished what she was doing to his hand would go on forever.

"No. Your *atman* can be liberated from the karmic wheel by achieving a state of perfection in life. This is *moksha*. It frees the *atman* from further incarnations. It is the ultimate goal of every *atman*."

"And eating beef would hold you back from *moksha*?" It sounded silly.

Kolabati seemed to read his mind again. "Not so odd, really. Jews and Moslems have a similar sanction against pork. For us, beef pollutes the karma."

" 'Pollutes.' "

"That's the word."

"Do you worry that much about your karma?"

"Not as much as I should. Certainly not as much as Kusum does." Her eyes clouded. "He's become obsessed with his karma . . . his karma and Kali."

That struck a dissonant chord in Jack. "Kali? Wasn't she worshipped by a bunch of stranglers?" Again, his source was *Gunga Din*.

Kolabati's eyes cleared and flashed as she dug her fingernails into his palm, turning pleasure to pain. "That wasn't Kali but a diminished avatar of her called Bhavani who was worshipped by Thugges— low-caste criminals! Kali is the Supreme Goddess!

"Whoops! Sorry."

She smiled. "Where do you live?"

"Not far."

"Take me there."

Jack hesitated, knowing it was his firm personal rule to never let people know where he lived unless he had known them for a good long while. But she was stroking his palm again.

THE TOMB

"Now?"

"Yes."

"Okay."

6.

For certain is death for the born
And certain is birth for the dead;
Therefore over the inevitable
Thou shouldst not grieve.

Kusum lifted his head from his study of the *Bhagavad Gita*. There it was again. That sound from below. It came to him over the dull roar of the city beyond the dock, the city that never slept, over the nocturnal harbor sounds, and the creaks and rattles of the ship as the tide caressed its iron hull and stretched the ropes and cables that moored it. Kusum closed the *Gita* and went to his cabin door. It was too soon. The Mother could not have caught the Scent yet.

He went out and stood on the small deck that ran around the aft superstructure. The officers' and crew's quarters, galley, wheelhouse and funnel were all clustered here at the stern. He looked forward along the entire length of the main deck, a flat surface broken only by the two hatches to the main cargo holds and the four cranes leaning out from the kingpost set between them. *His* ship. A good ship, but an old one. Small as freighters go—2,500 tons, running 200 feet prow to stern, 30 feet across her main deck. Rusted and dented but she rode high and true in the water. Her registry was Liberian, naturally.

Kusum had had her sailed here six months ago. No cargo at that time, only a sixty-foot enclosed barge towed 300 feet behind the ship as it made its way across the Atlantic from London. The cable securing the barge came loose the night the ship entered New York Harbor. The next morning the barge was found drifting two miles off shore. Empty. Kusum sold it to a garbage hauling outfit. U.S. Customs inspected the two empty cargo holds and allowed the ship to dock. Kusum had secured a slip for it in the barren area above Pier 97 on the West Side where there was little dock activity. It was moored nose first into the bulkhead. A rotting pier ran along its starboard flank. The crew had been paid and discharged. Kusum had been the only human aboard since.

The rasping sound came again. More insistent. Kusum went be-

97

low. The sound grew in volume as he neared the lower decks. Opposite the engine room, he came to a watertight hatch and stopped.

The Mother wanted to get out. She had begun scraping her talons along the inner surface of the hatch and would keep it up until she was released. Kusum stood and listened for a while, puzzled. He knew the sound well: long, grinding, irregular rasps in a steady, insistent rhythm. She showed all the signs of having caught the Scent. She was ready to hunt.

That puzzled him. It was too soon. The chocolates couldn't have arrived yet. He knew precisely when they had been posted from London—a telegram had confirmed it—and knew they'd be delivered tomorrow at the very earliest.

Could it possibly be one of those specially treated bottles of cheap wine he had been handing out to the winos downtown for the past six months? The derelicts had served as a food supply and good training fodder for the nest as it matured. He doubted there could be any of the treated wine left—those untouchables usually finished off the bottle within hours of receiving it.

But there was no fooling the Mother. She had caught the Scent and wanted to follow it. Although he had planned to continue training the brighter ones as crew for the ship—in the six months since their arrival in New York they had learned to handle the ropes and follow commands in the engine room—the hunt took priority. Kusum spun the wheel that retracted the lugs, then stood behind the hatch as it swung open. The Mother stepped out, an eight-foot, humanoid-shadow, lithe and massive in the dimness. One of the younglings, a foot shorter but almost as massive, followed on her heels. And then another. Without warning she spun and hissed and raked her talons through the air a bare inch from the second youngling's eyes. It retreated into the hold. Kusum closed the hatch and spun the wheel. Kusum felt the Mother's faintly glowing yellow eyes pass over him without seeing him as she turned and swiftly, silently led her adolescent offspring up the steps and into the night.

This was as it should be. The rakoshi had to be taught how to follow the Scent, how to find the intended victim and return with it to the nest so that all might share. The Mother taught them one by one. This was as it always had been. This was as it would be.

The Scent must be coming from the chocolates. He could think of no other explanation. The thought sent a thrill through him. Tonight would bring him one step closer to completing the vow. Then he could return to India.

On his way back to the upper deck, Kusum once again looked along the length of his ship, but this time his gaze lifted above and beyond to the vista spread out before him. Night was a splendid cosmetician for this city at the edge of this rich, vulgar, noisome, fulsome land. It hid the seaminess of the dock area, the filth collecting under the crumbling West Side Highway, the garbage swirling in the Hudson, the blank-faced warehouses and the human refuse that crept in and out and around them. The upper levels of Manhattan rose above all that, ignoring it, displaying a magnificent array of lights like sequins on black velvet.

It never failed to make him pause and watch. It was so unlike his India. Mother India could well use the riches in this land. Her people would put them to good use. They would certainly appreciate them more than these pitiful Americans who were so rich in material things and so poor in spirit, so lacking in inner resources. Their chrome, their dazzle, their dim-witted pursuit of "fun" and "experience" and "self." Only a culture such as theirs could construct such an architectural marvel as this city and refer to it as a large piece of fruit. They didn't deserve this land. They were like a horde of children given free run of the bazaar in Calcutta.

The thought of Calcutta made him ache to go home.

Tonight, and then one more.

One final death after tonight's and he would be released from his vow.

Kusum returned to his cabin to read his *Gita*.

7.

"I believe I've been *Kama Sutraed*."

"I don't think that's a verb."

"It just became one."

Jack lay on his back, feeling divorced from his body. He was numb from his hair down. Every fiber of nerve and muscle was being taxed just to support his vital functions.

"I think I'm going to die."

Kolabati stirred beside him, nude but for her iron necklace. "You did. But I resuscitated you."

"Is that what you call it in India?"

THE TOMB

They had arrived at his apartment after an uneventful walk from Beefsteak Charlie's. Kolabati's eyes had widened and she staggered a bit as she entered Jack's apartment. It was a common reaction. Some said it was the bric-a-brac and movie posters on the walls, others said it was the Victorian furniture with all the gingerbread carving and the wavy grain of the golden oak that did it.

"Your decor," she said, leaning against him. "It's so . . . interesting."

"I collect things—*things*. As for the furniture, hideous is what most people call it, and they're right. All that carving and such is out of style. But I like furniture that looks like human beings touched it at one time or another during its construction, even human beings of dubious taste."

Jack became acutely aware of the pressure of Kolabati's body against his flank. Her scent was unlike any perfume. He could not even be sure it was perfume. More like scented oil. She looked up at him and he wanted her. And in her eyes he could see she wanted him.

Kolabati stepped away and began to remove her dress.

In the past, Jack had always felt himself in control during lovemaking. It had not been a conscious thing, but he had always set the pace and moved into the positions. Not tonight. With Kolabati, it was different. It was all very subtle, but before long they were each cast in their roles. She was by far the hungrier of the two of them, the more insistent. And although younger, she seemed to be the more experienced. She became the director, he became an actor in her play.

And it was quite a play. Passion and laughter. She was skilled, yet there was nothing mechanical about her. She reveled in sensations, giggled, even laughed at times. She was a delight. She knew where to touch him, how to touch him in ways he had never known, lifting him to heights of sensation he had never dreamed possible. And though he knew he had brought her to thrashing peaks of pleasure numerous times, she was insatiable.

He watched her now as the light from the tiny leaded glass lamp in the corner of the bedroom cast a soft chiaroscuro effect over the rich color of her skin. Her breasts were perfect, their nipples the darkest brown he had ever seen. With her eyes still closed, she smiled and stretched, a slow, langorous movement that brought her dark and downy pubic mons against his thigh. Her hand crept across his chest, then trailed down over his abdomen toward his groin. He felt his

100

abdominal muscles tighten.

"That's not fair to do to a dying man."

"Where's there's life, there's hope."

"Is this your way of thanking me for finding the necklace?" He hoped not. He already been paid for the necklace.

She opened her eyes. "Yes . . . and no. You are a unique man in this world, Repairman Jack. I've travelled a lot, met many people. You stand out from all of them. Once my brother was like you, but he has changed. You are alone."

"Not at the moment."

She shook her head. "All men of honor are alone."

Honor. This was the second time she had spoken of honor this evening. Once at the Peacock Room, and now here in his bed. Strange for a woman to think in terms of honor. That was supposed to be men's territory, although nowadays the word rarely passed the lips of members of either sex. But when it did, it was most apt to be spoken by a man. Sexist, perhaps, but he could think of no exceptions to refute it.

"Can a man who lies, cheats, steals, and sometimes does violence to other people be a man of honor?"

Kolabati looked into his eyes. "He can if he lies to liars, cheats cheaters, steals from thieves, and limits his violence to those who are violent."

"You think so?"

"I know so."

An honorable man. He liked the sound of that. He liked the meaning that went with it. As Repairman Jack he had taken an honorable course without consciously setting out to do so. Autonomy had been his driving motive—to reduce to the barest minimum all external restraints upon his life. But honor . . . honor was an internal restraint. He hadn't recognized the role it had played all along in guiding him.

Kolabati's hand started moving again and thoughts of honor sank in the waves of pleasure washing over him. It was good to be aroused again.

He had led a monkish life since Gia had left him. Not that he had consciously avoided sex—he had simply stopped thinking about it. A number of weeks had gone by before he even realized what had happened to him. He had read that that was a sign of depression. Maybe. Whatever the cause, tonight made up for any period of abstention, no matter how long.

Her hand was gently working at him now, drawing responses from what he had thought was an empty well. He was rolling toward her when he caught the first whiff of the odor.

What the hell is that?

It smelled like a pigeon had got into the air conditioner and laid a rotten egg. Or died.

Kolabati stiffened beside him. He didn't know whether she had smelled it, too, or whether something had frightened her. He thought he heard her say something in a tense whisper that sounded like "Rakosh!" She rolled on top of him and clung like a drowning sailor to a floating spar.

An aura of nameless fear enveloped Jack. Something was terribly wrong, but he could not say what. He listened for a foreign sound, but all that came to him were the low hums, each in a different key, of the air conditioners in each of the three rooms. He reached for the .38 S&W Chief Special he always kept under the mattress, but Kolabati hugged him tighter.

"Don't move," she whispered in a voice he could barely hear. "Just lie here under me and don't say a word."

Jack opened his mouth to speak but she covered his lips with her own. The pressure of her bare breasts against his chest, her hips on his, the tingle of her necklace as it dangled from her neck against his throat, the caresses of her hands—all worked toward blotting out the odor.

Yet there was a desperation about her that prevented Jack from completely releasing himself to the sensations. His eyes kept opening and straying to the window, to the door, to the hall that led past the TV room to the darkened front room, then back to the window. There was no good reason for it, but a small part of him expected someone or something—a person, an animal—to come through the door. He knew it was impossible—the front door was locked, the windows were three stories up. Crazy. Yet the feeling persisted.

And persisted.

He did not know how long he lay there, tense and tight under Kolabati, itching for the comfortable feel of a pistol grip in his palm. It felt like half the night.

Nothing happened. Eventually, the odor began to fade. And with it the sensation of the presence of another. Jack felt himself begin to relax and, finally, begin to respond to Kolabati.

THE TOMB

But Kolabati suddenly had different ideas. She jumped up from the bed and padded into the front room for her clothes.

Jack followed and watched her slip into her underwear with brisk, almost frantic movements.

"What's wrong?"

"I have to get home."

"Back to D.C.?" His heart sank. Not yet. She intrigued him so.

"No. To my brother's. I'm staying with him."

"I don't understand. Is it something I—"

Kolabati leaned over and kissed him. "Nothing you did. Something *he* did."

"What's the hurry?"

"I must speak to him immediately."

She let the dress fall over her head and slipped her shoes on. She turned to go but the apartment door stopped her.

"How does this work?"

Jack turned the central knob that retracted the four bars, then pulled it open for her.

"Wait till I get some clothes on and I'll find you a cab."

"I haven't time to wait. And I can wave my arm in the air as well as anyone."

"You'll be back?" The answer was very important to him at the moment. He didn't know why. He hardly knew her.

"Yes, if I can be." Her eyes were troubled. For an instant he thought he detected a hint of fear in them. "I hope so. I really do."

She kissed him again, then was out the door and on her way down the stairs.

Jack closed the door, locked it, and leaned against it. If he weren't so exhausted from lack of sleep and from the strenuous demands Kolabati had made upon him tonight, he would have tried to make some sense out of the evening's events.

He headed for bed. This time to sleep.

But chase it as he might, sleep eluded him. The memory of the odor, Kolabati's bizarre behavior . . . he couldn't explain them. But it wasn't what had happened tonight that bothered him so much as the gnawing uneasy feeling that something awful had *almost* happened.

THE TOMB

8.

Kusum started out of his sleep, instantly alert. A sound had awakened him. His *Gita* slipped off his lap and onto the floor as he sprang to his feet and stepped to the cabin door. It was most likely the Mother and the young one returning, but it wouldn't hurt to be sure. One never knew what kind of scum might be lurking about the docks. He didn't care who came aboard in his absence—it would have to be a fairly determined thief or vandal because Kusum always kept the gangway raised. A silent beeper was needed to bring it down. But an industrious low-caste type who climbed one of the ropes and sneaked aboard would find little of value in the superstructure. And should he venture below decks to the cargo hold . . . that would mean one less untouchable prowling the streets.

But when Kusum was aboard—and he expected to be spending more time here than he wished now that Kolabati was in town—he liked to be careful. He didn't want any unpleasant surprises.

Kolabati's arrival had been a surprise. He had thought her safely away in Washington. She had already caused him an enormous amount of trouble this week and would undoubtedly cause him more. She knew him too well. He would have to avoid her whenever possible. And she must never learn of this ship or of its cargo.

He heard the sound again and saw two dark forms of unmistakable configuration lope along the deck. They should have been burdened with their prey, but they were not. Alarmed, Kusum ran down to the deck. He checked to make sure he was wearing the necklace, then stood in a corner and watched the rakoshi as they passed.

The youngling came first, prodded along by the Mother behind it. Both appeared agitated. If only they could talk! He had been able to teach the younglings a few words, but that was mere mimicry, not speech. He had never felt so much the need to communicate with the rakoshi as he did tonight. Yet he knew that was impossible. They were not stupid; they could learn simple tasks and follow simple commands—had he not been training them to act as crew for the ship?—but their minds did not operate on a level that permitted intelligent communication.

What had happened tonight? The Mother had never failed him before. When she caught the Scent, she invariably brought back the targeted victim. Tonight she had failed. Why?

Could there have been a mistake? Perhaps the chocolates hadn't arrived. But how then had the Mother caught the Scent? No one but Kusum controlled the source of the Scent. None of it made sense.

He padded down the steps that led belowdecks. The two rakoshi were waiting there, the Mother subdued by the knowledge that she had failed, the youngling restless, pacing about. Kusum slipped past them. The Mother raised her head, dimly aware of his presence, but the youngling only hissed and continued its pacing, oblivious to him. Kusum spun the wheel on the hatch and pulled it open. The youngling tried to retreat. It didn't like being on the iron ship and rebelled at returning to the hold. Kusum watched patiently. They all did this after their first run through the city. They wanted to be out in the air, away from the iron hold that weakened them, out among the crowds where they could pick and choose among the fattened human cattle.

The Mother would have none of it. She gave the youngling a brutal shove that sent it stumbling into the arms of its siblings waiting inside. Then she followed.

Kusum slammed the hatch closed, secured it, then pounded his fist against it. Would he never be done with this? He had thought he would be closer to fulfilling the vow tonight. Something had gone wrong. It worried him almost as much as it angered him. Had a new variable been added, or were the rakoshi to blame?

Why was there no victim?

One thing was certain, however: There would have to be punishment. That was the way it always had been. That was the way it would be tonight.

9.

Oh, Kusum! What have you done?

Kolabati's insides writhed in terror as she sat huddled in the rear of the cab. The ride was mercifully brief—directly across Central Park to a stately building of white stone on Fifth Avenue.

The night doorman didn't know Kolabati so he stopped her. He was old, his face a mass of wrinkles. Kolabati detested old people. She found the thought of growing old disgusting. The doorman questioned her until she showed him her key and her Maryland driver license, confirming her last name to be the same as Kusum's. She hurried through the marble lobby, past the modern low-backed couch and chairs and the uninspired abstract paintings on the walls, to the elevator. It stood open, waiting. She pressed 9, the top floor, and stood impatiently until the door closed and the car started up.

THE TOMB

Kolabati slumped against the rear wall and closed her eyes.

That odor! She had thought her heart would stop when she recognized it in Jack's apartment tonight. She thought she had left it behind forever in India.

A rakosh!

One had been outside Jack's apartment less than an hour ago. Her mind balked at the thought, yet there was no doubt in her mind. As sure as the night was dark, as sure as the number of her years—a rakosh! The knowledge nauseated her, made her weak inside and out. And the most terrifying part of it all: The only man who could be responsible—the only man in the world—was her brother.

But why Jack's apartment?

And how? By the Black Goddess, *how?*

The elevator glided to a smooth halt, the doors slid open, and Kolabati headed directly for the door numbered 98. She hesitated before inserting the key. This was not going to be easy. She loved Kusum but there was no denying that he intimidated her. Not physically—for he would never raise his hand against her—but morally. It hadn't always been so, but lately his righteousness had become impenetrable.

But not this time, she told herself. *This time he's wrong.*

She turned the key and went in.

The apartment was dark and silent. She flipped the light switch, revealing a huge, low ceilinged living room decorated by a hired professional. She had guessed that the first time she had walked in. There was no trace of Kusum in the decor. He hadn't bothered to personalize it, which meant he didn't intend to stay here very long.

"Kusum?"

She went down to two steps to the wool carpeted living room floor and crossed to the closed door that led to her brother's bedroom. It was dark and empty within.

She went back to the living room and called, louder now. "Kusum!"

No answer.

He had to be here! She had to find him! She was the only one who could stop him!

She walked past the door that led to the bedroom he had supplied for her and went to the picture window overlooking Central Park. The great body of the park was dark, cut at irregular intervals by lighted roads, luminescent serpents winding their way from Fifth

106

THE TOMB

Avenue to Central Park West.

Where are you, my brother, and what are you doing? What awfulness have you brought back to life?

10.

The two propane torches on either side of him were lit and roaring blue flame straight up. Kusum made a final adjustment on the air draw to each one—he wanted to keep them noisy but didn't want them to blow themselves out. When he was satisfied with the flames, he unclasped his necklace and laid it on the propane tank at the rear of the square platform. He had changed from his everyday clothes into his blood red ceremonial dhoti, arranging the one-piece sarong-like garment in the traditional *Maharatta* style with the left end hooked beneath his leg and the bulk gathered at his right hip, leaving his legs bare. He picked up his coiled bullwhip, then stabbed the Down button with his middle finger.

The lift—an open elevator platform floored with wooden planks—lurched, then started a slow descent along the aft corner of the starboard wall of the main hold. It was dark below. Not completely dark, for he kept the emergency lights on at all times, but these were so scattered and of such low wattage that the illumination they provided was nominal at best.

When the lift reached the halfway point, there came a shuffling sound from below as rakoshi moved from directly beneath him, wary of the descending platform and the fire it carried. As he neared the floor of the hold and the light from the torches spread among its occupants, tiny spots of brightness began to pick up and return the glare—a few at first, then more and more until more than a hundred yellow eyes gleamed from the darkness.

A murmur rose among the rakoshi to become a whispery chant, low, throaty, gutteral, the only word they could speak:

"*Kaka-jiiiiii! Kaka-jiiiiii!*"

Kusum loosed the coils of his whip and cracked it. The sound echoed like a gunshot through the hold. The chant stopped abruptly. They now knew he was angry; they would remain silent. As the platform and its roaring flames drew nearer the floor, they backed farther away. In all of heaven and earth, fire was all they feared—fire and their *Kaka-ji.*

He stopped the lift three or four feet above the floor, giving himself

107

THE TOMB

a raised platform from which to address the rakoshi assembled in a rough semicircle just beyond the reach of the torchlight. They were barely visible except for an occasional highlight off a smooth scalp or a hulking shoulder. And the eyes. All the eyes were focused on Kusum.

He began to speak to them in the Bengali dialect, knowing they could understand little of what he was saying, but confident they would eventually get his meaning. Although he was not directly angry with them, he filled his voice with anger, for that was an integral part of what was to follow. He did not understand what had gone wrong tonight, and knew from the confusion he had sensed in the Mother upon her return that she did not understand either. Something had caused her to lose the Scent. Something extraordinary. She was a skilled hunter and he could be sure that whatever had happened had been beyond her control. That did not matter, however. A certain form must be followed. It was tradition.

He told the rakoshi that there would be no ceremony tonight, no sharing of flesh, because those who had been entrusted to bring the sacrifice had failed. Instead of the ceremony, there would be punishment.

He turned and lowered the propane feed to the torches, constricting the semicircular pool of illumination, bringing the darkness—and the rakoshi—closer.

Then he called to the Mother. She knew what to do.

There came a scuffling and scraping from the darkness before him as the Mother brought forward the youngling that had accompanied her tonight. It came sullenly, unwillingly, but it came. For it knew it must. It was tradition.

Kusum reached back and lowered the propane farther. The young rakoshi were especially afraid of fire and it would be foolish to panic this one. Discipline was imperative. If he lost his control over them, even for an instant, they might turn on him and tear him to pieces. There must be no instance of disobedience—such an act must ever remain unthinkable. But in order to bend them to his will, he must not push them too hard against their instincts.

He could barely see the creature as it slouched forward in a posture of humble submission. Kusum gestured with the whip and the Mother turned the youngling around, facing its back to him. He raised the whip and lashed it forward—one—two—three times and more, putting his body into it so that each stroke ended with the meaty slap of braided rawhide on cold, cobalt flesh.

He knew the young rakosh felt no pain from the lash, but that was of little consequence. His purpose was not to inflict pain but to assert his position of dominance. The lashing was a symbolic act, just as a rakosh's submission to the lash was a reaffirmation of its loyalty and subservience to the will of Kusum, the *Kaka-ji*. The lash formed a bond between them. Both drew strength from it. With each stroke Kusum felt the power of Kali swell within him. He could almost imagine himself possessing two arms again.

After ten strokes, he stopped. The rakosh looked around, saw that he was finished, then slunk back into the group. Only the Mother remained. Kusum cracked the whip in the air. *Yes,* it seemed to say. *You, too.*

The Mother came forward, gave him a long look, then turned and presented her back to him. The eyes of the younger rakoshi grew brighter as they became agitated, shuffling their feet and clicking their talons together.

Kusum hesitated. The rakoshi were devoted to the Mother. They spent day after day in her presence. She guided them, gave order to their lives. They would die for her. Striking her was a perilous proposition. But a hierarchy had been established and it must be preserved. As the rakoshi were devoted to the Mother, so was the Mother devoted to Kusum. And to reaffirm the hierarchy, she must submit to the lash. For she was his lieutenant among the younglings and ultimately responsible for any failure to carry through the wishes of the *Kaka-ji*.

Yet despite her devotion, despite the knowledge that she would gladly die for him, despite the unspeakable bond that linked them— he had started the nest with her, nursing her, raising her from a mewing hatchling—Kusum was wary of the Mother. She was, after all, a rakosh—violence incarnate. Disciplining her was like juggling vials of high explosive. One lapse of concentration, one careless move . . .

Summoning his courage, Kusum let the whip fly, snapping its tip once against the floor far from where the Mother waited, and then he raised the whip no more. The hold had gone utterly still with the first stroke. All remained silent. The Mother continued to wait, and when no blow came, she turned toward the lift. Kusum had the bullwhip coiled by then, a difficult trick for a one-armed man, but he had long ago determined that there was a way to do almost anything with one hand. He held it out beside him, then dropped it onto the floor of the lift.

The Mother looked at him with shining eyes, her slit pupils dilating in worship. She had received no lashing, a public proclamation of the *Kaka-ji*'s respect and regard for her. Kusum knew this was a proud moment for her, one that would elevate her even higher in the eyes of her young. He had planned it this way.

He hit the Up switch and turned the torches to maximum as he rose. He was satisfied. Once more he had affirmed his position as absolute master of the nest. The Mother was more firmly in his grasp than ever before. And as he controlled her, so he controlled her young.

The field of brightly glowing eyes watched him from below, never leaving him until he reached the top of the hold. The instant they were blocked from view, Kusum reached for the necklace and clasped it around his throat.

CHAPTER FOUR

West Bengal, India
Friday, July 24, 1857

1.

Jaggernath the *svamin* and his mule train were due to appear any minute.

Tension was coiled like a snake around Captain Westphalen. If he failed to net the equivalent of 50,000 pounds sterling out of this little sortie, he might have to reconsider returning to England at all. Only disgrace and poverty would await him.

He and his men huddled behind a grassy hillock approximately two miles northwest of Bharangpur. The rain had ended at midday, but more was on the way. The summer monsoon was upon Bengal, bringing a year's rainfall in the space of a few months. Westphalen looked out along the rolling expanse of green that had been an arid wasteland only last month. An unpredictable land, this India.

As he waited beside his horse, Westphalen mentally reviewed the past four weeks. He had not been idle. Far from it. He had devoted part of each day to grilling every Englishman in Bharangpur on what he knew about the Hindu religion in general and the Temple-in-the-Hills in particular. And when he had exhausted the resources of his countrymen, he turned to local Hindus who had a decent command of English. They told him more than he wished to know about Hinduism and almost nothing about the temple.

He did learn a lot about Kali, though. Very popular in Bengal—even the name of the region's largest city, Calcutta, was an Anglicized

111

THE TOMB

form of Kalighata, the huge temple built to her there. The Black
Goddess. Not a diety to take comfort in. She was called Mother Night,
devouring all, slaying all, even Siva, her consort upon whose corpse
she stood in many of the pictures Westphalen had seen. Blood
sacrifices, usually goats and birds, were made regularly to Kali in her
many temples, but there were whispers of other sacrifices . . . human sacrifices.

No one in Bharangpur had ever seen the Temple-in-the-Hills, nor
known anyone who had. But he learned that every so often a
curiosity-seeker or a pilgrim would venture off into the hills to find the
temple. Some would follow Jaggernath at a discrete distance, others
would seek their own path. The few who returned claimed their
search had been fruitless, telling tales of shadowy beings creeping
about the hills at night, always just beyond the firelight, but unmistak-
ably there, watching. As to what happened to the rest, it was assumed
that the pilgrims true of heart were accepted into the temple order,
and that the adventurous and the merely curious became fodder for
the rakoshi who guarded the temple and its treasure. A rakosh, he
was assured by a colonel who was starting his third decade in India,
was some sort of flesh-eating demon, the Bengali equivalent of the
English Bogeyman—used to frighten children.

Westphalen had little doubt the temple was guarded, but by
human sentries, not demons. Guards would not deter him. He was
not a lone traveller wandering aimlessly through the hills—he was a
British officer leading six lancers armed with the new lightweight
Enfield rifle.

As he stood beside his mount, Westphalen ran a finger up and
down the stock of his Enfield. This simple construction of wood and
steel had been the precipitating factor in the sepoy rebellion.

All because of a tight-fitting cartridge.

Absurd, but true. The Enfield cartridge, like all other cartridges,
came wrapped in glazed paper which had to be bitten open to be
used. But unlike the heavier "Brown Bess" rifle the sepoys had been
using for forty years, the Enfield cartridge had to be greased to make
the tight fit into the barrel. There had been no problem until rumors
began circulating that the grease was a mixture of pork and bullock
fat. The Moslem troops would not bite anything that might be pork,
and the Hindus would not pollute themselves with cow grease.
Tension between British officers and their sepoy troops had built for
months, culminating on May 10, a mere eleven weeks ago, when the

112

sepoys had mutinied in Meerut, perpetrating atrocities on the white populace. The mutiny had spread like a grass fire across most of northern India, and the raj had not been the same since.

Westphalen had hated the Enfield for endangering him during what should have been a safe, peaceful tour of duty. Now he caressed it almost lovingly. If not for the rebellion he might still be far to the southeast in Fort William, unaware of the Temple-in-the-Hills and the promise of salvation it held for him and for the honor of the Westphalen name.

"I've spotted him, sir." It was an enlisted man named Watts speaking.

Westphalen stepped up to where Watts lay against the rise and took the field glasses from him. After refocusing to correct for his near-sightedness, he spotted the squat little man and his mules travelling north at a brisk pace.

"We'll wait until he's well into the hills, then follow. Keep down until then."

With the ground softened by monsoon rains, there would be no problem following Jaggernath and his mules. Westphalen wanted the element of surprise on his side when he entered the temple, but it wasn't an absolute necessity. One way or another he was going to find the Temple-in-the-Hills. Some of the tales said it was made of pure gold. Westphalen did not believe that for an instant—gold was not fit for buildings. Other tales said the temple housed urns full of precious jewels. Westphalen might have laughed at that too had he not seen the ruby Jaggernath had given MacDougal last month simply for not handling the supplies on the backs of his mules.

If the temple housed anything of value, Westphalen intended to find it . . . and to make all or part of it his own.

He glanced around at the men he had brought with him: Tooke, Watts, Russell, Hunter, Lang, and Malleson. He had combed his records carefully for individuals with the precise blend of qualities he required. He detested aligning himself so closely with their sort. They were worse than commoners. These were the toughest men he could find, the dregs of the Bharangpur garrison, the hardest drinking, most unscrupulous soldiers under his command.

Two weeks ago he had begun dropping remarks to his lieutenant about rumors of a rebel encampment in the hills. In the past few days he had begun to refer to unspecified intelligence reports confirming the rumors, saying it was thought that the pandies were receiving assistance from a religious order in the hills. And just yesterday he had begun picking men to accompany him on "a brief reconnaissance mission." The lieutenant had insisted on leading the patrol but Westphalen had overruled him.

During the entire time, Westphalen had grumbled incessantly about being so far from the fight, about letting all the glory of quelling the revolt go to others while he was stuck in northern Bengal battling administrative rubbish. His act had worked. It was now a common assumption among the officers and noncoms of the Bharangpur garrison that Captain Sir Albert Westphalen was not going to allow a post far from the battle lines prevent him from earning a decoration or two; perhaps he even had his eye on the brand new Victoria Cross.

He had also made a point of not wanting any support personnel. This would be a bare-bones scouting party, no pack animals, no *bhistis*—each trooper would carry his own food and water.

Westphalen went back and stood near his horse. He fervently prayed his plan would be successful, and swore to God that if things worked out the way he hoped, he would never turn another card or roll another die as long as he lived.

His plan *had* to work. If not, the great hall his family had called home since the eleventh century would be sold to pay his gambling debts. His profligate ways would be exposed to his peers, his reputation reduced to that of a wastrel, the Westphalen name dragged through the dirt ... commoners cavorting in his ancestral home ... better to remain here on the wrong side of the world than face disgrace of that magnitude.

He walked up the rise again and took the field glasses from Watts. Jaggernath was almost into the hills. Westphalen had decided to give him a half-hour lead. It was 4:15. Despite the overcast sky and the late hour of the day, there was still plenty of light left.

By 4:35 Westphalen could wait no longer. The last twenty minutes had dragged by with sadistic slowness. He mounted his men up and led them after Jaggernath at a slow walk.

As he had expected, the trail was easy to follow. There was no traffic into the hills and the moist ground held unmistakable evidence of the passage of six mules. The trail wound a circuitous path in and around the coarse outcroppings of yellow-brown rock that typified the hills in the region. Westphalen held himself in check with difficulty, resisting the urge to spur his mount ahead. *Patience* ... patience must be the order of the day. When he came to fear they might

THE TOMB

be gaining too much on the Hindu, he had his men dismount and continue following on foot.

The trail led on and on, always upward. The grass died away, leaving barren rock in all directions; he saw no other travellers, no homes, no huts, no signs of human habitation. Westphalen wondered at the endurance of the old man out of sight ahead of him. He now knew why no one in Bharangpur had been able to tell him how to reach the temple: the path was a deep, rocky gully, its walls rising at times to a dozen feet or more over his head on either side, so narrow that he had to lead his men in a single defile, so tortuous and obscure, with so many branches leading off in random directions, that even with a map he doubted he would have been able to keep on course.

The light was waning when he saw the wall. He was leading his horse around one of the countless sharp twists in the path, wondering how they were going to follow the trail once night came, when he looked up and saw that the gully opened abruptly into a small canyon. He immediately jumped back and signaled his men to halt. He gave his reins to Watts and peered around the edge of an outcropping of rock.

The wall sat 200 yards away, spanning the width of the canyon. It looked to be about ten feet high, made of black stone, with a single gate at its center. The gate stood open to the night.

"They've left the door open for us, sir." Tooke said at his side. He had crept up for a look of his own.

Westphalen snapped around to glare at him. "Back with the others!"

"Aren't we going in?"

"When I give the order and not before!"

Westphalen watched the soldier sulkily return to his proper place. Only a few hours away from the garrison and already discipline was showing signs of breaking down. Not unexpected with the likes of these. They had all heard the stories about the Temple-in-the-Hills. You couldn't be in Bharangpur barracks for more than a week without hearing them. Westphalen was sure there was not a man among them who had not used the hope of pocketing something of value from within the temple to spur him along as they had followed the trail into the hills; now they had reached their goal and wanted to know if the stories were true. The looter within them was rising to the surface like something rotten from the bottom of a pond. He could

115

THE TOMB

almost smell the foul odor of their greed.

And what about me? Westphalen thought grimly. *Do I reek as they do?*

He looked back toward the canyon. Behind the wall, rising above it, was the dim shape of the temple itself. Details were lost in the long shadows; all he could make out was a vaguely domelike shape with a spire on top.

As he watched, the door in the wall swung closed with a crash that echoed off the rocky mountain walls, making the horses shy and causing his own heart to skip a beat.

Suddenly it was dark. Why couldn't India have England's lingering twilight? Night fell like a curtain here.

What to do now? He hadn't planned on taking so long to reach the temple, hadn't planned on darkness and a walled-off canyon. Yet why hesitate? He knew there were no rebels in the temple compound—that had been a fiction he had concocted. Most likely only a few Hindu priests. Why not scale the walls and have done with it?

No ... he didn't want to do that. He could find no rational reason to hesitate, yet something in his gut told him to wait for the sun.

"We'll wait until morning."

The men glanced at each other, muttering. Westphalen searched for a way to keep them in hand. He could neither shoot nor handle a lance half as well as they, and he had been in command of the garrison less than two months, nowhere near enough time to win their confidence as an officer. His only recourse was to show himself to be their superior in judgement. And that should be no problem. After all, they were only commoners.

He decided to single out the most vocal of the grumblers.

"Do you detect some flaw in my decision, Mr. Tooke? If so, please speak freely. This is no time for formality."

"Begging your pardon, sir," the enlisted man said with a salute and exaggerated courtesy, "but we thought we'd be taking them right away. The morning's a long way off and we're anxious to be into the fighting. Aren't I right, men?"

There were murmurs of approval.

Westphalen made a show of seating himself comfortably on a boulder before speaking. *I hope this works.*

"Very well, Mr. Tooke," he said, keeping the mounting tension

116

out of his voice. "You have my permission to lead an immediate assault on the temple." As the men began to reach for their rifles, Westphalen added: "Of course, you realize that any pandies hiding within have been there for weeks and will know their way around the temple and its grounds quite well. Those of you who have never been on the other side of that wall will be lost in the dark."

He saw the men stop in their tracks and glance at each other. Westphalen sighed with relief. Now, if he could deliver the coup de grace, he would be in command again.

"Charge, Mr. Tooke?"

After a long pause, Tooke said, "I think we'll be waiting for morning, sir."

Westphalen slapped his hands on his thighs and stood up. "Good! With surprise and daylight on our side, we'll rout the pandies with a minimum of fuss. If all goes well, you'll be back in your barracks by this time tomorrow night."

If all goes well, he thought, *you will never see tomorrow night.*

CHAPTER FIVE

Manhattan
Saturday, August 4, 198-

1.

Gia stood inside the back door and let the air-conditioned interior cool and dry the fine sheen of perspiration coating her skin. Short, slick, blond curls were plastered against the nape of her neck. She was dressed in a Danskin body suit and jogging shorts, but even that was too much clothing. The temperature was pushing into the high eighties already and it was only 9:30.

She had been out in the back helping Vicky put up curtains in the new play house. Even with screens on the windows and the breeze off the East River, it was like an oven in that little thing. Vicky hadn't seemed to notice, but Gia was sure she would have passed out if she had stayed in there another minute.

9:30. It should have been noon by now. She was slowly going crazy here on Sutton Square. Nice to have a live-in maid to see to your every need, nice to have meals prepared for you, your bed made, and central air conditioning . . . but it was so boring. She was out of her routine and found it almost impossible to work. She needed her work to keep these hours from dragging so.

She had to get out of here!

The doorbell rang.

"I'll get it, Eunice!" she called as she headed for the door. Here was a break in the routine—a visitor. She was glad until she realized with a stab of apprehension that it could be someone from the police with bad news about Grace. She checked through the peephole before unlocking the deadbolt.

It was the mailman. Gia pulled open the door and was handed a flat box, maybe eight by twelve inches, weighing about a pound.

"Special delivery," he said, giving her a frank head-to-toe appraisal before returning to his truck. Gia ignored him.

The box—could it be from Grace? She checked and saw it had been mailed from England. The return address was someplace in London called "The Divine Obsession."

"Nellie! Package for you!"

Nellie was already halfway downstairs. "Is it word from Grace?"

"I don't think so. Not unless she's gone back to England."

Nellie's brow furrowed as she glanced at the return address, then she began tearing at the brown paper wrapper. As it pulled away, she gasped.

"Oh! Black Magic!"

Gia stepped around for a look at what was inside. She saw a black rectangular cardboard box with gold trim and a red rose painted on the lid. It was an assortment of dark chocolates.

"These are my favorites! Who could have—?"

"There's a card taped to the corner."

Nellie pulled it free and opened it. " 'Don't worry,' " she read. " 'I haven't forgotten you.' It's signed, 'Your favorite nephew, Richard!' "

Gia was aghast. "Richard?"

"Yes! What a dear sweet boy to think of me! Oh, he knows Black Magic has always been my favorite. What a thoughtful present!"

"Could I see the card, please?"

Nellie handed it over without looking at it again. She was pulling the rest of the wrapper off and lifting the lid. The strong odor of dark chocolate filled the foyer. As the older woman inhaled deeply, Gia studied the card, her anger rising.

It was written in a cutesy female hand, with round circles over the I's and little loops all over the place. Definitely not her ex-husband's scrawl. He'd probably called the shop, gave them the address, told them what to put on the card, then came by later and paid for it. Or better yet, sent his latest girlfriend around with the money. Yes, that would be more Richard's style.

Gia bottled the anger that had come to a full boil within her. Her ex-husband, controller of one-third of the huge Westphalen fortune,

120

had plenty of time to flit all over the world and send his aunt expensive chocolates from London, but not a penny to spare for child support, let alone the moment it would have taken to send his own daughter a birthday card back in April.

You sure can pick 'em, Gia.

She bent and picked up the wrapper. "The Divine Obsession." At least she knew what city Richard was living in. And probably not too far from this shop—he was never one to go out of his way for anyone, especially his aunts. They had never thought much of him and had never been reticent about letting him know it. Which raised the question: Why the candy? What was behind this thoughtful little gift out of the blue?

"Imagine!" Nellie was saying. "A gift from Richard! How lovely! Who'd have ever thought—"

They were both suddenly aware of a third person in the room with them. Gia glanced up and saw Vicky standing in the hallway in her white jersey with her bony legs sticking out of her yellow shorts and her feet squeezed sockless into her sneakers, watching them with wide blue eyes.

"Is that a present from my daddy?"

"Why, yes, love," Nellie said.

"Did he send one for me?"

Gia felt her heart break at those words. Poor Vickie . . .

Nellie glanced at Gia, her face distraught, then turned back to Vicky.

"Not yet, Victoria, but I'm sure one will be coming soon. Meanwhile, he said we should all share these chocolates until—" Nellie's hand darted to her mouth, realizing what she had just said.

"Oh, no," Vicky said. "My daddy would never send me chocolates. He knows I can't have any."

With her back straight and her chin high, she turned and walked quickly down the hall toward the backyard.

Nellie's face seemed to crumble as she turned toward Gia. "I forgot she's allergic. I'll go get her—"

"Let me," Gia said, putting a hand on her shoulder. "We've been over this ground before, and it looks like we'll have to go over it again."

She left Nellie standing there in the foyer, looking older than her years, unaware of the box of chocolates clutched so tightly in her spotted hands. Gia didn't know who to feel sorrier for: Vicky or Nellie.

121

THE TOMB

2.

Vicky hadn't wanted to cry in front of Aunt Nellie who always said what a big girl she was. Mommy said it was all right to cry, but Vicky never saw mommy cry. Well, hardly ever.

Vicky wanted to cry right now. It didn't matter if this was one of the all right times or not, it was going to come out anyway. It was like a big balloon inside her chest, getting bigger and bigger until she either cried or exploded. She held it in until she reached the playhouse. There was one door, two windows with new curtains, and room enough inside for her to spin around with her arms spread out all the way and not touch the walls. She picked up her Ms. Jelliroll doll and hugged it to her chest. Then it began.

The sobs came first, like big hiccups, then the tears. She didn't have a sleeve, so she tried to wipe them away with her arm but succeeded only in making her face and her arm wet and smeary.

Daddy doesn't care. It made her feel sick way down in the bottom of her stomach to think that, but she knew it was true. She didn't know why it should bother her so much. She couldn't much remember what he looked like. Mommy threw away all his pictures a long time ago and as time went by it became harder and harder to see his face in her mind. He hadn't been around at all in two years and Vicky didn't remember seeing much of him even before that. So why should it hurt to say that daddy didn't care? Mommy was the only one who really mattered, who really cared, who was always there.

Mommy cared. And so did Jack. But now Jack didn't come around anymore either. Except for yesterday. Thinking about Jack made her stop crying. When he had lifted her up and hugged her yesterday, she'd felt so good inside. Warm. And safe. For the short while he had been in the house yesterday she hadn't felt afraid. Vicky didn't know what there was to be scared of, but lately she felt afraid all the time. Especially at night.

She heard the door open behind her and knew it was mommy. That was okay. She had stopped crying now. She was all right now. But when she turned and saw that sad, pitying look on mommy's face, it all came out again and she burst into tears. Mommy squeezed into the little rocker and sat her on her knee and held her tightly until the sobs went away. This time for good.

122

THE TOMB

3.

"Why doesn't daddy love us anymore?"

The question startled Gia. Vicky had asked her countless times why daddy didn't live with them any more. But this was the first time she had mentioned love.

Answer a question with another question: "Why do you say that?"

But Vicky was not to be side-tracked.

"He doesn't love us, does he, mommy." It was not a question.

No. He doesn't. I don't think he ever did.

That was the truth. Richard had never been a father. As far as he was concerned, Vicky had been an accident, a terrible inconvenience to him. He had never shown affection to her, had never been a presence in their home when they had lived together. He might as well have phoned in his paternal duties.

Gia sighed and hugged Vicky tighter. What an awful time that had been . . . the worst years of her life. Gia had been brought up a strict Catholic, and although the days had become one long siege of Gia and Vicky alone against the world, and the nights—those nights when her husband bothered to come home—had been Richard and Gia against each other, she had never considered divorce. Not until the night when Richard, in a particularly vicious mood, had told her why he'd married her. She was as good as anyone else for rutting when he was randy, he had said, but the real reason was taxes. Immediately after the death of his father, Richard had gone to work transferring his assets out of Britain and into either American or international holdings, all the while looking for an American to marry. He'd found such an American in Gia, fresh in from the midwest looking to sell her commercial art talents to Madison Avenue. The urbane Richard Westphalen, with his refined British manners and accent, had swept her off her feet. They were married; he became an American citizen. There were other ways he could have acquired citizenship, but they were lengthy and this was more in keeping with his character. The taxes on the earnings of his portion of the Westphalen fortune would from then on be taxed at a maximum of seventy percent—which would drop to fifty percent starting in October, 1981—rather than the British government's ninety-plus percent. After that, he quickly lost interest in her. "We might have had some fun for a while," he said, "but you had to go and become a mother."

123

THE TOMB

Those words seared themselves onto her brain. She started divorce proceedings the following day, ignoring her lawyer's increasingly strident pleas for a whopping property settlement.

Perhaps she should have listened. She often would wonder about that later. But at the time all she wanted was out. She wanted nothing that came from his precious family fortune. She allowed her lawyer to ask for child support only because she knew she would need it until she revived her art career.

Was Richard contrite? Did the smallest mote of guilt come to rest on the featureless, diamond-hard surface of his conscience? No. Did he do anything to secure a future for the child he had fathered? No. In fact, he instructed his lawyer to fight for minimal child support.

"No, Vicky," Gia said, "I don't think he does."

Gia expected tears, but Vicky fooled her by smiling up at her.

"Jack loves us."

Not this again!

"I know he does, honey, but—"

"Then why can't *he* be my daddy?"

"Because" ... how was she going to say this? ... "because sometimes love just isn't enough. There have to be other things. You have to trust each other, have the same values—"

"What are values?"

"Ohhh ... you have to believe in the same things, want to live the same way."

"I like Jack."

"I know you do, honey. But that doesn't mean Jack is the right man to be your new father." Vicky's blind devotion to Jack undermined Gia's confidence in the child's character judgement. She was usually pretty astute.

She lifted Vicky off her lap and rose to a hands-on-knees crouch. The heat in the playhouse was suffocating.

"Let's go inside and get some lemonade."

"Not right now," Vicky said. "I want to play with Ms. Jelliroll. She's got to hide before Mr. Grape-grabber finds her."

"Okay. But come in soon. It's getting too hot."

Vicky didn't answer. She was already lost in a fantasy with her dolls. Gia stood outside the playhouse and wondered if Vicky might be spending too much time alone here. There were no children around Sutton Square for her to play with, just her mother, an elderly aunt, and her books and dolls. Gia wanted to get Vicky back home

THE TOMB

and into a normal routine as soon as possible.

"Miss Gia?" It was Eunice calling from the back door. "Mrs. Paton says lunch will be early today because of your trip to the dress shop."

Gia bit down on the middle knuckle of her right index finger, a gesture of frustration she had picked up from her grandmother many years ago.

The dress shop . . . the reception tonight . . . two places she most definitely did not want to go, but would have to because she had promised.

She had to get out of here!

4.

Joey Diaz placed the little bottle of green liquid on the table between them.

"Where'd you get ahold of this stuff, Jack?"

Jack was buying Joey a late lunch at a midtown Burger King. They had a corner booth, each was munching on a Whopper. Joey, a Filipino with a bad case of postadolescent acne, was a contact Jack treasured. He worked in the city Health Department lab. In the past, Jack had used him mostly for information and for suggestions on how to bring down the wrath of the Health Department upon the heads of certain targets of his fix-it work. Yesterday was the first time he had asked Joey to run an analysis for him.

"What's wrong with it?" Jack had been finding it hard to concentrate on Joey or the food. His mind had been on Kolabati and how she had made him feel last night. From there it flowed to the odor that had crept into the apartment and her bizarre reaction to it. His thoughts kept drifting away from Joey, and so it was easy to appear laid-back about the analysis. He had been playing everything low-key for Joey. No big thing—just see if there's anything really useful in it.

"Nothing wrong, exactly." Joey had a bad habit of talking with his mouth full. Most people would swallow, then talk before the next bite; Joey preferred to sip his Coke between swallows, take another big bite, then talk. As he leaned forward, Jack leaned back. "But it ain't gonna help you shit."

"Not a laxative? What *will* it help me do? Sleep?"

He shook his head and filled his mouth with fries. "Not a chance."

Jack drummed his fingers on the grease-patinaed, wood-grained Formica. *Damn!* It had occurred to him that the tonic might be some

125

THE TOMB

sort of sedative used to put Grace into a deep sleep so she wouldn't make a fuss when her abductors—if in fact she had been abducted—came by and snatched her. So much for that possibility. He waited for Joey to go on, hoping he would finish his Whopper first. No such luck.

"I don't think it does anything," he said around his last mouthful. "It's just a crazy conglomeration of odd stuff. None of it makes sense."

"In other words, somebody just threw a lot of junk together to sell for whatever ails you. Some sort of Dr. Feelgood tonic."

Joey shrugged. "Maybe. But if that's the case, they could have done it a lot cheaper. Personally, I think it was put together by someone who believed in the mixture. There are crude flavorings and a twelve per cent alcohol vehicle. Nothing special—I had them pegged in no time. But there was this strange alkaloid that I had the damnedest—"

"What's an alkaloid? Sounds like poison."

"Some of them are, like strychnine; others you take every day, like caffeine. They're almost always derived from plants. This one came from a doozy. Wasn't even in the computer. Took me most of the morning to track it down." He shook his head. "What a way to spend a Saturday morning."

Jack smiled to himself. Joey was going to ask a little extra for this job. That was okay. If it kept him happy, it was worth it.

"So where's it from?" he asked, watching with relief as Joey washed down the last of his lunch.

"It's from a kind of grass."

"Dope?"

"Naw. A nonsmoking kind called durba grass. And this particular alkaloid isn't exactly a naturally occurring thing. It was cooked in some way to add an extra amine group. That's what took me so long."

"So it's not a laxative, not a sedative, not a poison. What is it?"

"Beats hell out of me."

"This is not exactly a big help to me, Joey."

"What can I say?" Joey ran a hand through his lanky black hair, scratched at a pimple on his chin. "You wanted to know what was in it. I told you: some crude flavorings, an alcohol vehicle, and an alkaloid from an Indian grass."

Jack felt something twist inside him. Memories of last night

126

exploded around him. He said, "Indian? You mean American Indian, don't you?" knowing even as he spoke that Joey had not meant that at all.

"Of course not! American Indian grass would be North American grass. No, this stuff is from India, the subcontinent. A tough compound to track down. Never would have figured it out if the department computer hadn't referred me to the right textbook."

India! How strange. After spending a number of delirious hours last night with Kolabati, to learn that the bottle of liquid found in a missing woman's room was probably compounded by an Indian. Strange indeed.

Or perhaps not so strange. Grace and Nellie had close ties to the U.K. Mission and through there to the diplomatic community that centered around the U.N. Perhaps someone from the Indian Consulate had given Grace the bottle—perhaps Kusum himself. After all, wasn't India once a British colony?

"Afraid it's really an innocent little mixture, Jack. If you're looking to sic the Health Department on whoever's peddling it as a laxative, I think you'd be better off going to the Department of Consumer Affairs."

And Jack had been hoping the little bottle would yield a dazzling clue that would lead him directly to Aunt Grace, making him a hero in Gia's eyes.

So much for hunches.

He asked Joey what he thought his unofficial analysis was worth, paid the hundred and fifty, and headed back to his apartment with the little bottle in the front pocket of his jeans. As he rode the bus uptown, he tried to figure what he should do next on the Grace Westphalen thing. He had spent much of the morning tracking down and talking to a few more of his street contacts, but there had been no leads. No one had heard a thing. There had to be other avenues, but he couldn't think of any at the moment. Other thoughts pushed their way to the front.

Kolabati again. His mind was full of her. Why? As he tried to analyze it, he came to see that the sexual spell she had cast on him last night was only a small part of it. More important was the realization that she knew who he was, knew how he made a living, and somehow was able to accept it. No . . . accept wasn't the right word. It almost seemed as if she looked on his lifestyle as a perfectly natural way of living. One that she wouldn't mind for herself.

THE TOMB

Jack knew he was on the rebound from Gia, knew he was vulnerable, especially to someone who appeared to be as open-minded as Kolabati. Almost against his will, he had laid himself bare for her, and she had found him ... "honorable."

She wasn't afraid of him.

He had to call her.

But first he had to call Gia. He owed her some sort of progress report, even when there was no progress. He dialed the Paton number as soon as he reached his apartment.

"Any word on Grace?" he said after Gia was called to the other end.

"No." Her voice didn't seem nearly as cool as it had yesterday. Or was that just his imagination? "I hope you've got some good news. We could use it around here."

"Well ..." Jack grimaced. He really wished he had something encouraging to tell her. He was almost tempted to make up something, but couldn't bring himself to do it. "You know that stuff we thought was a laxative? It isn't."

"What is it, then?"

"Nothing. A dead end."

There was a pause on the other end, then, "Where do you go from here?"

"I wait."

"Nellie's already doing that. She doesn't need any help waiting."

Her sarcasm stung.

"Look, Gia, I'm not a detective—"

"I'm well aware of that."

"—and I never promised to do a Sherlock Holmes number on this. If there's a ransom note or something like that in the mail, I may be able to help. I've got people on the street keeping their ears open, but until something breaks ..."

The silence on the other end of the line was nerve-wracking.

"Sorry, Gia. That's all I can tell you now."

"I'll tell Nellie. Good-bye, Jack."

After a moment of deep breathing to calm himself, he dialed Kusum's number. A now-familiar female voice answered.

"Kolabati?"

"Yes?"

"This is Jack."

A gasp. "Jack! I can't talk now. Kusum's coming. I'll call you later!"

THE TOMB

She took his phone number and then hung up.

Jack sat and looked at the wall in bewilderment. Idly, he pressed the replay button on his answerphone. His father's voice came out of the speaker.

"Just want to remind you about the tennis match tomorrow. Don't forget to get here by ten. The tournament starts at noon."

This had all the makings of a very bad weekend.

5.

With trembling fingers, Kolabati pulled the jack clip from the back of the phone. Another minute or two from now and Jack's call would have ruined everything. She wanted no interruptions when she confronted Kusum. It was taking all her courage, but she intended to face her brother and wring the truth from him. She would need time to position him for her assault . . . time and concentration. He was a master dissembler and she would have to be as circumspect and as devious as he if she was going to trap him into the truth.

She had even chosen her attire for maximum effect. Although she played neither well nor often, she found tennis clothes comfortable. She was dressed in a white sleeveless shirt and shorts set by Boast. And she wore her necklace, of course, exposed through the fully open collar of her shirt. Much of her skin was exposed: another weapon against Kusum.

At the sound of the elevator door opening down the hall, the tension that had been gathering within her since she had seen him step from the taxi on the street below balled itself into a tight, hard knot in the pit of her stomach.

Oh, Kusum. Why does it have to be like this? Why can't you let it go?

As the key turned in the lock, she forced herself into an icy calm.

He opened the door, saw her, and smiled.

"Bati!" He came over as if to put his arm around her shoulders, then seemed to think better of it. Instead, he ran a finger along her cheek. Kolabati willed herself not to shrink from his touch. He spoke in Bengali. "You're looking better every day."

"Where were you all night, Kusum?"

He stiffened. "I was out. Praying. I have learned to pray again. Why do you ask?"

"I was worried. After what happened—"

"Do not fear for me on that account," he said with a tight smile.

129

THE TOMB

"Pity instead the one who tries to steal *my* necklace."

"Still I worry."

"Do not." He was becoming visibly annoyed now. "As I told you when you first arrived, I have a place I go to to read my *Gita* in peace. I see no reason to change my routines simply because you are here."

"I wouldn't expect such a thing. I have my life to lead, you have yours." She brushed past him and moved toward the door. "I think I'll go for a walk."

"Like that?" His eyes were racing up and down her minimally clad body. "With your legs completely exposed and your blouse unbuttoned?"

"This is America."

"But you are not an American! You are a woman of India! A *Brahmin*! I forbid it!"

Good—he was getting angry.

"You can't forbid, Kusum," she said with a smile. "You no longer tell me what to wear, what to eat, how to think. I am free of you. I'll make my own decisions today, just as I did last night."

"Last night? What did you do last night?"

"I had dinner with Jack." She watched him closely for his reaction. He seemed confused for an instant, and that wasn't what she expected.

"Jack who?" Then his eyes widened. "You don't mean—?"

"Yes. Repairman Jack. I owe him something, don't you think?"

"An American—!"

"Worried about my karma? Well, dear brother, my karma is already polluted, as is yours—*especially* yours—for reasons we both know too well." She averted her thoughts from that. "And besides," she said, tugging on her necklace, "what does karma mean to one who wears this?"

"A karma can be cleansed," Kusum said in a subdued tone. "I am trying to cleanse mine."

The sincerity of his words struck her and she grieved for him. Yes, he did want to remake his life; she could see that. But by what means was he going about it? Kusum had never shied away from extremes.

It suddenly occurred to Kolabati that this might be the moment to catch him off guard, but it passed. Besides, better to have him angry. She needed to know where he would be tonight. She did not intend to let him out of her sight.

"What are your plans for tonight, brother? More prayer?"

130

THE TOMB

"Of course. But not until late. I must attend a reception hosted by the U.K. Mission at eight."

"That sounds interesting. Would they mind if I came along?"

Kusum brightened. "You would come with me? That would be wonderful. I'm sure they would be glad to have you."

"Good." A perfect opportunity to keep an eye on him. Now ... to anger him. "But I'll have to find something to wear."

"You will be expected to dress like a proper Indian woman."

"In a sari?" She laughed in his face. "You *must* be joking!"

"I insist! Or I will not be seen with you!"

"Fine. Then I'll bring my own escort: Jack."

Kusum's face darkened with rage. "I forbid it!"

Kolabati moved closer to him. Now was the moment. She watched his eyes carefully.

"What will you do to stop it? Send a rakosh after him as you did last night?"

"A rakosh? After Jack?" Kusum's eyes, his face, the way the cords of his neck tightened—they all registered shock and bafflement. He was the consummate liar when he wished to be, but Kolabati knew she had caught him off guard, and everything in his reaction screamed the fact that he didn't know. *He didn't know!*

"There was one outside his apartment window last night!"

"Impossible!" His face still wore a bewildered expression. "I'm the only one who ..."

"Who what?"

"Who has an egg."

Kolabati reeled. "You have it *with* you?"

"Of course. Where could it be safer?"

"In Bengal!"

Kusum shook his head. He appeared to be regaining some of his composure. "No. I feel better when I know exactly where it is at all times."

"You had it with you when you were with the London Embassy, too?"

"Of course."

"What if it had been stolen?"

He smiled. "Who would even know what it was?"

With an effort, Kolabati mastered her confusion. "I want to see it. Right now."

"Certainly."

THE TOMB

He led her into his bedroom and pulled a small wooden crate from a corner of the closet. He lifted the lid, pushed the excelsior aside, and there it was. Kolabati recognized the egg. She knew every blue mottle on its gray surface, knew the texture of its cool, slippery surface like her own skin. She brushed her fingertips over the shell. Yes, this was it: a female rakosh egg.

Feeling weak, Kolabati backed up and sat on the bed.

"Kusum, do you know what this means? Someone has a nest of rakoshi here in New York!"

"Nonsense! This is the very last rakosh egg. It could be hatched, but without a male to fertilize the female, there could be no nest."

"Kusum, I know there was a rakosh there!"

"Did you see it? Was it male or female?"

"I didn't actually see it—"

"Then how can you say there are rakoshi in New York?"

"The odor!" Kolabati felt her own anger rise. "Don't you think I know the odor?"

Kusum's face had resolved itself into its usual mask. "You should. But perhaps you have forgotten, just as you have forgotten so many other things about our heritage."

"Don't change the subject."

"The subject is closed, as far as I'm concerned."

Kolabati rose and faced her brother. "Swear to me, Kusum. Swear that you had nothing to do with that rakoshi last night."

"On the grave of our mother and father," he said, looking her squarely in the eyes, "I swear that I did not send a rakosh after our friend Jack. There are people in this world I wish ill, but he is not one of them."

Kolabati had to believe him. His tone was sincere, and there was no more solemn oath for Kusum than the one he had just spoken.

And there, intact on its bed of excelsior, was the egg. As Kusum knelt to pack it away, he said:

"Besides, if a rakosh were truly after Jack, his life wouldn't be worth a paisa. I assume he is alive and well?"

"Yes, he's well. I protected him."

Kusum's head snapped toward her. Hurt and anger raced across his features. He understood exactly what she meant.

"Please leave me," he said in a low voice as he faced away and lowered his head. "You disgust me."

Kolabati spun and left the bedroom, slamming the door behind

132

her. Would she never be free of this man? She was sick of Kusum! Sick of his self-righteousness, his inflexibility, his monomania. No matter how good she felt—and she felt good about Jack—he could always manage to make her feel dirty. They both had plenty to feel guilty about, but Kusum had become obsessed with atoning for past transgressions and cleansing his karma. Not just his own karma, but hers as well. She had thought leaving India—to Europe first, then to America—would sever their relationship. But no. After years of no contact, he had arrived on these same shores.

She had to face it: She would never escape him. For they were bound by more than blood—the necklaces they wore linked them with a bond that went beyond time, beyond reason, even beyond karma.

But there had to be a way out for her, a way to free herself from Kusum's endless attempts to dominate her.

Kolabati went to the window and looked out across the green expanse of Central Park. Jack was over there on the other side of the Park. Perhaps he was the answer. Perhaps he could free her.

She reached for the phone.

6.

"Even the moon's frightened of me—frightened to death! The whole world's frightened to death!"

Jack was well into part three of the James Whale Festival—Claude Raines was getting ready to start his reign of terror as *The Invisible Man.*

The phone rang. Jack turned the sound down and picked it up before his answerphone began its routine.

"Where are you?" said Kolabati's voice.

"Home."

"But this is not the number on your phone."

"So you peeked, did you?"

"I knew I'd want to call you."

It was good to hear her say that. "I had the number changed and never bothered to change the label." Actually, he purposely had left the old label in place.

"I have a favor to ask you," she said.

"Anything." *Almost* anything.

"The U.K. Mission is holding a reception tonight. Will you accompany me?"

Jack mulled that for a few seconds. His first impulse was to refuse. He hated parties. He hated gatherings. And a gathering of U.N. types, the most useless people in the world . . . it was grim prospect.

"I don't know . . ."

"Please? As a personal favor? Otherwise I shall have to go with Kusum."

It was a choice then between seeing Kolabati and not seeing her. That wasn't a choice.

"Okay." Besides, it would be fun to see Burkes's face when he showed up at the reception. He might even rent a tux for the occassion. They set a time and a meeting place—for some reason, Kolabati didn't want to be picked up at Kusum's apartment—and then a question occurred to Jack.

"By the way, what's durba grass used for?"

He heard a sharp intake of breath on the other end of the line. "Where did you find durba grass?"

"I didn't find any. As far as I know, it only grows in India. I just want to know if it's used for anything."

"It has many uses in traditional Indian folk medicine." She was speaking very carefully. "But where did you even hear about it?"

"Came up in conversation this morning." Why was she so concerned?

"Stay away from it, Jack. Whatever it is you've found, stay away from it. At least until you see me tonight!"

She hung up. Jack stared uneasily at his big TV screen on which an empty pair of trousers was silently chasing a terrified woman down an English country lane. There had been something strange about Kolabati's voice at the end there. It had almost sounded as if she were afraid for him.

7.

"Stunning!" said the saleswoman.

Vicky looked up from her book. "You look pretty, mommy."

"Smashing!" Nellie said. "Absolutely smashing!"

She had brought Gia to La Chanson. Nellie had always liked this particular boutique because it didn't look like a dress shop. From the outside, with its canopied entrance, it looked more like a chic little restaurant. But the small display windows on either side of the door left little doubt as to what was sold within.

She watched Gia standing before a mirror, examining herself in a strapless cocktail dress. It was mauve and silk, and Nellie liked it best of the four Gia had tried on. Gia was making no bones, however, about what she thought of the idea of Nellie buying her a dress. But it had been part of the deal, and Nellie had insisted that Gia hold up her end.

Such a stubborn girl. Nellie had seen her examining all four dresses for a price tag, obviously intending to buy the cheapest one. But she hadn't found one.

Nellie smiled to herself. *Keep looking, dearie. They don't come with price tags here.*

It was only money, after all. And what was money?

Nellie sighed, remembering what her father had told her about money when she was a girl. Those who don't have enough of it are only aware of what it can buy them. When you finally have enough of it you become aware—*acutely* aware—of all the things it *can't* buy ... the really important things ... like youth, health, love, peace of mind.

She felt her lips quiver and tightened them into a firm line. All the Westphalen fortune could not bring her dear John back to life, nor bring Grace back from wherever she was.

Nellie glanced to her right on the sofa to where Victoria sat next to her, reading a collection of Peanuts cartoons. The child had been unusually quiet, almost withdrawn since the arrival of the chocolates this morning. She hoped she hadn't been too badly hurt. Nellie put her arm around her and squeezed. Victoria rewarded her with a smile.

Dear, dear, Victoria. How did Richard ever father you?

The thought of her nephew brought a bitter taste into her mouth. Richard Westphalen was living proof of what a curse wealth can be. Look what inheriting control of his father's share of the fortune at such a young age had done to him. He might have been a different person—a decent person—if her brother Teddy had lived longer.

Money! Sometimes she almost wished—

The saleswoman was speaking to Gia: "Did you see anything else you'd like to try on?"

Gia laughed. "About a hundred, but this is perfect." She turned to Nellie. "What do you think?"

Nellie studied her, delighted with the choice. The dress was perfect.

THE TOMB

The lines were clean, the color went well with her blond hair, and the silk clung everywhere it was supposed to.

"You'll be the toast of the diplomats."

"That's a classic, my dear," the saleswoman said.

And it was. If Gia kept to her current perfect size six, she could probably wear this dress ten years from now and still look good. Which would probably suit Gia just fine. To Nellie's mind, Gia's taste in clothing left a lot to be desired. She wished Gia would dress more fashionably. She had a good figure—enough bust and the long waist and long legs that dress designers dream about. She should have designer clothes.

"Yes," Gia said to the mirror. "This is the one."

The dress needed no alterations, so it was boxed up and Gia walked out with it under her arm. She hailed a cab for them on Third Avenue.

"I want to ask you something," Gia said *sotto voce* as they rode back to Sutton Square. "It's been bothering me for two days now. It's about the ... inheritance you're leaving Vicky; you mentioned something about it Thursday."

Nellie was startled for a moment. Had she spoken of the terms of her will? Yes ... yes, she had. Her mind was so foggy lately.

"What bothers you?" It wasn't at all like Gia to bring up the subject of money.

Gia smiled sheepishly. "Don't laugh, but you mentioned a curse that went along with the Westphalen fortune."

"Oh, dearie," Nellie said, relieved that was all that concerned her, "that's just talk!"

"You mean you made it up?"

"Not I. It was just something Sir Albert was heard to mutter when he was in his dotage and in his cups."

"Sir Albert?"

"My great-grandfather. He was the one who actually started the fortune. It's an interesting story. Back in the middle of the last century the family was in dire financial straits of some sort—I never knew the exact nature and I guess it doesn't matter. What does matter is that shortly after his return from India, Sir Albert found an old diagram of the cellar of Westphalen Hall which lead him to a huge cache of jewels hidden there since the Norman invasion. Westphalen Hall was saved. Most of the jewels were converted to cash which was carefully invested and the fortune has grown steadily for a century and a quarter.''

"But what about the curse?''

"Oh, pay no attention to that! I shouldn't even have mentioned it! Something about the Westphalen line ending 'in blood and pain,' about 'dark things' that would come for us. But don't worry, my dear. So far we've all lived long lives and died of natural causes.''

Gia's face relaxed. "That's good to know.''

"Don't give it another thought.''

But Nellie found her own thoughts dwelling on it. The Westphalen curse ... she and Grace and Teddy used to joke about it. But if some of the stories were to be believed, old Sir Albert had died a frightened old man, mortally afraid of the dark. It was said he spent his last years surrounded by guard dogs, and always kept a fire going in his room, even on the hottest nights.

Nellie shivered. It had been easy to make jokes back then when they were young and there were three of them. But Teddy was long dead of leukemia—at least he hadn't gone "in blood and pain''; more like fading away—and Grace was who knew where? Had some "dark thing'' come for her? Could there possibly be something to—

Rubbish! How can I let myself be frightened by the rantings of a crazy old man who's been dead for a century?

Still ... Grace was gone and there was no explaining that. Not yet.

As they neared Sutton Square, Nellie felt anticipation mounting within her. There had been news of Grace while she was out—she was sure of it! She hadn't budged from the house since Tuesday for fear of missing word from Grace. But wasn't staying in the house like watching a pot? It wouldn't boil until you turned your back on it. Leaving the house was the same thing: Grace had probably called as soon as they left Sutton Square.

Nellie hurried up to the front door and rang the bell while Gia paid the driver. Her fists clenched of their own volition as she waited impatiently for the door to open.

Grace is back! I know it! I just know it!

But the hope shriveled and died when the door opened and she saw Eunice's grim face.

"Any word?''

The question was unnecessary. The sad, slow shake of Eunice's head told Nellie what she already knew. Suddenly she felt exhausted, as if all her energy had been drained off.

She turned to Gia as she came in the door with Victoria. "I can't go tonight."

"You must." Gia said, throwing an arm around her shoulders. "What happened to that British stiff-upper-lip-and-all-that attitude? What would Sir Albert think if you just sat around and moped all night?"

Nellie appreciated what Gia was trying to do, but she truly did not give a damn about what Sir Albert might have thought.

"And what am I going to do with this dress?" Gia went on.

"The dress is yours," Nellie said morosely. She didn't have the will to put on a facade.

"Not if we don't go tonight, it isn't. I'll take it back to La Chanson right now unless you promise me we're going."

"That's not fair. I can't go. Can't you see that?"

"No, I can't see that at all. What would Grace think? You know she'd want you to go."

Would she? Nellie thought about that. Knowing Grace, she would want her to go. Grace was always one for keeping up appearances. No matter how bad you felt inside, you kept up your social obligations. And you never, *never* made a spectacle of your feelings.

"Do it for Grace," Gia said.

Nellie managed a little smile. "Very well, we shall go, although I can't guarantee how stiff my upper lip shall be."

"You'll do fine." Gia gave her one last hug, then released her. Victoria was calling from the kitchen, asking her mother to cut an orange for her. Gia hurried off, leaving Nellie alone in the foyer.

How will I do this? It has always been Grace-and-Nellie, Nellie-and-Grace, the two as one, always together. How will I do it without her?

Feeling very old, Nellie started up the stairs to her room.

8.

Nellie had neglected to tell her whom the reception was for, and Gia never did find out. She got the impression it was to welcome a new high-ranking official to the Mission.

The affair, while hardly exciting, was not nearly as deadly dull as Gia had expected. The Harley House where it was being held was convenient to the U.N. and a short drive from Sutton Square. Even Nellie seemed to enjoy herself after a while. Only the first fifteen

THE TOMB

minutes or so were rough on the old woman, for immediately upon her arrival she was surrounded by a score of people asking after Grace and expressing their concern. All were members of that unofficial club of wealthy British citizens living in New York, "the colony within the Colonies."

Buoyed by the sympathy and encouragement of her fellow Britons, Nellie perked up, drank some champagne, and actually began to laugh. Gia gave herself a pat on the back for refusing to allow her to cancel out tonight. This was her good deed for the day. The *year!*

Not such a bad crowd after all, Gia decided after an hour or so. There were numerous nationalities, all well-dressed, friendly, polite, offering a smorgasbord of accents. The new dress fit her beautifully and she felt very feminine. She was aware of the admiring glances she drew from more than a few of the guests, and she enjoyed that. She was nearly finished with her third fluted glass of champagne—she knew nothing about champagne but this was delicious—when Nellie grabbed her by the arm and pulled her toward two men standing off to the side. Gia recognized the shorter of the pair as Edward Burkes, security chief at the Mission. The taller man was dark, dressed all in white, including his turban. When he turned she noticed with a start that he had no left arm.

"Eddie, how are you?" Nellie said, extending her hand.

"Nellie! How good to see you!" Burkes took her hand and kissed it. He was a burly man of about fifty, with graying hair and a mustache. He looked at Gia and then smiled. "And Miss DiLauro! What an unexpected pleasure! You look wonderful! Allow me to introduce you both to Mr. Kusum Bahkti of the Indian delegation."

The Indian made a small bow at the waist but did not extend his hand. "A pleasure to meet you both."

Gia took an instant dislike to him. His dark, angular face was a mask, his eyes unreadable. He seemed to be hiding something. His gaze passed over her as if she were an ordinary piece of furniture, but came to rest and remain avidly on Nellie.

A waiter came around with a tray of champagne—filled glasses. Burkes gave one each to Nellie and Gia, then offered one to Mr. Bahkti who shook his head.

"Sorry, Kusum," Burkes said. "Forgot you don't drink. Can I get you anything else? A fruit punch?"

Mr. Bahkti shook his head. "Don't trouble yourself. Perhaps I'll examine the buffet table later and see if you've put out any of those

139

good English chocolates."

"Are you a chocolate fancier?" Nellie said. "I adore it."

"Yes. I developed a taste for it when I was with the London embassy. I brought a small supply with me when I came to this country, but that was six months ago, and it has long since been depleted."

"Just today I received a box of Black Magic from London. Have you ever had those?"

Gia saw genuine pleasure in Mr. Bahkti's smile. "Yes. Superior chocolates."

"You must come by some time and have some."

The smile widened. "Perhaps I shall do that."

Gia began to revise her opinion of Mr. Bahkti. He seemed to have gone from aloof to quite charming. Or was it simply an effect of her fourth glass of champagne? She tingled all over, felt almost giddy.

"I heard about Grace," Burkes said to Nellie. "If there's anything I can do ..."

"We're doing all we can," Nellie said with a brave smile, "but mostly it comes down to waiting."

"Mr. Bahkti and I were just discussing a mutual acquaintance, Jack Jeffers."

"I believe his surname is Nelson," the Indian said.

"No, I'm sure it's Jeffers. Isn't it, Miss DiLauro? You know him best, I believe."

Gia wanted to laugh. How could she tell them Jack's last name when she wasn't sure herself. "Jack is Jack," she said as tactfully as she could.

"He is that!" Burkes said with a laugh. "He recently helped Mr. Bahkti with a difficult matter."

"Oh?" Gia said, trying not to sound arch. "A security matter?" That was how Jack was first introduced to her: "a security consultant."

"Personal," the Indian said, and that was all.

Gia wondered about that. What had the U.K. Mission used Jack for? And Mr. Bahkti, a U.N. diplomat—why would he need Jack? These weren't the type of men who had use for someone like him. They were respectable members of the international diplomatic community. What could they want "fixed"? To her surprise, she detected an enormous amount of respect in their voices when they spoke of him. It baffled her.

"But anyway," Burkes said, "I was thinking perhaps he could be of use in finding your sister, Nellie."

Gia was looking at Mr. Bahkti as Burkes was speaking and she could have sworn she saw the Indian flinch. She did not have time to confirm the impression because she turned to give Nellie a quick warning look: They had promised Jack no one would know he was working for her.

"A marvelous idea, Eddie," Nellie said, catching Gia's glance and not missing a beat. "But I'm sure the police are doing all that can be done. However, if it—"

"Well, speak of the devil!" Burkes said, interrupting her and staring toward the entrance.

Before Gia turned to follow his gaze, she glanced again at Mr. Bahkti who was already looking in the direction Burkes had indicated. On his dark face she saw a look of fury so deep, so fierce, that she stepped away from him for fear that he might explode. She searched the other end of the room to see what could cause such a reaction. And then she saw him . . . and her.

It was Jack. He was dressed in an old fashioned tuxedo with tails, white tie, and winged collar. He looked wonderful. Against her will, her heart leaped at the sight of him—*That's only because he's a fellow American among all these foreigners*—and then crashed. For on his arm was one of the most striking women Gia had ever seen.

9.

Vicky was supposed to be asleep. It was way past her bedtime. She had tried to push herself into slumber, but it just wouldn't come. Too hot. She lay on top of the bedsheet to get cool. The air conditioning didn't work as well up here on the third floor as it did downstairs. Despite her favorite pink shorty pajamas, her dolls, and her new Wuppet to keep her company, she still couldn't sleep. Eunice had done all she could, from sliced oranges—Vicky loved oranges and couldn't get enough of them—to reading her a story. Nothing worked. Finally, Vicky had faked sleep just so Eunice wouldn't feel bad.

Usually when she couldn't sleep it was because she was worrying about mommy. There were times when mommy went out at night that she had a bad feeling, a feeling that she'd never come back, that she'd been caught in an earthquake or a tornado or a car wreck. On those nights she'd pray and promise to be good forever if only mommy got home safe. It hadn't failed yet.

But Vicky wasn't worried tonight. Mommy was out with Aunt Nellie and Aunt Nellie would take care of her. Worry wasn't keeping her awake.

It was the chocolates.

Vicky could not get those chocolates out of her mind. She had never seen a box like that—black with gold trim and a big red rose on the top. All the way from England. And the name: Black Magic! The name alone was enough to keep her awake.

She had to see them. It was as simple as that. She had to go down there and look in that box and see the ''Dark Assortment'' promised on the lid.

With Ms. Jelliroll tucked securely under her arm, she crawled out of bed and headed for the stairs. Down to the second floor landing without a sound, and then down to the first. The slate floor of the foyer was cool under her feet. Down the hall came voices and music and flickery light from where Eunice was watching television in the library. Vicky tiptoed across the foyer to the front parlor where she had seen Aunt Nellie put the box of chocolates.

She found it sitting on an end table. The cellophane was off. Vicky placed Ms. Jelliroll on the little couch, seated herself beside her, then pulled the Black Magic box onto her lap. She started to lift the lid, then stopped.

Mommy would have a fit if she came in now and found her sitting here. Bad enough that she was out of bed, but to have Aunt Nellie's chocolates, too!

Vicky felt no guilt, however. In a way, this box should be hers, even if she *was* allergic to chocolate. It was from her father, after all. She had hoped that when mommy stopped home today she would find a package there just for her. But no. Nothing from daddy.

Vicky ran her fingers over the rose on the lid. Pretty. Why couldn't this be hers? Maybe after Aunt Nellie finished the chocolates she'd let Vicky keep the box.

How many are left?

She lifted the lid. The rich, heavy smell of dark chocolate enveloped her, and with it the subtler odors of all the different fillings. And another smell, hiding just underneath the others, a smell she wasn't quite sure of. But that was of little concern. The chocolate overpowered everything else. Saliva poured into her mouth. She wanted one. Oh, how she wanted just one bite.

She tilted the box to better see the contents in the light from the foyer. No empty slots! None of the chocolates were missing! At this rate it would take forever before she got the empty box. But the box was really of secondary interest now. It was the chocolate she hungered for.

She picked up a piece from the middle, wondering what was inside. It was cool to the touch but within seconds the chocolate coating became soft. Jack had taught her how to poke her thumb into the bottom to see what color the middle was. But what if it was a liquid center? She had thumb-poked a chocolate-covered cherry once and wound up with a sticky mess all over her lap. No thumb-poking tonight.

She held it to her nose. It didn't smell quite so good up close. Maybe it had something yucky inside, like raspberry goo or some such awful stuff. One bite wouldn't hurt. Maybe just a nibble from the outer layer. That way she wouldn't have to worry about what was inside. And maybe no one would notice.

No.

Vicky put the piece back. She remembered the last time she had sneaked a nibble of chocolate—her face swelled up like a big red balloon and her eyelids got so puffy all the kids at school had said she looked Chinese. Maybe no one would notice the nibble she took, but mommy would sure notice her blown-up face. She took one last, longing look at the rows of dark lumps, then replaced the lid and put the box back on the table.

With Ms. Jelliroll under her arm again, she walked back to the bottom of the stairs and stood there looking up. It was dark up there. And she was scared. But she couldn't stay down here all night. Slowly she started up, carefully watching the dark at the top. When she reached the second floor landing she clung to the newel post and peered around. Nothing moved. With her heart beating wildly she broke into a scampering run around to the second flight and didn't slow until she had reached the third floor, jumped into her bed, and pulled the sheet over her head.

10.

"Working hard, I see."

Jack whirled at the sound of the voice, nearly spilling the two

143

glasses of champagne he had just lifted from the tray of a passing waiter.

"Gia!" She was the last person he expected to see here. And the last person he wanted to see. He felt he should be out looking for Grace instead of hob-nobbing with the diplomats. But he swallowed his guilt, smiled, and tried to say something brilliant. "Fancy meeting you here."

"I'm here with Nellie."

"Oh. That explains it."

He stood there looking at her, wanting to reach out his hand and have her take it the way she used to, knowing she'd only turn away if he did. He noticed a half-empty champagne glass in her hand and a glittery look in her eyes. He wondered how many she had had. She never was much of a drinker.

"So, what've you been doing with yourself?" she said, breaking the uncomfortable silence between them.

Yes—definitely too much to drink. Her voice was slightly slurred.

"Shoot anybody lately?"

Oh, swell. Here we go.

He answered in a quiet, soothing voice. He wasn't looking for an argument. "Reading a lot—"

"What? The Executioner series for the fourteenth time?"

"—and watching movies."

"A Dirty Harry Festival, I suppose."

"You look great," he said, refusing to let her irk him as he tried to turn the talk toward Gia. He wasn't lying. She filled her dress nicely, and the pinkish color, whatever it was, seemed made for her blond hair and blue eyes.

"You're not doing so bad yourself."

"It's my Fred Astaire suit. Always wanted to wear one of these. Like it?"

Gia nodded. "Is it as uncomfortable as it looks?"

"More so. Don't know how anyone ever tap danced in one of these. Collar's choking me."

"It's not your style, anyway."

"You're right." Jack preferred to be unobtrusive. He was happiest when he could walk past with no one noticing. "But something got into me tonight. Couldn't pass up the chance to be Fred Astaire just once."

"You don't dance and your date will never be mistaken for Ginger

Rogers.''

"I can dream, can't I?"

"Who is she?"

Jack studied Gia closely. Could there be just a trace of jealousy there? Was that possible?

"She's ..." he looked around the room until he spotted Kusum ... "that man's sister."

"Is she the 'personal matter' you helped him out with?"

"Oh?" he said with a slow smile. "You've been asking about me?"

Gia's eyes shifted away. "Burkes brought your name up. Not me."

"You know something, Gia?" Jack said, knowing he shouldn't but helpless to resist. "You're beautiful when you're jealous."

Her eyes flashed and her cheeks turned red. "Don't be absurd!" She turned and walked away.

Typical, Jack thought. She wanted nothing to do with him but didn't want to see him with anybody else.

He looked around for Kolabati—not a typical woman by any standard—and found her standing beside her brother who seemed to be doing his best to pretend she wasn't there.

As he walked toward the silent pair, Jack marveled at the way Kolabati's dress clung to her. It was made of a gauzy, dazzlingly white fabric that came across her right shoulder and wrapped itself around her breasts like a bandage. Her left shoulder was completely bare, exposing her dark, flawless skin for all to admire. And there were many admirers.

"Hello, Mr. Bahkti," he said as he handed Kolabati her glass.

Kusum glanced at the champagne, at Kolabati, then turned an icy smile on Jack.

"May I compliment you on the decadence of your attire."

"Thank you. I knew it wasn't stylish, but I'll settle for decadent. How's your grandmother?"

"Physically well, but suffering from a mental aberration. I fear."

"She's doing fine," Kolabati said with a scathing look at her brother. "I have the latest word and she's doing just fine." Then she smiled sweetly. "Oh, by the way, Kusum dear. Jack was asking about durba grass today. Anything you can tell him about it?"

Jack saw Kusum stiffen at the mention of durba grass. He knew Kolabati had been startled when he had asked her about it on the phone today. What did durba grass mean to these two?

Still smiling, Kolabati sauntered away as Kusum faced him.

THE TOMB

"What did you wish to know?"

"Nothing in particular. Except ... is it ever used as a laxative?"

Kusum's face remained impassive. "It has many uses, but I have never heard it recommended for constipation. Why do you ask?"

"Just curious. An old lady I know said she was using a concoction with a durba grass extract in it."

"I'm surprised. I didn't think you could find durba grass in the Americas. Where did she buy it?"

Jack was studying Kusum's face. Something there ... something he couldn't quite define.

"Don't know. She's away on a trip right now. When she comes back I'll ask her."

"Throw it away if you have any, my friend," Kusum said gravely. "Certain durba grass preparations have undesirable side-effects. Throw it away." Before Jack could say anything, Kusum gave one of his little bows. "Excuse me. There are some people I must speak to before the night is over."

Undesirable side-effects? What the hell did that mean?

Jack wandered around the room. He spotted Gia again but she avoided his eyes. Finally, the inevitable happened: He ran into Nellie Paton. He saw the pain behind her smile and suddenly felt absurd in his old-fashioned tuxedo. This woman had asked him to help find her missing sister and here he was dressed up like a gigolo.

"Gia tells me you're getting nowhere," she said in a low voice after brief amenities.

"I'm trying. If only I had more to go on. I'm doing what I—"

"I know you are, dear," Nellie said, patting his hand. "You were fair. You made no promises, and you warned me you might not be able to do any more than the police had already done. All I need to know is that someone is still looking."

"I am." He spread his arms. "I may not look like it, but I am."

"Oh, rubbish!" she said with a smile. "Everyone needs a holiday. And you certainly seem to have a beautiful companion for it."

Jack turned in the direction Nellie was looking and saw Kolabati approaching them. He introduced the two women.

"Oh, I met your brother tonight!" Nellie said. "A charming man."

"When he wants to be, yes," Kolabati replied. "By the way—has either of you seen him lately?"

Nellie nodded. "I saw him leave perhaps ten minutes ago."

Kolabati said a word under her breath. Jack didn't know Indian, but he could recognize a curse when he heard one.

"Something wrong?"

She smiled at him with her lips only. "Not at all. I just wanted to ask him something before he left."

"Speaking of leaving," Nellie said. "I think that's a good idea. Excuse me while I go find Gia." She bustled off.

Jack looked at Kolabati. "Not a bad idea. Had enough of the diplomatic crowd for one night?"

"For more than one night."

"Where shall we go?"

"How about your apartment? Unless you've got a better idea."

Jack could not think of one.

11.

Kolabati had spent most of the evening cudgeling her brain for a way to broach the subject to Jack. She had to find out about the durba grass! Where did he learn about it? Did he have any? She had to know!

She settled on the direct approach. As soon as they entered his apartment, she asked:

"Where's the durba grass?"

"Don't have any," Jack said as he took off his tailed coat and hung it on a hanger.

Kolabati glanced around the front room. She didn't see any growing in pots. "You must."

"Really, I don't."

"Then why did you ask me about it on the phone today?"

"I told you—"

"Truth, Jack." She could tell it was going to be hard getting a straight answer out of him. But she had to know. "Please. It's important."

Jack made her wait while he loosened his tie and unbuttoned the winged collar. He seemed glad to be out of it. He looked into her eyes. For a moment she thought he was going to tell her the truth. Instead, he answered her question with one of his own.

"Why do you want to know?"

"Just tell me, Jack."

"Why is it so important?"

She bit her lip. She had to tell him something. "Prepared in certain

147

ways it can be . . . dangerous.''

"Dangerous how?"

"Please, Jack. Just let me see what you've got and I'll tell you if there's anything to worry about.''

"Your brother warned me about it, too.''

"Did he?'' She still could not believe that Kusum was uninvolved in this. Yet he had warned Jack. "What did he say?''

"He mentioned side-effects. 'Undesirable' side-effects. Just what they might be, he didn't say. I was hoping maybe you could—''

"*Jack*! Why are you playing games with me?''

She was genuinely concerned for him. Frightened for him. Perhaps that finally got through to him. He stared at her, then shrugged.

"Okay, okay.'' He went to the giant Victorian breakfront, removed a bottle from a tiny drawer hidden in the carvings, and brought it over to Kolabati. Instinctively, she reached for it. Jack pulled it away and shook his head as he unscrewed the top. "Smell first.''

He held it under her nose. At the first whiff, Kolabati thought her knees would fail her. *Rakoshi elixir!* She snatched at it but Jack was quicker and held it out of her reach. She had to get it away from him!

"Give that to me, Jack.'' Her voice was trembling with the terror she felt for him.

"Why?''

Kolabati took a deep breath and began to walk around the room. *Think!*

"Who gave it to you? And please don't ask me why I want to know. Just answer me.''

"All right. Answer: no one.''

She glared at him. "I'll rephrase the question. Where did you get it?''

"From the dressing room of an old lady who disappeared between Monday night and Tuesday morning and hasn't been seen or heard from since.''

So the elixir was *not* meant for Jack! He had come by it second hand. She began to relax.

"Did you drink any?''

"No.''

That didn't make sense. A rakosh had come here last night. She was sure of that. The elixir must have drawn it. She shuddered at what might have happened had Jack been here alone.

THE TOMB

"You must have."

Jack's brow furrowed. "Oh, yes ... I tasted it. Just a drop."

She moved closer, feeling a tightness in her chest. "When?"

"Yesterday."

"And today?"

"Nothing. It's not exactly a soft drink."

Relief. "You must never let a drop of that pass your lips again—or anybody else's for that matter."

"Why not?"

"Flush it down the toilet! Pour it down a sewer! Anything! But don't let any of it get into your system again!"

"What's wrong with it?" Jack was becoming visibly annoyed now. Kolabati knew he wanted answers and she couldn't tell him the truth without him thinking her insane.

"It's a deadly poison," she said off the top of her head. "You were lucky you took only a tiny amount. Any more and you would have—"

"Not true," he said, holding up the still unstoppered bottle. "I had it analyzed today. No toxins in here."

Kolabati cursed herself for not realizing that he'd have it analyzed. How else could he have known it contained durba grass?

"It's poisonous in a different way," she said, improvising poorly, knowing she wasn't going to be believed. If only she could lie like Kusum! She felt tears of frustration fill her eyes. "Oh, Jack, please listen to me! I don't want to see anything happen to you! Trust me!"

"I'll trust you if you'll tell me what's going on. I find this stuff among the possessions of a missing woman and you tell me it's dangerous but you won't say how or why. What's going on?"

"I don't *know* what's going on! Really. All I can tell you is something awful will happen to anyone who drinks that mixture!"

"Is that so?" Jack looked at the bottle in his hand, then looked at Kolabati.

Believe me! Please, believe me!

Without warning, he tipped the bottle up to his mouth.

"*No!*" Kolabati leaped at him, screaming.

Too late. She saw his throat move. He had swallowed some.

"*You idiot!*"

She raged at her own foolishness. *She* was the idiot! She hadn't been thinking clearly. If she had she would have realized the inevitability of what had just happened. Next to her brother, Jack was the

149

THE TOMB

most relentlessly uncompromising man she had ever met. Knowing that, what could have made her think he would surrender the elixir without a full explanation as to what it was? Any fool could have foreseen that he would bring matters to a head this way. The very reasons she was attracted to Jack might have doomed him.

And she was so attracted to him. She learned with an explosive shock the true depth of her feelings when she saw him swallow the rakoshi elixir. She had had more than her share of lovers. They had wandered in and out of her life in Bengal and Europe, and in Washington. But Jack was someone special. He made her feel complete. He had something the others didn't have . . . a purity—was that the proper word?—that she wanted to make her own. She wanted to be with him, stay with him, keep him for herself.

But first she had to find a way to keep him alive through tonight.

12.

The vow was made . . . the vow must be kept . . . the vow was made . . .

Kusum repeated the words over and over in his mind.

He sat in his cabin with his *Gita* spread out on his lap. He had stopped reading it. The gently rocking ship was silent but for the familiar rustlings from the main hold amidships. He didn't hear them. Thoughts poured through his mind in a wild torrent. That woman he had met tonight, Nellie Paton. He knew her maiden name: Westphalen. A sweet, harmless old woman with a passion for chocolate, worrying about her missing sister, unaware that her sister was far beyond her concern, and that her worry should be reserved for herself. For her days were numbered on the fingers of a single hand. Perhaps a single finger.

And that blond woman, not a Westphalen herself, yet the mother of one. Mother of a child who would soon be the last Westphalen. Mother of a child who must die.

Am I sane?

When he thought of the journey he had embarked upon, the destruction he had already wrought, he shuddered. And he was only half done.

Richard Westphalen had been the first. He had been sacrificed to the rakoshi during Kusum's stay at the London embassy. He remembered dear Richard: the fear-bulged eyes, the crying, the whimper-

THE TOMB

ing, the begging as he cringed before the rakoshi and answered in detail every question Kusum put to him about his aunts and daughter in the United States. He remembered how piteously Richard Westphalen had pleaded for his life, offering anything—even his current consort in his place—if only he would be allowed to live.

Richard Westphalen had not died honorably and his karma would carry that stain for many incarnations.

The pleasure Kusum had taken in delivering the screaming Richard Westphalen over to the rakoshi had dismayed him. He was performing a duty. He was not supposed to enjoy it. But he had thought at the time that if all three of the remaining Westphalens were creatures as reprehensible as Richard, fulfilling the vow would be a service to humanity.

It was not to be so, he had learned. The old woman, Grace Westphalen, had been made of sterner stuff. She had acquitted herself well before fainting. She had been unconscious when Kusum gave her over to the rakoshi.

But Richard and Grace had been strangers to Kusum. He had seen them only from afar before their sacrifices. He had investigated their personal habits and studied their routines, but he had never come close to them, never spoken to them.

Tonight he had stood not half a meter from Nellie Paton discussing English chocolates with her. He had found her pleasant and gracious and unassuming. And yet she must die by his design.

Kusum ground his only fist into his eyes, forcing himself to think about the pearls he had seen around her neck, the jewels on her fingers, the luxurious townhouse she owned, the wealth she commanded, all bought at a terrible price of death and destruction to his family. Nellie Paton's ignorance of the source of her wealth was of no consequence.

A vow had been made . . .

And the road to a pure karma involved keeping that vow. Though he had fallen along the way, he could make everything right again by being true to his first vow, his *vrata*. The Goddess had whispered to him in the night. Kali had shown him the way.

Kusum wondered at the price others had paid—and soon would have to pay—for the purification of his karma. The soiling of that karma had been no one's fault but his own. He had freely taken a vow of *Brahmacharya* and for many years had held to a life of chastity and sexual continence. Until . . .

151

THE TOMB

His mind shied away from the days that ended his life as a *Brahmachari*. There were sins—*patakas*—that stained every life. But he had committed a *mahapataka*, thoroughly polluting his karma. It was a catastrophic blow to his quest for *moksha*, the liberation from the karmic wheel. It meant he would suffer greatly before being born again as an evil man of low caste. For he had forsaken his vow of *Brahmacharya* in the most abominable fashion.

But the *vrata* to his father he would not forsake: Although the crime was more than a century in the past, all the descendents of Sir Albert Westphalen must die for it. Only two were left.

A new noise rose from below. The Mother was scraping on the hatch. She had caught the Scent and wanted to hunt.

He rose and stepped to his cabin door, then stopped, uncertain of what to do. He knew the Paton woman had received the candies. Before leaving London he had injected each piece with a few drops of the elixir and had left the wrapped and addressed parcel in the care of an embassy secretary to hold until she received word to mail it. And now it had arrived. All would be perfect.

Except for Jack.

Jack obviously knew the Westphalens. A startling coincidence but not outlandish when one considered that both the Westphalens and Kusum knew Jack through Burkes at the U.K. Mission. And Jack had apparently come into possession of the small bottle of elixir Kusum had arranged for Grace Westphalen to receive last weekend. Had it been mere chance that he had picked that particular bottle to investigate? From what little Kusum knew of Jack, he doubted it.

For all the considerable risk Jack represented—his innate intuitive abilities and his capacity and willingness to do physical damage made him a very dangerous man—Kusum was loathe to see him come to harm. He was indebted to him for returning the necklace in time. More importantly, Jack was too rare a creature in the Western World—Kusum did not want to be responsible for his extinction. And finally, there was a certain kinship he felt toward the man. He sensed Repairman Jack to be an outcast in his own land, just as Kusum had been in his until recently. True, Kusum had an ever-growing following at home and now moved in the upper circles of India's diplomatic corps as if he belonged there, but he was still an outcast in his heart. For he would never—could never—be a part of the "new" India.

The "new" India indeed! Once he had fulfilled his vow he would return home with his rakoshi. And then he would begin the task of

152

transforming the "new" India back into a land true to its heritage.

He had the time.

And he had the rākoshi.

The Mother's scraping against the hatch door became more insistent. He would have to let her hunt tonight. All he could hope for was that the Paton woman had eaten a piece of the candy and that the Mother would lead her youngling there. He was quite sure Jack had the bottle of elixir, and that he had tasted it some time yesterday—a single drop was enough to draw a rakosh. It was unlikely he would taste it twice. And so it must be the Paton woman who now carried the scent.

Anticipation filled Kusum as he started below to free the Mother and her youngling.

13.

They were entwined on the couch, Jack sitting, Kolabati sprawled across him, her hair a dark storm cloud across her face. It was a replay of last night, only this time they hadn't made it to the bedroom.

After Kolabati's initial frightened reaction to seeing him swallow the liquid, Jack had waited to see what she would say. Taking that swig had been a radical move on his part, but he had butted heads against this thing long enough. Maybe now he would get some answers.

But she had said nothing. Instead, she started undressing him. When he protested, she began doing things to him with her fingernails that drove all questions about mysterious liquids from his mind.

Questions could wait. Everything could wait.

Jack floated now on a langorous river of sensation, leading he knew not where. He had tried to take the helm but had given up, yielding to her superior knowledge of the various currents and tributaries along the way. As far as he was concerned, Kolabati could steer him wherever she wished. They had explored new territories last night and more tonight. He was ready to push the frontiers back even further. He only hoped he could stay afloat during the ensuing excursions.

Kolabati was just beginning to guide him into the latest adventure when the odor returned. Just a trace, but enough to recognize as the same unforgettable stench as last night.

If Kolabati noticed it, too, she said nothing. But she immediately rose to her knees and swung her hips over him. As she settled astride his lap with a little sigh, she clamped her lips over his. This was the most conventional position they had used all night. Jack found her rhythm and began moving with her but, just like last night when the odor had invaded the apartment, he sensed a strange tension in her that took the edge off his ardor.

And the odor ... it was nauseating, growing stronger and stronger, filling the air around them. It seemed to flow from the TV room. Jack raised his head from Kolabati's throat where he had been nuzzling around her iron necklace. Over the rise and fall of her right shoulder he could look into the dark of that room. He saw nothing—

A noise.

A click, really, much like the whirring air conditioner in the TV room made from time to time. But different. Slightly louder. A little more solid. Something about it alerted Jack. He kept his eyes open ...

And as he watched, two pairs of yellow eyes began to glow outside the TV room window.

It had to be a trick of the light. He squinted for a better look, but the eyes remained. They moved around, as if searching for something. One of the pair fixed on Jack for an instant. An icy fingernail scored the outer wall of his heart as he stared into those glowing yellow orbs ... like looking into the very soul of evil. He felt himself wither inside Kolabati. He wanted to throw her off, run to the old oak secretary, pull out every gun behind the panel in its base and fire them out the window two at a time.

But he could not move! Fear as he had never known it gripped him in a clammy fist and pinned him to the couch. He was paralyzed by the alienness of those eyes and the sheer malevolence behind them.

Kolabati had to be aware that something was wrong—there was no way she could not be. She leaned back and looked at him.

"What do you see?" Her eyes were wide and her voice barely audible.

"Eyes," Jack said. "Yellow eyes. Two pairs."

She caught her breath. "In the other room?"

"Outside the window."

"Don't move, don't say another word."

"But—"

"For both our sakes. Please."

Jack neither moved nor spoke. He stared at Kolabati's face, trying to read it. She was afraid, but anything beyond that was closed off to him. Why hadn't she been surprised when he told her there were eyes watching them from the other side of a third-story window with no fire escape?

He glanced over her shoulder again. The eyes were still there, still searching for something. What? They appeared confused, and even when they looked directly at him, they did not seem to see him. Their gaze slid off him, slithered around him, passed through him.

This is crazy! Why am I sitting here?

He was angry with himself for yielding so easily to fear of the unknown. There was some sort of animal out there—two of them. Nothing he couldn't deal with.

As Jack started to lift Kolabati off him, she gave a little cry. She wrapped her arms around his neck in a near stranglehold and dug her knees into his hips.

"Don't move!" Her voice was hushed and frantic.

"Let me up." He tried to slide out from under but she twisted around and pulled him down on top of her. It would have been comical but for her very genuine terror.

"Don't leave me!"

"I'm going to see what's out there."

"No! If you value your life you'll stay right where you are!"

This was beginning to sound like a bad movie.

"Come *on*! What could be out there?"

"Better you never find out."

That did it. He gently but firmly tried to disengage himself from Kolabati. She protested all the way and would not let go of his neck. Had she gone crazy? What was wrong with her?

He finally managed to gain his feet with Kolabati still clinging to him, and had to drag her with him to the TV room door.

The eyes were gone.

Jack stumbled to the window. Nothing there. And nothing visible in the darkness of the alley below. He turned within the circle of Kolabati's arms.

"What was out there?"

Her expression was charmingly innocent. "You saw for yourself: nothing."

She released him and walked back into the front room, completely unselfconscious in her nakedness. Jack watched the swaying flare of her hips silhouetted in the light as she walked away. Something had happened here tonight and Kolabati knew what it was. But Jack was at a loss as to how to make her tell him. He had failed to learn

155

anything about Grace's tonic—and now this.

"Why were you so afraid?" he said, following her.

"I wasn't afraid." She began to slip into her underwear.

He mimicked her: " 'If you value your life' and whatever else you said. You were scared! Of what?"

"Jack, I love you dearly," she said in a voice that did not quite carry all the carefree lightness she no doubt intended it to, "but you can be so silly at times. It was just a game."

Jack could see the pointlessness of pursuing this any further. She had no intention of telling him anything. He watched her finish dressing—it didn't take long; she hadn't been wearing much—with a sense of *deja-vu*. Hadn't they played this scene last night?

"You're leaving?"

"Yes. I have to—"

"—See your brother?"

She looked at him. "How did you know?"

"Lucky guess."

Kolabati stepped up to him and put her arms around his neck. "I'm sorry to run off like this again." She kissed him. "Can we meet tomorrow?"

"I'll be out of town."

"Monday, then?"

He held back from saying yes.

"I don't know. I'm not too crazy about our routine: We come here, we make love, a stink comes into the room, you get up-tight and cling to me like a second skin, the stink goes away, you take off."

Kolabati kissed him again and Jack felt himself begin to respond. She had her ways, this Indian woman. "It won't happen again. I promise."

"How can you be so sure?"

"I just am," she said with a smile.

Jack let her out, then locked the door behind her. Still naked, he went back to the window in the TV room and stood there looking out at the dark. The beach scene was barely visible on the shadowed wall across the alley. Nothing moved, no eyes glowed. He wasn't crazy and he didn't do drugs. Something—two somethings—had been out there tonight. Two pairs of yellow eyes had been looking in. Something about those eyes were familiar but he couldn't quite make the connection. Jack didn't push it. It would come sooner or later.

His attention was drawn to the sill outside his window where he saw three long white scratches in the concrete. He was sure they had never been there before. He was puzzled and uneasy, angry and frustrated—and what could he do? She was gone.

He walked through the front room to get a beer. On the way, he glanced at the shelf on the big hutch where he had left the bottle of herbal mixture after taking the swallow.

It was gone.

14.

Kolabati hurried toward Central Park West. This was a residential district with trees near the curb and cars lining both sides of the street. Nice in the daytime, but at night there were too many deep shadows, too many dark hiding places. It was not rakoshi she feared—not while she wore her necklace. It was humans. And with good reason: Look what had happened Wednesday night because a hoodlum thought an iron and topaz necklace looked valuable.

She relaxed when she reached Central Park West. There was plenty of traffic there despite the lateness of the hour, and the sodium lamps high over the street made the very air around her seem to glow. Empty cabs cruised by. She let them pass. There was something she had to do before she flagged one down.

Kolabati walked along the curb until she found a sewer grate. She reached into her purse and removed the bottle of rakoshi elixir. She hadn't liked stealing it from Jack, for she would have to fabricate a convincing explanation later. But it was his safety that counted, and to assure that, she would steal from him again and again.

She unscrewed the cap and poured the green mixture down the sewer, waiting until the last drop fell.

She sighed with relief. Jack was safe. No more rakoshi would come looking for him.

She sensed someone behind her and turned. An elderly woman stood a few dozen feet away, watching her bend over the sewer grate. A nosey old biddy. Kolabati found her wrinkles and stooped posture repulsive. She never wanted to be that old.

As Kolabati straightened up, she recapped the bottle and returned it to her purse. She would save that for Kusum.

Yes, dear brother, she thought with determination, *I don't know how, or to what end, but I know you're involved. And soon I'll have the answers.*

THE TOMB

15.

Kusum stood in the engine room at the stern of his ship, every cell in his body vibrating in time to the diesel monstrosities on either side of him. The drone, the roar, the clatter of twin engines capable of generating a total of nearly 3,000 b.h.p. at peak battered his eardrums. A man could die screaming down here in the bowels of the ship and no one on the deck directly above would hear him; with the engines running, he wouldn't even hear himself.

Bowels of the ship . . . how apt. Pipes like masses of intestines coursed through the air, along the walls, under the catwalks, vertically, horizontally, diagonally.

The engines were warm. Time to get the crew.

The dozen or so rakoshi he had been training to run the ship had been doing well, but he wanted to keep them sharp. He wanted to be able to take his ship to sea on short notice. Hopefully that necessity would not arise, but the events of the past few days had made him wary of taking anything for granted. Tonight had only compounded his unease.

His mood was grim as he left the engine room. Again the Mother and her youngling had returned empty-handed. That meant only one thing. Jack had tried the elixir again and Kolabati had been there to protect him . . . with her body.

The thought filled Kusum with despair. Kolabati was destroying herself. She had spent too much time among westerners. She had already absorbed too many of their habits of dress. What other foul habits had she picked up? He had to find a way to save her from herself.

But not tonight. He had his own personal concerns: His evening prayers had been said; he had made his thrice-daily offering of water and sesame . . . he would make an offering more to the Goddess's taste tomorrow night. Now he was ready for work. There would be no punishment for the rakoshi tonight, only work.

Kusum picked up his whip from where he had left it on the deck and rapped the handle on the hatch that led to the main hold. The Mother and the younglings that made up the crew would be waiting on the other side. The sound of the engines was their signal to be ready. He released the rakoshi. As the dark, rangy forms swarmed up the steps to the deck, he relocked the hatch and headed for the wheelhouse.

THE TOMB

Kusum stood before his controls. The green-on-black CRTs with their flickering graphs and read-outs would have been more at home on a lunar lander than on this old rustbucket. But they were familiar to Kusum by now. During his stay in London he had had most of the ship's functions computerized, including navigation and steering. Once on the open sea, he could set a destination, phase in the computer, and tend to other business. The computer would choose the best course along the standard shipping lanes and leave him sixty miles off the coast of his target destination, disturbing him during the course of the voyage only if other vessels came within a designated proximity.

And it all worked. In its test run across the Atlantic—with a full human crew as back-up and the rakoshi towed behind in a barge—there had not been a single hitch.

But the system was useful only on the open sea. No computer was going to get him out of New York Harbor. It could help, but Kusum would have to do most of the work—without the aid of a tug or a pilot. Which was illegal, of course, but he could not risk allowing anyone, even a harbor pilot, aboard his ship. He was sure if he timed his departure carefully he could reach international waters before anyone could stop him. But should the Harbor Patrol or the Coast Guard pull alongside and try to board, Kusum would have his own boarding party ready.

The drills were important to him; they gave him peace of mind. Should something go awry, should his freighter's living cargo somehow be discovered, he needed to know he could leave on short notice. And so he ran the rakoshi through their paces regularly, lest they forget.

The river was dark and still, the wharf deserted. Kusum checked his instruments. All was ready for tonight's drill. A single blink of the running lights and the rakoshi leaped into action, loosening and untying the mooring ropes and cables. They were agile and tireless. They could leap to the wharf from the gunwales, cast off the ropes from the pilings, and then climb up those same ropes back to the ship. If one happened to fall in, it was of little consequence. They were quite at home in the water. After all, they had swum behind the ship after their barge had been cut loose off Staten Island and had climbed aboard after it had docked and been cleared by customs.

Within minutes, the Mother scrambled to the center of the forward hatch cover. This was the signal that all ropes were clear. Kusum threw the engines into reverse. The twin screws below began to pull the prow away from the pier. The computer aided Kusum in making tiny corrections for tidal drift, but most of the burden of the task was directly on his shoulders. With a larger freighter such a maneuver would have been impossible. But with this particular vessel, equipped as it was and with Kusum at the wheel, it could be done. It had taken Kusum many tries over the months, many crunches against the wharf and one or two nerve-shattering moments when he thought he had lost all control over the vessel, before he had become competent. Now it was routine.

The ship backed toward New Jersey until it was clear of the wharf. Leaving the starboard engine in reverse, Kusum threw the port engine into neutral, and then into forward. The ship began to turn south. Kusum had searched long and hard to find this ship—few freighters this size had twin screws. But his patience had paid off. He now had a ship that could turn 360 degrees within its own length.

When the prow had swung ninety degrees and was pointing toward the Battery, Kusum idled the engines. Had it been time to leave, he would have thrown both into forward and headed for the Narrows and the Atlantic Ocean beyond. If only he could! If only his duty here were done! Reluctantly, he put the starboard into forward and the port into reverse. The nose swung back toward the dock. Then it was alternating forward and reverse for both until the ship eased back into its slip. Two blinks of the running lights and the rakoshi were leaping to the pier and securing the ship in place.

Kusum allowed himself a smile of satisfaction. Yes, they were ready. It wouldn't be long before they left this obscene land forever. Kusum would see to it that the rakoshi did not return empty-handed tomorrow night.

CHAPTER SIX

West Bengal, India
Saturday, July 25, 1857

1.

People were going to die today. Of that Sir Albert Westphalen had no doubt.

And he might be one of them.

Here, high up on this ledge, with the morning sun on his back, with the mythical Temple-in-the-Hills and its walled courtyard spread out below him, he wondered at his ability to carry his plans through to completion. The abstract scheme that had seemed so simple and direct in his office in Bharangpur had become something quite different in these forbidding hills under the cold light of dawn.

His heart ground against his sternum as he lay on his belly and peered at the temple through his field glasses. He must have been daft to think this would work! How deep and cold was his desperation that it could lead him to this? Was he willing to risk his own death to save the family name?

Westphalen glanced down at his men, all busy checking their gear and mounts. With their stubbly faces, their rumpled uniforms caked with dirt, dried sweat and rain, they certainly didn't look like Her Majesty's finest this morning. They seemed not to notice, however. And well they might not, for Westphalen knew how these men lived—like animals in cramped quarters with a score and ten of their fellows, sleeping on canvas sheets changed once a month and eating and washing out of the same tin pot. Barracks life brutalized the best

161

of them, and when there was no enemy to fight they fought each other. The only thing they loved more than battle was liquor, and even now, when they should have been fortifying themselves with food, they were passing a bottle of raw spirits spiked with chopped capsicin. He could find no trace of his own disquiet in their faces; only anticipation of the battle and looting to come.

Despite the growing warmth of the sun, he shivered—the after-effect of a sleepless night spent huddled away from the rain under a rocky overhang, or simple fear of what was to come? He had certainly had his fill of fear last night. While the men had slept fitfully, he had remained awake, sure that there were wild things skulking about in the darkness beyond the small fire they had built. Occasionally he had glimpsed yellow glints of light in the dark, like pairs of fireflies. The horses, too, must have sensed something, for they were skittish all night.

But now it was day, and what was he to do?

He turned back to the temple and studied it anew through his field glasses. It sat hunched in the center of its courtyard behind the wall, alone but for a compound of some sort to its left against the base of a rocky cliff. The temple's most striking feature was its blackness—not dull and muddy, but proud and gleaming, deep and shiny, as if it were made of solid onyx. It was an oddly-shaped affair, boxlike with rounded corners. It seemed to have been made in layers, with each higher level dripping down over the ones below. The temple walls were ringed with friezes and studded along their length with gargoylelike figures, but Westphalen could make out no details from his present position. And atop it all was a huge obelisk, as black as the rest of the structure, pointing defiantly skyward.

Westphalen wondered how—short of a daguerreotype—he would ever do justice to any description of the Temple-in-the-Hills. It was simply alien. It looked ... it looked as if someone had driven a spike through an ornate block of licorice and left it out in the sun to melt.

As he watched, the door in the wall swung open. A man, younger than Jaggernath but swathed in a similar dhoti, came out carrying a large urn on his shoulder. He walked to the far corner of the wall, emptied the liquid contents of the urn onto the ground, and returned to the compound.

The door remained open behind him.

There was no longer any reason to delay, and no way in hell or on

THE TOMB

earth to turn his men back now. Westphalen felt as if he had started a huge juggernaut on its way down an incline; he had been able to guide it at first, but now its momentum was such that it was completely out of his control.

He clambered off the ledge and faced his men.

"We shall advance at full gallop in a double column with lances at the ready. Tooke will lead one column and take it left around the temple after entering the courtyard; Russell will lead the other column and go right. If there is no immediate resistance, you will all dismount and ready your rifles. We will then search the grounds for any pandies that might be hiding within. Any questions?"

The men shook their heads. They were more than ready—they were slavering for the fight. All they needed was someone to unleash them.

"Mount up!" Westphalen said.

The approach began orderly enough. Westphalen let the six lancers lead the way while he gladly brought up the rear. The detail trotted up the path until they were in sight of the temple, then broke into a gallop as planned.

But something happened on the road leading down to the wall. The men started to whoop and yell, whipping themselves and each other into a frenzy. Soon their lances were lowered and clamped under their arms in battle position as they leaned low over the necks of their mounts, bloodying the flanks as they spurred them to greater and greater speed.

They had been told that a band of rebel sepoys were quartered beyond that wall; the lancers had to be ready to kill as soon as they cleared the gate. Westphalen alone knew that their only resistance would come from a handful of surprised and harmless Hindu priests.

Only that knowledge allowed him to keep up with them. *Nothing to worry about,* he told himself as the wall drew nearer and nearer. *Only a few unarmed priests in there. Nothing to worry about.*

He had a glimpse of bas-relief murals on the surrounding wall as he raced toward the gate, but his mind was too full of the uncertainty of what they might find on the other side to make any sense of them. He drew his sabre and charged into the courtyard behind his howling lancers.

Westphalen saw three priests standing in front of the temple, all unarmed. They ran forward waving their hands in the air in what appeared to be an attempt to shoo the soldiers away.

163

THE TOMB

The lancers never hesitated. Three of them fanned out on the run and drove their lances through the priests. They then circled the temple and came to a halt at its front entrance where they dismounted, dropping their lances and pulling their Enfields from their saddle boots.

Westphalen remained mounted. He was uncomfortable at making himself an easy target, but felt more secure with his horse under him, able to wheel and gallop out the gate at an instant's notice should something go wrong.

There was a brief lull during which Westphalen directed the men toward the temple entrance. They were almost to the steps when the *svamin* counterattacked from two directions. With shrill cries of rage, a half dozen or so charged out from the temple; more than twice that number rushed from the compound. The former were armed with whips and pikes, the latter with curved swords much like sepoy talwars.

It was not a battle—it was a slaughter. Westphalen almost felt sorry for the priests. The soldiers first took aim at the closer group emerging from the temple. The Enfields left only one priest standing after the first volley; he ran around their flank to join the other group which had slowed its advance after seeing the results of the withering fire. From his saddle, Westphalen directed his men to retreat to the steps of the black temple where the light weight and rapid reloading capacity of the Enfield allowed them second and third volleys that left only two priests standing. Hunter and Malleson picked up their lances, remounted, and ran down the survivors.

And then it was over.

Westphalen sat numb and silent in his saddle as he let his gaze roam the courtyard. So easy. So final. They had all died so quickly. More than a score of bodies lay sprawled in the morning sun, their blood pooling and soaking into the sand as India's omnipresent opportunists, the flies, began to gather. Some of the bodies were curled into limp parodies of sleep, others, still transfixed by lances, looked like insects pinned to a board.

He glanced down at his pristine blade. He had bloodied neither his hands nor his sword. Somehow, that made him feel innocent of what had just happened all around him.

"Don't look like pandies to me," Tooke was saying as he rolled a corpse over onto its back with his foot.

"Never mind them," Westphalen said, dismounting at last.

164

THE TOMB

"Check inside and see if there's any more hiding around."

He ached to explore the temple, but not until it had been scouted by a few of the men. After watching Tooke and Russell disappear into the darkness within, he sheathed his sword and took a moment to inspect the temple close up. It was not made of stone as he had originally thought, but of solid ebony that had been cut and worked and polished to a gloss. There did not seem to be a square inch anywhere on its surface that had not been decorated with carvings.

The friezes were the most striking—four-foot high belts of illustration girding each level up to the spire. He tried to follow one from the right of the temple door. The art was crudely stylized and he found whatever story it was telling impossible to follow. But the violence depicted was inescapable. Every few feet there were killings and dismemberments and demonlike creatures devouring the flesh.

He felt a chill despite the growing heat of the day. What sort of a place had he invaded?

Further speculation was cut off by a cry from within the temple. It was Tooke's voice, telling everyone that he'd found something.

Westphalen led the rest of the men inside. It was cool within, and very dark. Oil lamps set on pedestals along the ebony walls gave scant, flickering illumination. He had the impression of cyclopean sculptures rising against the black walls all around him, but could make out only an occasional highlight where pinpoints of light gleamed from a shiny surface. After seeing the friezes outside, he was quite content to let the details remain in shadow.

He turned his thoughts to other matters more immediately pressing. He wondered if Tooke and Russell had found the jewels. His mind raced over various strategies he would have to employ to keep what he needed for himself. For all he knew, he might need it all.

But the two scouts had found no jewels. Instead, they had found a man. He was seated in one of two chairs high on a dais in the center of the temple. Four oil lamps, each set on a pedestal placed every ninety degrees around the dais, lit the scene.

Rising above and behind the priest was an enormous statue made of the same black wood as the temple. It was a four-armed woman, naked but for an ornate headdress and a garland of human skulls. She was smiling, protruding her pointed tongue between her filed teeth. One hand held a sword, another a severed human head; the third and fourth hands were empty.

Westphalen had seen this diety before, but as a book-sized

drawing—not as a giant. He knew her name.

Kali.

With difficulty, Westphalen tore his gaze away from the statue and brought it to bear on the priest. He had typical Indian coloring and features but was a little heavier than most of his fellow countrymen Westphalen had seen. His hairline was receding. He looked like a Buddha dressed in a white robe. And he showed no trace of fear.

"I been talking to 'im, captain," Tooke said, "but 'e aint' been—"

"I was merely waiting," the priest suddenly said in deep tones that resonated through the temple, "for someone worth speaking to. Whom am I addressing, please?"

"Captain Sir Albert Westphalen."

"Welcome to the temple of Kali, Captain Westphalen." There was no hint of welcome in his voice.

Westphalen's eye was caught by the priest's necklace—an intricate thing, silvery, inscribed with strange script, with a pair of yellow stones with black centers spaced by two links at the front.

"So, you speak English, do you?" he said for want of something better. This priest—the high priest of the temple, no doubt—unsettled him with his icy calm and penetrating gaze.

"Yes. When it appeared that the British were determined to make my country a colony, I decided it might be a useful language to know."

Westphalen put down his anger at the smug arrogance of this heathen and concentrated on the matter at hand. He wanted to find the jewels and leave this place.

"We know you are hiding rebel sepoys here. Where are they?"

"There are no sepoys here. Only devotees of Kali."

"Then what about this?" It was Tooke. He was standing by a row of waist-high urns. He had slashed through the waxy fabric that sealed the mouth of the nearest one and now held up his dripping knife. "Oil! Enough for a year. And there's sacks of rice over there. More than any twenty 'devotees' need!"

The high priest never looked in Tooke's direction. It was as if the soldier didn't exist.

"Well?" Westphalen said at last. "What about the rice and oil?"

"Merely stocking in provisions against the turmoil of the times, captain," the high priest said blandly. "One never knows when supplies might be cut off."

"If you won't reveal the whereabouts of the rebels, I shall be forced

THE TOMB

to order my men to search the temple from top to bottom. This will cause needless destruction."

"That will not be necessary, captain."

Westphalen and his men jumped at the sound of the woman's voice. As he watched, she seemed to take form out of the darkness behind the statue of Kali. She was shorter than the high priest, but well-proportioned. She too wore a robe of pure white.

The high priest rattled something in a heathen tongue as she joined him on the dais; the woman replied in kind.

"What did they say?" Westphalen said to anyone who was listening.

Tooke replied: "He asked about the children; she said they were safe."

For the first time, the priest admitted Tooke's existence by looking at him, nothing more.

"What you seek, Captain Westphalen," the woman said quickly, "lies beneath our feet. The only way to it is through that grate."

She pointed to a spot beyond the rows of oil urns and sacks of rice. Tooke hopped over them and knelt down.

"Here it is! But"—he jumped to his feet again—"*whoosh!* The stink!"

Westphalen pointed to the soldier nearest him. "Hunter! Watch those two. If they try to escape, shoot them!"

Hunter nodded and aimed his Enfield at the pair on the dais. Westphalen joined the rest of the men at the grate.

The grate was square, measuring perhaps ten feet on a side. It was made of heavy iron bars criss-crossing about six inches apart. Damp air, reeking of putrefaction, wafted up through the bars. The darkness below was impenetrable.

Westphalen sent Malleson for one of the lamps from the dais. When it was brought to him, he dropped it through the grate. Its copper body rang against the bare stone floor fifteen feet below as it bounced and landed on its side. The flame sputtered and almost died, then wavered to life again. The brightening light flickered off the smooth stone surfaces on three sides of the well. A dark, arched opening gaped in the wall opposite them. They were looking down into what appeared to be the terminus of a subterranean passage.

And there in the two corners flanking the tunnel mouth stood small urns filled with colored stones—some green, some red, and some crystal clear.

167

THE TOMB

Westphalen experienced an instant of vertigo. He had to lean forward against the grate to keep himself from collapsing.

Saved!

He quickly glanced around at his men. They had seen the urns, too. Accommodations would have to be made. If those urns were full of jewels, there would be plenty for all. But first they had to get them up here.

He began barking orders: Malleson was sent out to the horses for a rope; the remaining four were told to spread out around the grate and lift it off. They bent to it, strained until their faces reddened in the light filtering up from below, but could not budge it. Westphalen was about to return to the dais and threaten the priest when he noticed simple sliding bolts securing the grate to rings in the stone floor at two of the corners; on the far side along one edge was a row of hinges. As Westphalen freed the bolts—which were chained to the floor rings— it occurred to him how odd it was to lock up a treasure with such simple devices. But his mind was too full of the sight of those jewels below to dwell for long on bolts.

The grate was raised on its hinges and propped open with an Enfield. Malleson arrived with the rope then. At Westphalen's direction he tied it to one of the temple's support columns and tossed it into the opening. Westphalen was about to ask for a volunteer when Tooke squatted on the rim.

"Me father was a jeweler's assistant," he announced. "I'll tell ye if there be anything down there to get excited about."

He grasped the rope and began to slide down. Westphalen watched Tooke reach the floor and fairly leap upon the nearest urn. He grabbed a handful of stones and brought them over to the sputtering lamp. He righted it, then poured the stones from one hand to the other in the light.

"They're real!" he shouted. "B'God, they're real!"

Westphalen was speechless for a moment. Everything was going to be all right. He could go back to England, settle his debts, and never, never gamble again. He tapped Watts, Russell and Lang on the shoulders and pointed below.

"Give him a hand."

The three men slid down the rope in rapid succession. Each made a personal inspection of the jewels. Westphalen watched their long shadows interweaving in the lamplight as they scurried around below. It was all he could do to keep from screaming at them to send up the jewels. But he could not appear too eager. No, that wouldn't do at all. He had to be calm. Finally they dragged an urn over to the side and tied the rope around its neck. Westphalen and Malleson hauled it up, lifted it over the rim and sent it on the floor.

Malleson dipped both hands into the jewels and brought up two fistfuls. Westphalen restrained himself from doing the same. He picked up a single emerald and studied it, outwardly casual, inwardly wanting to crush it against his lips and cry for joy.

"C'mon, up there!" said Tooke from below. "Let's 'ave the rope, what? There be plenty more to come up and it stinks down 'ere. Let's 'urry it up."

Westphalen gestured to Malleson who untied the rope from the urn and tossed the end over the edge. He continued to study the emerald, thinking it the most beautiful thing he had ever seen, until he heard one of the men say:

"What was that?"

"What was what?"

"A noise. I thought I 'eard a noise in the tunnel there."

"Yer daft, mate. Nothing in that black 'ole but stink."

"I 'eard something, I tell you."

Westphalen stepped up to the edge and looked down at the four men. He was about to tell them to stop talking and keep working when the priest and the woman broke into song. Westphalen whirled at the sound. It was like no music he had ever heard. The woman's voice was a keening wail, grating against the man's baritone. There were no words to the song, only disconnected notes, and none of the notes they sang seemed to belong together. There was no harmony, only discord. It set his teeth on edge.

They stopped abruptly.

And then came another sound. It rose from below, seeping from the mouth of the tunnel that terminated in the pit, growing in volume. A grumbled cacophony of moans and grunts and snarls that made each hair on the nape of his neck stand up one by one.

The sounds from the tunnel ceased, to be replaced by the dissonant singing of the priest and priestess. They stopped and the inhuman sounds from the tunnel answered, louder still. It was a litany from hell.

Suddenly the singing was joined by a scream of pain and terror from below. Westphalen looked over the edge and saw one of the men—Watts, he thought—being dragged by his legs into the black maw of the tunnel, shrieking, *"It's got me! It's got me!"*

169

THE TOMB

But *what* had him? The tunnel mouth was a darker shadow within the shadows below. What was pulling him?

Tooke and Russell had him by the arms and were trying to hold him back, but the force drawing him into the dark was as inexorable as the tide. It seemed Watts's arms would be pulled from their sockets at any moment when a dark shape leaped from the tunnel and grabbed Tooke around the neck. It had a lean body and towered over Tooke. Westphalen could make out no details in the poor light and dancing shadows of the pandemonium below. But what little he saw was enough to make his skin tighten and shrink against his insides, and set his heart to beating madly.

The priest and the woman sang again. He knew he should stop them, but he couldn't speak, couldn't move.

Russell let go of Watts, who was quickly swallowed by the tunnel, and rushed to Tooke's aid. But as soon as he moved, another dark figure leaped from the shadows and pulled him into the tunnel. With a final convulsive heave, Tooke too was dragged off.

Westphalen had never heard grown men scream in such fear. The sound sickened him. Yet he could not react.

And still the priest and the woman sang, no longer stopping for an answering phrase from the tunnel.

Only Lang remained below. He had the rope in his fists and was halfway up the wall, his face a white mask of fear, when two dark shapes darted out of the darkness and leaped upon him, pulling him down. He screamed for help, his eyes wild as he was dragged twisting and kicking into the blackness below. Westphalen managed to break the paralysis that had gripped him since his first glimpse of the denizens of the tunnel. He pulled his pistol from its holster. Beside him, Malleson had already moved into action—he aimed his Enfield and fired at one of the creatures. Westphalen was sure he saw it take the hit, but it seemed to take no notice of the bullet. He fired three shots into the two creatures before they disappeared from sight, taking the howling Lang with them.

Behind him the ghastly song went on, playing counterpoint to the agonized screams from the tunnel below, and all around him the stench ... Westphalen felt himself teetering on the edge of madness. He charged up to the dais.

"Stop it!" he screeched. "Stop it or I'll have you shot!"

But they only smiled and continued their hellish song.

He gestured to Hunter, who had been guarding them. Hunter

170

didn't hesitate. He raised his Enfield to his shoulder and fired.

The shot rang like an explosion through the temple. A red splatter bloomed upon the priest's chest as he was thrown back against his chair. Slowly he slid to the floor. His mouth worked, his glazing eyes blinked twice, and then he lay still. The woman cried out and knelt beside him.

The song had stopped. And so had the screams from below.

Once again silence ruled the temple. Westphalen drew a tremulous breath. If he could just have a moment to think, he could—

"Captain! They're coming up!" There was an edge of hysteria to Malleson's voice as he backed away from the pit. "They're coming *up!*"

Panic clutching at him, Westphalen ran to the opening. The chamber below was filled with shadowy forms. There were no growls or barks or hissing noises from down there, only the slither of moist skin against moist skin, and the rasp of talon against stone. The lamp had been extinguished and all he could see were dark milling bodies crowded against the walls—

—and climbing the rope!

He saw a pair of yellow eyes rising toward him. One of the things was almost to the top!

Westphalen holstered his pistol and drew his sword. With shaking hands he raised it above his head and chopped down with all his strength. The heavy rope parted cleanly and the distal end whipped away into the darkness below.

Pleased with his swordplay, he peered over the edge to see what the creatures would do now. Before his disbelieving eyes they began to climb the wall. But that was impossible. Those walls were as smooth as—

Now he saw what they were doing: the things were scrambling over and upon each other, reaching higher and higher, like a wave of black, foul water filling a cistern from below. He dropped his sword and turned to run, then forced himself to hold his position. If those things got out, there would be no escape for him. And he couldn't die here. Not now. Not with a fortune sitting in the urn at his feet.

Westphalen mustered all his courage and stepped over to where Tooke's Enfield propped up the grate. With teeth clenched and sweat springing out along the length of his body, he gingerly extended a foot and kicked the rifle into the pit. The grate slammed down with a resounding clang as Westphalen stumbled back against a pillar, sagging with relief. He was safe now.

The grate rattled, it shook, it began to rise.

Moaning with terror and frustration, Westphalen edged back toward the grate.

The bolts had to be fastened!

As he drew nearer, Westphalen witnessed a scene of relentless, incalculable ferocity. He saw dark bodies massed beneath the grate, saw talons gripping, raking, scoring the bars, saw teeth sharp and white gnash at the iron, saw flashes of utterly feral yellow eyes, devoid of fear, of any hint of mercy, consumed by a bloodthirst beyond reason and sanity. And the stench . . . it was almost overpowering.

Now he understood why the grate had been fastened as it had.

Westphalen sank to his knees, then to his belly. Every fiber of his being screamed at him to run, but he would not. He had come too far! He would *not* be robbed of his salvation! He could order his two remaining men toward the grate, but he knew Malleson and Hunter would rebel. That would waste time and he had none to waste. *He* had to do it!

He began to crawl forward, inching his way toward the nearest bolt where it lay chained to the steel eye driven into the floor. He would have to wait until the corresponding ring on the shuddering, convulsing grate became aligned with the floor ring, and then shove the bolt home through both of them. Then and only then would he feel it safe to run.

Stretching his arm to the limit, he grasped the bolt and waited. The blows against the underside of the grate were coming with greater frequency and greater force. The ring on the grate rarely touched the floor, and when it did clank down next to the floor ring, it was there for but an instant. Twice he shoved the bolt through the first and missed the second. In desperation, he rose up and placed his left hand atop the corner of the grate and threw all his weight against it. He had to lock this down!

It worked. The grate slammed against the floor and the bolt slid home, locking one corner down. But as he leaned against the grate, something snaked out between the bars and clamped on his wrist like a vise. It was a hand of sorts, three-fingered, each finger tapering to a long yellow talon; the skin was blue-black, its touch cold and wet against his skin.

Westphalen screamed in terror and loathing as his arm was pulled toward the seething mass of shadows below. He reared up and placed both boots against the edge of the grate, trying with all his strength to pull himself free. But the hand only tightened its grip. Out of the corner of his eye he caught sight of his sabre on the floor where he had dropped it, not two feet from where he stood. With a desperate lunge, he grabbed it by the hilt and started hacking at the arm that held him. Blood as dark as the skin that covered it spouted from the arm. Westphalen's tenth swing severed the arm and he fell back onto the floor. He was free—

Yet the taloned hand still gripped his wrist with a life of its own!

Westphalen dropped the sword and pried at the fingers. Malleson rushed over and helped. Together they pulled the fingers far enough apart to allow Westphalen to extricate his arm. Malleson hurled it onto the grate where it clung to one of the bars until pulled loose by one of the fiends below.

As Westphalen lay gasping on the ground trying to massage life back into the crushed and bruised tissues of his wrist, the woman's voice rose over the clatter of the shaking grate.

"Pray to your god, Captain Westphalen. The rakoshi will not let you leave the temple alive!"

She was right. Those things—What had she called them? Rakoshi?—would rip the lone securing eye from the stone floor and have that grate up in a minute if he didn't find some means to weight it down. His eyes ranged the small area of the temple visible to him. There had to be a way! His gaze came to rest on the urns of lamp oil. They looked heavy enough. If he, Malleson and Hunter could set enough of them on the grate. No . . . wait . . .

Fire! Nothing could withstand burning oil! He leapt to his feet and ran to the urn Tooke had opened with his knife.

"Malleson! Here! We'll pour it through the grate!" He turned to Hunter and pointed to one of the lamps around the dais. "Bring that over here!"

Groaning under the weight, Westphalen and Malleson dragged the urn across the floor and upended it on the shuddering grate, pouring its contents onto the things below. Directly behind them came Hunter who didn't have to be told what to do with the lamp. He gave it a gentle underhand toss onto the grate.

The oil on the iron bars caught first, the flames licking along the upper surfaces to form a meshwork of fire, then dropping in a fine rain onto the creatures directly beneath. As dark, oil-splashed bodies burst into flame, a caterwauling howl arose from the pit. The thrash-

173

ing below became more violent. And still the flames spread. Black, acrid smoke began to rise toward the ceiling of the temple.

"More!" Westphalen shouted above the shrieking din. He used his sabre to slice open the tops, then watched as Malleson and Hunter poured the contents of a second urn, and then a third into the pit. The howls of the creatures began to fade away as the flames leapt higher and higher.

He bent his own back to the task, pouring urn after urn through the grate, flooding the pit and sending a river of fire into the tunnel, creating an inferno that even Shadrach and his two friends would have shied from.

"Curse you, Captain Westphalen!"

It was the woman. She had risen from beside the priest's corpse and was pointing a long, red-nailed finger at a spot between Westphalen's eyes. "Curse you and all who spring from you!"

Westphalen took a step toward her, his sword raised. "Shut up!"

"Your line shall die in blood and pain, cursing you and the day you set your hand against this temple!"

The woman meant it, there was no denying that. She really believed she was laying a curse upon Westphalen and his progeny, and that shook him. He gestured to Hunter.

"Stop her!"

Hunter unslung his Enfield and aimed it at her. "You 'eard what 'e said."

But the woman ignored the certain death pointed her way and kept ranting.

"You've slain my husband, desecrated the temple of Kali! There will be no peace for you, Captain Albert Westphalen! Nor for you"—she pointed to Hunter—"or you!"—then to Malleson. "The rakoshi shall find you all!"

Hunter looked at Westphalen, who nodded. For the second time that day, a rifle shot rang out in the Temple-in-the-Hills. The woman's face exploded as the bullet tore into her head. She fell to the floor beside her husband.

Westphalen glanced at her inert form for a moment, then turned away toward the jewel-filled urn. He was forming a plan on how to arrange a three-way split that would give him the largest share, when a shrill screech of rage and an agonized grunt swung him around again.

Hunter stood stiff and straight at the edge of the dais, his face the color of soured whey, his shoulders thrown back, eyes wide, mouth working soundlessly. His rifle clattered to the floor as blood began to trickle from a corner of his mouth. He seemed to lose substance. Slowly, like a giant festival balloon leaking hot air from all its seams, he crumbled, his knees folding beneath him as he pitched forward onto his face.

It was with a faint sense of relief that Westphalen saw the bloody hole in the center of Hunter's back—he had died by physical means, not from a heathen woman's curse. He was further relieved to see the dark-eyed, barefoot boy, no more than twelve years old, standing behind Hunter, staring down at the fallen British soldier. In his hand was a sword, the distal third of its blade smeared red with blood.

The boy lifted his gaze from Hunter and saw Westphalen. With a high-pitched cry, he raised his sword and charged forward. Westphalen had no time to reach for his pistol, no choice but to defend himself with the oil-soaked sabre he still clutched in his hand.

There was no cunning, no strategy; no skill to the boy's swordplay, only a ceaseless, driving barrage of slashing strokes, high and low, powered by blind, mindless rage. Westphalen gave way, as much from the ferocity of the attack as from the maniacal look on the boy's tear-streaked face: his eyes were twin slits of fury, spittle flecked his lips and dribbled onto his chin as he grunted with each thrust of his blade. Westphalen saw Malleson standing off to the side with his rifle raised.

"For God's sake, shoot him!"

"Waiting for a clear shot!"

Westphalen backpedaled faster, increasing the distance between himself and the boy. Finally, after what seemed like an eternity, Malleson fired.

And *missed!*

But the boom of the rifle shot startled the boy. He dropped his guard and looked around. Westphalen struck then, a fierce, downward cut aimed at the neck. The boy saw it coming and tried to dodge, but too late. Westphalen felt the blade slide through flesh and bone, saw the boy go down in a spray of crimson. That was enough. He jerked his sabre free and turned away in the same motion. He felt sick. He found he much preferred to let others do the actual killing.

Malleson had dropped his rifle and was scooping handfuls of gems into his pockets. He looked up at his commanding officer. "It's all right, isn't it, sir?" He gestured toward the priest and his wife. "I mean, they won't be needing 'em."

Westphalen knew he'd have to be very careful now. He and Malleson were the only survivors, accomplices in what would surely be described as mass murder should the facts ever come to light. If neither of them spoke a word of what had happened here today, if they were both extremely careful as to how they turned the jewels into cash over the next few years, if neither got drunk enough for guilt or boastfulness to cause the story to spill out, they could both live out their lives as rich, free men. Westphalen was quite sure he could trust himself; he was equally sure that trusting Malleson would be a catastrophic mistake.

He put on what he hoped was a sly grin. "Don't waste your time with pockets," he told the soldier. "Get a couple of saddle bags."

Malleson laughed and jumped up. "Right, sir!"

He ran out the entry arch. Westphalen waited uneasily. He was alone in the temple—at least he prayed he was. He hoped all those things, those monsters, were dead. They had to be. Nothing could have survived that conflagration in the pit. He glanced over to the dead bodies of the priest and priestess, remembering her curse. Empty words of a crazed heathen woman. Nothing more. But those things in the pit . . .

Malleson finally returned with two sets of saddlebags. Westphalen helped him fill the four large pouches, then each stood up with a pair slung over a shoulder.

"Looks like we're rich, sir," Malleson said with a smile that faded when he saw the pistol Westphalen was pointing at his middle.

Westphalen didn't let him begin to plead. It would only delay matters without changing the outcome. He simply couldn't let the future of his name and his line depend on the discretion of a commoner who would doubtlessly get himself sotted at the first opportunity upon his return to Bharangpur. He aimed at where he assumed Malleson's heart would be, and fired. The soldier reeled back with outflung arms and fell flat on his back. He gasped once or twice as a red flower blossomed on the fabric of his tunic, then lay still.

Holstering his pistol, Westphalen went over and gingerly removed the saddlebags from Malleson's shoulder, then looked around him. All remained still. Foul, oily smoke still poured from the pits; a shaft of sunlight breaking through a vent in the vaulted ceiling pierced the spreading cloud. The remaining lamps flickered on their pedestals. He went to the two nearest oil urns, sliced open their tops, and kicked them over. Their contents spread over the floor and washed up against the nearest wall. He then took one of the remaining lamps and threw it into the center of the puddle. Flame spread quickly to the wall where the wood began to catch.

He was turning to leave when a movement over by the dais caught his eye, frightening him and causing him to drop one of the saddlebags as he clawed for his pistol again.

It was the boy. He had somehow managed to crawl up the dais to where the priest lay. He was reaching for the necklace around the man's throat. As Westphalen watched, the fingers of the right hand closed around the two yellow stones. Then he lay still. The whole of the boy's upper back was soaked a deep crimson. He had left a trail of red from where he had fallen to where he now lay. Westphalen returned his pistol to his holster and picked up the fallen saddlebag. There was no one and nothing left in the temple to do him any harm. He remembered that the woman had mentioned "children," but he could not see them as a threat, especially with the way the fire was eating up the ebony. Soon the temple would be a smoldering memory.

He strode from the smoke-filled interior into the morning sunlight, already planning where he would bury the saddlebags and plotting the story he would tell of how they had become lost in the hills and were ambushed by a superior force of sepoy rebels. And how he alone escaped.

After that, he would have to find a way to maneuver himself into a trip back to England as soon as possible. Once home, it would not be too long before he would just happen to find a large cache of uncut gems behind some stonework in the basement level of Westphalen Hall.

Already he was blotting the memory of the events of the morning from his mind. It would do no good to dwell on them. Better to let the curse, the demons, and the dead float away with the black smoke rising from the burning temple, a temple that was now a pyre and a tomb for that nameless sect. He had done what he had to do and that was that. He felt good as he rode away from the temple. He did not look back. Not once.

CHAPTER SEVEN

Manhattan
Sunday, August 5, 198-

1.

Tennis!

Jack rolled out of bed with a groan. He'd almost forgotten. He had been lying there dreaming of a big brunch at the Perkins Pancakes down on Seventh Avenue when he remembered the father-son tennis match he'd promised to play in today.

And he had no racquet. He'd lent it to someone in April and couldn't remember who. Only one thing to do: Call Abe and tell him it was an emergency.

Abe said he would meet him at the store right away. Jack showered, shaved, pulled on white tennis shorts, a dark blue jersey, sneakers and socks, and hurried down to the street. The morning sky had lost the humid haze it had carried for most of the week. Looked like it was going to be a nice day.

As he neared the Isher Sports Shop, he saw Abe waddling up from the other direction. Abe looked him up and down as they met before the folding iron grille that protected the store during off-hours.

"Tennis balls! You're going to tell me you want a can of tennis balls, are you?"

Jack shook his head and said, "Naw. I wouldn't get you up early on a Sunday morning for tennis balls."

"Glad to hear it." He unlocked the grille and pushed it back far enough to expose the door. "Did you see the business section of the

THE TOMB

Times this morning? All that talk about the economy picking up? Don't believe it. We're on the *Titanic* and the iceberg's straight ahead."

"It's too nice a day for an economic holocaust, Abe."

"All right," he said, unlocking the door and pushing it open. "Go ahead, close your eyes to it. But it's coming and the weather has nothing to do with it."

After disarming the alarm system, Abe headed for the back of the store. Jack didn't follow. He went directly to the tennis racquets and stood before a display of the oversized Prince models. After a moment's consideration, he rejected them. Jack figured he'd need all the help he could get today, but he still had his pride. He'd play with a normal size racquet. He picked out a Wilson Triumph—the one with little weights on each side of the head that were supposed to enlarge the sweet spot. The grip felt good in his hand, and it was already strung.

He was about to call out that he'd take this one when he noticed Abe glaring at him from the end of the aisle.

"For this you took me away from my breakfast? A tennis racquet?"

"And balls, too. I'll need some balls."

"Balls you've got! Too much balls to do such a thing to me! You said it was an emergency!"

Jack had been expecting this reaction. Sunday was the only morning Abe allowed himself the forbidden foods: lox and bagels. The first was *verboten* because of his blood pressure, the second because of his weight.

"It is an emergency. I'm supposed to be playing with my father in a couple of hours."

Abe's eyebrows rose and wrinkled his forehead all the way up to where his hairline had once been.

"Your father? First Gia, now your father. What is this—National Masochism Week?"

"I like my dad."

"Then why are you in such a black mood every time you return from one of these jaunts into Jersey?"

"Because he's a good guy who happens to be a pain in the ass."

They both knew that wasn't the whole story but by tacit agreement neither said any more. Jack paid for the racquet and a couple of cans of Penn balls. "I'll bring you back some tomatoes," he said as the grille was locked across the storefront again.

THE TOMB

Abe brightened. "That's right! Beefsteaks are in season. Get me some."

Next stop was Julio's where Jack picked up Ralph, the car Julio kept for him. It was a '63 Corvair, white with a black convertible top and a rebuilt engine. An unremarkable, everyday kind of car. Not at all Julio's style, but Julio hadn't paid for it. Jack had seen it in the window of a "classic" car store; he had given Julio the cash to go make the best deal he could and have it registered in his name. Legally it was Julio's car, but Jack paid the insurance and the garage fee and reserved preemptive right of use for the rare occasions when he needed it.

Today was such an occasion. Julio had it gassed up and waiting for him. He had also decorated it a bit since the last time Jack had taken it out: There was a "Hi!" hand waving from the left rear window, fuzzy dice hanging from the mirror, and in the rear window a little dog whose head wobbled and whose eyes blinked red in unison with the tail lights.

"You expect me to ride around with those?" Jack said, giving Julio what he hoped was a withering stare.

Julio did his elaborate shrug. "What can I say, Jack? It's in the blood."

Jack didn't have time to remove the cultural paraphernalia, so he took the car as it was. Armed with the finest New York State driver license money could buy—in the name of Jack Howard—he slipped the Semmerling and its holster into the special compartment under the front seat and began a leisurely drive crosstown.

Sunday morning is a unique time in midtown Manhattan. The streets are deserted. No buses, no cabs, no trucks being unloaded, no Con Ed crews tearing up the streets, and only a rare pedestrian or two here and there. Quiet. It would all change as noon approached, but at the moment Jack found it almost spooky.

He followed Fifty-eighth Street all the way to its eastern end and pulled in to the curb before 8 Sutton Square.

2.

Gia answered the doorbell. It was Eunice's day off and Nellie was still asleep, so the job was left to her. She wrapped her robe more tightly around her and walked slowly, carefully from the kitchen to the front of the house. The inside of her head felt too big for her skull;

181

her tongue was thick, her stomach slightly turned. Champagne ... why should something that made you feel so good at night leave you feeling so awful the next day?

A look through the peephole showed Jack standing there in white shorts and a dark blue shirt.

"Tennis anyone?" he said with a lopsided grin as she opened the door.

He looked good. Gia had always liked a lean, wiry build on a man. She liked the linear cords of muscle in his forearms, and the curly hair on his legs. Why did he look so healthy when she felt so sick?

"Well? Can I come in?"

Gia realized she had been staring at him. She had seen him three times in the past four days. She was getting used to having him around again. That wasn't good. But there would be no defense against it until Grace was found—one way or another.

"Sure." When the door was closed behind him, she said, "Who're you playing? Your Indian lady?" She regretted that immediately, remembering his crack last night about jealousy. She wasn't jealous ... just curious.

"No. My father."

"Oh." Gia knew from the past how painful it was for Jack to spend time with his father.

"But the reason I'm here ..." He paused uncertainly and rubbed a hand over his face. "I'm not sure how to say this, but here goes: Don't drink anything strange."

"What's that supposed to mean?"

"No tonics or laxatives or anything new you find around the house."

Gia was not in the mood for games. "I may have had a little too much champagne last night, but I don't go around swigging from bottles."

"I'm serious, Gia."

She could see that, and it made her uneasy. His gaze was steady and concerned.

"I don't understand."

"Neither do I. But there was something bad about that laxative of Grace's. Just stay away from anything like it. If you find any more of it, lock it away and save it for me."

"Do you think it has anything to do—?"

"I don't know. But I want to play it safe."

182

THE TOMB

Gia could sense a certain amount of evasiveness in Jack. He wasn't telling her everything. Her unease mounted.

"What do you know?"

"That's just it—I don't know anything. Just a gut feeling. So play it safe and stay away from anything strange." He gave her a slip of paper with a telephone number on it. It had a 201 area code. "Here's my father's number. Call me there if you need me or there's any word from Grace." He glanced up the stairs and toward the rear of the house. "Where's Vicks?"

"Still in bed. She had a hard time falling asleep last night, according to Eunice." Gia opened the front door. "Have a good game."

Jack's expression turned sour. "Sure."

She watched him drive back to the corner and turn downtown on Sutton Place. She wondered what was going on in his mind; why the odd warning against drinking "anything strange." Something about Grace's laxative bothered him but he hadn't said what. Just to be sure, Gia went up to the second floor and checked through all the bottles on Grace's vanity and in her bathroom closet. Everything had a brand name. There was nothing like the unlabeled bottle Jack had found on Thursday.

She took two Tylenol Extra Strength capsules and a long hot shower. The combination worked to ease her headache. By the time she had dried off and dressed in plaid shorts and a blouse, Vicky was up and looking for breakfast.

"What do you feel like eating?" she asked as they passed the parlor on their way to the kitchen. She looked cute in her pink nightie and her fuzzy pink Dearfoams.

"Chocolate!"

"Vicki!"

"But it looks so good!" She pointed to where Eunice had set out a candy dish full of the Black Magic pieces from England before going out for the day.

"You know what it does to you."

"But it would be *delicious!*"

"All right," Gia said. "Have a piece. If you think a couple of bites in a couple of minutes is worth a whole day of swelling up and itching and feeling sick, go ahead and take one."

Vicky looked up at her, and then at the chocolates. Gia held her breath, praying Vicky would make the right choice. If she chose the chocolate, Gia would have to stop her, but there was a chance she

183

would use her head and refuse. Gia wanted to know which it would be. Those chocolates would be sitting there for days, a constant temptation to sneak one behind her mother's back. But if Vicky could overcome the temptation now, Gia was sure she would be able to resist for the rest of their stay.

"I think I'll have an orange, mom."

Gia swept her up into her arms and swung her around.

"I'm so proud of you, Vicky! That was a very grown-up decision."

"Well, what I'd really like is a chocolate-covered orange."

Laughing, she led Vicky by the hand to the kitchen, feeling pretty good about her daughter and about herself as a mother.

3.

Jack had the Lincoln Tunnel pretty much to himself. He passed the stripe which marked the border of New York and New Jersey, remembering how his brother and sister and he used to cheer whenever they crossed the line after spending a day in The City with their parents. It had always been a thrill then to be back in good ol' New Jersey. Those days were gone with the two-way toll collections. Now they charged you a double toll to get to Manhattan and let you leave for nothing. And he didn't cheer as he crossed the line.

He cruised out of the tunnel mouth, squinting into the sudden glare of the morning sun. The ramp made a nearly circular turn up to and through Union City, then down to the meadowlands and the New Jersey Turnpike. Jack collected his ticket from the "Cars Only" machine, set his cruise control for 50 miles per hour and settled into the right hand lane for the trip. He was running a little late, but the last thing he wanted was to be stopped by a state cop.

The olfactory adventure began as the Turnpike wound its way through the swampy lowlands, past the Port of Newark and all the surrounding refineries and chemical plants. Smoke poured from stacks and torchlike flames roared from ten-story discharge towers. The odors he encountered on the strip between Exits 16 and 12 were varied and uniformly noxious. Even on a Sunday morning.

But as the road drifted inland, the scenery gradually turned rural and hilly and sweet-smelling. The farther south he drove, the further his thoughts were pulled into the past. Images streaked by with the mile markers: Mr. Canelli and his lawn . . . early fix-it jobs around Burlington County during his late teens, usually involving vandals,

THE TOMB

always contracted *sub rosa* . . . starting Rutgers but keeping his repairs business going on the side . . . the first trips to New York to do fix-it work for relatives of former customers . . .

Tension began building in him after he passed Exit 7. Jack knew the reason: He was approaching the spot where his mother was killed.

It was also the spot where he had—how had Kolabati put it?—"drawn the line between yourself and the rest of the human race."

It had happened during his third year at Rutgers. A Sunday night in early January. Jack was on semester break. He and his parents were driving south on the Turnpike after visiting his Aunt Doris in Hightstown; Jack was in the back seat, his parents in the front, his father driving. Jack had offered to take the wheel, but his mother said the way he wove in and out of all those trucks made her nervous. As he remembered it, he and his father had been discussing the upcoming Super Bowl while his mother watched the speedometer to make sure it didn't stray too far over 55. The easy, peaceful feeling that comes with a full stomach after a lazy winter afternoon spent with relatives was shattered as they cruised under an overpass. With a crash like thunder and an impact that shook the car, the right half of the windshield exploded into countless flying, glittering fragments. He heard his father shout with surprise, his mother scream in pain, felt a blast of icy air rip through the car. His mother moaned and vomited.

As his father swerved the car to the side of the road, Jack jumped into the front seat and realized what had happened: A cinderblock had crashed through the windshield and landed against his mother's lower ribs and upper abdomen. Jack didn't know what to do. As he watched helplessly, his mother passed out and slumped forward. He shouted to get to the nearest hospital. His father drove like a demon, flooring the pedal, blowing the horn, and blinking the headlights while Jack pushed his mother's limp body back and pulled the cinderblock off her. Then he removed his coat and wrapped it around her as protection against the cold gale whistling through the hole in the windshield. His mother vomited once more—this time it was all blood and it splattered the dashboard and what was left of the windshield. As he held her, Jack could feel her growing cold, could almost feel the life slipping out of her. He knew she was bleeding internally, but there was nothing he could do about it. He screamed at his father to hurry, but he was already driving as fast as he could without risking loss of control of the car.

185

THE TOMB

She was in deep shock by the time they got her to the emergency room. She died in surgery of a lacerated liver and a ruptured spleen. She had exsanguinated into her abdominal cavity.

The incalculable grief. The interminable wake and funeral. And afterwards, questions: *Who? Why?* The police didn't know and doubted very much that they would ever find out. It was common for kids to go up on the overpasses at night and drop things through the cyclone fencing onto the cars streaming by below. By the time an incident was reported, the culprits were long gone. The State Police response to any and all appeals from Jack and his father was a helpless shrug.

His father's response was withdrawal: the senselessness of the tragedy had thrown him into a sort of emotional catatonia in which he appeared to function normally but felt absolutely nothing. Jack's response was something else: cold, nerveless, consuming rage. He was faced with a new kind of fix-it job. He knew where it had happened. He knew how. All he had to do was find out who.

He would do nothing else, think of nothing else, until that job was done.

And eventually it *was* done.

It was long over now, a part of the past. Yet as he approached that overpass he felt his throat constrict. He could almost see a cinderblock falling . . . falling toward the windshield . . . crashing through in a blizzard of glass fragments . . . crushing him. Then he was under and in shadow, and for an instant it was nighttime and snowing, and hanging off the other side of the overpass he saw a limp, battered body dangling from a rope tied to its feet, swinging and spinning crazily. Then it was gone and he was back in the August sun again.

He shivered. He hated New Jersey.

4.

Jack got off at Exit 5. He took 541 through Mount Holly and continued south on the two lane blacktop through towns that were little more than groups of buildings clustered along a stretch of road like a crowd around an accident. The spaces between were all open cultivated field. Fresh produce stands advertising Jersey Beefsteak tomatoes "5 lbs/$1" dotted the roadside. He reminded himself to pick up a basketful for Abe on the way back.

186

THE TOMB

He passed through Lumberton, a name that always conjured up ponderous images of morbidly obese people waddling in and out of oversized stores and houses. Next came Fostertown which should have been populated by a horde of homeless runny-nosed waifs, but wasn't.

And then he was home, turning the corner by what had been Mr. Canelli's house; Canelli had died and the new owner must have been trying to save water because the lawn had burnt to a uniform shade of pale brown. He pulled into the driveway of the three-bedroom ranch in which he, his brother, and sister had all grown up, turned off the car, and sat a moment wishing he were someplace else.

But there was no sense in delaying the inevitable so he got out and walked up to the door. Dad pushed it open just as he reached it.

"Jack!" He thrust out his hand. "You had me worried. Thought you'd forgotten."

His father was a tall, thin, balding man tanned a dark brown from daily workouts on the local tennis courts. His beakish nose was pink and peeling from sunburn, and the age spots on his forehead had multiplied and coalesced since the last time Jack had visited. But his grip was firm and his blue eyes bright behind the steel-rimmed glasses as Jack shook hands with him.

"Only a few minutes late."

Dad reached down and picked up his tennis racquet from where it had been leaning against the door molding. "Yeah, but I reserved a court so we could warm up a little before the match." He closed the door behind him. "Let's take your car. You remember where the courts are?"

"Of course."

As he slid into the front seat, dad glanced around the interior of the Corvair. He touched the dice, either to see if they were fuzzy or if they were real.

"You really drive around in this?"

"Sure. Why?"

"It's ..."

"Unsafe at Any Speed?"

"Yeah. That, too."

"Best car I ever owned." Jack pushed the little lever in the far left of the dashboard into reverse and pulled out of the driveway.

For a couple of blocks they made inconsequential small talk about the weather and how smoothly Jack's car was running after twenty

187

years and the traffic on the Turnpike. Jack tried to keep the conversation on neutral ground. He and dad hadn't had much to say to each other since he quit college nearly fifteen years ago.

"How's business?"

Dad smiled. "Great. You've been buying any of those stocks I told you about?"

"I bought two thousand of Arizona Petrol at one-and-an-eighth. It was up to four last time I looked."

"Closed at four-and-a-quarter on Friday. Hold onto it."

"Okay. Just let me know when to dump it."

A lie. Jack couldn't own stock. He needed a Social Security number for that. No broker would open an account for him without it. So he lied to his father about following his stock tips and looked up the NASDAQ listings every so often to see how his imaginary investments were doing.

They were all doing well. Dad had a knack for finding low-priced, out-of-the-way OTC stocks that were undervalued. He'd buy a few thousand shares, watch the price double, triple, or quadruple, then sell off and find another. He had done so well at it over the years that he finally quit his accounting job to see if he could live off his stock market earnings. He had an Apple Lisa with a Wall Street hookup and spent his days wheeling and dealing. He was happy. He was making as much as he had as an accountant, his hours were his own, and no one could tell him he had to stop when he reached sixty-five. He was living by his wits and seemed to love it, looking more relaxed than Jack could ever remember.

"If I come up with something better, I'll let you know. Then you can parlay your AriPet earnings into even more. By the way, did you buy the stock through a personal account or your IRA?"

"Uh . . . the IRA." Another lie. Jack couldn't have an IRA account either. Sometimes he wearied of lying to everybody, especially people he should be able to trust.

"Good! When you don't think you'll be holding them long enough to qualify for capital gains, use the IRA."

He knew what his father was up to. Dad figured that as an appliance repairman, Jack would wind up depending on Social Security after he retired, and nobody could live off that. He was trying to help his prodigal son build up a nest egg for his old age.

They pulled into the lot by the two municipal courts. Both were occupied.

THE TOMB

"Guess we're out of luck."

Dad waved a slip of paper. "No worry. This says court two is reserved for us between 10:00 and 11:00."

While Jack fished in the back seat for his new racquet and the can of balls, his father went over to the couple who now occupied court two. The fellow was grumpily packing up their gear as Jack arrived. The girl—she looked to be about nineteen—glared at him as she sipped from a half-pint container of chocolate milk.

"Guess it's who you know instead of who got here first."

Jack tried a friendly smile. "No. Just who thinks ahead and gets a reservation."

She shrugged. "It's a rich man's sport. Should've known better than to try to take it up."

"Let's not turn this into a class war, shall we?"

"Who? Me?" she said with an innocent smile. "I wouldn't think of it."

With that she poured the rest of her chocolate milk onto the court just behind the baseline.

Jack set his teeth and turned his back on her. What he really wanted to do was see if she could swallow a tennis racquet. He relaxed a little after she and her boyfriend left and he began to rally with his father. Jack's tennis game had long since stabilized at a level of mediocrity he felt he could live with.

He was feeling fit today; he liked the balance of the racquet, the way the ball came off the strings, but the knowledge that there was a puddle of souring chocolate milk somewhere behind him on the asphalt rippled his concentration.

"You're taking your eye off the ball!" dad yelled from the other end of the court after Jack's third wild shot in a row.

I know!

The last thing he needed now was a tennis lesson. He concentrated fully on the next ball, backpedaling, watching it all the way up to his racquet strings. He threw his body into the forehand shot, giving it as much top spin as he could to make it go low over the net and kick when it bounced. Suddenly his right foot was slipping. He went down in a spray of warm chocolate milk.

Across the net, his father returned the ball with a drop shot that rolled dead two feet from the service line. He looked at Jack and began to laugh.

It was going to be a very long day.

189

THE TOMB

5.

Kolabati paced the apartment, clutching the empty bottle that had once held the rakoshi elixir, waiting for Kusum. Again and again her mind ranged over the sequence of events last night: First, her brother disappeared from the reception; then the rakoshi odor at Jack's apartment and the eyes he said he had seen. There had to be a link between Kusum and the rakoshi. And she was determined to find it. But first she had to find Kusum and keep track of him. Where did he go at night?

The morning wore on. By noon, when she had begun to fear he would not show up at all, there came the sound of his key in the door.

Kusum entered, looking tired and preoccupied. He glanced up and saw her.

"Bati. I thought you'd be with your American lover."

"I've been waiting all morning for you."

"Why? Have you thought of a new way to torment me since last night?"

This wasn't going the way Kolabati wanted. She had planned a rational discussion with her brother. To this end, she had dressed in a long-sleeved, high-collared white blouse and baggy white slacks.

"No one has tormented you," she said with a small smile and a placating tone. "At least not intentionally."

He made a gutteral sound. "I sincerely doubt that."

"The world is changing. I've learned to change with it. So must you."

"Certain things never change."

He started toward his room. Kolabati had to stop him before he locked himself away in there.

"That's true. I have one of those unchanging things in my hand."

Kusum stopped and looked at her questioningly. She held up the bottle, watching his face closely. His expression registered nothing but puzzlement. If he recognized the bottle, he hid it well.

"I'm in no mood for games, Bati."

"I assure you, my brother, this is no game." She removed the top and held the bottle out to him. "Tell me if you recognize the odor."

Kusum took the bottle and held it under his long nose. His eyes widened.

"This cannot be! It's impossible!"

190

THE TOMB

"You can't deny the testament of your senses."

He glared at her. "First you embarrass me, now you try to make a fool of me as well!"

"It was in Jack's apartment last night!"

Kusum held it up to his nose again. Shaking his head, he went to an overstuffed couch nearby and sank into it.

"I don't understand this," he said in a tired voice.

Kolabati seated herself opposite him. "Of course you do."

His head snapped up, his eyes challenging her. "Are you calling me a liar?"

Kolabati looked away. There were rakoshi in New York. Kusum was in New York. She possessed a logical mind and could imagine no circumstances under which these two facts could exist independently of each other. Yet she sensed that now was not the right time to let Kusum know how certain she was of his involvement. He was already on guard. Any more signs of suspicion on her part and he would shut her out completely.

"What am I supposed to think?" she told him. "Are we not Keepers? The *only* Keepers?"

"But you saw the egg. How can you doubt me?"

There was a note of pleading in his voice, of a man who wanted very much to be believed. He was so convincing. Kolabati was sorely tempted to take his word.

"Then explain to me what you smell in that bottle."

Kusum shrugged. "A hoax. An elaborate, foul hoax."

"Kusum, they were there! Last night and the night before as well!"

"Listen to me." He rose and stood over her. "Did you ever actually see a rakosh these last two nights?"

"No, but there was the odor. There was no mistaking that."

"I don't doubt there was an odor, but an odor can be faked—"

"There was something *there!*"

"—and so we're left with only your impressions. Nothing tangible."

"Isn't that bottle in your hand tangible enough?"

Kusum handed it to her. "An interesting imitation. It almost had me fooled, but I'm quite sure it's not genuine. By the way, what happened to the contents?"

"Poured down a sewer."

His expression remained bland. "Too bad. I could have had it analyzed and perhaps we could learn who is perpetrating this hoax. I want to know that before I do another thing."

"Why would someone go to all the trouble?"

His gaze penetrated her. "A political enemy, perhaps. One who has uncovered our secret."

Kolabati felt the clutch of fear at her throat. She shook it off. This was absurd! It was Kusum behind it all. She was sure of it. But for a moment there he almost had her believing him.

"That isn't possible!"

He pointed to the bottle in her hand. "A few moments ago I would have said the same about that."

Kolabati continued to play along.

"What do we do?"

"We find out who is behind this." He started for the door. "And I'll begin right now."

"I'll come with you."

He paused. "No. You'd better wait here. I'm expecting an important call on Consulate business. That's why I came home. You'll have to wait here and take the message for me."

"All right. But won't you need me?"

"If I do, I'll call you. And don't follow me—you know what happened last time."

Kolabati allowed him to leave. She watched through the peephole in the apartment door until he entered the elevator. As soon as the doors slid closed behind him, she ran into the hall and pressed the button for the second elevator. It opened a moment later and took her down to the lobby in time to see Kusum stroll out the front entrance of the building.

This will be easy, she thought. *There should be no problem trailing a tall, slender, turbaned Indian through midtown Manhattan.*

Excitement pushed her on. At last she would find where Kusum spent his time. And there, she was quite sure, she would find what should not be. She still did not see how it was possible, but all the evidence pointed to the existence of rakoshi in New York. And despite all his protests to the contrary, Kusum was involved. She knew it.

Staying half a block behind, she followed Kusum down Fifth Avenue to Central Park South with no trouble. The going became rougher after that. Sunday shoppers were out in force and the sidewalks became congested. Still she managed to keep him in view until he entered Rockefeller Plaza. She had been here once in the winter when the area had been mobbed with ice skaters and Christmas shoppers wandering about the huge Rockefeller Center tree. Today there was a different kind of crowd, but no less dense. A jazz group was playing imitation Coltrane and every few feet there were men with pushcarts selling fruit, candy, or balloons. Instead of ice skating, people were milling about or taking the sun with their shirts off.

Kusum was nowhere to be seen.

Kolabati frantically pushed her way through the crowd. She circled the dry, sun-drenched ice rink. Kusum was gone. He must have spotted her and ducked into a cab or down a subway entrance.

She stood amid the happy, carefree crowd, biting her lower lip, so frustrated she wanted to cry.

6.

Gia picked up the phone on the third ring. A soft, accented voice asked to speak to Mrs. Paton.

"Who shall I say is calling?"

"Kusum Bahkti."

She thought the voice sounded familiar. "Oh, Mr. Bahkti. This is Gia DiLauro. We met last night."

"Miss DiLauro—a pleasure to speak to you again. May I say you looked very beautiful last night."

"Yes, you may. As often as you wish." As he laughed politely, Gia said, "Wait a second and I'll get Nellie."

She was in the third floor hall. Nellie was in the library watching one of those public affairs panels that dominate Sunday afternoon television. Shouting down to her seemed more appropriate to a tenement than a Sutton Square townhouse. Especially when an Indian diplomat was on the phone. So Gia hurried down to the first floor.

As she descended the stairs she told herself that Mr. Bahkti was a good lesson on not trusting one's first impressions. She had disliked him immediately upon meeting him, yet he had turned out to be quite a nice man. She smiled grimly. No one should count on her as much of a judge of character. She had thought Richard Westphalen charming enough to marry, and look how he had turned out. And after that there had been Jack. Not an impressive track record.

Nellie took the call from her seat in front of the TV. As the older woman spoke to Mr. Bahkti, Gia turned her attention to the screen where the Secretary of State was being grilled by a panel of reporters.

"Such a nice man," Nellie said as she hung up. She was chewing on something.

"Seems to be. What did he want?"

"He said he wished to order some Black Magic for himself and wanted to know where I got it. The Divine Obsession, wasn't it?"

"Yes." Gia had committed the address to memory. "In London."

"That's what I told him." Nellie giggled. "He was so cute: He wanted me to taste one and tell him if it was as good as I remembered. So I did. They're lovely! I think I'll have another." She held up the dish. "Do help yourself."

Gia shook her head. "No, thanks. With Vicky allergic to it, I've kept it out of the house for so long I've lost my taste for it."

"That's a shame," Nellie said, holding another between a thumb and forefinger with her pinky raised and taking a dainty bite out of it. "These are simply lovely."

7.

Match point at the Mount Holly Lawn Tennis Club:

Jack was drenched with sweat. He and his father had scraped through the first elimination on a tie-breaker: 6-4, 3-6, 7-6. After a few hours of rest they started the second round. The father-son team they now faced was much younger—the father only slightly older than Jack, and the son no more than twelve. But they could play! Jack and his father won only one game in the first set, but the easy victory must have lulled their opponents into a false sense of security for they made a number of unforced errors in the second set and lost it 4-6.

So with one set apiece it was now 4-5 and Jack was losing his serve. It was deuce with the advantage to the receiver. Jack's right shoulder was on fire. He had been putting everything he had into his serves but the pair facing him across the net had returned every single one. This was it. If he lost that point, the match was over and he and dad would be out of the tournament. Which would not break Jack's heart. If they won it meant he'd have to return next Sunday. He didn't relish that thought. But he wasn't going to throw the match. His father had a right to one hundred per cent and that was what he was going to get.

He faced the boy. For three sets now Jack had been trying to find a weakness in the kid's game. The twelve-year old had a Borg topspin forehand, a flat, two-handed Connors backhand, and a serve that could challenge Tanner's for pace. Jack's only hope lay in the kid's short legs which made him relatively slow, but he hit so many winners that Jack had been unable to take advantage of it.

Jack served to the kid's backhand and charged the net, hoping to take a weak return and put it away. The return came back strong and Jack made a weak volley to the father who slammed it up the alley to Jack's left. Without thinking, Jack shifted the racquet to his left hand and lunged. He made the return, but then the kid passed dad up the other alley.

The boy's father came up to the net and shook Jack's hand.

"Good game. If your dad had your speed he'd be club champ." He turned to Jack's father. "Look at him, Tom—not even breathing hard. And did you see that last shot of his? That left-handed volley? You trying to slip a ringer in on us?"

His father smiled. "You can tell by his ground strokes he's no ringer. But I never knew he was ambidextrous."

They all shook hands, and as the other pair walked off, Jack's father looked at him intently.

"I've been watching you all day. You're in good shape."

"I try to stay healthy." His father was a shrewd cookie and Jack was uncomfortable under the scrutiny.

"You move fast. Damn fast. Faster than any appliance repairman I've ever known."

Jack coughed. "What say we have a beer or two. I'm buying."

"Your money's no good here. Only members can sign for drinks. So the beer's on me." They began to walk toward the clubhouse. His father was shaking his head. "I've got to say, Jack, you really surprised me today."

Gia's hurt and angry face popped into Jack's mind.

"I'm full of surprises."

8.

Kusum could wait no longer. He had watched sunset come and go, hurling orange fire against the myriad empty windows of the Sunday-silent office towers. He had seen darkness creep over the city with agonizing slowness. And now, with the moon rising above the skyscrapers, night finally ruled.

Time for the Mother to take her youngling on the hunt.

THE TOMB

It was not yet midnight, but Kusum felt it safe to let them go. Sunday night was a relatively quiet time in Manhattan. The stores closed early, the theatres had no evening performances, and most people were home, resting in anticipation of the coming week.

The Paton woman would be taken tonight, of that he was certain. Kolabati had unwittingly cleared the way by taking the bottle of rakoshi elixir from Jack and disposing of its contents. And had not the Paton woman eaten one of the treated chocolates as she spoke to him on the phone this morning?

Tonight he would be one step closer to fulfilling the vow. He would follow the same procedures with the Paton woman as he had with her nephew and her sister. Once she was in his power, he would reveal to her the origin of the Westphalen fortune and allow her a day to reflect on her ancestor's atrocities.

Tomorrow evening her life would be offered to Kali, and she would be given over to the rakoshi.

9.

Something was rotten somewhere.

Nellie had never thought one could be awakened by an odor, but this . . .

She lifted her head from the pillow and sniffed the air in the darkened room . . . a carrion odor. Warm air brushed by her. The French doors out to the balcony were ajar. She could have sworn they had been closed all day, what with the air conditioner going. But that had to be where the odor was coming from. It smelled as if some dog had unearthed a dead animal in the garden directly below the balcony.

Nellie sensed movement by the doors. No doubt the breeze on the curtains. Still . . .

She pulled herself up, reaching to the night table for her glasses. She found them and held them up to her eyes without bothering to fit the endpieces over her ears. Even then she wasn't sure what she saw.

A dark shape was moving toward her as swiftly and as soundlessly as a puff of smoke in the wind. It couldn't be real. A nightmare, an hallucination, an optical illusion—nothing so big and solid-looking could move so smoothly and silently.

But there was no illusion about the odor that became progressively worse at the shadow's approach.

THE TOMB

Nellie was suddenly terrified. This was no dream! She opened her mouth to scream but a cold, clammy hand sealed itself over the lower half of her face before a sound could escape.

The hand was huge, it was incredibly foul, and it was not human.

In a violent spasm of terror, she struggled against whatever held her. It was like fighting the tide. Bright colors began to explode before her eyes as she fought for air. Soon the explosions blotted out everything else. And then she saw no more.

10.

Vicky was awake. She shivered under the sheet, not from cold but from the dream she had just lived through in which Mr. Grape-grabber had kidnapped Ms. Jelliroll and was trying to bake her in a pie. With her heart pounding in her throat she peered through the darkness at the night table next to the bed. Moonlight filtered through the curtains on the window to her left, enough to reveal Ms. Jelliroll and Mr. Grape-grabber resting peacefully where she had left them. Nothing to worry about. Just a dream. Anyway, didn't the package say that Mr. Grape-grabber was Ms. Jelliroll's "friendly rival"? And he didn't want Ms. Jelliroll herself for his jams, just her grapes.

Still, Vicky trembled. She rolled over and clung to her mother. This was the part she liked best about staying here at Aunt Nellie's and Aunt Grace's—she got to sleep with mommy. Back at the apartment she had her own room and had to sleep alone. When she got scared from a dream or during a storm she could always run in and huddle with mommy, but most of the time she had to keep to her own bed.

She tried to go back to sleep but found it impossible. Visions of the tall, lanky Mr. Grape-grabber putting Ms. Jelliroll into a pot and cooking her along with her grapes kept popping into her head. Finally, she let go of her mother and turned over to face the window.

The moon was out. She wondered if it was full. She liked to look at its face. Slipping out of bed, she went to the window and parted the curtains. The moon was almost to the top of the sky, and nearly full. And there was its smiling face. It made everything so bright. Almost like daytime.

With the air conditioner on and the windows closed against the heat, all the outside sounds were blocked out. Everything was so still and quiet out there, like a picture.

She looked down at her playhouse roof, white with moonlight. It

197

looked so small from up here on the third floor.

Something moved in the shadows below. Something tall and dark and angular, manlike yet very unmanlike. It moved across the backyard with a fluid motion, a shadow among the shadows, looking as if it were carrying something. And there seemed to be another of its kind waiting for it by the wall. The second one looked up and seemed to be gazing right at her with glowing yellow eyes. There was hunger in them . . . hunger for her.

Vicky's blood congealed in her veins. She wanted to leap back into bed with her mother but could not move. All she could do was stand there and scream.

11.

Gia awoke on her feet. There was a moment of complete disorientation during which she had no idea where she was or what she was doing. The room was dark, a child was screaming, and she could hear her own terror-filled voice shouting a garbled version of Vicky's name.

Frantic thoughts raced through her slowly-awakening mind.

Where's Vicky . . . the bed's empty . . . where's Vicky? She could hear her but couldn't see her. *Where in God's name is Vicky?*

She stumbled to the switch by the door and turned on the light. The sudden glare blinded Gia for an instant, and then she saw Vicky standing by the window, still screaming. She ran over and lifted the child against her.

"It's all right, Vicky! It's all right!"

The screaming stopped but not the trembling. Gia held her tighter, trying to absorb Vicky's shudders into her own body. Finally the child was calm, only an occasional sob escaping from where she had her face buried between Gia's breasts.

Night horrors. Vicky had had them frequently during her fifth year, but only rarely since. Gia knew how to handle them: wait until Vicky was fully awake and then talk to her quietly and reassuringly.

"Just a dream, honey. That's all. Just a dream."

"No! It wasn't a dream!" Vicky lifted her tear-streaked face. "It was Mr. Grape-grabber! I saw him!"

"Just a dream, Vicky."

"He was stealing Ms. Jelliroll!"

"No, he wasn't. They're both right behind you." She turned Vicky

198

THE TOMB

around and faced her toward the night table. "See?"

"But he was outside by the playhouse! I saw him!"

Gia didn't like the sound of that. There wasn't supposed to be anyone in the backyard.

"Let's take a look. I'll turn out the light so we can see better."

Vicky's face twisted in sudden panic. "Don't turn out the lights! *Please* don't!"

"Okay. I'll leave them on. But there's nothing to worry about. I'm right here."

They both pressed their faces against the glass and cupped their hands around their eyes to shut off the glare from the room light. Gia quickly scanned the yard, praying she wouldn't see anything.

Everything was as they had left it. Nothing moved. The backyard was empty. Gia sighed with relief and put her arm around Vicky.

"See? Everything's fine. It was a dream. You just thought you saw Mr. Grape-grabber."

"But I *did!*"

"Dreams can be very real, honey. And you know Mr. Grape-grabber is just a doll. He can only do what you want him to. He can't do a single thing on his own."

Vicky said no more but Gia sensed that she remained unconvinced.

That settles it, she thought. *Vicky's been here long enough.*

The child needed her friends—real, live, flesh and blood friends. With nothing else to occupy her time, she had been getting too involved with these dolls. Now they were even in her dreams.

"What do you say we go home tomorrow? I think we've stayed here long enough."

"I like it here. And Aunt Nellie will be lonely."

"She'll have Eunice back again tomorrow. And besides, I have to get back to my work."

"Can't we stay a little longer?"

"We'll see."

Vicky pouted. "'We'll see.' Whenever you say 'we'll see' it ends up meaning 'no.'"

"Not always," Gia said with a laugh, knowing that Vicky was right. The child was getting too sharp for her. "But we'll see. Okay?"

Reluctantly: "Okay."

She put Vicky back between the covers. As she went to the door to switch off the light she thought of Nellie in the bedroom below. She

THE TOMB

could not imagine anyone sleeping through Vicky's screams, yet Nellie had not called up to ask what was wrong. Gia turned on the hall light and leaned over the bannister. Nellie's door was open and her bedroom dark. It didn't seem possible she could still be asleep.

Uneasy now, Gia started down the stairs.

"Where're you going, mommy?" Vicky asked with a frightened voice from the bed.

"Just down to Aunt Nellie's room for a second. I'll be right back."

Poor Vicky, she thought. *She really got a scare.*

Gia stood at Nellie's door. It was dark and still within. Nothing out of the ordinary except an odor ... a faint whiff of putrefaction. Nothing to fear, yet she was afraid. Hesitantly, she tapped on the door jamb.

"Nellie?"

No answer.

"Nellie, are you all right?"

When only silence answered her, she reached inside the door and found the light switch. She hesitated, afraid of what she might find. Nellie wasn't young. What if she had died in her sleep? She seemed to be in good health, but you never knew. And that odor, faint as it was, made her to think of death. Finally she could wait no longer. She flipped the switch.

The bed was empty. It obviously had been slept in—the pillow was rumpled, the covers pulled down—but there was no sign of Nellie. Gia stepped around to the far side of the bed, walking as if she expected something to rise out of the rug and attack her. No ... Nellie was not lying on the floor. Gia turned to the bathroom. It stood open and empty.

Frightened now, she ran downstairs, going from room to room, turning on all the lights in each, calling Nellie's name over and over. She headed back upstairs, checking Grace's empty room on the second floor, and the other guest room on the third.

Empty. All empty.

Nellie was gone—just like Grace!

Gia stood in the hall, shivering, fighting panic, unsure of what to do. She and Vicky were alone in a house from which people disappeared without a sound or a trace—

Vicky!

Gia rushed to their bedroom. The light was still on. Vicky lay curled up under the sheet, sound asleep. Thank God! She sagged against the doorframe, relieved yet still afraid. What to do now? She went out to the phone on the hall table. She had Jack's number and he had said to call if she needed him. But he was in South Jersey and couldn't be here for hours. Gia wanted somebody here now. She didn't want to stay alone with Vicky in this house for a minute longer than she had to.

With a trembling finger she dialed 911 for the police.

12.

"You still renting in the city?"

Jack nodded. "Yep."

His father grimaced and shook his head. "That's like throwing your money away."

Jack had changed into the shirt and slacks he had brought along, and now they were back at the house after a late, leisurely dinner at a Mount Holly seafood restaurant. They sat in the living room sipping Jack Daniel's in near-total darkness, the only light coming in from the adjoining dining room.

"You're right, dad. No argument there."

"I know houses are ridiculously expensive these days, and a guy in your position really doesn't need one, but how about a condo? Get ahold of something you can build up equity in."

It was an oft-held discussion, one they had whenever they got together. Dad would go on about the tax benefits of owning your own home while Jack lied and hedged, unable to say that tax deductions were irrelevant to a man who didn't pay taxes.

"I don't know why you stay in that city, Jack. Not only've you got federal and state taxes, but the goddamn city sticks its hand in your pocket, too."

"My business is there."

His father stood up and took both glasses into the dining room for refills. When they returned to the house after dinner, he hadn't asked Jack what he wanted; he'd simply poured a couple of fingers on the rocks and handed him one. Jack Daniel's wasn't something he ordered much, but by the end of the first glass he found himself enjoying it. He didn't know how many glasses they had had since the first.

Jack closed his eyes and absorbed the feel of the house. He had grown up here. He knew every crack in the walls, every squeaky step, every hiding place. This living room had been so big then; now it seemed tiny. He could still remember that man in the next room carrying him around the house on his shoulders when he was about five. And when he was older they had played catch out in the backyard. Jack had been the youngest of the three kids. There had been something special between his father and him. They used to go everywhere together on weekends, and whenever he had the chance, his father would float a little propaganda toward him. Not lectures really, but a pitch on getting into a profession when he grew up. He worked on all the kids that way, telling them how much better it was to be your own boss rather than be like him and have to work for somebody else. They had been close then. Not any more. Now they were like acquaintances ... near-friends ... almost-relatives.

His father handed him the glass of fresh ice and sour mash, then returned to his seat.

"Why don't you move down here?"

"Dad—"

"Hear me out. I'm doing better than I ever dreamed. I could take you in with me and show you how it's done. You could take some business courses and learn the ropes. And while you're going to school I could manage a portfolio for you to pay your expenses. 'Earn while you learn,' as the saying goes."

Jack was silent. His body felt leaden, his mind sluggish. Too much Jack Daniel's? Or the weight of all those years of lying? He knew dad's bottom line: He wanted his youngest to finish college and establish himself in some sort of respectable field. Jack's brother was a judge, his sister a pediatrician. What was Jack? In his father's eyes he was a college drop-out with no drive, no goals, no ambition, no wife, no children; he was somebody who was going to drift through life putting very little in and getting very little out, leaving no trace or evidence that he had even passed through. In short: a failure.

That hurt. He wanted more than almost anything else for his father to be proud of him. Dad's disappointment in him was like a festering sore. It altered their entire relationship, making Jack want to avoid a man he loved and respected.

He was tempted to lay it out for him—put all the lies aside and tell him what his son really did for a living.

Alarmed at the trend of his thoughts, Jack straightened up in his chair and got a grip on himself. That was the Jack Daniel's talking.

THE TOMB

Leveling with his father would accomplish nothing. First off, he wouldn't believe it; and if he believed it, he wouldn't understand; and if he believed and understood, he'd be horrified . . . just like Gia.

"You like what you're doing, don't you, dad?" he said finally.

"Yes. Very much. And you would, too, if—"

"I don't think so." After all, what was his father making besides money? He was buying and selling, but he wasn't producing anything. Jack didn't mention this to his father—it would only start an argument. The guy was happy, and the only thing that kept him from being completely at peace with himself was his youngest son. If Jack could have helped him there he would have. But he couldn't. So he only said, "I like what *I'm* doing. Can't we leave it at that?"

Dad said nothing.

The phone rang. He went into the kitchen to answer it. A moment later he came out again.

"It's for you. A woman. She sounds upset."

The lethargy that had been slipping over Jack suddenly dropped away. Only Gia had this number. He pushed himself out of the chair and hurried to the phone.

"Nellie's gone, Jack!"

"Where?"

"Gone! Disappeared! Just like Grace! Remember Grace? She was the one you were supposed to find instead of going to diplomatic receptions with your Indian lady-friend."

"Calm down will you? Did you call the cops?"

"They're on their way."

"I'll see you after they leave."

"Don't bother. I just wanted you to know what a good job you've done!"

She hung up.

"Something the matter?" his father asked.

"Yeah. A friend's been hurt." Another lie. But what was one more added to the mountain of lies he had told people over the years? "Gotta get back to the city." They shook hands. "Thanks. It's been great. Let's do it again soon."

He had his racquet and was out to his car before dad could warn him about driving after all those drinks. He was fully alert now. Gia's call had evaporated all effects of the alcohol.

Jack was in a foul mood as he drove up the turnpike. He'd really blown this one. It hadn't even occurred to him that if one sister

203

disappeared, the other might do the same. He wanted to push the car to eighty but didn't dare. He turned on the Fuzzbuster and set the cruise control at 59. The best radar detector in the world wouldn't protect you from the cop driving behind you at night and clocking you on his speedometer. Jack figured no one would bother him if he kept it just under 60.

At least the traffic was light. No trucks. The night was clear. The near-full moon hanging over the road was flat on one edge, as a grapefruit someone had dropped and left on the floor too long.

As he passed Exit 6 and approached the spot where his mother had been killed, his thoughts began to flow backwards in time. He rarely permitted that. He preferred to keep them focused on the present and the future; the past was dead and gone. But in his present state of mind he allowed himself to remember a snowy winter night almost a month after his mother's death . . .

13.

He had been watching the fatal overpass every night, sometimes in the open, sometimes in the bushes. The January wind ate at his face, chapped his lips, numbed his fingers and toes. Still he waited. Cars passed, people passed, time passed, but no one threw anything off.

February came. A few days after the official groundhog had supposedly seen its shadow and returned to its burrow for another six weeks of winter, it snowed. An inch was on the ground already and at least half a dozen more predicted. Jack stood on the overpass looking at the thinning southbound traffic slushing along beneath him. He was cold, tired, and ready to call it a night.

As he turned to go, he saw a figure hesitantly approaching through the snow. Continuing his turning motion, Jack bent, scooped up some wet snow, packed it into a ball, and lobbed it over the cyclone fencing to drop on a car below. After two more snowballs, he glanced again at the figure and saw it was approaching more confidently now. Jack stopped his bombardment and stared at the traffic as if waiting for the newcomer to pass. But he didn't. He stopped next to Jack.

"Whatcha putting in them?"

Jack looked at him. "Putting in what?"

"The snowballs."

"Get lost."

The guy laughed. "Hey, it's all right. Help yourself." He held out a handful of walnut-sized rocks.

Jack sneered. "If I wanted to throw rocks, I could sure as hell do better'n those."

"This is just for starters."

The newcomer, who said his name was Ed, laid his stones atop the guard rail and together they formed new snowballs with rocky cores. Then Ed showed him a spot where the fencing could be stretched out over the road to allow room for a more direct shot . . . a space big enough to slip a cinderblock through. Jack managed to hit the tops of trucks with his rock-centered snowballs or miss completely. But Ed landed a good share of his dead center on oncoming windshields.

Jack watched his face as he threw. Not much was visible under the knitted cap pulled down to pale eyebrows and above the navy peacoat collar turned up around his fuzzy cheeks, but there was a wild light in Ed's eyes as he threw his snowballs, and a smile as he saw them smash against the windshields. He was getting a real thrill out of this.

That didn't mean Ed was the one who had dropped the cinderblock that killed his mother. He could be just another one of a million petty terrorists who got their jollies destroying or disfiguring something that belonged to someone else. But what he was doing was dangerous. The road below was slippery. The impact of one of his special snowballs—even if it didn't shatter the windshield—could cause a driver to swerve or slam on his brakes. And that could be lethal under the present conditions.

Either that had never crossed Ed's mind, or it was what had brought him out tonight.

It could be him.

Jack fought to think clearly. He had to find out. And he had to be absolutely sure.

Jack made a disgusted noise. "Fucking waste of time. I don't think we even cracked one." He turned to go. "See ya."

"Hey!" Ed said, grabbing his arm. "I said we're just getting started."

"This is diddley-shit."

"Follow me. I'm a pro at this."

Ed led him down the road to where a 280-Z was parked. He opened the trunk and pointed to an icy cinderblock wedged up against the spare tire.

"You call that diddley-shit?"

THE TOMB

It took all of Jack's will to keep from leaping upon Ed and tearing his throat out with his teeth. He had to be sure. What Jack was planning left no room for error. There could be no going back and apologizing for making a mistake.

"I call that big trouble," Jack managed to say. "You'll get the heat down on you somethin' awful."

"Naw! I dropped one these bombs last month. You shoulda seen it—perfect shot! Right in somebody's lap!"

Jack felt himself begin to shake. "Hurt bad?"

Ed shrugged. "Who knows? I didn't hang around to find out." He barked a laugh. "I just wish I coulda been there to see the look on their faces when that thing came through the windshield. Blam! Can you see it?"

"Yeah," Jack said. "Let's do it."

As Ed leaned over to grab the block, Jack slammed the trunk lid down on his head. Ed yelled and tried to straighten up but Jack slammed it down again. And again. He kept on slamming it down until Ed stopped moving. Then he ran to the bushes where twenty feet of heavy duty rope had lain hidden for the past month.

* * *

"Wake up!"

Jack had tied Ed's hands behind his back. He had cut a large opening in the cyclone wire and now held him balanced on the top rung of the guard rail. A rope ran from Ed's ankles to the base of one of the guard rail supports. They were on the south side of the overpass; Ed's legs dangled over the southbound lanes.

Jack rubbed snow in Ed's face.

"Wake *up!*"

Ed sputtered and shook his head. His eyes opened. He looked dully at Jack, then around him. He looked down and stiffened. Panic flashed in his eyes.

"Hey! What—?"

"You're dead, Ed. Ed is dead. It rhymes, Ed. That's 'cause it's meant to be."

Jack was barely in control. He would look back in later years and know what he was doing was crazy. A car could have come down the road and along the overpass at any time, or someone in the northbound lanes could have looked up and spotted them through the

206

THE TOMB

heavy snow. But good sense had fled along with mercy, compassion, and forgiveness.

This man had to die. Jack had decided that after talking to the State Police before his mother's funeral. It had been clear then that even if they learned the name of whoever had dropped the cinderblock, there was no way to convict him short of an eyewitness to the incident or a full confession freely given in the presence of the defendant's attorney.

Jack refused to accept that. The killer had to die—not just any way, but Jack's way. He had to know he was going to die. And why.

Jack's voice sounded flat in his ears, and as cold as the snow drifting out of the featureless night sky.

"You know who's lap your 'bomb' landed in last month, Ed? My mother's. You know what? She's dead. A lady who never hurt anyone in her whole life was riding along minding her own business and you killed her. Now she's dead and you're alive. That's not fair, Ed."

He took bleak satisfaction from the growing horror in Ed's face.

"Hey, look! It wasn't me! It wasn't me!"

"Too late, Ed. You already told me it was."

Ed let out a scream as he slid off the guard rail, but Jack held him by the back of his coat until his tied feet found purchase on the ledge.

"Please don't do this! I'm sorry! It was an accident! I didn't mean for anyone to get hurt! I'll do anything to make it up! Anything!"

"Anything? Good. Don't move."

Together they stood over the right southbound lane, Jack inside the guard rail, Ed outside. Both watched the traffic roar out from beneath the overpass and flee down the turnpike away from them. With his hand gripping the collar of Ed's peacoat to steady him, Jack glanced over his shoulder at the oncoming traffic.

As the snow had continued to fall, the traffic had slowed and thinned. The left lane had built up an accumulation of sluch and no one was using it, but there were still plenty of cars and trucks in the middle and right lanes, most doing 45 or 50. Jack saw the headlights and clearance lights of a tractor-semitrailer approaching down the right lane. As it neared the overpass he gave a gentle shove.

Ed toppled forward slowly, gracefully, his bleat of terror rising briefly above the noise of the traffic echoing from below. Jack had measured the rope carefully. Ed fell feet first until the rope ran out of slack, then his feet were jerked up as the rest of his body snapped

THE TOMB

downward. Ed's head and upper torso swung over the cab of the oncoming truck and smashed against the leading edge of the trailer with a solid *thunk,* then his body bounced and dragged limply along the length of the trailer top, then swung into the air, spinning and swaying crazily from the rope around its feet.

The truck kept going, its driver undoubtedly aware that something had struck his trailer but probably blaming it on a clump of wet snow that had shaken loose from the overpass and landed on him. There was another truck rolling down the lane but Jack didn't wait for the second impact. He walked to Ed's car and removed the cinderblock from the trunk. He threw it into a field as he walked the mile farther down the road to his own car. There would be no connection to his mother's death, no connection to him.

It was over.

He went home and put himself to bed, secure in the belief that starting tomorrow he could pick up his life again where he had left off.

He was wrong.

He slept into the afternoon of the following day. When he awoke, the enormity of what he had done descended on him with the weight of the earth itself. He had killed. More that that: He had executed another man.

He was tempted to cop an insanity plea, say it hadn't been him up there on the overpass but a monster wearing his skin. Someone else had been in control.

It wouldn't wash. It hadn't been someone else. It had been him. Jack. No one else. And he hadn't been in a fog or a fugue or consumed by a red haze of rage. He remembered every detail, every word, every move with crystal clarity.

No guilt. No remorse. That was the truly frightening part: The realization that if he could go back and relive those moments he wouldn't change a thing.

He knew that afternoon as he sat hunched on the edge of the bed that his life would never be the same. The young man in the mirror today was not the same one he had seen there yesterday. Everything looked subtly different. The angles and curves of his surroundings hadn't changed; faces and architecture and geography all stayed the same topographically. But someone had shifted the lighting. There were shadows where there had been light before.

Jack went back to Rutgers but college no longer seemed to make any sense. He could sit and laugh and drink with his friends, but he no longer felt a part of them. He was one step removed. He could still see and hear them, but could no longer touch them, as if a glass wall had risen between him and everyone he thought he knew.

He searched for a way to make some sense of it all. He went through the existentialist canon, devouring Camus and Sartre and Kierkegaard. Camus seemed to know the questions Jack was asking, but he gave no answers.

Jack flunked most of his second semester courses. He drifted away from his friends. When summer came he took all his savings and moved to New York where the fix-it work continued with a gradually escalating level of danger and violence. He learned how to pick locks and pick the right gun and ammo for any given situation, how to break into a house and break an arm. He had been there ever since.

Everyone, including his father, blamed the change on the death of his mother. In a very roundabout way, they were right.

14.

The overpass receded in his rear-view mirror, and with it the memory of that night. Jack wiped his sweaty palms against his slacks. He wondered where he'd be and what he'd be doing now if Ed had dropped that cinderblock a half-second earlier or later, letting it bounce relatively harmlessly off the hood or roof of his folks' car. Half a second would have meant the difference between life and death for his mother—and for Ed. Jack would by now have finished school, had a regular job with regular hours, a wife, kids, stability, identity, security. He'd be able to drive under that overpass without reliving two deaths.

Jack arrived in Manhattan via the Lincoln Tunnel and went directly crosstown. He drove past Sutton Square and saw a black-and-white parked outside Nellie's townhouse. After making a U-turn under the bridge, he drove back down to the mid-fifties and parked near a hydrant on Sutton Place South. He waited and watched. Before too long he saw the black-and-white pull out of Sutton Square and head uptown. He cruised around until he found a working pay phone and used it to call Nellie's.

"Hello?" Gia's voice was tense, expectant.

"It's Jack, Gia. Everything okay?"

"No." She seemed to relax. Now she just sounded tired.

"Police gone?"

"Just left."

"I'm coming over—that is, if you don't mind."

Jack expected an argument and some abuse; instead, Gia said, "No, I don't mind."

"Be there in a minute."

He got back into the car, pulled the Semmerling from under the seat and strapped it to his ankle. Gia hadn't given him an argument. She must be terrified.

15.

Gia had never thought she would be glad to see Jack again. But when she opened the door and he was standing there on the top step, it required all her reserve to keep from leaping into his arms. The police had been no help. In fact, the two officers who finally showed up in response to her call had acted as if she were wasting their time. They had given the house a cursory once-over inside and out, had seen no sign of forced entry, had hung around asking a few questions, then had gone, leaving her alone with Vicky in this big empty house.

Jack stepped into the foyer. For a moment it seemed he would lift his arms and hold them out to her. Instead, he turned and closed the door behind him. He looked tired.

"You all right?" he asked.

"Yes. I'm fine."

"Vicky, too?"

"Yes. She's asleep." Gia felt as ill at ease as Jack looked.

"What happened?"

She told him about Vicky's nightmare and her subsequent search of the house for Nellie.

"The police find anything?"

"Nothing. 'No sign of foul play,' as they so quaintly put it. I believe they think Nellie's gone off to meet Grace somewhere on some kind of senile lark!"

"Is that possible?"

Gia's immediate reaction was anger that Jack could even consider such a thing, then realized that to someone who didn't know Nellie and Grace the way she did, it might seem as good an explanation as any.

"No! Utterly impossible!"

THE TOMB

"Okay. I'll take your word for it. How about the alarm system?"

"The first floor was set. As you know, they had the upper levels disconnected."

"So it's the same as with Grace: *The Lady Vanishes.*"

"I don't think this is the time for cute movie references, Jack."

"I know," he said apologetically. "It's just my frame of reference. Let's take a look at her room."

As Gia led him up to the second floor, she realized that for the first time since she had seen Nellie's empty bed, she was beginning to relax. Jack exuded competence. There was an air about him that made her feel that things were finally under control here, that nothing was going to happen without his say-so.

He wandered through Nellie's bedroom in a seemingly nonchalant manner, but she noticed that his eyes constantly darted about, and that he never touched anything with his fingertips—with the side or back of a hand, with the flat edge of a fingernail or knuckle, but never in any way that might conceivably leave a print. All of which served as an uncomfortable reminder of Jack's state of mind and his relationship with the law.

He nudged the French doors open with a foot. Warm humid air swam into the room.

"Did the cops unlock this?"

Gia shook her head. "No. It wasn't even latched, just closed over."

Jack stepped out onto the tiny balcony and looked over the railing.

"Just like Grace's," he said. "Did they check below?"

"They were out there with flashlights—said there was no sign that a ladder or the like had been used."

"Just like Grace." He came in and elbowed the doors closed. "Doesn't make sense. And the oddest part is that you wouldn't have found out she was gone until sometime tomorrow if it hadn't been for Vicky's nightmare." He looked at her. "You're sure it was a nightmare? Is it possible she heard something that woke her up and scared her and you only thought it was a nightmare?"

"Oh, it was a nightmare, all right. She thought Mr. Grape-grabber was stealing Ms. Jelliroll." Gia's insides gave a small lurch as she remembered Vicky's scream—"She even thought she saw him in the backyard."

Jack stiffened. "She saw someone?"

"Not someone. Mr. Grape-grabber. Her doll."

"Go through it all step by step, from the time you awoke until you called the police."

"I went through it all for those two cops."

"Do it again for me. Please. It may be important."

Gia told him of awakening to Vicky's screams, of looking out the window and seeing nothing, of going down to Nellie's room ...

"One thing I didn't mention to the police was the smell in the room."

"Perfume? After shave?"

"No. A rotten smell." Recalling the odor made her uneasy. "Putrid."

Jack's face tightened. "Like a dead animal?"

"Yes. Exactly. How did you know?"

"Lucky guess." He suddenly seemed tense. He went into Nellie's bathroom and checked all the bottles. He didn't seem to find what he was looking for. "Did you catch that odor anywhere else in the house?"

"No. What's so important about an odor?"

He turned to her. "I'm not sure. But remember what I told you this morning?"

"You mean about not drinking anything strange like Grace's laxative?"

"Right. Did Nellie buy anything like that? Or did anything like it come to the house?"

Gia thought for a moment. "No ... the only thing we've received lately is a box of chocolates from my ex-husband."

"For you?"

"Hardly! For Nellie. They're her favorite. Seem to be a pretty popular brand. Nellie mentioned them to your Indian lady's brother last night." *Was last night Saturday night? It seemed so long ago.* "He called today to find out where he could order some."

Jack's eyebrows rose. "Kusum?"

"You sound surprised."

"Just that he doesn't strike me as a chocolate fan. More like a brown-rice-and-water type."

Gia knew what he meant. Kusum had ascetic written all over him.

As they walked back into the hall, Jack said, "What's this Mr. Grape-grabber look like?"

"Like a purple Snidely Whiplash. I'll get it for you."

She led Jack up to the third floor and left him outside in the hall while she tiptoed over to the night table and picked up the doll.

THE TOMB

"Mommy?"

Gia started at the unexpected sound. Vicky had a habit of doing that. Late at night, when she should be sound asleep, she would let her mother walk in and bend over to kiss her good night; at the last moment she would open her eyes and say, "Hi." It was spooky sometimes.

"Yes, honey?"

"I heard you talking downstairs. Is Jack here?"

Gia hesitated, but could see no way to get out of telling her.

"Yes. But I want you to lie there and go back to—"

Too late. Vicky was out of bed and running for the hall.

"Jack-Jack-Jack!"

He had her up in his arms and she was hugging him by the time Gia reached the hall.

"Hiya, Vicks."

"Oh, Jack, I'm so glad you're here! I was so scared before."

"So I heard. Your mommy said you had a bad dream."

As Vicky launched into her account of Mr. Grape-grabber's plots against Ms. Jelliroll, Gia marveled again at the rapport between Jack and her daughter. They were like old friends. At a time like this she sorely wished Jack were a different sort of man. Vicky needed a father so, but not one whose work required guns and knives.

Jack held his hand out to Gia for the doll. Mr. Grape-grabber was made of plastic; a lean, wiry fellow with long arms and legs, entirely purple but for his face and a black top hat. Jack studied the doll.

"He does sort of look like Snidely Whiplash. Put a crow on his shoulder and he'd be Will Eisner's Mr. Carrion." He held the doll up to Vicky. "Is this the guy you thought you saw outside?"

"Yes," Vicky said, nodding. "Only he wasn't wearing his hat."

"What was he wearing?"

"I couldn't see. All I could see was his eyes. They were yellow."

Jack started violently, almost dropping Vicky. Gia instinctively reached out a hand to catch her daughter in case she fell.

"Jack, what's the matter?"

He smiled—weakly, she thought.

"Nothing. Just a spasm in my arm from playing tennis. Gone now." He looked at Vicky. "But about those eyes—it must have been a cat you saw. Mr. Grape-grabber doesn't have yellow eyes."

Vicky nodded vigorously. "He did tonight. So did the other one."

Gia was watching Jack and could swear a sick look passed over his

213

face. It worried her because it was not an expression she ever expected to see there.

"Other one?" he said.

"Uh-huh. Mr. Grape-grabber must have brought along a helper."

Jack was silent a moment, then he hefted Vicky in his arms and carried her back into the bedroom.

"Time for sleep, Vicks. I'll see you in the morning."

Vicky made some half-hearted protests as he left the bedroom, then rolled over and lay quiet as soon as Gia tucked her in. Jack was nowhere in sight when Gia returned to the hall. She found him downstairs in the walnut paneled library, working on the alarm box with a tiny screwdriver.

"What are you doing?"

"Reconnecting the upper floors. This should have been done right after Grace disappeared. There! Now no one gets in or out without raising Cain."

Gia could tell he was hiding something from her and that was unfair.

"What do you know?"

"Nothing." He continued to study the insides of the box. "Nothing that makes any sense, anyway."

That wasn't what Gia wanted to hear. She wanted someone—anyone—to make some sense out of what had happened here in the past week. Something Vicky said had disturbed Jack. Gia wanted to know what it was.

"Maybe it will make sense to me."

"I doubt it."

Gia flared into anger. "I'll be the judge of that! Vicky and I have been here most of the week and we'll probably have to stay here a few more days in case there's any word from Nellie. If you've got any information about what's going on here, I want to hear it!"

Jack looked at her for the first time since she had entered the room.

"Okay. Here it is: There's been a rotten smell that has come and gone in my apartment for the last two nights. And last night there were two sets of yellow eyes looking in the window of my TV room."

"Jack, you're on the third floor!"

"They were there."

Gia felt something twist inside her. She sat down on the settee and shivered.

"God! That gives me the creeps!"

THE TOMB

"It had to be cats."

Gia looked at him and knew that he didn't believe that. She pulled her robe more tightly about her. She wished she hadn't demanded to know what he was thinking, and wished even more that he hadn't told her.

"Right," she said, playing along with the game. "Cats. Had to be."

Jack stretched and yawned as he moved toward the center of the room. "It's late and I'm tired. Think it'd be all right if I spent the night here?"

Gia bottled a sudden gush of relief to keep it from showing on her face.

"I suppose so."

"Good." He settled into Nellie's recliner and pushed it all the way back. "I'll just bed down right here while you go up with Vicky."

He turned on the reading lamp next to the chair and reached for a magazine from the pile next to the dish full of the Black Magic chocolates. Gia felt a lump swell in her throat at the thought of Nellie's childlike glee at receiving that box of candy.

"Need a blanket?"

"No. I'm fine. I'll just read for a little while. Good night."

Gia rose and walked toward the door.

"Good night."

She flipped off the room lights, leaving Jack in a pool of light in the center of the darkened room. She hurried up to Vicky's side and snuggled against her, hunting sleep. But despite the quiet and the knowledge that Jack was on guard downstairs, sleep never came.

Jack ... he had come when needed and had single-handedly accomplished what the New York Police Force had been unable to do: He had made her feel safe tonight. Without him she would have spent the remaining hours till daylight in a shuddering panic. She had a growing urge to be with him. She fought it but found herself losing. Vicky breathed slowly and rhythmically at her side. She was safe. They all were safe now that the alarm system was working again—no window or outer door could be opened without setting it off.

Gia slipped out of bed and stole downstairs, taking a lightweight summer blanket with her. She hesitated at the door to the library. What if he rejected her? She had been so cold to him ... what if he . . .?

Only one way to find out.

She stepped inside the door and found Jack looking at her. He must have heard her come down.

"Sure you don't need a blanket?" she asked.

His expression was serious. "I could use someone to share it with me."

Her mouth dry, Gia went to the chair and stretched herself alongside Jack who spread the blanket over both of them. Neither spoke. There was nothing to say, at least for her. All she could do was lie beside him and contain the hunger within her.

After an eternity, Jack lifted her chin and kissed her. It must have taken him as much courage to do that as it had taken her to come down to him. Gia let herself respond, releasing all the pent-up need in her. She pulled at his clothes, he lifted her nightgown, and then nothing separated them. She clung to him as if to keep him from being torn away from her. This was it, this was what she needed, this was what had been missing from her life.

God help her, this was the man she wanted.

16.

Jack lay back in the recliner and tried unsuccessfully to sleep. Gia had taken him completely by surprise tonight. They had made love twice—furiously the first time, more leisurely the second—and now he was alone, more satisfied and content than he could ever remember. For all her knowledge and inventiveness and seemingly inexhaustible passion, Kolabati hadn't left him feeling like this. This was special. He had always known that he and Gia belonged together. Tonight proved it. There had to be a way for them to get back together and stay that way.

After a long time of drowsy, sated snuggling, Gia had gone back upstairs, saying she didn't want Vicky to find them both down here in the morning. She had been warm, loving, passionate . . . everything she hadn't been the past few months. It baffled him, but he wasn't fighting it. He must have done something right. Whatever it was, he wanted to keep doing it.

The change in Gia wasn't all that was keeping him awake, however. The events of the night had sent a confusion of facts, theories, guesses, impressions, and fears whirling through his mind.

Vicky's description of the yellow eyes had shocked him. Until then he had almost been able to convince himself that the eyes outside his window had been some sort of illusion. But first had come Gia's casual mention of the putrid smell in Nellie's room—it had to be the same odor that had invaded his apartment Friday and Saturday nights. Then the mention of the eyes. The two phenomena together on two different nights in two different locations could not be mere coincidence.

There was a link between what had happened last night at his apartment and Nellie's disappearance from here tonight. But Jack was damned if he knew what it was. Tonight he had looked for more of the herbal liquid he had found in Grace's room last week. He had been disappointed when he could not find any. He couldn't say why he thought so, and he certainly couldn't say how, but he was sure the odor, the eyes, the liquid, and the disappearances of the two old women were connected.

Idly, he picked up a piece of chocolate from the candy dish beside his chair. He really wasn't hungry, but he wouldn't mind something sweet right now. Trouble with these things was you never knew what was inside. There was always the old thumb-puncture-on-the-bottom trick, but that didn't seem right on a missing person's candy. He dropped it back in the bowl and returned to his musings.

If he had found some more of the liquid among Nellie's effects, he would have had one more piece of the puzzle. He wouldn't have been any closer to a solution but at least he would have had a firmer base to work from. Jack reached down and checked the position of the little Semmerling where he had squeezed it and its ankle holster between the seat cushion and arm rest of the recliner. It was still handy. He closed his eyes and thought of other eyes . . . yellow eyes . . .

And then it struck him—the thought that had eluded him last night. Those eyes . . . yellow with dark pupils . . . why they had seemed vaguely familiar to him: They resembled the pair of black-centered topazes on the necklaces worn by Kolabati and Kusum and on the one he had retrieved for their grandmother!

He should have seen it before! Those two yellow stones had been staring at him for days, just as the eyes had stared at him last night. His spirits rose slightly. He didn't know what the resemblance meant, but now he had a link between the Bahktis and the eyes, and perhaps the disappearance of Grace and Nellie. It might well turn out to be pure coincidence, but at least he had a path to follow.

Jack knew what he'd be doing in the morning.

CHAPTER EIGHT

Monday, August 6

1.

Gia watched Jack and Vicky playing with their breakfasts. Vicky had been up at dawn and delighted to find Jack asleep in the library. Before long she had her mother up and making breakfast for them.

As soon as they were all seated Vicky had begun a chant: "We want Moony! We want Moony!" So Jack had dutifully borrowed Gia's lipstick and a felt-tipped pen and drawn a face, Señor Wences-style, on his left hand. The hand then became a very rude, boisterous entity known as Moony. Jack was presently screeching in a falsetto voice as Vicky stuffed Cheerios into Moony's mouth. She was laughing so hard she could barely breathe. Vicky had such a good laugh, an unselfconscious belly-laugh from the very heart of her being. Gia loved to hear it and was in turn laughing at Vicky.

When was the last time she and Vicky had laughed at breakfast?

"Okay. That's enough for now," Jack said at last. "Moony's got to rest and I've got to eat." He went to the sink to wash Moony away.

"Isn't Jack funny, mom?" Vicky said, her eyes bright. "Isn't he the *funniest?*"

As Gia replied, Jack turned around at the sink and mouthed her words in perfect synchronization: "He's a riot, Vicky." Gia threw her napkin at him. "Sit down and eat."

Gia watched Jack finish off the eggs she had fried for him. There was happiness at this table, even after Vicky's nightmare and Nellie's

219

THE TOMB

disappearance—Vicky hadn't been told yet. She had a warm, contented feeling inside. Last night had been so good. She didn't understand what had come over her, but was glad she had given in to it. She didn't know what it meant ... maybe a new beginning ... maybe nothing. If only she could go on feeling this way. If only ...

"Jack," she said slowly, not knowing how she was going to phrase this, "have you ever thought of switching jobs?"

"All the time. And I will—or at least get out of this one."

A small spark of hope ignited in her. "When?"

"Don't know," he said with a shrug. "I know I can't do it forever, but ..." He shrugged again, obviously uncomfortable with the subject.

"But what?"

"It's what I do. I don't know how to say it any better than that. It's what I do and I do it well. So I want to keep on doing it."

"You like it."

"Yeah," he said, concentrating on the last of his eggs. "I like it."

The growing spark winked out as the old resentment returned with an icy blast. For want of something to do with her hands, Gia got up and began clearing the table. *Why bother?* she thought. *The man's a hopeless case.*

And so, breakfast ended on a tense note.

Afterwards, Jack caught her alone in the hallway.

"I think you ought to get out of here and back to your own place."

Gia would have liked nothing better. "I can't. What about Nellie? I don't want her to come back to an empty house."

"Eunice will be here."

"I don't know that and neither do you. With Nellie and Grace gone, she's officially unemployed. She may not want to stay here alone, and I can't say I'd blame her."

Jack scratched his head. "I guess you're right. But I don't like the idea of you and Vicks here alone, either."

"We can take care of ourselves," she said, refusing to acknowledge his concern. "You do your part and we'll do ours."

Jack's mouth tightened. "Fine. Just fine. What was last night, then? Just a roll in the hay?"

"Maybe. It could have meant something, but I guess nothing's changed, not you, not me. You're the same Jack I left, and I still can't accept what you do. And you are what you do."

THE TOMB

He walked out, and she found herself alone. The house suddenly seemed enormous and ominous. She hoped Eunice would show up soon.

2.

A day in the life of Kusum Bahkti . . .

Jack had buried the hurt of his most recent parting with Gia and attacked the task of learning all he could about how Kusum spent his days. It had come down to a choice between trailing Kusum or Kolabati, but Kolabati was just a visitor from Washington, so Kusum won.

His first stop after leaving Sutton Square had been his apartment where Jack had called Kusum's number. Kolabati had answered and they'd had a brief conversation during which he learned that Kusum could probably be found either at the consulate or the U.N. Jack had also managed to wrangle the apartment address out of her. He might need that later. He called the Indian Consulate and learned that Mr. Bahkti was expected to be at the U.N. all day.

And so he stood in line in the General Assembly Building of the United Nations and waited for the tour to start. The morning sun stung the sunburned nose and forearms he had acquired yesterday on the tennis courts in Jersey. He knew nothing about the U.N. Most people he knew in Manhattan had never been here unless it was to show a visiting friend or relative.

He was wearing dark glasses, a dark blue banlon buttoned up to the neck, an "I Love NY" button pinned to his breast pocket, light blue Bermudas, knee-high black socks and sandals. A Kodak disk camera and a pair of binoculars were slung around his neck. He had decided his best bet was to look like a tourist. He blended perfectly.

The tombstonelike Secretariat Building was off limits to the public. An iron fence surrounded it and guards checked IDs at all the gates. In the General Assembly Building there were airport-style metal detectors. Jack had reluctantly resigned himself to being an unarmed tourist for the day.

The tour began. As they moved through the halls the guide gave them a brief history and a glowing description of the accomplishments and the future goals of the United Nations. Jack only half-listened. He kept remembering a remark he had once heard that if all the diplomats were kicked out, the U.N. could be turned into the finest bordello in the world and do just as much, if not more, for international harmony.

The tour served to give him an idea of how the building was laid out. There were public areas and restricted areas. Jack decided his best bet was to sit in the public gallery of the General Assembly, which was in session all day due to some new international crisis somewhere. Soon after seating himself, Jack learned that the Indians were directly involved in the matter under discussion: escalating hostile incidents along the Sino-Indian border. India was charging Red China with aggression.

He suffered through endless discussions that he was sure he had heard a thousand times. Every dinky little country, most unknown to him, had to have its say and usually it said the same thing as the dinky little country before it. Jack finally turned his headphones off. But he kept his binoculars trained on the area around the Indian delegation's table. So far he had seen no sign of Kusum. He found a public phone and called the Indian Consulate again: No, Mr. Bahkti was with the delegation at the U.N. and was not expected back for hours.

He was just about to nod off when Kusum finally appeared. He walked in with a dignified, businesslike stride and handed a sheaf of papers to the chief delegate, then seated himself in one of the chairs to the rear.

Jack was immediately alert, watching him closely through the glasses. Kusum was easy to keep track of: He was the only member of the delegation wearing a turban. He exchanged a few words with the other diplomate seated near him, but for the most part kept to himself. He seemed aloof, preoccupied, almost as if he were under some sort of strain, fidgeting in his seat, crossing and uncrossing his legs, tapping his toes, glancing repeatedly at the clock, twisting a ring on his finger: the picture of a man with something on his mind, a man who wanted to be somewhere else.

Jack wanted to know where that somewhere else was.

He left Kusum sitting in the General Assembly and went out to the U.N. Plaza. A brief reconnaissance revealed the location of the diplomats' private parking lot in front of the Secretariat. Jack fixed the image of the Indian flag in his mind, then found a shady spot across the street that afforded a clear view of the exit ramp.

THE TOMB

3.

It took most of the afternoon. Jack's eyes burned after hours of being trained on the exit ramp from the diplomats' parking lot. If he hadn't happened to glance across the Plaza toward the General Assembly Building at a quarter to four, he might have spent half the night waiting for Kusum. For there he was, looking like a mirage as he walked through the shimmering heat rising from the sun-baked concrete. For some reason, perhaps because he was leaving before the session was through, Kusum had by-passed an official car and was walking to the curb. He hailed a cab and got in.

Fearful he might lose him, Jack ran to the street and flagged down a cab of his own.

"I hate to say this," he said to the driver as he jumped into the rear seat, "but follow that cab."

The driver didn't even look back. "Which one."

"It's just pulling away over there—the one with the *Times* ad on the back."

"Got it."

As they moved into the uptown flow of traffic on First Avenue, Jack leaned back and studied the driver's ID photo taped to the other side of the plastic partition that separated him from the passenger area. It showed a beefy black face sitting on a bull neck. Arnold Green was the name under it. A hand-lettered sign saying The Green Machine was taped to the dashboard. The Green Machine was one of the extra-roomy Checker Cabs. A vanishing breed. They weren't making them any more. Compact cabs were taking over. Jack would be sad to see the big ones go.

"You get many 'Follow-that-cab' fares?" Jack asked.

"Almost never."

"You didn't act surprised."

"As long as you're paying, I'll follow. Drive you around and around the block till the gas runs out if you want. As long as the meter's running."

Kusum's cab turned west on Sixty-sixth, one of the few streets that broke the "evens-run-east" rule of Manhattan, and Green's Machine followed. Together they crawled west to Fifth Avenue. Kusum's apartment was in the upper Sixties on Fifth. He was going home. But the cab ahead turned downtown on Fifth. Kusum emerged at the

223

corner of Sixty-fourth and began to walk east. Jack followed in his cab. He saw Kusum enter a doorway next to a brass plaque that read: New India House. He checked the address of the Indian Consulate he had jotted down that morning. It matched. He had expected something looking like a Hindu temple. Instead, this was an ordinary building of white stone and iron-barred windows with a large Indian flag—orange, white, and green stripes with a wheellike mandala in the center—hanging over double oak doors.

"Pull over," he told the cabbie. "We're going to wait a while."

The Green Machine pulled into a loading zone across the street from the building. "How long?"

"As long as it takes."

"That could run into money."

"That's okay. I'll pay you every fifteen minutes so the meter doesn't get too far ahead. How's that sound?"

He stuck a huge brown hand through the slot in the plastic partition. "How about the first installment?"

Jack gave him a five dollar bill. Arnold turned off the engine and slouched down in the seat.

"You from around here?" he asked without turning around.

"Sort of."

"You look like you're from Cleveland."

"I'm in disguise."

"You a detective?"

That seemed like a reasonable explanation for following cabs around Manhattan, so Jack said, "Sort of."

"You on an expense account?"

"Sort of." Not true: He was on his own time and using his own money, but it sounded better to agree.

"Well, sort of let me know when you sort of want to get moving again."

Jack laughed and got himself comfortable. His only worry was that there might be a back way out of the building.

People began drifting out of the building at 5:00. Kusum wasn't among them. Jack waited another hour and still no sign of Kusum. By 6:30, Arnold was sound asleep in the front seat and Jack feared that Kusum had somehow slipped out of the building unseen. He decided to give it another half hour. If Kusum didn't show by then, Jack would either go inside or find a phone and call the Consulate.

THE TOMB

It was nearly 7:00 when two Indians in business suits stepped through the door and onto the sidewalk. Jack nudged Arnold.

"Start your engine. We may be rolling soon."

Arnold grunted and reached for the ignition. The Green Machine grumbled to life.

Another pair of Indians came out. Neither was Kusum. Jack was edgy. There was still plenty of light, no chance for Kusum to slip past him, yet he had a feeling that Kusum could be a pretty slippery character if he wanted to be.

Come out, come out, wherever you are.

He watched the two Indians walk up toward Fifth Avenue. They were walking west! With a flash of dismay, Jack realized that he was parked on a one-way street going east. If Kusum followed the same path as these last two, Jack would have to leave this cab and find another on Fifth Avenue. And the next cabbie might not be as easy-going as Arnold.

"We've got to get onto Fifth!" he told Arnold.

"Okay."

Arnold put his cab in forward and started to pull out into the crosstown traffic.

"No, wait! It'll take too long to go around the block. I'll miss him."

Arnold gave him a baleful stare through the partition. "You're not telling me to go the wrong way on a one-way street, are you?"

"Of course not," Jack said. Something in the cabbie's voice told him to play along. "That would be against the law."

Arnold smiled. "Just wanted to make sure you wasn't telling."

Without warning he threw the Green Machine into reverse and floored it. The tires screeched, terrified pedestrians leaped for the curb, cars coming out of the Central Park traverse swerved and honked angrily while Jack hung on to the passenger straps as the car lunged the hundred feet or so back to the corner, skewed to a halt across the mouth of the street, then nosed along the curb on Fifth Avenue.

"This okay?" Arnold said.

Jack peered through the rear window. He had a clear view of the doorway in question.

"It'll do. Thanks."

"Welcome."

And suddenly Kusum was there, pushing through the door and walking up toward Fifth Avenue. He crossed Sixty-fourth and walked

225

THE TOMB

Jack's way. Jack pressed himself into a corner of the seat so he could see without being seen. Kusum came closer. With a start Jack realized that Kusum was angling across the sidewalk directly toward the Green Machine.

Jack slapped his hand against the partition. "Take off! He thinks you're looking for a fare!"

The Green Machine slipped away from the curb just as Kusum was reaching for the door handle. Jack peeked through the rear window. Kusum didn't seem the least bit disturbed. He merely held his hand up for another cab. He seemed far more intent on getting where he was going than on what was going on around him.

Without being told to, Arnold slowed to a halt half a block down and waited until Kusum got in his cab. When the cab went by, he pulled into traffic behind it.

"On the road again, Momma," he said to no one in particular.

Jack leaned forward intently and fixed his eyes on Kusum's cab. He was almost afraid to blink for fear of losing sight of it. Kusum's apartment was only a few blocks uptown from the Indian Consulate—walking distance. But he was taking a cab downtown. This could be what Jack had been waiting for. They chased it down to Fifty-seventh where it turned right and headed west along what used to be known as Art Gallery Row.

They followed Kusum farther and farther west. They were nearing the Hudson River docks. With a start, Jack realized that this was the area where Kusum's grandmother had been mugged. The cab went as far west as it could and stopped at Twelfth Avenue and Fifty-seventh. Kusum got out and began to walk.

Jack had Arnold pull in to the curb. He stuck his head out the window and squinted against the glare of the sinking sun as Kusum crossed Twelfth Avenue and disappeared into the shadows under the partially-repaired West Side Highway.

"Be back in a second," he told Arnold.

He walked to the corner and saw Kusum hurry along the crumbling waterside pavement to a rotting pier where a rustbucket freighter was moored. As Jack watched, a gangplank lowered itself as if by magic. Kusum climbed aboard and disappeared from view. The gangplank hoisted itself back to the raised position after he was gone.

A ship. What the hell could Kusum be doing on a floating heap like that? It had been a long, boring day, but now things were getting interesting.

226

THE TOMB

Jack went back to the Green Machine.

"Looks like this is it," he said to Arnold. He glanced at the meter, calculated what he still owed of the total, added twenty dollars for good will, and handed it to Arnold. "Thanks. You've been a big help."

"This ain't such a good neighborhood during the day," Arnold said, glancing around. "And after dark it really gets rough, especially for someone dressed like you."

"I'll be okay," he said, grateful for the concern of a man he had known for only a few hours. He slapped the roof of the car. "Thanks again."

Jack watched the Green Machine until it disappeared into the traffic, then he studied his surroundings. There was a vacant lot on the corner across the street, and an old, boarded-up brick-warehouse next to him.

He felt exposed standing there in an outfit that shouted "Mug me" to anyone so inclined. And since he hadn't dared to bring a weapon to the U.N., he was unarmed. Officially, unarmed. He could permanently disable a man with a ballpoint pen and knew half a dozen ways to kill with a key ring, but didn't like to work that close unless he had to. He would have been much more comfortable knowing the Semmerling was strapped against his leg.

He had to hide. He decided his best bet would be under the West Side Highway. He jogged over and perched himself high up in the notch of one of the supports. It offered a clear view of the pier and the ship. Best of all, it would keep him out of sight of any troublemakers.

Dusk came and went. The streetlights came on as night slipped over the city. He was away from the streets, but he saw the traffic to the west and south of him thin out to a rare car cruising by. There was still plenty of rumbling on the West Side Highway overhead, however, as the cars slowed for the ramp down to street level just two blocks from where he crouched. The ship remained silent. Nothing moved on its decks, no lights showed from the superstructure. It had all the appearances of a deserted wreck. What was Kusum doing in there?

Finally, when full darkness settled in at nine o'clock, Jack could wait no longer. In the dark he was pretty sure he could reach the deck and do some hunting around without being seen.

He jumped down from his perch and crossed over to the shadows by the pier. The moon was rising in the east. It was big and low now,

227

slightly rounder than last night, glowing ruddily. He wanted to get aboard and off again before it reached full brightness and started lighting up the waterfront.

At the water's edge, Jack crouched against a huge piling under the looming shadow of the freighter and listened. All was quiet but for the lapping of the water under the pier. A sour smell—a mixture of sea salt, mildew, rotting wood, creosote, and garbage—permeated the air. Movement to the left caught his eye: a lone wharf rat scurried along the bulkhead in search of dinner. Nothing else moved.

He jumped as something splashed near the hull. An automatic bilge pump was spewing a stream of water out a small port near the waterline of the hull.

He was edgy and couldn't say why. He had done clandestine searches under more precarious conditions than these. And with less apprehension. Yet the nearer he got to the boat, the less he felt like boarding her. Something within him was warning him away. Through the years he had come to recognize a certain instinct for danger; listening to it had kept him alive in a dangerous profession. That instinct was ringing frantically with alarm right now.

Jack shrugged off the feeling of impending disaster as he took the binoculars and camera from around his neck and laid them at the base of the piling. The rope that ran from the piling up to the bow of the ship was a good two inches thick. It would be rough on his hands but easy to climb.

He leaned forward, got a firm two-handed grip on the rope, then swung out over the water. As he hung from the rope, he raised his legs until his ankles locked around it. Now began the climb: Hanging from a branch like an orangutan with his face to the sky and his back to the water below, he pulled himself up hand-over-hand while his heels caught the finger-thick strands of the rope and pushed from behind.

The angle of ascent steepened and the climb got progressively tougher as he neared the gunwale of the ship. The tiny fibers of the rope were coarse and stiff. His palms were burning; each handful of rope felt like a handful of thistles, especially painful where he had started a few blisters playing tennis yesterday. It was a pleasure to grab the smooth, cool steel of the gunwale and pull himself up to eye-level with its upper edge. He hung there and scanned the deck. Still no sign of life.

He pulled himself over the gunwale and onto the deck, then ran in

THE TOMB

a crouch to the anchor windlass.

His skin prickled in warning—danger here. But where? He peered over the windlass. There was no sign that he had been seen, no sign that there was anyone else aboard. Still the feeling persisted, a nagging sensation, almost as if he were being watched.

Again, he shrugged it off and set his mind to the problem of reaching the deckhouse. Well over a hundred feet of open deck lay between him and the aft superstructure. And aft was where he wanted to go. He couldn't imagine much going on in the cargo holds.

Jack set himself, then sprinted around the forward cargo hatch to the kingpost and crane assembly that stood between the two holds. He waited. Still no sign that he had been seen . . . or that there was anyone here to see him. Another sprint took him to the forward wall of the deckhouse.

He slid along the wall to the port side where he found some steps and took these up to the bridge. The wheelhouse was locked, but through the side window he could see a wide array of sophisticated controls.

Maybe this tub was more seaworthy than it looked.

He crossed in front of the bridge and began checking all the doors. On the second deck on the starboard side he found one open. The hallway within was dark but for a single, dim emergency bulb glowing at the far end. One by one he checked the three cabins on this deck. They looked fairly comfortable—probably for the ship's officers. Only one looked like it had been recently occupied. The bed was rumpled and a book written in an exotic-looking language lay open on a table. That at least confirmed Kusum's recent presence.

Next he checked the crew's quarters below. They were deserted. The galley showed no signs of recent use.

What next? The emptiness, the silence, the stale, musty air were getting on Jack's nerves. He wanted to get back to dry land and fresh air. But Kusum was aboard and Jack wasn't leaving until he found him.

He descended to the deck below and found a door marked Engine Room. He was reaching for the handle when he heard it.

A sound . . . barely audible . . . as a baritone chorus chanting in a distant valley. And it came not from the engine room but from somewhere behind him.

Jack turned and moved silently to the other end of the short corridor. There was a watertight hatch there. A central wheel retracted the lugs at its edges. Hoping it still had some oil in its works, Jack grasped the wheel and turned it counterclockwise, half-expecting a loud screech to echo throughout the ship and give him away. But there came only a soft scrape and a faint squeak. When the wheel had turned as far as it would go, he gently swung the door open.

The odor struck him an almost physical blow, rocking him back on his heels. It was the same stink of putrescence that had invaded his apartment two nights in a row, only now a hundred, a thousand times stronger, gripping him, jamming itself against his face like a graverobber's glove.

Jack gagged and fought the urge to turn and run. This was it! This was the source, the very heart of the stench. It was here he would learn whether the eyes he had seen outside his window Saturday night were real or imagined. He couldn't let an odor, no matter how nauseating, turn him back now.

He forced himself to step through the hatch and into a dark, narrow corridor. The dank air clung to him. The corridor walls stretched into the blackness above him. And with each step the odor grew stronger. He could taste it in the air, almost touch it. Faint, flickering light was visible maybe twenty feet ahead. Jack fought his way toward it, passing small, room-sized storage areas on either side. They seemed empty—he hoped they were.

The chant he had dimly heard before had ceased, but there were rustling noises ahead, and as he neared the light, the sound of a voice speaking in a foreign language.

Indian, I'll bet.

He slowed his advance as he neared the end of the corridor. The light was brighter in a larger, open area ahead. He had been travelling forward from the stern. By rough calculation he figured he should be almost to the main cargo hold.

The corridor opened along the port wall of the hold; across the floor in the forward wall was another opening, no doubt a similar passage leading to the forward hold. Jack reached the end and cautiously peeked around the corner. What he saw stopped breath. Shock swept through him front to back, like a storm front.

The high, black-iron walls of the hold rose and disappeared into the darkness above. Wild shadows cavorted on them. Glistening beads of moisture clung to their oily surfaces, catching and holding the light from the two roaring gas torches set upon an elevated platform at the

THE TOMB

other end of the hold. The wall over there was a different color, a bloody red, with the huge form of a many-armed goddess painted in black upon it. And between the two torches stood Kusum, naked but for some sort of long cloth twisted and wrapped around his torso. Even his necklace was off. His left shoulder was horribly scarred where he had lost his arm, his right arm was raised, as he shouted in his native tongue to the crowd assembled before him.

But it wasn't Kusum who seized and held Jack's attention in a stranglehold, who made the muscles of his jaw bunch with the effort to hold back a cry of horror, who made his hands grip the slimy walls so fiercely.

It was his audience. There were four or five dozen of them, cobalt-skinned, six or seven feet tall, all huddled in a semicircular crowd before Kusum. Each had a head, a body, two arms and two legs—but they weren't human. They weren't even close to human. Their proportions, the way they moved, everything about them was all wrong. There was a bestial savagery about them combined with a reptilian sort of grace. They were reptiles but something more, humanoid but something less . . . an unholy mongrelization of the two with a third strain that could not, even in the wildest nightmare delirium, be associated with anything of this earth. Jack caught flashes of fangs in the wide, lipless mouths beneath their blunt, sharklike snouts, the glint of talons at the end of their three-digit hands, and the yellow glow of their eyes as they stared at Kusum's ranting, gesticulating figure.

Beneath the shock and revulsion that numbed his mind and froze his body, Jack felt a fierce, instinctive hatred of these things. It was a subrational reaction, like the loathing a mongoose must feel toward a snake. Instantaneous enmity. Something in the most remote and primitive corner of his humanity recognized these creatures and knew there could be no truce, no coexistence with them.

Yet this inexplicable reaction was overwhelmed by the horrid fascination of what he saw. And then Kusum raised his arm and shouted something. Perhaps it was the light, but he looked older to Jack. The creatures responded by starting the same chant he had faintly heard moments ago. Only now he could make out the sounds. Gruff, grumbling voices, chaotic at first, then with growing unity, began repeating the same word over and over:

"Kaka-jiiiiiii! Kaka-jiiiiiii! Kaka-jiiiiiii! Kaka-jiiiiiii!"

Then they were raising their taloned hands in the air, and clutched

231

in each was a bloody piece of flesh that glistened redly in the wavering light.

Jack didn't know how he knew, but he was certain he was looking at all that remained of Nellie Paton.

It was all he could take. His mind refused to accept any more. Terror was a foreign sensation to Jack, unfamiliar, almost unrecognizable. All he knew was that he had to get away before his sanity completely deserted him. He turned and ran back down the corridor, careless of the noise he made, not that much could be heard over the din in the hold. He closed the hatch behind him, spun the wheel to lock it, then ran up the steps to the deck, dashed along its moonlit length to the prow where he straddled the gunwale, grabbed the mooring rope and slid down to the dock, burning the skin from his palms.

He grabbed his binoculars and camera and fled toward the street. He knew where he was going: to the only other person besides Kusum who could explain what he had just seen.

4.

Kolabati reached the intercom on the second buzz. Her first thought was that it might be Kusum, then she realized he would have no need of the intercom, which operated only from the lobby. She had neither seen nor heard from her brother since losing him in Rockefeller Plaza yesterday, and had not moved from the apartment all day in the hope of catching him as he stopped by to change his clothes. But he had never appeared.

"Mrs. Bahkti?" It was the doorman's voice.

"Yes?" She didn't bother to correct him about the "Mrs."

"Sorry to bother you, but there's a guy down here says he has to see you." His voice sank to a confidential tone. "He doesn't look right, but he's really been bugging me."

"What's his name?"

"Jack. That's all he'll tell me."

A rush of warmth spread over her skin at the mention of his name. But would it be wise to allow him to come up? If Kusum returned and found the two of them together in his apartment . . .

Yet she sensed that Jack would not show up without calling first unless it was something important.

"Send him up."

THE TOMB

She waited impatiently until she heard the elevator open, then she went to the door. When she saw Jack's black knee socks, sandals, and shorts, she broke into a laugh. No wonder the doorman wouldn't let him up!

Then she saw his face.

"Jack! What's wrong?"

He stepped through the door and closed it behind him. His face was pale beneath a red patina of sunburn, his lips drawn into a tight line, his eyes wild.

"I followed Kusum today ..."

He paused, as if waiting for her to react. She knew from his expression that he must have found what she had suspected all along, but she had to hear it from his lips. Hiding the dread of what she knew Jack would say, she set her face into an impassive mask and held it that way.

"And?"

"You really don't know, do you?"

"Know what, Jack?" She watched him run a hand through his hair and noticed that his palms were dirty and bloody. "What happened to your hands?"

He didn't answer. Instead he walked past her and stepped down into the living room. He sat on the couch. Without looking at her, he began to speak in a dull monotone.

"I followed Kusum from the U.N. to this boat on the West Side—a big boat, a freighter. I saw him in one of the cargo holds leading some sort of ceremony with these" ... his face twisted with the memory ... "these things. They were holding up pieces of raw flesh. I think it was human flesh. And I think I know whose."

Strength flowed out of Kolabati like water down a drain. She leaned against the foyer wall to steady herself. *It was true!* Rakoshi in America! And Kusum behind them—resurrecting the old dead rites that should have been left dead. But how? The egg was in the other room!

"I thought you might know something about it," Jack was saying. "After all, Kusum is your brother and I figured—"

She barely heard him.

The egg ...

She pushed herself away from the wall and started toward Kusum's bedroom.

"What's the matter?" Jack said, finally looking up at her. "Where are you going?''

Kolabati didn't answer him. She had to see the egg again. How could there be rakoshi without using the egg? It was the last surviving egg. And that alone was not enough to produce a nest—a male rakosh was needed.

It simply couldn't be!

She opened the closet in Kusum's room and pulled the square crate out into the room. It was so light. Was the egg gone? She pulled the top up. No . . . the egg was still there, still intact. But the box had been so light. She remembered that egg weighing at least ten pounds . . .

She reached into the box, placed a hand on each side of the egg and lifted it. It almost leaped into the air. It weighed next to nothing! And on its underside her fingers felt a jagged edge.

Kolabati turned the egg over. A ragged opening gaped at her. Bright smears showed where cracks on the underside had been repaired with glue.

The room reeled and spun about her.

The rakosh egg was empty! It had hatched long ago!

5.

Jack heard Kolabati cry out in the other room. Not a cry of fear or pain—more like a wail of despair. He found her kneeling on the floor of the bedroom, rocking back and forth, cradling a mottled, football-sized object in her arms. Tears were streaming down her face.

''What happened?''

''It's empty!'' she said through a sob.

''What was in it?'' Jack had seen an ostrich egg once. That had been white; this was about the same size but its shell was swirled with gray.

''A female rakosh.''

Rakosh. This was the second time Jack had heard her say that word. The first had been Friday night when the rotten odor had seeped into his apartment. He didn't need any further explanation to know what had hatched from that egg: It had dark skin, a lean body with long arms and legs, a fanged mouth, taloned hands, and bright yellow eyes.

Moved by her anguish, he knelt opposite Kolabati. Gently he pulled the empty egg from her grasp and he took her two hands in his.

THE TOMB

"Tell me about it."

"I can't."

"You must."

"You wouldn't believe ..."

"I've already seen them. I believe. Now I've got to understand. What are they?"

"They are rakoshi."

"I gathered that. But the name means nothing."

"They are demons. They people the folk tales of Bengal. They're used to spice up stories told at night to frighten children or to make them behave—'The rakoshi will get you!' Only a select few through the ages have known that they are more than mere superstition."

"And you and Kusum are two of those select few, I take it."

"We are the only ones left. We come from a long line of high priests and priestesses. We are the last of the Keepers of the Rakoshi. Through the ages the members of our family have been charged with the care of the rakoshi—to breed them, control them, and use them according to the laws set down in the old days. And until the middle of the last century we discharged that duty faithfully."

She paused, seemingly lost in thought. Jack impatiently urged her on.

"What happened then?"

"British soldiers sacked the temple of Kali where our ancestors worshipped. They killed everyone they could find, looted what they could, poured burning oil into the rakoshi cave, and set the temple afire. Only one child of the priest and priestess survived." She glanced at the empty shell. "And only one intact rakosh egg was found in the fire-blasted caves. A female egg. Without a male egg, it meant the end of the rakoshi. They were extinct."

Jack touched the shell gingerly. So this was where those horrors came from. Hard to believe. He lifted the shell and held it so the light from the lamp shown through the hole into the interior. Whatever had been in here was long gone.

"I can tell you for sure, Kolabati: They aren't extinct. There were a good fifty of them in that ship tonight." *Fifty of them* ... he tried to blank out the memory. *Poor Nellie!*

"Kusum must have found a male egg. He hatched them both and started a nest."

Kolabati baffled him. Could it be true that she hadn't known until now? He hoped so. He hated to think she could fool him so com-

235

pletely.

"That's all well and fine, but I still don't know what they are. What do they do?"

"They're demons—"

"Demons, *shmemons*! Demons are supernatural! There was nothing supernatural about those things. They were flesh and blood!"

"No flesh like you have ever seen before, Jack. And their blood is almost black."

"Black, red—blood is blood."

"No, Jack!" She rose up on her knees and gripped his shoulders with painful intensity. "You must never underestimate them! Never! They appear slow-witted but they are cunning. And they are almost impossible to kill."

"The British did a good job, it seems."

Her face twisted. "Only by sheer luck! They chanced upon the only thing that will kill rakoshi—fire! Iron weakens them, fire destroys them."

"Fire and iron . . ." Jack suddenly understood the two jets of flame Kusum had stood between, and the reason for housing the monsters in a steel-hulled ship. Fire and iron: the two age-old protections against night and the dangers it held. "But where did they come from?"

"They have always been."

Jack stood up and pulled her to her feet. Gently. She seemed so fragile right now.

"I can't believe that. They're built like humans, but I can't see that we ever had a common ancestor. They're too—" he remembered the instinctive animosity that had surged to life within him as he had watched them— "different."

"Tradition has it that before the Vedic gods, and even before the pre-Vedic gods, there were other gods, the Old Ones, who hated mankind and wanted to usurp our place on earth. To do this they created blasphemous parodies of humans embodying the opposite of everything good in humans, and called them rakoshi. They are us, stripped of love and decency and everything good we are capable of. They are hate, lust, greed, and violence incarnate. The Old Ones made them far stronger than humans, and planted in them an insatiable hunger for human flesh. The plan was to have rakoshi take humankind's place on earth."

"Do you believe that?" It amazed him to hear Kolabati talking like

236

THE TOMB

a child who believed in fairy tales.

She shrugged. "I think so. At least it will do for me until a better explanation comes along. But as the story goes, it turned out that humans were smarter than the rakoshi and learned how to control them. Eventually, all rakoshi were banished to the Realm of Death."

"Not all."

"No, not all. My ancestors penned the last nest in a series of caves in northern Bengal and built their temple above. They learned ways to bend the rakoshi to their will and they passed those ways on, generation after generation. When our parents died, our grandmother passed the egg and the necklaces on to Kusum and me."

"I knew the necklaces came in somewhere."

Kolabati's voice was sharp as her hand flew to her throat. "What do you know of the necklace?"

"I know those two stones up front there look an awful lot like rakoshi eyes. I figured it was some sort of membership badge."

"It's more than that," she said in a calmer voice. "For want of a better term, I'll say it's magic."

As Jack walked back to the living room, he laughed softly.

"You find this amusing?" Kolabati said from behind him.

"No." He dropped into a chair and laughed again, briefly. The laughter disturbed him—he seemed to have no control over it. "It's just that I've been listening to what you've been telling me and accepting every word without question. That's what's funny—I *believe* you! It's the most ridiculous, fantastic, far-fetched, implausible, impossible story I've ever heard, and I believe every word of it!"

"You should. It's true."

"Even the part about the magic necklace?" Jack held up his hand as she opened her mouth to elaborate. "Never mind. I've swallowed too much already. I might choke on a magic necklace."

"It's *true!*"

"I'm far more interested in your part in all this. Certainly you must have known."

She sat down opposite him. "Friday night in your room I knew there was a rakosh outside the window. Saturday night, too."

Jack had figured that out by now. But he had other questions: "Why me?"

"It came to your apartment because you tasted the durba grass elixir that draws a hunting rakosh to a particular victim."

Grace's so-called laxative! A rakosh must have carried her off

THE TOMB

between Monday night and Tuesday morning. And Nellie last night. But Nellie—those pieces of flesh held on high in the flickering light ... he swallowed the bile that surged into his throat—Nellie was dead. Jack was alive.

"Then how come I'm still around?"

"My necklace protected you."

"Back to that again? All right—tell me."

She lifted the front of the necklace as she spoke, holding it on either side of the pair of eyelike gems. "This has been handed down through my family for ages. The secret of making it is long gone. It has ... powers. It is made of iron, which traditionally has power over rakoshi, and renders its wearer invisible to a rakosh."

"Come on, Kolabati—" This was too much to believe.

"It's true! The only reason you are able to sit here and doubt is because I covered you with my body on both occasions when the rakosh came in to find you! I made you disappear! As far as a rakosh was concerned, your apartment was empty. If I hadn't, you would be dead like the others!"

The others ... Grace and Nellie. Two harmless old ladies.

"But why the others? Why—?"

"To feed the nest! Rakoshi must have human flesh on a regular basis. In a city like this it must have been easy to feed a nest of fifty. You have your own caste of untouchables here—winos, derelicts, runaways, people no one would miss or bother to look for even if their absence was noticed."

That explained all those missing winos the newspapers had been blabbering about. Jack jumped to his feet. "I'm not talking about them! I'm talking about two well-to-do ladies who have been made victims of these things!"

"You must be mistaken."

"I'm not."

"Then it must have been an accident. A missing-person's search is the last thing Kusum would want. He would pick faceless people. Perhaps those women came into the possession of some of the elixir by mistake."

"Possible." Jack was far from satisfied, but it was possible. He wandered around the room.

"Who were they?"

"Two sisters: Nellie Paton last night and Grace Westphalen last week."

THE TOMB

Jack thought he heard a sharp intake of breath, but when he turned to Kolabati her face was composed. "I see," was all she said.

"He's got to be stopped."

"I know," Kolabati said, clasping her hands in front of her. "But you can't call the police."

The thought hadn't entered Jack's mind. Police weren't on his list of possible solutions for anything. But he didn't tell Kolabati that. He wanted to know her reasons for avoiding them. Was she protecting her brother?

"Why not? Why not get the cops and the harbor patrol and have them raid that freighter, arrest Kusum, and wipe out the rakoshi?"

"Because that won't accomplish a thing! They can't arrest Kusum because of diplomatic immunity. And they'll go in after the rakoshi not knowing what they're up against. The result will be a lot of dead men; instead of being killed, the rakoshi will be scattered around the city to prey on whomever they can find, and Kusum will go free."

She was right. She had obviously given the matter a lot of thought. Perhaps she had even considered blowing the whistle on Kusum herself. Poor girl. It was a hideous burden of responsibility to carry alone. Maybe he could lighten the load.

"Leave him to me."

Kolabati rose from her chair and came to stand before Jack. She put her arms around his waist and laid the side of her head against his shoulder.

"No. Let me speak to him. He'll listen to me. I can stop him."

I doubt that very much, Jack thought. *He's crazy, and nothing short of killing's going to stop him.*

But he said: "You think so?"

"We understand each other. We've been through so much together. Now that I know for sure he has a nest of rakoshi, he'll have to listen to me. He'll have to destroy them."

"I'll wait with you."

She jerked back and stared at him, terror in her eyes. "No! He mustn't find you here! He'll be so angry he'll never listen to me!"

"I don't—"

"I'm serious, Jack! I don't know what he might do if he found you here with me and knew you had seen the rakoshi. He must never know that. Please. Leave now and let me face him alone."

Jack didn't like it. His instincts were against it. Yet the more he thought about it, the more reasonable it sounded. If Kolabati could convince her brother to eradicate his nest of rakoshi, the touchiest part of the problem would be solved. If she couldn't—and he doubted very much that she could—at least she might be able to keep Kusum off balance long enough for Jack to find an opening and make his move. Nellie Paton had been a spirited little lady. The man who killed her was not going to walk away.

"All right," he said. "But you be careful. You never know—he might turn on you."

She smiled and touched his face. "You're worried about me. I need to know that. But don't worry. Kusum won't turn on me. We're too close."

As he left the apartment, Jack wondered if he was doing the right thing. Could Kolabati handle her brother? Could anyone? He took the elevator down to the lobby and walked out to the street.

The park stood dark and silent across Fifth Avenue. Jack knew that after tonight he would never feel the same about the dark again. Yet horse-drawn hansom cabs still carried lovers through the trees, taxis, cars and trucks still rushed past on the street, late workers, party-goers, prowling singles walked by, all unaware that a group of mon-sters was devouring human flesh in a ship tied to a West Side dock.

Already the horrors he had witnessed tonight were taking on an air of unreality. Was what he had seen real?

Of course it was. It just didn't seem so standing here amid the staid normalcy of Fifth Avenue in the upper Sixties. Maybe that was good. Maybe that seeming unreality would let him sleep at night until he took care of Kusum and his monsters.

He caught a cab and told the driver to go around the park instead of through it.

6.

Kolabati watched through the peephole until Jack stepped into the elevator and the doors closed behind him. Then she slumped against the door.

Had she told him too much? What had she said? She couldn't remember what she might have blurted out in the aftermath of the shock of finding that hole in the rakosh egg. Probably nothing too damaging—she'd had such long experience at keeping secrets from people that it was now an integral part of her nature. Still, she wished she could be sure.

THE TOMB

Kolabati straightened up and pushed those concerns aside. What was done was done. Kusum would be coming back tonight. After what Jack had told her, she was sure of that.

It was all so clear now. That name: *Westphalen*. It explained everything. Everything except where Kusum found the male egg. And what he intended to do next.

Westphalen . . . she thought Kusum would have forgotten that name by now. But then, why should she have thought that? Kusum forgot nothing, not a favor, certainly not a slight. He would never forget the name Westphalen. Nor the time-worn vow attached to it.

Kolabati ran her hands up and down her arms. Captain Sir Albert Westphalen had committed a hideous crime and deserved an equally hideous death. But not his descendents. Innocent people should not be given into the hands of the rakoshi for a crime committed before they were born.

But she could not worry about them now. She had to decide how to handle Kusum. To protect Jack she would have to know more than she did. She tried to remember the name of the woman Jack said had disappeared last night . . . Paton, wasn't it? Nellie Paton. And she needed a way to put Kusum on the defensive.

She went into the bedroom and brought the empty egg back to the tiny foyer. There she dropped the shell just inside the door. It shattered into a thousand pieces.

Tense and anxious, she found herself a chair and tried to get comfortable.

7.

Kusum stood outside his apartment door a moment to compose himself. Kolabati was certainly waiting within with questions as to his whereabouts last night. He had his answers ready. What he had to do now was mask the elation that must be beaming from his face. He had disposed of the next to the last Westphalen—one more and he would be released from the vow. Tomorrow he would set the wheels in motion to secure the last of Albert Westphalen's line. Then he would set sail for India.

He keyed the lock and opened the door. Kolabati sat facing him from a living room chair, her arms and legs crossed, her face impassive. As he smiled and stepped forward, something crunched under his foot. He looked down and saw the shattered rakoshi egg. A thousand thoughts hurtled through his shocked mind, but the one that leaped to the forefront was: *How much does she know?*

"So," he said as he closed the door behind him. "You know."

"Yes, brother. I know."

"How—?"

"That's what *I* want to know!" she said sharply.

She was being so oblique! She knew the egg had hatched. What else did she know? He didn't want to give anything away. He decided to proceed on the assumption that she knew only of the empty egg and nothing more.

"I didn't want to tell you about the egg," he said finally. "I was too ashamed. After all, it was in my care when it broke, and—"

"Kusum!" Kolabati leaped to her feet, her face livid. "Don't lie to me! I know about the ship and I know about the Westphalen women!"

Kusum felt as if he had been struck by lightning. She knew everything!

"How? . . ." was all he could manage to say.

"I followed you yesterday."

"You followed me?" He was sure he had eluded her. She had to be bluffing. "Didn't you learn your lesson last time?"

"Forget the last time. I followed you to your ship last night."

"Impossible!"

"So you thought. But I watched and waited all last night. I saw the rakoshi leave. I saw them return with their captive. And I learned from Jack today that Nellie Paton, a Westphalen, disappeared last night. That was all I needed to know." She glared at him. "No more lies, Kusum. It's my turn to ask, 'how?'"

Stunned, Kusum stepped down into the living room and sank into a chair. He would have to bring her into it now . . . tell her everything. *Almost* everything. There was one part he could never tell her—he could barely think about that himself. But he could tell her the rest. Maybe she could see his side.

He began his tale.

8.

Kolabati scrutinized her brother closely as he spoke, watching for lies. His voice was clear and cool, his expression calm with just a hint of guilt, as a husband confessing a minor dalliance with another

THE TOMB

woman.

"I felt lost after you left India. It was as if I had lost my other arm. Despite all my followers clustered around me, I spent much time alone—too much time, you might say. I began to review my life and all I had done and not done with it. Despite my growing influence, I felt unworthy of the trust so many were placing in me. What had I truly accomplished except to filthy my karma to the level of the lowest caste? I confess that for a time I wallowed in self-pity. Finally I decided to journey back to Bharangpur, to the hills there, to the temple ruins that are now the tomb of our parents and heritage."

He paused and looked directly at her. "The foundation is still there, you know. The ashes of the rest are gone, washed into the sand or blown away, but the stone foundation remains, and the rakoshi caves beneath are intact. The hills are still uninhabited. Despite all the crowding at home, people still avoid those hills. I stayed there for days in an effort to renew myself. I prayed, I fasted, I wandered the caves . . . yet nothing happened. I felt as empty and as worthless as before.

"And then I found it!"

Kolabati saw a light begin to glow in her brother's eyes, growing steadily, as if someone were stoking a fire within his brain.

"A male egg, intact, just beneath the surface of the sand in a tiny alcove in the caves! At first I did not know what to make of it, or what to do with it. Then it struck me: I was being given a second chance. There before me lay the means to accomplish all that I should have with my life, the means to cleanse my karma and make it worthy of one of my caste. I saw it then as my destiny. I was to start a nest of rakoshi and use them to fulfill the vow."

A male egg. Kusum continued to talk about how he manipulated the foreign service and managed to have himself assigned to the London embassy. Kolabati barely heard him. A male egg . . . she remembered hunting through the ruins of the Temple and the caves beneath as a child, searching everywhere for a male egg. In their youth they both had felt it their duty to start a new nest and they had desperately wanted a male egg.

"After I established myself at the embassy," Kusum was saying, "I searched for Captain Westphalen's descendents. I learned that there were only four of his bloodline left. They were not a prolific family and a number of them were killed off in the World Wars. To my dismay, I learned that only one, Richard Westphalen, was still in Britain. The

243

other three were in America. But that did not deter me. I hatched the eggs, mated them, and started the nest. I have since disposed of three of the four Westphalens. There is only one left."

Kolabati was relieved to hear that only one remained—perhaps she could prevail upon Kusum to give it up.

"Aren't three lives enough? *Innocent* lives, Kusum?"

"The vow, Bati," he said as if intoning the name of a diety. "The *vrata*. They carry the blood of that murderer, defiler, and thief in their veins. And that blood must be wiped from the face of the earth."

"I can't let you, Kusum. It's wrong!"

"It's *right*!" He leapt to his feet. "There's never been anything so right!"

"No!"

"Yes!" He came toward her, his eyes bright. "You should see them, Bati! So beautiful! So willing! Please come with me and look at them! You'll know then that it was the will of Kali!"

A refusal rose immediately to Kolabati's lips, yet did not pass them. The thought of seeing a nest of rakoshi here in America repulsed and fascinated her at the same time. Kusum must have sensed her uncertainty, for he pressed on:

"They are our birthright! Our heritage! You can't turn your back on them—or on your past!"

Kolabati wavered. After all, she did wear the necklace. And she was one of the last two remaining Keepers. In a way she owed it to herself and her family to at least go and see them.

"All right," she said slowly. "I'll come see them with you. But only once."

"Wonderful!" Kusum seemed elated. "It will be like going back in time. You'll see!"

"But that won't change my mind about killing innocent people. You must promise me that will stop."

"We'll discuss it," Kusum said, leading her toward the door. "And I want to tell you about my other plans for the rakoshi—plans that do not involve what you call 'innocent' lives."

"What?" She didn't like the sound of that.

"I'll tell you after you've seen them."

Kusum was silent during the cab ride to the docks while Kolabati tried her best to appear as if she knew exactly where they were going. After the cab dropped them off, they walked through the dark until they were standing before a small freighter. Kusum led her around to

THE TOMB

the starboard side.

"If it were daylight you could see the name across the stern: *Ajit-Rupobati*—in Vedic!"

She heard a click from where his hand rested in his jacket pocket. With a whir and a hum, the gangplank began to lower toward them. Dread and anticipation grew as she climbed to the deck. The moon was high and bright, illuminating the surface of the deck with a pale light made all the more stark by the depths of the shadows it cast.

He stopped at the aft end of the second hatch and knelt by a belowdecks entry port.

"They're in the hold below," he said as he pulled up the hatch.

Rakoshi-stench poured out of the opening. Kolabati turned her head away. How could Kusum stand it? He didn't even seem to notice the odor as he slid his feet into the port.

"Come," he said.

She followed. There was a short ladder down to a square platform nestled into a corner high over the empty hold. Kusum hit a switch and the platform began to descend with a jerk. Startled, Kolabati grabbed Kusum's arm.

"Where are we going?"

"Down just a little way." He pointed below with his bearded chin. "Look."

Kolabati squinted into the shadows, futilely at first. Then she saw their eyes. A garbled murmur arose from below. Kolabati realized that until this instant, despite all the evidence, all that Jack had told her, she had not truly believed there could be rakoshi in New York. Yet here they were.

She shouldn't have been afraid—she was a Keeper—yet she was terrified. The closer the platform sank to the floor of the hold, the greater her fear. Her mouth grew dry as her heart pounded against the wall of her chest.

"Stop it, Kusum!"

"Don't worry. They can't see us."

Kolabati knew that, but it gave her no comfort.

"Stop it now! Take me back up!"

Kusum hit another button. The descent stopped. He looked at her strangely, then started the platform back up. Kolabati sagged against him, relieved to be moving away from the rakoshi but knowing she had deeply disappointed her brother.

It couldn't be helped. She had changed. She was no longer the

245

THE TOMB

recently-orphaned little girl who had looked up to her older brother as the nearest thing to a god on earth, who had planned with him to find a way to bring the rakoshi back, and through them restore the ruined temple to its former glory. That little girl was gone forever. She had ventured into the world and found that life could be good outside India. She wanted to stay there.

Not so Kusum. His heart and his mind had never left those blackened ruins in the hills outside Bharangpur. There was no life for him outside India. And even in his homeland his rigid Hindu fundamentalism made him something of a stranger. He worshipped India's past. That was the India in which he wished to live, not the land India was striving to become.

With the belowdecks port shut and sealed behind them, Kolabati relaxed, reveling in the outside air. Whoever would have thought muggy New York City air could smell so sweet? Kusum led her to a steel door in the forward wall of the superstructure. He opened the padlock that secured it. Inside was a short hallway and a single furnished cabin.

Kolabati sat on the cot while Kusum stood and looked at her. She kept her head down, unable to meet his eyes. Neither had said a word since leaving the hold. Kusum's air of disapproval rankled her, made her feel like an errant child, yet she could not fight it. He had a right to feel the way he did.

"I brought you here hoping to share the rest of my plans with you," he said at last. "I see now that was a mistake. You have lost all touch with your heritage. You would become like the millions of soulless others in this place."

"Tell me your plans, Kusum," she said, feeling his hurt. "I want to hear them."

"You'll hear. But will you listen?" He answered his own question without waiting for her. "I don't think so. I was going to tell you how the rakoshi could be used to aid me back home. They could help eliminate those who are determined to change India into something she was never intended to be, who are bent on leading our people away from the true concerns of life in a mad drive to make India another America."

"Your political ambitions."

"Not ambitions! A mission!"

Kolabati had seen that feverish light shining in her brother's eyes before. It frightened her almost as much as the rakoshi. But she kept

246

her voice calm.

"You want to use the rakoshi for political ends."

"I do *not*! But the only way to bring India back onto the True Path is through political power. It came to me that I have not been allowed to start this nest of rakoshi for the mere purpose of fulfilling a vow. There is a grander scheme here, and I am part of it."

With a sinking feeling, Kolabati realized where all this was leading. A single word said it all:

"*Hindutvu.*"

"Yes—*Hindutvu*! A reunified India under Hindu rule. We will undo what the British did in 1947 when they made the Punjab into Pakistan and vivisected Bengal. If only I had had the rakoshi then— Lord Mountbatten would never have left India alive! But he was out of my reach, so I had to settle for the life of his collaborator, the revered Hindu traitor who legitimized the partition of our India by persuading the people to accept it without violence."

Kolabati was aghast. "Gandhi? It couldn't have been you—!"

"Poor Bati." He smiled maliciously at the shock that must have shown on her face. "I'm truly disappointed that you never guessed. Did you actually think I would sit idly by after the part he played in the partition?"

"But Savarkar was behind—!"

"Yes. Savarkar was behind Godse and Apte, the actual assassins. He was tried and executed for his part. But who do you think was behind Savarkar?"

No! It couldn't be true! Not her brother—the man behind what some called The Crime of the Century!

But he was still talking. She forced herself to listen:

"... the return of East Bengal—it belongs with West Bengal. Bengal shall be whole again!"

"But East Bengal is Bangladesh now. You can't possibly think—"

"I'll find a way. I have the time. I have the rakoshi. I'll find a way, believe me."

The room spun about Kolabati. Kusum, her brother, her surrogate parent for all these years, the steady, rational cornerstone of her life, was slipping further and further from the real world, indulging himself in the revenge and power fantasies of a maladjusted adolescent.

Kusum was mad. The realization sickened her. Kolabati had fought against the admission all night but the truth could no longer be denied. She had to get away from him.

THE TOMB

"If anyone can find a way, I'm sure you will," she told him, rising and turning towards the door. "And I'll be glad to help in any way I can. But I'm tired now and I'd like to go back to the—"

Kusum stepped in front of the door, blocking her way.

"No, my sister. You will stay here until we sail away together."

"Sail?" Panic clutched at her throat. She had to get off this ship! "I don't want to sail anywhere!"

"I realize that. And that's why I had this room, the pilot's cabin, sealed off." There was no malice in his voice or his expression. He was more like an understanding parent talking to a child. "I'm bringing you back to India with me."

"No!"

"It's for your own good. During the voyage back home I'm sure you'll see the error of the life you've chosen to lead. We have a chance to do something for India, an unprecedented chance to cleanse our karmas. I do this for you as much as for myself." He looked at her knowingly. "For your karma is as polluted as mine."

"You have no right!"

"I've more than a right. I've a duty."

He darted out of the room and shut the door behind him. Kolabati lunged forward but heard the lock click before she reached the handle. She pounded on its sturdy oak panels.

"Kusum, let me out! Please let me out!"

"When we're at sea," he said from the far side of the door.

She heard him walk down the hall to the steel hatch that led to the deck and felt a sense of doom settle over her. Her life was no longer her own. Trapped on this ship . . . weeks at sea with a madman, even if it was her brother. She had to get out of here! She became desperate.

"Jack will be looking for me!" she said on impulse, regretting it immediatley. She hadn't wanted to involve Jack in this.

"Why would he be looking for you?" Kusum said slowly, his voice faint.

"Because . . ." She couldn't let him know that Jack had found the ship and knew about the rakoshi. "Because we've been together every day. Tomorrow he'll want to know where I am."

"I see." There was a lengthy pause. "I believe I will have to talk to Jack."

"Don't you harm him, Kusum!" The thought of Jack falling victim to Kusum's wrath was more than she could bear. Jack was certainly

248

capable of taking care of himself, but she was sure he had never run up against someone like Kusum ... or a rakoshi.

She heard the steel door clang shut.

"Kusum?"

There was no reply. Kusum had left her alone on the ship.

No ... not alone.

There were rakoshi below.

9.

"SAHNKchewedday! SAHNKchewedday!"

Jack had run out of James Whale films—he had been searching unsuccessfully for a tape of Whale's *The Old Dark House* for years—so he had put on the 1939 version of *The Hunchback of Notre Dame*. Charles Laughton, playing the part of the ignorant, deformed Parisian, had just saved Maureen O'Hara and was shouting in an upper class British accent from the walls of the church. Ridiculous. But Jack loved the film and had watched it nearly a hundred times. It was like an old friend, and he needed an old friend here with him now. The apartment seemed especially empty tonight.

So with the six-foot projection TV providing a sort of visual musak, he sat and pondered his next move. Gia and Vicky were all right for the time being, so he didn't have to worry about them. He had called the Sutton Square house as soon as he had arrived home. It had been late and Gia had obviously been awakened by the phone. She had grouchily told him that no word had been received from either Grace or Nellie and assured him that everyone was fine and had been sleeping peacefully until his call.

On that note, he had let her go back to sleep. He wished he could do the same. But tired as he was, sleep was impossible. *Those things!* He could not drive the images out of his mind! Nor the possibility that if Kusum learned that he had been on the ship and had seen what it held, he might send them after him.

With that thought, he got up and went to the old oak secretary. From behind the false panel in its lower section he removed a Ruger Security Six .357 magnum revolver with a four-inch barrel. He loaded it with jacketed 110-grain hollow-points, bullets that would shatter upon entry causing incredible internal devastation: little hole going in, huge hole coming out. Kolabati had said the rakoshi were unstoppable except for fire. He'd like to see anything stand up to a couple of these in the chest. But the features that made them so lethal on impact with a body made them relatively safe to use indoors—a miss lost all its killing power once it hit a wall or even a window. He loaded five chambers and left the hammer down on the empty sixth.

As an extra precaution, Jack added a silencer—Kusum and the rakoshi were *his* problem. He didn't want to draw any of his neighbors into it if he could avoid it. Some of them would surely be hurt or killed.

He was just settling down in front of the TV again when there was a knock on the door. Startled and puzzled, Jack flipped the Betamax off and padded to the door, gun in hand. There was another knock as he reached it. He could not imagine a rakoshi knocking, but he was very uneasy about this night caller.

"Who is it?"

"Kusum Bahkti," said a voice on the other side.

Kusum! Muscles tightened across Jack's chest. Nellie's killer had come calling. Holding himself in check, he cocked the Ruger and unlocked the door. Kusum stood there alone. He appeared perfectly relaxed and unapologetic despite the fact that dawn was only a few hours away. Jack felt his finger tighten on the trigger of the pistol he held behind his right leg. A bullet in Kusum's brain right now would solve a number of problems, but might be difficult to explain. Jack kept his pistol hidden. *Be civil!*

"What can I do for you?"

"I wish to discuss the matter of my sister with you."

10.

Kusum watched Jack's face. His eyes had widened slightly at the mention of "my sister." Yes, there was something between these two. The thought filled Kusum with pain. Kolabati was not for Jack, or any casteless westerner. She deserved a prince.

Jack stepped back and let the door swing open wider, keeping his right shoulder pressed against the edge of the door. Kusum wondered if he was hiding a weapon.

As he stepped into the room he was struck by the incredible clutter. Clashing colors, clashing styles, bric-a-brac and memorabilia filled every wall and niche and corner. He found it at once offensive and entertaining. He felt that if he could sift through everything in this room he might come to know to the man who lived here.

THE TOMB

"Have a seat."

Kusum hadn't seen Jack move, yet now the door was closed and Jack was sitting in an overstuffed armchair, his hands clasped behind his head. He couldn't kick him in the throat now and end it all. One kick and Kolabati would no longer be tempted. Quick, easier than using a rakoshi. But Jack appeared to be on guard, ready to move. Kusum warned himself that he should not underestimate this man. He sat down on a short sofa across from him.

"You live frugally," he said, continuing to inspect the room around him. "With the level of income I assume you to have, I would have thought your quarters would be more richly appointed."

"I'm content the way I live," Jack said. "Besides, conspicuous consumption is contrary to my best interests."

"Perhaps. Perhaps not. But at least you have resisted the temptation to join the big car, yacht, and country club set. A lifestyle too many of your fellow countrymen would find irresistible." He sighed. "A lifestyle too many of my own countrymen find irresistible as well, much to India's detriment."

Jack shrugged. "What's this got to do with Kolabati."

"Nothing, Jack," Kusum said. He studied the American: a self-contained man; a rarity in this land. He does not need the adulation of his fellows to give him self-worth. He finds it within. I admire that. Kusum realized he was giving himself reasons why he should not make Jack a meal for the rakoshi.

"How'd you get my address?"

"Kolabati gave it to me." In a sense this was true. He had found Jack's address on a slip of paper on her bureau the other day.

"Then let's get to the subject of Kolabati, shall we?"

There was an undercurrent of hostility running through Jack. Perhaps he resented being disturbed at his hour. No ... Kusum sensed it was more than that. Had Kolabati told him something she shouldn't have? That idea disturbed him. He would have to be wary of what he said.

"Certainly. I had a long talk with my sister tonight and have convinced her that you are not right for her."

"Interesting," Jack said. A little smile played about his lips. What did he know? "What arguments did you use?"

"Traditional ones. As you may or may not know, Kolabati and I are of the *Brahmin* caste. Do you know what that means?"

"No."

251

"It is the highest caste. It is not fitting for her to consort with someone of a lower caste."

"That's a little old-fashioned, isn't it?"

"Nothing that is of such vital concern to one's karma can be considered 'old-fashioned.'"

"I don't worry about karma," Jack said. "I don't believe in it."

Kusum allowed himself to smile. What ignorant children these Americans were.

"Your believing or not believing in karma has no effect on its existence, nor on its consequences to you. Just as a refusal to believe in the ocean would not prevent you from drowning."

"And you say that because of your arguments about caste and karma, Kolabati was convinced that I am not good enough for her?"

"I did not wish to state it so bluntly. May I just say that I prevailed upon her not to see or even speak to you ever again." He felt a warm glow begin within him. "She belongs to India. India belongs to her. She is eternal, like India. In many ways, she *is* India."

"Yeah," Jack said as he reached out with his left hand and placed the phone in his lap. "She's a good kid." Cradling the receiver between his jaw and his left shoulder, he dialed with his left hand. His right hand rested quietly on his thigh. Why wasn't he using it?

"Let's call her and see what she says."

"Oh, she's not there," Kusum said quickly. "She has packed her things and started back to Washington."

Jack held the phone against his ear for a long time. Long enough for at least twenty rings. Finally, he replaced the receiver in its cradle with his left hand—

—and suddenly there was a pistol in his right hand, the large bore of its barrel pointing directly between Kusum's eyes.

"Where is she?" Jack's voice was a whisper. And in the eyes sighting down the barrel of that pistol Kusum saw his own death—the man holding the gun was quite willing and even anxious to pull the trigger.

Kusum's heart hammered in his throat. Not now! I can't die now! I've too much still to do!

11.

Jack saw the fear spring onto Kusum's face. *Good!* Let the bastard squirm. Give him a tiny taste of what Grace and Nellie must have felt

252

before they died.

It was all Jack could do to keep from pulling the trigger. Practical considerations held him back. Not that anyone would hear the silenced shot; and the possibility that anyone knew Kusum had come here was remote. But disposing of the body would be a problem.

And there was still Kolabati to worry about. What had happened to her? Kusum seemed to care too much for his sister to harm her, but any man who could lead a ceremony like the one Jack had seen tonight on that hellship was capable of anything.

"Where is she?" he repeated.

"Out of harm's way, I assure you," Kusum said in measured tones. "And out of yours." A muscle throbbed in his cheek, as if someone were tapping insistently against the inside of his face.

"Where?"

"Safe . . . as long as I am well and able to return to her."

Jack didn't know how much of that to believe, and yet he dared not take it too lightly.

Kusum stood up.

Jack kept the pistol trained on his face. "Stay where you are!"

"I have to go now."

Kusum turned his back and walked to the door. Jack had to admit the bastard had nerve. He paused there and faced Jack. "But I want to tell you one more thing: I spared your life tonight."

Incredulous, Jack rose to his feet. "What?" He was tempted to mention the rakoshi but remembered Kolabati's plea to say nothing of them. Apparently she hadn't told Kusum that Jack had been on the boat tonight.

"I believe I spoke clearly. You are alive now only because of the service you performed for my family. I now consider that debt paid."

"There was no debt. It was fee-for-service. You paid the price, I rendered the service. We've always been even."

"That is not the way I choose to see it. However, I am informing you now that all debts are cancelled. And do not follow me. Someone might suffer for that."

"Where is she?" Jack said, leveling the pistol. "If you don't tell me, I'm going to shoot you in the right knee. If you still won't talk, I'll shoot you in the left knee."

Jack was quite ready to do what he said but Kusum made no move to escape. He continued facing him calmly.

"You may begin," he told Jack. "I have suffered pain before."

253

THE TOMB

Jack glanced at Kusum's empty left sleeve, then looked into his eyes and saw the unbreakable will of a fanatic. Kusum would die before uttering a word.

After an interminable silence, Kusum smiled thinly, stepped into the hall, and closed the door behind him. Containing the urge to hurl the .357 against the door, Jack lined up the empty chamber and gently let the hammer down on it. Then he went over and locked the door—but not before giving it a good kick.

Was Kolabati really in some kind of danger, or had Kusum been bluffing? He had a feeling he had been outplayed, but still did not feel he could have risked calling the bluff.

The question was: *Where was Kolabati?* He would try to trace her tomorrow. Maybe she really was on her way back to Washington. He wished he could be sure.

Jack kicked the door again. Harder.

CHAPTER NINE

"For I am become death, destroyer of worlds."

From The *Bhagavad Gita*

Tuesday, August 7

1.

With a mixture of anger, annoyance and concern, Jack slammed the phone back into its cradle. For the tenth time this morning he had called Kusum's apartment and listened to an endless series of rings. He had alternated those calls with others to Washington, D.C. information and had found no listing for Kolabati in the District or in northern Virginia, but a call to Maryland information had turned up a number for a K. Bahkti in Chevy Chase, the fashionable Washington suburb.

There had been no answer there all morning, either. It was only a four-hour drive from here to the Capital. She had had plenty of time to make it—if she really had left New York. Jack didn't accept that. Kolabati had struck him as far too independent to knuckle under to her brother.

Visions of Kolabati bound and gagged in a closet somewhere plagued him. She was probably more comfortable than that, but he was sure she was Kusum's prisoner. It was because of her relationship with Jack that her brother had taken action against her. He felt responsible.

Kolabati ... his feelings for her were confused at this point. He

255

cared for her, but he couldn't say he loved her. She seemed, rather, to be a kindred spirit, one who understood him and accepted—even admired—him for what he was. Augment that with an intense physical attraction and the result was a unique bond that was exhilarating at times. But it wasn't love.

He had to help her. So why had he spent most of the morning on the phone? Why hadn't he gone over to the apartment and tried to find her?

Because he had to get over to Sutton Square. Something within had been nudging him in that direction all morning. He wouldn't fight it. He had learned through experience to obey those nudgings. It wasn't prescience. Jack didn't buy ESP or telepathy. The nudgings meant his subconscious mind had made correlations as yet inapparent to his conscious mind and was trying to let him know.

Somewhere in his subconscious, two and two and two had added up to Sutton Place. He should go there today. This morning. *Now.*

He pulled on some clothes and slipped the Semmerling into its ankle holster. Knowing he probably would need it later in the day, he stuffed his housebreaking kit—a set of lock picks and a thin plastic ruler—into a back pocket and headed for the door.

It felt good to be doing something at last.

2.

"Kusum?"

Kolabati heard a rattling down the hall. She pressed an ear against the upper panel of her cabin door. The noise definitely came from the door that led to the deck. Someone was unlocking it. It could only be Kusum.

She prayed he had come to release her.

It had been an endless night, quiet except for faint rustlings from within the depths of the ship. Kolabati knew she was safe, that she was sealed off from the rakoshi; and even if one or more did break free of the cargo areas, the necklace about her throat would protect her from detection. Yet her sleep had been fitful at best. She thought about the awful madness that had completely overtaken her brother; she worried about Jack and what Kusum might do to him. Even if her mind had been at peace, sleep would have been difficult. The air had grown thick through the night. The ventilation in the cabin was poor and with the rising of the sun the temperature had risen steadily. It was now like a sauna. She was thirsty. There was a sink in the tiny head attached to her cabin but the water that dribbled from the tap was brackish and musty-smelling.

She twisted the handle on the cabin door as she had done a thousand times since Kusum had locked her in here. It turned but would not open no matter how hard she pulled on it. A close inspection had revealed that Kusum had merely reversed the handle and locking apparatus—the door that was supposed to have locked from the inside now locked from the outside.

The steel door at the end of the hall clanged. Kolabati stepped back as her cabin door swung open. Kusum stood there with a flat box and a large brown paper sack cradled in his arm. His eyes held genuine compassion as he looked at her.

"What have you done to Jack?" she blurted as she saw the look on his face.

"Is that your first concern?" Kusum asked, his face darkening. "Does it matter that he was ready to kill me?"

"I want you *both* alive!" she said, meaning it.

Kusum seemed somewhat mollified. "We are that—both of us. And Jack will stay that way as long as he does not interfere with me."

Kolabati felt weak with relief. And in light of the knowledge that Jack had not been harmed, she felt free to concentrate on her own plight. She took a step toward her brother.

"Please let me out of here, Kusum," she said. She hated to beg but dreaded the thought of spending another night locked in this cabin.

"I know you had an uncomfortable night," he said, "and I'm sorry for that. But it won't be long now. Tonight your door shall be unlocked."

"Tonight? Why not now?"

He smiled. "Because we have not yet sailed."

Her heart sank. "We're sailing tonight?"

"The tide turns after midnight. I've made arrangements for apprehending the last Westphalen. As soon as she is in my hands, we will sail."

"Another old woman?"

Kolabati saw a queasy look flicker across her brother's face.

"Age has no bearing. She is the last of the Westphalen line. That is all that matters."

Kusum set the bag on the fold-out table and began unpacking it. He pulled out two small jars of fruit juice, a square Tupperware container filled with some sort of salad, eating utensils, and paper cups. At the bottom of the bag was a small selection of newspapers and magazines, all in Hindi. He opened the container and released the scent of curried vegetables and rice into the room.

"I've brought you something to eat."

Despite the cloud of depression and futility that enveloped her, Kolabati felt her mouth filling with saliva. But she willed her hunger and thirst to be still and glanced toward the open cabin door. If she got a few steps lead on Kusum she could perhaps lock him in here and escape.

"I'm famished," she said, approaching the table on an angle that would put her between Kusum and the door. "It smells delicious. Who made it?"

"I bought it for you at a little Indian restaurant on Fifth Avenue in the Twenties. A Bengali couple run it. Good people."

"I'm sure they are."

Her heart began to pound as she edged closer to the door. What if she failed to get away? Would he hurt her? She glanced to her left. The door was only two steps away. She could make it but she was afraid to try.

It had to be now!

She leaped for the doorway, a tiny cry of terror escaping her as she grabbed the handle and pulled the door closed behind her. Kusum was at the door the instant it slammed shut. Kolabati fumbled with the catch and shouted with joy when it clicked into the locked position.

"Bati, I command you to open this door immediately!" Kusum shouted from the other side, his voice heavy with anger.

She ran for the outer door. She knew she wouldn't feel truly free until there was a layer of steel between herself and her brother. A crash behind her made Kolabati glance over her shoulder. The wooden door was exploding outward. She saw Kusum's foot flash through as the door dissolved into a shower of splintered wood. Kusum stepped into the hall and started after her.

Terror spurred her on. Sunlight, fresh air, and freedom beckoned to her from beyond the steel hatch. Kolabati darted through and pushed it shut, but before she could lock it, Kusum threw all his weight against the other side, sending her flying onto her back.

Without a word, he stepped out onto the deck and pulled her to her feet. With a viselike grip that bruised her wrist, he dragged her back to her cabin. Once there, he spun her around and gripped the front of her blouse.

"Don't *ever* try that again!" he said, his eyes nearly bulging with rage. "It was idiotic! Even if you had managed to lock me up, you would have no way to reach the dock—unless you know how to slide down a rope."

She felt herself jerked forward, heard the fabric of her blouse rip as buttons flew in all directions.

"Kusum!"

He was like a mad beast, his breathing harsh, his eyes wild.

"*And take*—"

He reached into the open front of her blouse, grabbed her bra between the cups, and tore the center piece, exposing her breasts . . .

"—*off*—"

. . . then pushed her down on the bed and yanked brutally at the waistband of her skirt, bursting the seams and pulling it from her . . .

"—*these*—"

. . . then tore her panties off . . .

"—*obscene*—"

. . . then tore away the remnants of her blouse and bra.

"—*rags!*"

He threw down the ruined clothes and ground them into the floor with his heel.

Kolabati lay frozen in panic until he finally calmed himself. As his breathing and complexion returned to normal, he stared at her as she huddled naked before him, an arm across her breasts, a hand over the pubic area between her tightly-clenched thighs.

Kusum had seen her unclothed countless times before; she had often paraded nude before him to see his reaction, but at this moment she felt exposed and degraded, and tried to hide herself.

His sudden smile was sardonic. "Modesty doesn't become you, dear sister." He reached for the flat box he had brought with him and tossed it to her. "Cover yourself."

Afraid to move, yet more afraid of disobeying him, Kolabati drew the box across her lap and awkwardly pulled it open. It contained a light blue sari with gold stitching. Fighting back tears of humiliation and impotent rage, she slipped the tight upper blouse over her head, then wrapped the silk fabric around herself in the traditional manner. She fought the hopelessness that threatened to engulf her. There had to be a way out.

THE TOMB

"Let me go!" she said when she felt she could trust her voice. "You have no right to keep me here!"

"There will be no further discussion as to what I have a right to do. I am doing what I *must* do. Just as I must see my vow through to its fulfillment. Then I can go home and stand before those who believe in me, who are willing to lay down their lives to follow me in bringing Mother India back to the True Path. I will not deserve their trust, nor be worthy of leading them to *Hindutvu,* until I can stand before them with a purified karma."

"But that's *your* life!" she screamed. "*Your* karma!"

Kusum's shook his head slowly, sadly. "Our karmas are entwined, Bati. Inextricably. And what *I* must do, *you* must do." He stepped through the ruined door and looked back at her. "Meanwhile, I am due at an emergency session of the Security Council. I shall return with your dinner this evening."

He turned, stepped through the remains of the shattered door, and was gone. Kolabati didn't bother calling his name or looking after him. The outer door to the deck closed with a loud clang.

More than fear, more than misery at being incarcerated on this ship, she felt a great sadness for her brother and the mad obsession that drove him. She went to the table and tried to eat but could not even bring herself to taste the food.

Finally the tears came. She buried her face in her hands and wept.

3.

For the first time since Gia had known him, Jack looked his age. There were dark rings under his eyes and a haunted look hovering within them. His dark brown hair needed combing and he had been careless shaving.

"I didn't expect you," she said as he stepped into the foyer.

It annoyed her that he could just show up like this without warning. On the other hand, she was glad to have him around. It had been a very long, fearful night. And a lonely one. She began to wonder if she would ever straighten out her feelings about Jack.

Eunice closed the door and looked questioningly at Gia. "I'm about to fix lunch, mum. Shall I set an extra place?" The maid's voice was lifeless. Gia knew she missed her mistresses. Eunice had kept busy, talking incessantly of Grace and Nellie's imminent return. But even she seemed to be running out of hope.

260

THE TOMB

Gia turned to Jack. "Staying for lunch?"

He shrugged. "Sure."

As Eunice bustled off, Gia said, "Shouldn't you be out looking for Nellie?"

"I wanted to be here," he said. It was a simple statement.

"You won't find her here."

"I don't think I'll ever find her. I don't think anyone will."

The note of finality in his voice shocked Gia. "W-what do you know?"

"Just a feeling," he said, averting his eyes as if embarrassed to admit acting on feelings. "Just as I've had this other feeling all morning that I should be here today."

"That's all you're going on—feelings?"

"Humor me, Gia" he said with an edge on his voice she had never heard before. "All right? Humor me."

Gia was about to press him for a more specific answer when Vicky came running in. Vicky missed Grace and Nellie, but Gia had kept her daughter's spirits up by telling her that Nellie had gone to find Grace. Jack picked her up and swung her to his hip, but his responses to her chatter consisted mainly of noncommittal grunts. Gia could not remember ever seeing him so preoccupied. He seemed worried, almost unsure of himself. That upset her the most. Jack was always a rock of self-assurance. Something was terribly wrong here and he wasn't telling her about it.

The three of them trailed into the kitchen where Eunice was preparing lunch. Jack slumped into a chair at the kitchen table and stared morosely into space. Vicky apparently noticed that he wasn't responding to her in his usual manner so she went out to the back yard to her playhouse. Gia sat across from him, watching him, dying to know what he was thinking but unable to ask with Eunice there.

Vicky came running in from the back with an orange in her hand. Gia idly wondered where she had got it. She thought they had run out of oranges.

"Do the orange mouth! Do the orange mouth!"

Jack straightened up and put on a smile that wouldn't have fooled a blind man.

"Okay, Vicks. The orange mouth. Just for you."

He glanced at Gia and made a sawing motion with his hand. Gia got up and found him a knife. When she returned to the table, he was shaking his hand as if it were wet.

"What's the matter?"

"This thing's leaking. Must be a real juicy one." He sliced the orange in half. Before quartering it, he rubbed the back of his hand along his cheek. Suddenly he was on his feet, his chair tipping over backwards behind him. His face was putty-white as he held his fingers under his nose and sniffed.

"No!" he cried as Vicky reached for one of the orange halves. He grabbed her hand and roughly pushed it away. "Don't touch it!"

"Jack! What's wrong with you?" Gia was furious at him for treating Vicky that way. And poor Vicky stood there staring at him with her lower lip trembling.

But Jack was oblivious to both of them. He was holding the orange halves up to his nose, inspecting them, sniffing at them like a dog. His face grew steadily whiter.

"Oh, God!" he said, looking as if he was about to be sick. "Oh, my God!"

As he stepped around the table, Gia pulled Vicky out of his way and clutched her against her. His eyes were wild. Three long strides took him to the kitchen garbage can. He threw the orange in it, then pulled the Hefty bag out, twirled it, and twisted the attached tie around the neck. He dropped the bag on the floor and came back to kneel before Vicky. He gently laid his hands on her shoulders.

"Where'd you get that orange, Vicky?"

Gia noted the "Vicky" immediately. Jack never called her by that name. She was always "Vicks" to him.

"In ... in my playhouse."

Jack jumped up and began pacing around the kitchen, frantically running the fingers of both hands through his hair. Finally he seemed to come to a decision.

"All right—we're getting out of here."

Gia was on her feet. "What are you—?"

"Out! All of us! And no one eat anything! Not a thing! That goes for you, too, Eunice!"

Eunice puffed herself up. "I beg your pardon?"

Jack got behind her and firmly guided her toward the door. He was not rough with her, but there was no hint of playfulness about him. He came over to Gia and pulled Vicky away from her.

"Get your toys together. You and your mommy are going on a little trip."

Jack's sense of urgency was contagious. Without a backward

THE TOMB

glance at her mother, Vicky ran outside.

Gia shouted angrily: "Jack, you can't do this! You can't come in here and start acting like a fire marshall. You've no right!"

"Listen to me!" he said in a low voice as he grasped her left biceps in a grip that bordered on pain. "Do you want Vicky to end up like Grace and Nellie? Gone without a trace?"

Gia tried to speak but no words came out. She felt as if her heart had stopped. *Vicky gone? NO*—!

"I didn't think so," Jack said. "If we're here tonight, that might happen."

Gia still couldn't speak. The horror of the thought was a hand clutching at her throat.

"Go!" he said, pushing her toward the front of the house. "Pack up and we'll get out of here."

Gia stumbled away from him. It was not so much what Jack said, but what she had seen in his eyes ... something she had never seen nor ever expected to see: fear.

Jack afraid—it was almost inconceivable. Yet he was; she was sure of it. And if Jack was afraid, what should she be?

Terrified, she ran upstairs to pack her things.

4.

Alone in the kitchen, Jack sniffed his fingers again. At first he had thought he was hallucinating, but then he had found the needle puncture in the orange skin. There could be no doubt—rakoshi elixir. Even now he wanted to retch. Someone—Someone? Kusum!—had left a doctored orange for Vicky.

Kusum wanted Vicky for his monsters!

The worst part was realizing that Grace and Nellie had not been accidental victims. There was purpose here. The two old women had been intended targets. And Vicky was next!

Why? In God's name, *why?* Was it this house? Did he want to kill everyone who lived here? He had Grace and Nellie already, but why Vicky next? Why not Eunice or Gia? It didn't make sense. Or maybe it did and his brain was too rattled right now to see the pattern.

Vicky came up the back steps and hurried through the kitchen carrying something that looked like a big plastic grape. She walked by with her chin out and her nose in the air, without even once glancing Jack's way.

THE TOMB

She's mad at me.

To her mind she had ample reason to be upset with him. After all, he had frightened her and everyone else in the house. But that could not be helped. He could not remember a shock like the one that had blasted through him when he recognized the odor on his hands. Orange juice, yes, but tainted by the unmistakable herbal smell of rakoshi elixir.

Fear trickled down his chest wall and into his abdomen.

Not my Vicky. *Never* my Vicky!

He walked over to the sink and looked out the window as he washed the smell off his hands. The house around him, the playhouse out there, the yard, the whole neighborhood had become tainted, sinister.

But where to go? He couldn't let Gia and Vicky go back to their own apartment. If Kusum knew of Vicky's passion for oranges, surely he knew her address. And Jack's place was definitely out. On impulse he called Isher Sports.

"Abe? I need help."

"So what else is new?" came the lighthearted reply.

"This is serious, Abe. It's Gia and her little girl. I've got to find them a safe place to stay. Somewhere not connected with me."

The banter was suddenly gone from Abe's voice. "Hotel no good?"

"As a last resort it'll do, but I'd feel better in a private place."

"My daughter's apartment is empty until the end of the month. She's on sabbatical in Europe for the summer."

"Where is it?"

"Queens. On the border of Astoria and Long Island City."

Jack glanced out the kitchen window to the jumble of buildings directly across the East River. For the first time since cutting the orange open, he felt he had a chance of controlling the situation. The sick dread that weighed so relentlessly upon him lifted a little.

"Perfect! Where's the key?"

"In my pocket."

"I'll be right over to get it."

"I'll be here."

Eunice came in as he hung up. "You really have no right to send us all on our way," she said sternly. "But if I must go, at least let me clean up the kitchen."

"I'll clean it up," Jack said, blocking her way as she reached for the

THE TOMB

sponge in the sink. She turned and picked up the Hefty bag that contained the tainted orange. Jack gently pulled it from her grasp. "I'll take care of that, too."

"Promise?" she said, eyeing him with unconcealed suspicion. "I wouldn't want the two ladies of the house coming back and finding a mess."

"They won't find a mess here," Jack told her, feeling sorry for this loyal little woman who had no idea that her employers were dead. "I promise you."

Gia came down the stairs as Jack ushered Eunice out the front door. Gia seemed to have composed herself since he had chased her upstairs.

"I want to know what all this means," she said after Eunice was gone. "Vicky's upstairs. You tell me what's going on here before she comes down."

Jack searched for something to say. He could not tell her the truth—she'd lose all confidence in his sanity. She might even call the nut patrol to take him down to pillow city in Bellevue. He began to improvise, mixing truth and fiction, hoping he made sense.

"I think Grace and Nellie were abducted."

"That's ridiculous!" Gia said, but her voice did not carry much conviction.

"I wish it were."

"But there was no sign of a break-in or a struggle—"

"I don't know how it was done, but I'm sure the liquid I found in Grace's bathroom is a link." He paused for effect. "Some of it was in that orange Vicky brought in to me."

Gia's hand clutched his arm. "The one you threw away?"

Jack nodded. "And I bet if we had the time we could find something of Nellie's that's laced with the stuff, something she ate."

"I can't think of anything ..." Her voice trailed off, then rose again. "What about the chocolates?" Gia grabbed his arm and dragged him to the parlor. "They're in here. They came last week."

Jack went to the candy bowl on the table beside the recliner where they had spent Sunday night. He took a chocolate off the top and inspected it. No sign of a needle hole or tampering. He broke it open and held it up to his nose ... and there it was: the odor. Rakoshi elixir. He held it out to Gia.

"Here. Take a whiff. I don't know if you remember what Grace's laxative smelled like, but it's the same stuff." He led her to the kitchen

265

where he opened the garbage bag and took out Vicky's orange. "Compare."

Gia sniffed them both, then looked up at him. Fear was growing in her eyes. "What is it?"

"I don't know," Jack lied as he took the candy and orange from her and threw them both into the bag. Then he brought the dish from the parlor and dumped the rest of the chocolates.

"But it's got to do *some*thing!" Gia said, persistent as always.

So that Gia couldn't see his eyes as he spoke, Jack made a show of concentrating on twisting the tie around the neck of the bag as tightly as he could.

"Maybe it has some sedative properties that keeps people quiet while they're being carried off."

Gia stared at him, a mystified look on her face. "This is crazy! Who would want to—?"

"That's my next question: Where'd she get the candy?"

"From England." Gia's face blanched. "Oh, no! From Richard!"

"Your ex?"

"He sent them from London."

With his mind working furiously, Jack took the garbage bag outside and dumped it in a can in the narrow alley alongside the house.

Richard Westphalen? Where the hell did he fit in? But hadn't Kusum mentioned that he had been in London last year? And now Gia says her ex-husband sent these chocolates from London. It all fits, but it made no sense. What possible link could he have to Kusum? Certainly not financial. Kusum hadn't struck Jack as a man to whom money meant much.

This was making less and less sense every minute.

"Could your ex be behind this?" he asked as he returned to the kitchen. "Could he be thinking he's going to inherit something if Grace and Nellie disappear?"

"I wouldn't put much past Richard," Gia said, "but I can't see him getting involved in a serious crime. Besides, I happen to know that he's not going to inherit a thing from Nellie."

"But does *he* know that?"

"I don't know." She glanced around and appeared to shiver. "Let's get out of here, shall we?"

"Soon as you're ready."

Gia went upstairs to get Vicky. Before long, mother and daughter were standing in the foyer, Vicky with a little suitcase in one hand and

THE TOMB

her plastic grape carrying case in the other.

"What's in there?" Jack asked, pointing to the grape.

Vicky held it out of his reach behind her back. "Just my Ms. Jelliroll doll."

"I should have known." *At least she's talking to me.*

"Can we go now?" Gia said. She had been transformed from a reluctant evictee to someone anxious to be as far away from this house as possible. He was glad for that.

Jack took the large suitcase and led the two of them up to Sutton Place where he hailed a cab and gave the address of Isher Sports.

"I want to get home," Gia said. She was in the middle, Vicky on her left and Jack on her right. "That's in *your* neighborhood."

"You can't go home," he told her. As she opened her mouth to protest he added: "You can't go to my place, either."

"Then where?"

"I've found a place in Queens."

"Queens? I don't want to—"

"No one'll find you in a million years. Just hang out there for a couple of days until I see if I can put a stop to this."

"I feel like a criminal." Gia put an arm around Vicky and hugged her close.

Jack wanted to hug both of them and tell them they'd be all right, that he'd see to it that nothing ever hurt them. But it would be awkward here in the back seat of a cab, and after his outburst this morning with the orange, he wasn't sure how they'd react.

The cab pulled up in front of Abe's store. Jack ran in and found him at his usual station reading his usual science fiction novel. There was mustard on his tie; poppy seeds peppered his ample shirt front.

"The key's on the counter and so's the address," he said, glancing over his reading glasses without moving from his seat. "This won't be messy, I hope. Already my relationship with Sarah is barely civil."

Jack pocketed the key but kept the address in hand.

"If I know Gia, she'll leave the place spotless."

"If I know my daughter, Gia will have her work cut out for her." He stared at Jack. "I suppose you have some running around to do tonight?"

Jack nodded. "A lot."

"And I suppose you want I should come over and baby sit the two ladies while you're out of the apartment? Don't even ask," he said, holding up a hand, "I'll do it."

267

THE TOMB

"I owe you one, Abe," Jack said.

"I'll add it to the list," he replied with a deprecating wave of his hand.

"Do that."

Back in the cab, Jack gave the driver the address of Abe's daughter's apartment. "Take the Midtown Tunnel," he said.

"The bridge is better for where you're going," the cabbie said.

"Take the tunnel," Jack told him. "And go through the park."

"It's quicker around."

"The park. Enter at Seventy-second and head downtown."

The cabbie shrugged. "You're paying for it."

They drove over to Central Park West, then turned into the park. Jack stayed twisted around in his seat the whole way, tensely watching through the back window for any car or cab that followed them. He had insisted on taking the route through the park because it was narrow and winding, curving through the trees and beneath the overpasses. Anyone tailing would want to stay close for fear of losing them.

There was no one following. Jack was sure of that by the time they reached Columbus Circle, but he kept his eyes fixed out the rear window until they reached the Queens Midtown Tunnel.

As they slid into that tiled fluorescent gullet, Jack faced front and allowed himself to unwind. The East River was above them, Manhattan was rapidly falling behind. Soon he'd have Gia and Vicky lost in the mammoth beehive of apartments called Queens. He was putting the whole island of Manhattan between Kusum and his intended victims. Kusum would never find them. With that worry behind him, Jack would be free to concentrate his efforts on finding a way to deal with the crazy Indian.

Right now, however, he had to mend his relationship with Vicky who was sitting on the far side of her mother with her big plastic grape sitting in her lap. He began by leaning around Gia and making the kind of faces mothers always tell their children not to make because you never know when your face'll get stuck that way.

Vicky tried to ignore him but soon was laughing and crossing her eyes and making faces, too.

"Stop that, Vicky!" Gia said. "Your face could get stuck that way!"

THE TOMB

5.

Vicky was glad Jack was acting like his old self. He had frightened her this morning with his yelling and grabbing her orange and throwing it away. That had been mean. He had never done anything like that before. Not only had it frightened her, but her feelings had been hurt. She had got over being scared right away, but her feelings had remained hurt until now. Silly Jack. He was making her laugh. He just must have been grouchy this morning.

Vicky shifted her Ms. Jelliroll Carry Case on her lap. There was room in it for the doll and extra things like doll clothes.

Vicky had something extra in there now. Something special. She hadn't told Jack or mommy that she had found two oranges in the playhouse. Jack had thrown the first away. But the second was in her carry case, safely hidden beneath the doll clothes. She was saving that for later and not telling anybody. That was only right. It was her orange. She had found it, and she wasn't going to let anybody throw it away.

6.

Apartment 1203 was hot and stuffy. The stale smell of cigarette smoke had become one with the upholstery, rugs, and wallpaper. Dust bunnies under the front room coffee table were visible from the door.

So this was the hide-out: Abe's daughter's place.

Gia had met Abe briefly once. He hadn't looked too neat—had little bits of food all over him, in fact. Like father, like daughter, apparently.

Jack went to the big air conditioner in the window. "Could use some of this."

"Just open the windows," Gia told him. "Let's get a change of air in here."

Vicky was prancing around, swinging her strawberry carry case, delighted to be in a new place. Nonstop chatter:

"Are we staying here mommy how long are we staying is this going to be my room can I sleep in this bed? ooh look how high we are you can see the Umpire State Building over there and there's Chrysler's building it's my favorite 'cause it's pointy and silvery at the top . . ."

And on and on. Gia smiled at the memory of how hard she had worked coaxing Vicky to say her first words, how she had agonized over the completely unfounded notion that her daughter might never speak. Now she wondered if she would ever stop.

Once the windows on both sides of the apartment were open, the wind began to flow through, removing all the old trapped odors and bringing in new ones.

"Jack, I've got to clean this place up if I'm going to stay here. I hope no one minds."

"No one'll mind," he said. "Just let me make a couple of calls and I'll help you."

Gia located the vacuum cleaner while he dialed and listened, then dialed again. Either it was busy or he got no answer, because he hung up without saying anything.

They spent the better part of the afternoon cleaning the apartment. Gia took pleasure in the simple tasks of scouring the sink, cleaning the counters, scrubbing the inside of the refrigerator, washing the kitchen floors, vacuuming the rugs. Concentrating on the minutiae kept her mind off the formless threat she felt hanging over Vicky and herself.

Jack wouldn't let her out of the apartment so he took the bed-clothes down to the laundry area and washed them. He was a hard worker and not afraid to get his hands dirty. They made a good team. She found she enjoyed being with him, something up until a few days ago she thought she'd never enjoy again. The certain knowledge that there was a gun hidden somewhere on his body and that he was the sort of man quite willing and able to use it effectively did not cause the revulsion it would have a few days ago. She couldn't say she approved of the idea, but she found herself taking reluctant comfort from it.

It wasn't until the sun was leaning into the west toward the Manhattan skyline that she finally declared the apartment habitable. Jack went out and found a Chinese restaurant and brought back egg rolls, hot and sour soup, spare ribs, shrimp fried rice, and moo shi pork. In a separate bag, he had an Entenmann's almond ring coffee cake. That didn't strike Gia as a fitting dessert for a Chinese meal, but she didn't say anything.

She watched as he tried to teach Vicky how to use the chopsticks he had picked up at the restaurant. The riff between those two had apparently healed without a scar. They were buddies again, the trauma of the morning forgotten—at least by Vicky.

"I have to go out," he told her as they cleared the dishes.

270

THE TOMB

"I figured that," Gia said, hiding her unease. She knew they were lost in this apartment complex among other apartment complexes—the proverbial needle in the haystack—but she didn't want to be alone tonight, not after what she had learned this morning about the chocolates and the orange. "How long will you be out?"

"Don't know. That's why I asked Abe to come and stay with you until I get back. Hope you don't mind."

"No. I don't mind at all." From what she remembered of Abe, he seemed an unlikely protector, but any port in a storm. "Anyway, how could I object? He has more of a right to be here than we do."

"I wouldn't be too sure of that," Jack said.

"Oh?"

"Abe and his daughter are barely on speaking terms." Jack turned and faced her, leaning his back against the sink. He glanced over her shoulder to where Vicky sat alone at the table munching on a fortune cookie, then spoke in a low voice, his eyes fixed on her. "You see, Abe's a criminal. Like me."

"Jack—" She didn't want to get into this now.

"Not exactly like me. Not a *thug.*" His emphasis on the word she had used on him was a barb in her heart. "He just sells illegal weapons. He also sells legal weapons, but he sells them illegally."

Portly, voluble Abe Grossman—a gunrunner? It wasn't possible! But the look in Jack's eyes said it was.

"Was it necessary to tell me that?" What was he trying to do?

"I just want you to know the truth. I also want you to know that Abe is the most peace-loving man I've ever met."

"Then why does he sell guns?"

"Maybe he'll explain it to you someday. I found his reasons pretty convincing—more convincing than his daughter did."

"She doesn't approve, I take it."

"Barely speaks to him."

"Good for her."

"Didn't stop her from letting him pay the tuition for her bachelor and graduate degrees, though."

There was a knock on the door. A voice in the hall said, "It's me—Abe."

Jack let him in. He looked the same as he had the last time Gia had seen him: An overweight man dressed in a short-sleeved white shirt, black tie, and black pants. The only difference was the nature of the food stains up and down his front.

THE TOMB

"Hello," he said, shaking Gia's hand. She liked a man to shake her hand. "Nice to see you again." He also shook Vicky's hand, which elicited a big smile from her.

"Just in time for dessert, Abe," Jack said. He brought out the Entenmann's cake.

Abe's eyes widened. "Almond coffee ring! You shouldn't have!" He made a show of searching the table top. "What are the rest of you having?"

Gia laughed politely, not knowing how seriously to take the remark, then watched with wonder as Abe consumed three-quarters of the cake, all the while talking eloquently and persuasively of the imminent collapse of western civilization. Although he had failed to persuade Vicky to call him "Uncle Abe" by the time dessert was over, he had Gia half convinced she should flee New York and build an underground shelter in the foothills of the Rockies.

Finally, Jack stood up and stretched. "I have to go out for a little bit. Shouldn't be long. Abe will stay here until I get back. And if you don't hear from me, don't worry."

Gia followed him to the door. She didn't want to see him go, but couldn't bring herself to tell him so. A persistent knot of hostility within her always veered her away from the subject of Gia and Jack.

"I don't know if I can be with him too much longer," she whispered to Jack. "He's so *depressing!*"

Jack smiled. "You ain't heard nuthin' yet. Wait till the network news comes on and he gives you his analysis of what *every* story *really* means." He put his hand on her shoulder and drew her close. "Don't let him bother you. He means well."

Before she knew what was happening he leaned forward and kissed her on the lips.

"Bye!" And he was out the door.

Gia turned back to the apartment: There was Abe squatting before the television. There was a Special Report about the Chinese border dispute with India.

"Did you hear that?" Abe was saying. "Did you hear? Do you know what this means?"

Resignedly, Gia joined him before the set. "No. What does it mean?"

THE TOMB

7.

Finding a cab took some doing, but Jack finally nabbed a gypsy to take him back into Manhattan. He still had a few hours of light left; he wanted to make the most of them. The worst of the rush hour was over and he was heading the opposite way of much of the flow, so he made good time getting back into the city.

The cab dropped him off between Sixty-seventh and Sixty-eighth on Fifth Avenue, one block south of Kusum's apartment building. He crossed to the Park side of Fifth and walked uptown, inspecting the building as he passed. He found what he wanted: a delivery alley along the left side secured by a wrought iron gate with pointed rails curved over and down toward the street. Next step was to see if anybody was home.

He crossed over and stepped up to the doorman who wore a pseudomilitary cap and sported a handlebar mustache.

"Would you ring the Bahkti apartment, please?"

"Surely," the doorman said. "Whom shall I say is calling?"

"Jack. Just Jack."

The doorman buzzed on the intercom and waited. And waited. Finally he said, "I do not believe Mr. Bahkti is in. Shall I leave a message?"

No answer did not necessarily mean no one was home.

"Sure. Tell him Jack was here and that he'll be back."

Jack sauntered away, not sure of what his little message would accomplish. Perhaps it would rattle Kusum, although he doubted it. It would probably take a hell of a lot to rattle a guy with a nest of rakoshi.

He walked to the end of the building. Now came the touchy part: getting over the gate unseen. He took a deep breath. Without looking back, he leaped up and grabbed two of the curved iron bars near their tops. Bracing himself against the side wall, he levered himself over the spikes and jumped down to the other side. Those daily workouts paid off now and then. He stepped back and waited but no one seemed to have noticed him. He exhaled. So far, so good. He ran around to the rear of the building.

There he found a double door wide enough for furniture deliveries. He ignored this—they were almost invariably wired with alarms. The narrow little door at the bottom of a short stairwell was more interesting. He pulled the leather-cased lock-picking kit out of his pocket as he descended the steps. The door was solid, faced with sheet metal,

273

no windows. The lock was a Yale, most likely an inter-grip rim model. While his hands worked two of the slim black picks into the keyhole, his eyes kept watch along the rear of the building. He didn't have to look at what he was doing—locks were picked by feel.

And then it came—the click of the tumblers within the cylinder. There was a certain grim satisfaction in that sound, but Jack didn't take time to savor it. A quick twist and the bolt snapped back. He pulled the door open and waited for an alarm bell. None came. A quick inspection showed that the door wasn't wired for a silent alarm either. He slipped inside and locked it after him.

It was dark in the basement. As he waited for his eyes to adjust, he ran over a mental picture of the layout of the lobby one floor above. If his memory was accurate, the elevators should be straight ahead and slightly to the left. He moved forward and found them right where he had figured. The elevator came down in response to the button and he took it straight up to the ninth floor.

There were four doors facing on the small vestibule outside the elevator. Jack went immediately to 9B and withdrew the thin, flexible plastic ruler from his pocket. Tension tightened the muscles at the back of his neck. This was the riskiest part. Anyone seeing him now would call the police immediately. He had to work fast. The door was double-locked: a Yale deadbolt and a Quikset with a keyhole in the handle. He had cut a right-triangular notch half an inch into the edge of the ruler about an inch from the end. Jack slipped the ruler in between the door and the jamb and ran it up and down past the Yale. It moved smoothly—the deadbolt had been left open. He ran the ruler down to the Quikset, caught the notch on the latch bolt, wiggled and pulled on the ruler . . . and the door swung inward.

The entire operation had taken ten seconds. Jack jumped inside and quietly closed the door behind him. The room was bright within—the setting sun was pouring orange light through the living room windows. All was quiet. The apartment had an empty feel to it.

He looked down and saw the smashed egg. Thrown in anger or dropped during a struggle? He moved quickly, silently through the living room to the bedrooms, searching the closets, under the beds, behind the chairs, into the kitchen and the utility room.

Kolabati was not here. There was a closet in the second bedroom half-filled with women's clothes; he recognized a dress as the one Kolabati had worn in Peacock Alley; another was the one she had worn to the Consulate reception. She wouldn't have gone back to

THE TOMB

Washington without her clothes.

She was still in New York.

He went to the window and looked out over the park. The orange sun was still bright enough to hurt his eyes. He stood there and stared west for a long time. He had desperately hoped to find Kolabati here. It had been against all logic, but he had had to see for himself so he could cross this apartment off his short list of possibilities.

He turned and picked up the phone and dialed the number of the Indian Embassy. No, Mr. Bahkti was still at the U.N., but was expected back shortly.

That did it. There were no more excuses left to him. He had to go to the only other place Kolabati could be.

Dread rolled back and forth in his stomach like a leaden weight.

That ship. That godawful floating piece of hell. He had to go back there.

8.

"I'm thirsty, mommy."

"It's the Chinese food. It always makes you thirsty. Have another drink of water."

"I don't want water. I'm tired of water. Can't I have some juice?"

"I'm sorry, honey, but I didn't get a chance to do any shopping. The only thing to drink around here is some wine and you can't have that. I'll get you some juice in the morning. I promise."

"Oh, okay."

Vicky slumped in her chair and folded her arms over her chest. She wanted juice instead of water and she wanted to watch something else besides these dumb news shows. First the six o'clock news, then something called the network news, and Mr. Grossman—he wasn't her uncle; why did he want her to call him Uncle Abe?—talking, talking, talking. She'd much rather be watching "The Brady Bunch." She had seen them all at least twice, some three or four times. She liked the show. Nothing bad ever happened. Not like the news.

Her tongue felt dry. If only she had some juice . . .

She remembered the orange—the one she had saved from her playhouse this morning. That would taste so delicious now.

Without a word she got up from her chair and slipped into the bedroom she and mommy would be sharing tonight. Her Ms. Jelliroll Carry Case was on the floor of the closet. Kneeling in the dim light of the room, she opened it and pulled the orange out. It felt so cool in her hand. Just the smell made her mouth water. This was going to taste so good.

She went over by the screened window and dug her thumb into the thick skin until it broke through, then she began peeling. Juice squirted all over her hands as she tore a section loose and bit into it. Juice, sweet and tangy gushed onto her tongue. *Delicious!* She pushed the rest of the section into her mouth and was tearing another free when she noticed something funny about the taste. It wasn't a bad taste, but it wasn't a good taste either. She took a bite of the second section. It tasted the same.

Suddenly she was frightened. What if the orange was rotten? Maybe that's why Jack wouldn't let her have any this morning. What if it made her sick?

Panicked, Vicky bent and shoved the rest of the orange under the bed—she'd sneak it into the garbage later when she had a chance. Then she strolled as casually as she could out of the room and over to the bathroom where she washed the juice off her hands and drank a Dixie Cup full of water.

She hoped she didn't get a stomach ache. Mommy would be awfully mad if she found out about sneaking the orange. But more than anything Vicky prayed she didn't throw up. Throwing up was the worst thing in the world.

Vicky returned to the living room, averting her face so no one could see it. She felt guilty. One look at her and mommy would know something was wrong. The weather lady was saying that tomorrow was going to be hot and dry and sunny again, and Mr. Grossman started talking about drought and people fighting over water. She sat down and hoped they'd let her watch "The Partridge Family" after this.

9.

The dark bow of the freighter loomed over Jack, engulfing him in its shadow as he stood on the dock. The sun was sinking over New Jersey but there was still plenty of light. Traffic rushed by above and behind him. He was oblivious to everything but the ship before him and the clatter of his heart against his ribs.

He had to go in. There was no way around it. For an instant, he actually considered calling the police, but rejected the idea immediately. As Kolabati had said, Kusum was legally untouchable. And even if Jack managed to convince the police that such things as rakoshi existed, all they were likely to do was get themselves killed and loose the rakoshi upon the city. Probably get Kolabati killed, too.

No, the police didn't belong here, for practical reasons and for reasons of principle: This was his problem and he would solve it by himself. Repairman Jack always worked alone.

He had put Gia and Vicky out of harm's way. Now he had to find Kolabati and see her to safety before he made a final move against her brother.

As he followed the wharf around to the starboard side of the ship, he pulled on a pair of heavy work gloves he had bought on his way over from Fifth Avenue. There were also three brand new Cricket butane lighters—three for $1.47 at the department store—scattered through his pockets. He didn't know what good they would do but Kolabati had been emphatic about fire and iron being the only weapons against rakoshi. If he needed fire, at least he would have a little of it available.

There was too much light to climb up the same rope he had last time—it was in plain view of the traffic on the West Side Highway. He would have to enter by way of a stern line this time. He looked longingly at the raised gangplank. If he had had the time he could have stopped at his apartment and picked up the variable frequency beeper he used for getting into garages with remote control door openers. He was sure the gangplank operated on a similar principle.

He found a heavy stern line and tested his tautness. He saw the name across the stern but couldn't read the lettering. The setting sun was warm against his skin. Everything seemed so normal and mundane out here. But in that ship . . .

He stilled the dread within and forced himself up the rope monkey-style as he had last night. As he pulled himself over the gunwale and onto the deck at the rear of the superstructure, he realized that the darkness of last night had hidden a multitude of sins. The boat was filthy. Rust grew where paint had thinned or peeled away; everything was either nicked or dented or both. And overlaying all was a thick coat of grease, grime, soot, and salt.

The rakoshi are below, Jack told himself as he entered the superstructure and began his search of the cabins. They're sealed in the cargo areas. I won't run into one up here. I won't.

He kept repeating it over and over, like a litany. It allowed him to concentrate on his search instead of constantly looking over his shoulder.

THE TOMB

He started at the bridge and worked his way downward. He found no sign of Kolabati in any of the officers' cabins. He was going through the crew's quarters on the main deck level when he heard a sound. He stopped. A voice—a woman's voice—calling a name from somewhere inside the wall. Hope began to grow in him as he followed that wall around to the main deck where he found a padlocked iron door.

The voice was coming from behind the door. Jack allowed himself a self-congratulatory grin. The voice was Kolabati's. He had found her.

He examined the door. The shackle of a laminated steel padlock had been passed through the swivel eye of a heavy-slotted hasp welded firmly to the steel of the door. Simple but very effective.

Jack dug out his pick kit and went to work on the lock.

10.

Kolabati had started calling Kusum's name when she heard the footsteps on the deck above her cabin; she stopped when she heard him rattle the lock on the outer door. She wasn't hungry or thirsty, she just wanted to see another human face—even Kusum's. The isolation of the pilot's cabin was getting to her.

She had spent all day wracking her brain for a way to appeal to her brother. But pleas would be of no avail. How could you plead with a man who thought he was salvaging your karma? How could you convince that man to alter a course of action he was pursuing for what he was certain was your own good?

She had even gone so far as to look for something she might conceivably use for a weapon but had discarded the notion. Even with one arm, Kusum was too quick, too strong, too agile for her. He had proved that beyond a doubt this morning. And in his unbalanced state of mind, a physical assault might drive him over the edge.

And still she worried for Jack. Kusum had said he was unharmed, but how could she be sure after all the lies he had already told her?

She heard the outer door open—Kusum seemed to have been fumbling with it—and footsteps approaching her cabin. A man stepped through the splinters of the door. He stood there smiling, staring at her sari.

"Where'd you get the funny dress?"

THE TOMB

"Jack!" She leaped into his arms, her joy bursting within her. "You're alive!"

"You're surprised?"

"I thought Kusum might have . . ."

"No. It was almost the other way around."

"I'm so glad you found me!" She clutched him, reassuring herself that he was really here. "Kusum is going to sail back to India tonight. Get me out of here!"

"My pleasure." He turned toward the shattered door and paused. "What happened to that?"

"Kusum kicked it out after I locked him in."

She saw Jack's eyebrows rise. "How many kicks?"

"One, I think." She wasn't sure.

Jack pursed his lips as if to whistle but made no sound. He began to speak but was interrupted by a loud clang from down the hall.

Kolabati went rigid. *No! Not Kusum! Not now!*

"The door!"

Jack was already out in the hall. She followed in time to see him slam his shoulder full force against the steel door.

Too late. It was locked.

Jack pounded once on the door with his fist, but said nothing.

Kolabati leaned against the door beside him. She wanted to scream with frustration. Almost free—and now locked up again!

"Kusum, let us out!" she cried in Bengali. "Can't you see this is useless?"

There was no reply. Only taunting silence on the other side. Yet she sensed her brother's presence.

"I thought you wanted to keep us apart!" she said in English, purposely goading him. "Instead you've locked us in here together with a bed and nothing but each other to fill the empty hours."

There followed a lengthy pause, and then an answer—also in English. The deadly precision in Kusum's voice chilled Kolabati.

"You will not be together long. There are crucial matters that require my presence at the Consulate now. The rakoshi will separate the two of you when I return."

He said no more. And although Kolabati had not heard his footsteps retreating across the deck, she was sure he had left them. She glanced at Jack. Her terror for him was a physical pain. It would be so easy for Kusum to bring a few rakoshi onto the deck, open this door and send them in after Jack.

279

Jack shook his head. "You've got a real way with words."

He seemed so calm. "Aren't you frightened?"

"Yeah. Very." He was feeling the walls, rubbing his fingers over the low ceiling.

"What are we going to do?

"Get out of here, I hope."

He strode back to the cabin and began to tear the bed apart. He threw the pillow, mattress and bedclothes on the floor, then pulled at the iron spring frame. It came free with a screech. He worked at the bolts that held the frame together; amid a constant stream of muttered curses he managed to loosen one of them. After that it took him only a moment to twist one of the L-formed iron sides off the frame.

"What are you going to do with that?"

"Find a way out."

He jabbed the six-foot iron bar against the cabin ceiling. Paint chips flew in accompaniment to the unmistakable sound of metal against metal. It was the same with the ceiling and the walls in the hall.

The floor, however, was made of heavily varnished, two-inch oak boards. He began to work the corner of the bar between two of them.

"We'll go through the floor," he said, grunting with the effort.

Kolabati recoiled at the thought.

"The rakoshi are down there!"

"If I don't meet them now, I'll have to meet them later. I'd rather meet them on my terms than on Kusum's." He looked at her. "You going to stand there or are you going to help?"

Kolabati added her weight to the bar. A board splintered and popped up.

11.

Jack tore at the floor boards with grim determination. It wasn't long before his shirt and his hair were soaked with perspiration. He removed the shirt and kept working. Breaking through the floor seemed a futile, almost suicidal gesture—like a man trying to escape from a burning plane by jumping into an active volcano. But he had to do something. Anything was better than sitting and waiting for Kusum to return

The rotten odor of rakoshi wafted up from below, engulfing him, making him gag. And the larger the hole in the flooring, the stronger the smell. Finally the opening was big enough to admit his shoulders.

THE TOMB

He stuck his head through for a look. Kolabati knelt beside him, peering over his shoulder.

It was dark down there. By the light of a solitary ceiling emergency lamp off to his right he could see a number of large insulated pipes to each side of the hole, running along just under the steel beams that supported the flooring. Directly below was a suspended walkway that led to an iron-runged ladder.

He was ready to cheer until he realized he was looking at the *upper* end of the ladder. It went *down* from there. Jack did not want to go down. Anywhere but down.

An idea struck him. He lifted his head and turned to Kolabati.

"Does that necklace really work?"

She started and her expression became guarded. "What do you mean, 'work'?"

"What you told me. Does it really make you invisible to the rakoshi?"

"Yes, of course. Why?"

Jack couldn't imagine how such a thing could be, but then he had never imagined that such a thing as a rakosh could be. He held out his hand.

"Give it to me."

"No!" she said, her hand darting to her throat as she jumped to her feet and stepped back.

"Just for a few minutes. I'll sneak below, find my way up to the deck, unlock the door and let you out."

She shook her head violently. "No, Jack!"

Why was she being so stubborn?

"Come on. You don't know how to pick a lock. I'm the only one who can get us both out of here."

He stood up and took a step toward her but she flattened herself against the wall and screamed.

"No! Don't touch it!"

Jack froze, confused by her response. Kolabati's eyes were wide with terror.

"What's *wrong* with you?"

"I can't take it off," she said in a calmer voice. "No one in the family is *ever* allowed to take it off."

"Oh, come—"

"I can't, Jack! Please don't ask me!" The terror was creeping back into her voice.

THE TOMB

"Okay-okay!" Jack said quickly, raising his hands, palms out, and stepping back. He didn't want any more screaming. It might attract a rakosh.

He walked over to the hole in the floor and stood there thinking. Kolabati's reaction baffled him. And what she had told him about no one in the family allowed to take the necklace off was untrue—he remembered seeing Kusum without it just last night. But it had been obvious then that Kusum had wanted to be seen by his rakoshi.

Then he remembered something else.

"The necklace will protect two of us, won't it?"

Kolabati's brow furrowed. "What do you—oh, I see. Yes, I think so. At least it did in your apartment."

"Then we'll both go down," he said, pointing to the hole.

"Jack, it's too dangerous! You can't be sure it will protect you!"

He realized that and tried not to think about it. He had no other options.

"I'll carry you on my back—piggyback. We won't be quite as close as we were in the apartment, but it's my only chance." As she hesitated, Jack played what he hoped was his ace: "Either you come down with me or I go alone with no protection at all. I'm not waiting here for your brother."

Kolabati stepped forward. "You can't go down there alone."

Without another word, she kicked off her sandals, hiked up her sari, and sat on the floor. She swung her legs into the hole and began to lower herself through.

"Hey!"

"I'll go first. I'm the one with the necklace, remember?"

Jack watched in amazement as her head disappeared below the level of the floor. Was this the same woman who had screamed in abject terror a moment ago? Going first through that hole took a lot of courage—with or without a "magic" necklace. It didn't make sense. Nothing seemed to make much sense anymore.

"All right," she said, popping her head back through. "It's clear."

He followed her into the darkness below. When he felt his feet touch the suspended walkway, he eased himself into a tense crouch.

They were at the top of a high, narrow, tenebrous corridor. Through the slats of the walkway Jack could see the floor a good twenty feet below. Abruptly, he realized where he was: This was the same corridor he had followed to the aft cargo hold last night.

Kolabati leaned toward him and whispered. Her breath tickled his ear.

"It's good you're wearing sneakers. We must be quiet. The necklace clouds their vision but does not block their hearing." She glanced around. "Which way do we go?"

Jack pointed to the ladder barely visible against the wall at the end of the walkway. Together they crawled toward it. Kolabati led the way down.

Halfway to the floor she paused and he stopped above her. Together they scanned the floor of the corridor for any shape, any shadow, any movement that might indicate the presence of a rakosh. All clear. He found scant relief in that. The rakoshi could not be far away.

As they descended the rest of the way, the rakoshi stench grew ever stronger. Jack felt his palms grow slick with sweat and begin to slip as they clung to the iron rungs of the ladder. He had come through this same corridor in a state of ignorance last night, blithely unaware of what waited in the cargo hold at its end. Now he knew, and with every step closer to the floor his heart increased its pounding rhythm.

Kolabati stepped off the ladder and waited for Jack. During his descent he had been orienting himself as to his position in the ship. He had determined that the ladder lay against the starboard wall of the corridor, which meant that the cargo hold and the rakoshi were forward to his left. As soon as his feet hit the floor he grabbed her arm and pulled her in the opposite direction. Safety lay toward the stern . . .

Yet a knot of despair began to coil in his chest as he neared the watertight hatch through which he had entered and exited the corridor. He had secured that hatch behind him last night. He was sure of it. But perhaps Kusum had used it since. Perhaps he had left it unlocked. He ran the last dozen feet to the hatch and fairly leaped upon the handle.

It wouldn't budge. Locked!

Damn!

Jack wanted to shout, to pound his fists against the hatch. But that would be suicide. So he pressed his forehead against the cold, unyielding steel and began a slow mental count from one. By the time he reached six he had calmed himself. He turned to Kolabati and drew her head close to his.

"We've got to go the other way," he whispered.

THE TOMB

Her eyes followed his pointing finger, then turned back to him. She nodded.

"The rakoshi are there," he said.

Again she nodded.

Kolabati was a pale blur beside him as Jack stood there in the dark and strained for another solution. He could not find one. A dim rectangle of light beckoned from the other end of the corridor where it opened into the main hold. They had to go through the hold. He was willing to try almost any other route but that one. But it was either back up the ladder to the dead end of the pilot's cabin or straight ahead.

He lifted Kolabati, cradling her in his arms, and began to carry her toward the hold, praying that whatever power her necklace had over the rakoshi would be conducted to him as well. Halfway down the corridor he realized that his hands were entirely useless this way. He put Kolabati back on her feet and took two of the Cricket lighters from his pockets, then motioned to her to hop on his back. She gave him a small, tight, grim smile and did as directed. With an arm hooked behind each of her knees, he carried her piggyback style, leaving his hands free to clutch a Cricket in each. They seemed ridiculously inadequate, but he derived an odd sort of comfort from the feel of them in his palms.

He came to the end of the corridor and stopped. Ahead and to their right, the hold opened before them. It was brighter than the passageway behind them, but not by much; darker than Jack remembered from last night. But Kusum had been on the elevator then with his two gas torches roaring full force.

There were other differences. Details were scarce and nubilous in the murky light, but Jack could see that the rakoshi were no longer clustered around the elevator. Instead, some forty or fifty of them were spread throughout the hold, some crouched in the deepest shadows, others slumped against the walls in somber poses, still others in constant motion, walking, turning, stalking. The air was hazed with humidity and with the stink of them. The glistening black walls rose and disappeared into the darkness above. The high wall lamps gave off meager, dreary light, such as a gibbous moon might provide on a foggy night. Movements were slow and languorous. It was like looking in on a huge, candle-lit opium den in a forgotten corner of hell.

A rakosh began to walk toward where they stood at the mouth of the corridor. Though the temperature was much cooler down here than it had been up in the pilot's cabin, Jack felt his body break out from head to toe in a drenching sweat. Kolabati's arms tightened around his neck and her body tensed against his back. The rakosh looked directly at Jack but gave no sign that it saw him or Kolabati. It veered off aimlessly in another direction.

It worked! The necklace worked! The rakosh had looked right at them and hadn't seen either of them!

Directly across from them, in the forward port corner of the hold, Jack saw an opening identical to the one in which they stood. He assumed it led to the forward hold. A steady stream of rakoshi of varying sizes wandered in and out of the passage.

"There's something wrong with these rakoshi," Kolabati whispered over his shoulder and into his ear. "They're so lazy-looking. So lethargic."

You should have seen them last night, Jack wanted to say, remembering how Kusum had whipped them into a frenzy.

"And they're smaller than they should be," she said. "Paler, too."

At seven feet tall and the color of night, the rakoshi were already bigger and darker than Jack wanted them.

An explosion of hissing, scuffling, and scraping drew their attention to the right. Two rakoshi circled each other, baring their fangs, raking the air with their talons. Others gathered around, joining in the hissing. It looked as if a fight had begun.

Suddenly one of Kolabati's arms tightened on his throat in a stranglehold as she pointed across the hold with the other.

"There!" she whispered. "There's a *true* rakosh!"

Even though he knew he was invisible to the rakosh, Jack took an involuntary step backward. This one was huge, fully a foot taller and darker than the rest, moving with greater ease, greater determination.

"It's a female," Kolabati said. "That must be the one that hatched from our egg! The mother rakosh! Control her and you control the nest!"

She seemed almost as awed and excited as she was terrified. Jack guessed it was part of her heritage. Hadn't she been raised to be what she called a "Keeper of the Rakoshi"?

Jack looked again at the Mother. He found it hard to call her a female—there was nothing feminine about her, not even breasts—which probably meant that rakoshi did not suckle their young. She looked like a huge body-builder whose arms, legs, and torso had been stretched to grotesque lengths. There was not an ounce of fat on her; each cord of her musculature could be seen rippling under her inky skin. Her face was the most alien, however, as if someone had taken a shark's head, shortened the snout and moved the eyes slightly forward, leaving the fanged slash of a mouth almost unchanged. But the cold, remote gaze of the shark had been replaced by a soft pale glow of pure malevolence.

She even moved like a shark, gracefully, sinuously. The other rakoshi made way for the Mother, parting before her like mackerel before a great white. She headed directly for the two fighters, and when she reached them, tore them apart and hurled them aside as if they weighed nothing. Her children accepted the rough treatment meekly.

He watched the Mother make a circuit of the chamber and return to the passage leading to the forward hold.

How do we get out of here?

Jack looked up toward the ceiling of the hold—actually the underside of the hatch cover, invisible in the dark. He had to get up there, to the deck. How?

He poked his head into the hold and scanned the slick walls for a ladder. There was none. But there, at the top of the starboard aft corner of the hold—the elevator! If he could bring that down . . .

But to do that he would have to enter the hold and cross its width.

The thought was paralyzing. To walk among them . . .

Every minute he delayed in getting off this ship increased his danger, yet a primal revulsion held him back. Something within him preferred to crouch here and wait for death rather than venture into the hold.

He fought against it, not with reason but with anger. *He* was in charge here, not some mindless loathing. Jack finally mastered himself, although with greater effort than he could ever remember.

"Hold on!" he whispered to Kolabati. Then he stepped out of the corridor and into the hold.

He moved slowly, with the utmost care and caution. Most of the rakoshi were caliginous lumps scattered over the floor. He had to step over some of the sleeping ones and wind his way between the alert ones. Although his sneakered feet made no sound, occasionally a head would lift and look around as they passed. Jack could barely make out the details of their faces and would not know a puzzled rakoshi expression if he saw one, but they had to be confused. They sensed a presence yet their eyes told them nothing was there.

He could sense their pure, naked aggression, their immaculate evil. There was no pretense about their savagery—it was all on the surface, surrounding them like an aura.

Jack still felt his heart trip and fumble a beat every time one of the creatures looked his way with its yellow eyes. His mind still resisted complete acceptance of the fact that he was invisible to them.

The reek of the things thickened to a nauseating level as he wound his way across the floor. They must have looked a comical pair, tiptoeing piggyback through the dark. Laughable unless it was remembered how precarious their position was: one wrong move and they would be torn to shreds.

If negotiating a path through the recumbent rakoshi was harrowing, dodging the wandering ones was utterly nerve-wracking. Jack had little or no warning as to when they would appear. They would loom out of the shadows and pass within inches, some pausing, some even stopping to look around, sensing humans but not seeing them.

He was three-quarters of the way across the floor of the hold when a seven-foot shadow suddenly rose from the floor and stepped toward him. Jack had nowhere to go. Dark forms reclined on either side and the space where he stood between them would not allow a rakoshi to pass. Instinctively he jerked back—and began to lose his balance. Kolabati must have sensed this for she pressed her weight rigidly against his spine.

In a desperate move to keep from toppling over, Jack lifted his left leg and pivoted on his right foot. He swiveled in a semicircle to wind up facing the way he had come, straddling a sleeping rakosh. As it shuffled past, the creature brushed Jack's arm.

With a sound somewhere between a growl and a hiss, the rakosh whirled with raised talons, baring its fangs. Jack didn't think he had ever seen anything move so fast. He clenched his jaw, not daring to move or breathe. The creature asleep between and beneath his legs stirred. He prayed it would not awaken. He could feel a scream building within Kolabati; he tightened his grip around her legs—silent encouragement to hold on.

The rakosh facing him rotated its head back and forth quickly, warily at first, then more slowly. Soon it calmed itself and lowered its talons. Finally it moved off, but not without a long, searching look over its shoulder in their direction.

Jack allowed himself to breathe again. He swung back into the

THE TOMB

path of clear floor between the rakoshi and continued the endless trek toward the starboard wall of the hold. As he neared the aft corner, he spotted an electrical conduit leading upward from a small box on the wall. He headed for that, and smiled to himself when he saw the three buttons on the box.

The shallow well directly under the elevator was clear of rakoshi. Perhaps they had learned during the time they had been here that this was not a good place to rest—sleep too deeply and too long and you might be crushed.

Jack didn't hesitate. As soon as he was close enough, he reached out and jabbed the Down button.

There came a loud clank—almost deafening as it echoed through the gloomy, enclosed hold—followed by a high-pitched hum. The rakoshi—all of them—were instantly alert and on their feet, their glowing yellow eyes fixed as one on the descending platform.

Movement at the far side of the hold caught Jack's eye: the Mother rakosh was heading their way. All the rakoshi began to shuffle forward to stand in a rough semicircle less than a dozen feet from where Jack stood with Kolabati on his back. He had backed up as far as he could without actually stepping into the foot-deep elevator well.

The Mother pushed her way to the front and stood there with the rest, eyes upward. When the descending platform reached the level of ten feet or so from the floor, the rakoshi began a low chant, barely audible above the steadily growing whine of the elevator.

"They're speaking!" Kolabati whispered in his ear. "Rakoshi can't speak!"

With all the other noise around them, Jack felt it safe to turn his head and answer her.

"You should have seen it last night—like a political rally. They were all shouting something like, *Kaka-ji! Kaka-ji!* It was—"

Kolabati's fingernails dug into his shoulders like claws, her voice rising in pitch and volume that he feared would alert the rakoshi.

"What? What did you say?"

"*Kaka-ji.* They were saying, '*Kaka-ji*'. What's—?"

Kolabati let out a small cry that sounded like a word, but not an English word. And suddenly the chant stopped.

The rakoshi had heard her.

THE TOMB

12.

Kusum stood at the curb with his arm outstretched. All the taxis on Fifth Avenue seemed to be taken tonight. He tapped his foot impatiently. He wanted to get back to the ship. Night was here and there was work to be done. There was work to be done at the Consulate, too, but he had found it impossible to stay there a minute longer, emergency meeting or no. He had excused himself amid frowns from the senior diplomats, but he could afford their displeasure now. After tonight he would no longer need the shield of diplomatic immunity. The last Westphalen would be dead and he would be at sea, on his way back to India with his rakoshi to take up where he had left off.

There was still the matter of Jack to contend with. He had already decided how to deal with him. He would allow Jack to swim ashore later tonight after he had put to sea. Killing him would serve no purpose at that point.

He still had not figured out how Jack had found the ship. That question had nagged him for hours, distracting him throughout the meeting at the Consulate. No doubt Kolabati had told him about it, but he wanted to know for sure.

An empty taxi finally pulled up before him. Kusum swung into the back seat.

"Where to, Mac?"

"West on Fifty-seventh Street. I will tell you when to stop."

"Gotcha."

He was on his way. Soon the Mother and a youngling would be on *their* way to bring him the last Westphalen, and then he would be rid of this land. His followers awaited. A new era was about to dawn for India.

13.

Jack froze as the creatures began milling around, searching for the source of the cry. Behind him he could feel Kolabati's body bucking gently against him as if she were sobbing soundlessly into the nape of his neck.

What had he said to shock her so? It had to be *Kaka-ji*. What did it mean?

The top of the elevator's wooden platform had descended to chest level by now. With his left arm still hooked around one of Kolabati's

289

knees, Jack freed his right and hauled himself and his burden onto the platform. He struggled to his knees and staggered to the control panel next to one of the propane torches, punching the Up button as soon as he reached it.

With an abrupt lurch and a metallic screech, the elevator reversed direction. The attention of all the rakoshi was once again focused on the elevator. With Kolabati still clinging to him, Jack sagged to his knees at the edge of the platform and stared back at them.

When they were a dozen feet off the floor, he let go of Kolabati's legs. Without a word she released her grip on his neck and slid away toward the inner corner of the platform. As soon as she broke contact with him, a chorus of enraged growls and hisses broke from the floor. The rakoshi could see him now.

They surged forward like a Stygian wave, slashing the air with their talons. Jack watched them in mute fascination, stunned by the intensity of their fury. Suddenly three of them lunged into the air, long arms stretched to the limit, talons extended. Jack's first impulse was to laugh at the futility of the attempt—the platform was easily fifteen feet from the floor now. But as the rakoshi hurtled up at him, he realized to his horror that they weren't going to fall short. He rolled back and sprang to his feet as their talons caught the edge of the platform. Their strength had to be enormous!

The rakosh in the middle fell short of the other two. Its yellow talons had hooked into the very edge of the platform; the ends of the wooden planks cracked and splintered under its weight. As jagged pieces broke loose, the middle rakosh dropped back to the floor.

The other two had a better grip and were pulling themselves up onto the platform. Jack leaped to his left where the rakosh was raising its face above the level of the platform. He saw gnashing fangs, a snouted, earless head. Loathing surged up in him as he aimed a flying kick at its face. The impact of the blow vibrated up his leg. Yet the creature hadn't even flinched. It was like kicking a brick wall!

Then he remembered the lighters in his hands. He thumbed the flame regulator on each to maximum and flicked the switches. As two thin wavering pencils of flame shot up, he shoved both lighters at the rakosh's face, aiming for the eyes. It hissed in rage and jerked its head back. The sudden movement caused a backward shift in its center of gravity. Its talons raked inch-deep gouges in the wood but to no avail. It was over-balanced. Like the first rakosh, its weight caused the wood to crack and give way. It toppled back to the shadows below.

THE TOMB

Jack swung toward the last rakosh and saw that it had pulled its body waist-high to the platform, just then lifting a knee over the edge. It was almost up! He leaped toward it with his lighters outstretched. Without warning, the rakosh leaned forward and slashed at him with extended talons that brushed Jack's right hand. He had under-estimated both the length of the creature's arm and its agility. Pain lanced up his arm from his palm as the Cricket went flying and Jack fell back out of reach.

The rakosh had slipped back after its attempt at Jack, almost losing its grip entirely. It had to use both hands to keep itself from falling off, but it held on and began to pull itself up to the platform again.

Jack's mind raced. The rakosh would be up on the platform in a second or two. The elevator had been rising continuously but would never make it to the top in time. He could rush back to where Kolabati crouched in a daze by the propane tank and take her in his arms. The necklace would hide him from the rakosh, but the elevator platform was too small to keep it from finding them eventually—sooner or later it would bump into them and that would be the end.

He was trapped.

Desperately, his eyes ranged the platform looking for a weapon. They came to rest on the propane torches Kusum used for his foul ceremony with the rakoshi. He remembered how the flames had roared six feet into the air last night. There was a fire to reckon with!

The rakosh had both knees up on the platform now.

"Turn on the gas!" he shouted to Kolabati.

She looked at him blank-eyed. She seemed to be in a state of shock.

"The gas!" He flung his second Cricket lighter at her, striking her in the shoulder. "Turn it on!"

Kolabati shook herself and reached slowly for the handle atop the tank. *Come on!* He wanted to scream at her. He turned to the torch. It was a hollow metal cylinder, six inches across, supported by four slender metal legs. As he wrapped an arm around it and tilted it toward the oncoming rakosh, he heard the propane rushing through the gas port at the lower end of the cylinder, filling it, smelled the gas seeping into the air around him.

The rakosh had reared up to its full height and was leaping toward him, seven feet of bared fangs, outstretched arms, and fully-extended talons. Jack almost quailed at the sight. His third Cricket was slippery with blood from the gash on his palm, but he found the touch hole at

291

the base of the torch, flicked the lighter and jammed it in.

The gas exploded with a near deafening roar, shooting a devastating column of flame directly into the face of the oncoming rakosh.

The creature reeled back, its arms outflung, its head ablaze. It spun, lurched crazily to the edge of the platform, and fell off.

"Yes!" Jack shouted, raising his fists in the air, exultant and amazed at his victory. "Yes!"

Down below he saw the Mother rakosh, darker, taller than her young, staring upward, her cold yellow eyes never leaving him as he rose farther and farther from the floor. The intensity of the hatred in those eyes made him turn away.

He coughed as smoke began to fill the air around him. He looked down and saw the wood of the platform blackening and catching fire where the flame of the fallen torch seared it. He quickly stepped over to the propane tank and shut off the flow. Kolabati crouched next to the tank, her expression still dazed.

The elevator came to an automatic halt at the top of its run. The hold hatch-cover sat six feet above them. Jack guided Kolabati over to the ladder that led up to a small trap door in the cover. He went up first, half expecting it to be locked. Why not? Every other escape route was blocked. Why should this one be any different? He pushed, wincing with pain as his bloody right palm slipped on the wood. But the door moved up, letting in a puff of fresh air. Momentarily weak with relief, Jack rested his head on his arm.

Made it!

Then he threw open the trap door, and thrust his head through.

It was dark. The sun had set, stars were out, the moon was rising. The humid air and the normal stink of Manhattan's waterfront was like ambrosia after being in the hold with the rakoshi.

He looked across the deck. Nothing moved. The gangway was up. There was no sign that Kusum had returned.

Jack turned and looked down at Kolabati. "It's clear. Let's go."

He pulled himself up onto the deck and turned to help her out. But she was still standing on the elevator platform.

"Kolabati!" He yelled her name and she jumped, looked at him, and started up the ladder.

When they were both on deck, he led her by the hand to the gangway.

"Kusum operates it electronically," she told him.

He searched the top of the gangway with his hands until he found the motor, then followed the wires back to a small control box. On the undersurface of that he found a button.

"This should do it."

He pressed: A click, a hum, and the gangway began its slow descent. Too slow. An overwhelming sense of urgency possessed him. He had to be off this ship!

He didn't wait for the gangway to reach the dock. As soon as it passed the three-quarter mark in its descent he was on the treads, heading down, pulling Kolabati behind him. They jumped the last three feet and began to run. Some of his urgency must have transferred to her—she was running right beside him.

They stayed away from Fifty-seventh street on the chance that they might run into Kusum coming back to the docks. Instead they ran up Fifty-eighth. Three taxis passed them by despite Jack's shouts. Perhaps the cabbies didn't want to get involved with two haggard-looking people—a shirtless man with a bloody right hand and a woman in a rumpled sari—looking as if they were running for their lives. Jack couldn't say he blamed them. But he wanted to get off the street. He felt vulnerable out here.

A fourth taxi stopped and Jack leaped in, dragging Kolabati after him. He gave the address of his apartment. The driver wrinkled his nose at the stench that clung to him and floored his gas peddle. He seemed to want to be rid of this fare as soon as possible.

During the ride Kolabati sat in a corner of the back seat and stared out the window. Jack had a thousand questions he wanted to ask her but restrained himself. She wouldn't answer him in the presence of the cab driver and he wasn't sure he wanted her to. But as soon as they were in the apartment ...

14.

The gangway was down.

Kusum froze on the dock when he saw it. It was no illusion. Moonlight glinted icy blue from its aluminum steps and railings.

How? He could not imagine—

He broke into a run, taking the steps two at a time and sprinting across the deck to the door to the pilot's quarters. The lock was still in place. He pulled on it—still intact and locked.

He leaned against the door and waited for his pounding heart to slow. For a moment he had thought someone had come aboard and released Jack and Kolabati.

THE TOMB

He tapped on the steel door with the key to the lock.

"Bati? Come to the door. I wish to speak to you."

Silence.

"Bati?"

Kusum pressed an ear to the door. He sensed more than silence on the other side. There was an indefinable feeling of emptiness there. Alarmed, he jammed the key into the padlock—

—and hesitated.

He was dealing with Repairman Jack here and was wary of underestimating him. Jack was probably armed and unquestionably dangerous. He might well be waiting in there with a drawn pistol ready to blast a hole in whoever opened the door.

But it *felt* empty. Kusum decided to trust his senses. He twisted the key, removed the padlock, and pulled the door open.

The hallway was empty. He glanced into the pilot's cabin—empty! But how—?

And then he saw the hole in the floor. For an instant he thought a rakosh had broken through into the compartment, then he saw part of the iron bed frame on the floor and understood.

The audacity of that man! He had escaped into the heart of the rakoshi quarters—and had taken Kolabati with him! He smiled to himself. They were probably still down there somewhere, cowering on a catwalk. Bati's necklace would protect her. But Jack might well have fallen victim to a rakosh by now.

Then he remembered the lowered gangplank. Cursing in his native tongue, he hurried from the pilot's quarters to the hatch over the main hold. He lifted the entry port and peered below.

The rakoshi were agitated. Through the murky light he could see their dark forms mixing and moving about chaotically on the floor of the hold. Half a dozen feet below him was the elevator platform. Immediately he noticed the torch on its side, the scorched wood. He leaped through the trap door to the elevator and started it down.

Something lay on the floor of the hold. When he had descended halfway to the floor, he saw that it was a dead rakosh. Rage suffused Kusum. *Dead!* Its head—what was left of it—was a mass of charred flesh!

With a trembling hand, Kusum reversed the elevator.

That man! That thrice-cursed American! How had he done it? If only the rakoshi could speak! Not only had Jack escaped with Kolabati, he had killed a rakosh in the process! Kusum felt as if he had lost a part of himself.

As soon as the elevator reached the top, Kusum scrambled onto the deck and rushed back to the pilot's quarters. Something he had seen on the floor there . . .

Yes! Here it was, near the hole in the floor, a shirt—the shirt Jack had been wearing when Kusum had last seen him. Kusum picked it up. It was still damp with sweat.

He had planned to let Jack live, but all that was changed now. Kusum had known Jack was resourceful, but had never dreamed him capable of escaping through the midst of a nest of rakoshi. The man had gone too far tonight. And he was too dangerous to be allowed to roam free with what he now knew.

Jack would have to die.

He could not deny a trace of regret in the decision, yet Kusum was sure Jack had good karma and would shortly be reincarnated into a life of quality.

A slow smile stretched Kusum's thin lips as he hefted the sweaty shirt in his hand. The Mother rakosh would do it, and Kusum already had a plan for her. The irony of it was delicious.

15.

"I have to wash up," Jack said, indicating his injured hand as they entered his apartment. "Come into the bathroom with me."

Kolabati looked at him blankly. "What?"

"Follow me." Wordlessly, she complied.

As he began to wash the dirt and clotted blood from the gash, he watched her in the mirror over the sink. Her face was pale and haggard in the merciless light of the bathroom. His own looked ghoulish.

"Why would Kusum want to send his rakoshi after a little girl?"

She seemed to come out of her fugue. Her eyes cleared. "A little girl?"

"Seven years old."

Her hand covered her mouth. "Is she a Westphalen?" she said between her fingers.

Jack stood numb and cold in the epiphany that burst upon him.

That's it! My God, that's the link! Nellie, Grace, and Vicky—all Westphalens!

"Yes." He turned to face her. "The last Westphalen in America, I

295

believe. But why the Westphalens?"

Kolabati leaned against the wall beside the sink and spoke to the opposite wall. She spoke slowly, carefully, as if measuring every word.

"About a century and a quarter ago, Captain Sir Albert Westphalen pillaged a temple in the hills of northern Bengal—the temple I told you about last night. He murdered the high priest and priestess along with all their acolytes, and burned the temple to the ground. The jewels he stole became the basis of the Westphalen fortune.

"Before she died the priestess laid a curse upon Captain Westphalen, saying that his line would end in blood and pain at the hands of the rakoshi. The captain thought he had killed everyone in the temple but he was wrong. A child escaped the fire. The eldest son was mortally wounded, but before he died he made his younger brother vow to see that their mother's curse was carried out. A single female rakosh egg—you saw the shell in Kusum's apartment—was found in the caves beneath the ruins of the temple. That egg and the vow of vengeance have been handed down from generation to generation. It became a family ceremony. No one took it seriously—until Kusum."

Jack stared at Kolabati in disbelief. She was telling him that Grace and Nellie's deaths and Vicky's danger were all the result of a family curse begun in India over a century ago. She was not looking at him. Was she telling the truth? Why not? It was far less fantastic than much of what had happened to him today.

"You've got to save that little girl," Kolabati said, finally looking up and meeting his eyes.

"I already have." He dried his hand and began rubbing some Neosporin ointment from the medicine cabinet into the wound. "Neither your brother nor his monsters will find her tonight. And by tomorrow he'll be gone."

"What makes you think that?"

"You told me so an hour ago."

She shook her head, very slowly, very definitely. "Oh, no. He may leave without me, but he will never leave without that little Westphalen girl. And ..." she paused ... "you've earned his undying enmity by freeing me from his ship."

" 'Undying enmity' is a bit much, isn't it?"

"Not where Kusum is concerned."

THE TOMB

"What is it with your brother?" Jack placed a couple of four-by-four gauze pads in his palm and began to wrap it with cling. "I mean, didn't any of the previous generations try to kill off the Westphalens?"

Kolabati shook her head.

"What made Kusum decide to take it all so seriously?"

"Kusum has problems—"

"You're telling me!" He secured the cling with an inch of adhesive tape.

"You don't understand. He took a vow of *Brahmacharya*—a vow of lifelong chastity—when he was twenty. He held to that vow and remained a steadfast *Brahmachari* for many years." Her gaze wavered and wandered back to the wall. "But then he broke that vow. To this day he's never forgiven himself. I told you the other night about his growing following of Hindu purists in India. Kusum doesn't feel he has a right to be their leader until he has purified his karma. Everything he has done here in New York has been to atone for desecrating his vow of *Brahmacharya*."

Jack hurled the roll of adhesive tape against the wall. He was suddenly furious.

"That's *it?*" he shouted. "Kusum has killed Nellie and Grace and who knows how many winos, all because he got laid? Give me a *break!*"

"It's true!"

"There's got to be more to it than that!"

Kolabati still wasn't looking at him. "You've got to understand Kusum—"

"No, I don't! All I have to understand is that he's trying to kill a little girl I happen to love very much. Kusum's got a problem all right: *me!*"

"He's trying to cleanse his karma."

"Don't tell me about karma. I heard enough about karma from your brother last night. He's a mad dog!"

Kolabati turned on him, her eyes flashing. "Don't say that!"

"Can you honestly deny it?"

"No! But don't say that about him! Only I can say it!"

Jack could understand that. He nodded. "Okay. I'll just think it."

She started to turn around to leave the bathroom but Jack gently pulled her back. He wanted very badly to get to the phone to call Gia and check on Vicky, but he needed the answer to one more question.

"What happened to you in the hold? What did I say back there to

297

shock you so?"

Kolabati's shoulders slumped, her head tilted to the side. Silent sobs caused small quakes at first but soon grew strong enough to wrack her whole body. She closed her eyes and began to cry.

Jack was startled at first. He had never imagined the possibility of seeing Kolabati reduced to tears. She had always seemed so self-possessed, so worldly. Yet here she was standing before him and crying like a child. Her anguish touched him. He took her in his arms.

"Tell me about it. Talk it out."

She cried for a while longer, then she began to talk, keeping her face buried against his shoulder as she spoke.

"Remember how I said these rakoshi were smaller and paler than they should be? And how shocked I was that they could speak?"

Jack nodded against her hair. "Yes."

"Now I understand why. Kusum lied to me again! And again I believed him. But this is so much worse than a lie. I never thought even Kusum would go *that* far!"

"What are you talking about?"

"Kusum lied about finding a male egg!" An hysterical edge was creeping onto her voice.

Jack pushed her to arm's length. Her face was tortured. He wanted to shake her but didn't.

"Talk sense!"

"*Kaka-ji* is Bengali for 'father'!"

"So?"

Kolabati only stared at him.

"Oh, jeez!" Jack leaned back against the sink, his mind reeling with the idea of Kusum impregnating the Mother rakosh. Visions of the act half-formed in his brain and then quickly faded to merciful black.

"How could your brother have fathered those rakoshi? *Kaka-ji* has to be a title of respect or something like that."

Kolabati shook her head slowly, sadly. She appeared emotionally and physically drained.

"No. It's true. The changes in the younglings are evidence enough."

"But how?"

"Probably when she was very young and docile. He needed only one brood from her. From there on the rakoshi would mate with each other and bring the nest to full size."

"I can't believe it. Why would he even try?"

THE TOMB

"Kusum . . ." her voice faltered, "Kusum sometimes thinks Kali speaks to him in dreams. He may believe she told him to mate with the female. There are many dark tales of rakoshi mating with humans."

"Tales! I'm not talking about tales! This is real life! I don't know much about biology but I know cross-species fertilization is impossible!"

"But the rakoshi aren't a different species, Jack. As I told you last night, legend has it that the ancient evil gods—the Old Ones—created the rakoshi as obscene parodies of humanity. They took a man and a woman and reshaped them in their image—into rakoshi. That means that somewhere far, far up the line there's a common genetic ancestor between human and rakosh." She gripped Jack's arms. "You've got to stop him, Jack!"

"I could have stopped him last night," he said, remembering how he had sighted down the barrel of the .357 at the space between Kusum's eyes. "Could have killed him."

"It's not necessary to kill him to stop him."

"I don't see any other way."

"There is: his necklace. Take it from him and he will lose his hold on the rakoshi."

Jack smiled ruefully. "Sort of like the mice deciding to bell the cat, isn't it?"

"No. You can do it. You are his equal . . . in more ways than you know."

"What's that supposed to mean?"

"Why didn't you shoot Kusum when you had the chance?"

"Worried about you I guess, and . . . I don't know . . . couldn't pull the trigger." Jack had wondered about the answer to that question, too.

Kolabati came close and leaned against his chest. "That's because Kusum's like you and you're like him."

Resentment flared like a torch. He pushed her away. "That's crazy!"

"Not really," she said, her smile seductive. "You're carved from the same stone. Kusum is you—gone mad."

Jack didn't want to hear that. The idea repulsed him . . . frightened him. He changed the subject.

"If he comes tonight, will it be alone or will he bring some rakoshi?"

"It depends," she said, moving closer again. "If he wants to take

299

me with him, he'll come in person since a rakosh will never find me. If he only wants to even the score with you for making a fool of him by stealing me away from under his nose, he'll send the Mother rakosh."

Jack swallowed, his throat going dry at the memory of the size of her.

"Swell."

She kissed him. "But that won't be for a while. I'm going to shower. Why don't you come in with me? We both need one."

"You go ahead," he said, gently releasing himself from her. He did not meet her gaze. "Someone has to stay on guard. I'll shower after you."

She studied him a moment with her dark eyes, then turned and walked toward the bathroom. Jack watched her until the door closed behind her, then let out a long sigh. He felt no desire for her tonight. Was it because of Sunday night with Gia? It had been different when Gia was rejecting him. But now . . .

He was going to have to cool it with Kolabati. No more rolls in her *Kama Sutra*-hay. But he had to tread softly here. He did not wish to weather the wrath of a scorned Indian woman.

He went to the secretary and removed the silenced Ruger with the hollow-point bullets; he also took out a snub-nosed Smith & Wesson .38 Chief Special and loaded it. Then he sat down to wait for Kolabati to come out of the shower.

16.

Kolabati blotted herself dry, wrapped the towel around her, and came out into the hall. She found Jack sitting on the bed—just where she wanted him. Desire surged up at the sight of him.

She needed a man right now, someone to lie beside her, to help her lose herself in sensation and wash away all thought. And of all the men she knew, she needed Jack the most. He had pulled her from Kusum's clutches, something no man she had ever known could have done. She wanted Jack very much right now.

She dropped the towel and fell onto the bed beside him.

"Come," she said, caressing his inner thigh. "Lie down with me. We'll find a way to forget what we've been through tonight."

"We can't forget," he said, pulling away. "Not if he's coming after us."

"We have time, I'm sure." She wanted him so. "Come."

THE TOMB

Jack held his hand out to her. She thought it was an invitation to pull him down and she reached up. But his hand was not empty.

"Take it," he said, placing something cold and heavy in her palm.

"A gun?" The sight of it jolted her. She had never held one before ... so heavy. The dark blue of its finish glinted in the subdued light of the bedroom. "What for? This won't stop a rakosh."

"Maybe not. I've yet to be convinced of that. But I'm not giving it to you for protection against rakoshi."

Kolabati pulled her eyes away from the weapon in her hand to look at him. "Then what? . . ." His grim expression provided a chilling answer to her question. "Oh, Jack. I don't know if I could."

"You don't have to worry about it now. It may never come to that. On the other hand it may come down to a choice between being dragged off to that ship again and shooting your brother. It's a decision you'll have to make at the time."

She looked back at the gun, hating it and yet fascinated by it—much the same as she had felt when Kusum had given her that first look into the ship's hold last night.

"But I've never ..."

"It's double-action: You've got to cock it before you can fire." He showed her how. "You've got five shots."

He began to undress and Kolabati put the gun aside as she watched him, thinking he was about to join her on the bed. Instead he went to the bureau. When he turned to face her again he had fresh underwear in one hand and in the other a long-barreled pistol that dwarfed hers.

"I'm taking a shower," he said. "Stay alert and use that"—he gestured to her pistol on the night stand—"if you have to. Don't start thinking of ways to get your brother's necklace. Shoot first, then worry about the necklace."

He stepped out into the hall and soon she heard the shower running.

Kolabati laid back and pulled the sheet over her. She moved her legs around, spreading and closing them, enjoying the touch of the sheets on her skin. She needed Jack very much tonight. But he seemed so distant, immune to her nakedness.

There was another woman. Kolabati had sensed her presence in Jack the very first night they met. Was it the attractive blonde she had seen him talking to at the U.K. reception? It had not concerned her then because the influence had been so weak. Now it was strong.

301

THE TOMB

No matter. She knew how to have her way with a man, knew ways to make him forget the other women in his life. She would make Jack want her and only her. She had to, for Jack was important to her. She wanted him beside her always.

Always ...

She fingered her necklace.

She thought of Kusum and looked at the pistol on the night stand. Could she shoot her brother if he came in now?

Yes. Most definitely, yes. Twenty-four hours ago her answer would have been different. Now ... the loathing crawled up from her stomach to her throat ... *"Kaka-ji!"* ... the rakoshi called her brother *"Kaka-ji!"* Yes, she could pull the trigger. Knowing the level of depravity to which he had sunk, knowing that his sanity was irredeemable, killing Kusum could almost be looked on as an act of compassion, done to save him from any further acts of depravity and self-degradation.

More than anything she wanted his necklace. Possessing it would end his threat to her forever—and allow her to clasp it about the throat of the only man worthy to spend the rest of his days with her—Jack.

She closed her eyes and nestled her head deeper into the pillow. After only a few minutes of fitful slumber on that wafer-thin mattress in the pilot's cabin last night, she was tired. She'd just close her eyes for a few minutes until Jack came out of the shower, then she would make him hers again. He'd soon forget the other woman on his mind.

17.

Jack lathered himself vigorously in the shower, scrubbing his skin to cleanse it of the stink of the hold. His .357 was wrapped in a towel on a shelf within easy reach of the shower. His eyes repeatedly wandered to the outline of the door, hazily visible through the light blue translucency of the shower curtain. His mind's eye kept replaying a variation on the shower scene from *Psycho*. Only here it wasn't Norman Bates in drag coming in and slashing away with a knife—it was the Mother rakosh using the built-in knives of her taloned hands.

He rinsed quickly and stepped out to towel off.

Everything was okay in Queens. A call to Gia while Kolabati was in the shower had confirmed that Vicky was safe and sound asleep.

THE TOMB

Now he could get on with business here.

Back in the bedroom he found Kolabati sound asleep. He grabbed some fresh clothes and studied her sleeping face as he got dressed. She looked different in repose. The sensuousness was gone, replaced by a touching innocence.

Jack pulled the sheet up over her shoulder. He liked her. She was lively, she was fun, she was exotic. Her sexual skills and appetite were unparalleled in his experience. And she seemed to find things in him she truly admired. They had the basis for a long relationship. But . . .

The eternal but!

. . . despite the intimacies they had shared, he knew he was not for her. She would want more of him than he was willing to give. And he knew in his heart he would never feel for her what he felt for Gia.

Closing the bedroom door behind him, Jack went into the front room and prepared to wait for Kusum. He pulled on a T-shirt and slacks, white socks and tennis shoes—he wanted to be ready to move at an instant's notice. He put an extra handful of hollow-point bullets in his right front pocket and, on impulse, stuck the remaining Cricket lighter in the left. He set his wing-backed chair by the front window and faced the door. He pulled the matching hassock up and seated himself with the loaded Ruger .357 in his lap.

He hated waiting for an opponent to make the next move. It left him on the defensive, and the defensive side had no initiative.

But why play defensively? That was just what Kusum expected him to do. Why let crazy Kusum call the shots? Vicky was safe. Why not take the war to Kusum?

He snatched up the phone and dialed. Abe answered with a croak on the first ring.

"It's me—Jack. Did I wake you?"

"No, of course not. I sit up next to the phone every night waiting for you to call. Should tonight be any different?"

Jack didn't know whether he was joking or not. At times it was hard to tell with Abe.

"Everything okay on your end?"

"Would I be sitting here so calmly talking to you if it wasn't?"

"Vicky's all right?"

"Of course. Can I go back to sleep on this wonderfully comfortable couch now?"

"You're on the couch? There's another bedroom."

"I know all about the other bedroom. I just thought maybe I'd

303

sleep here between the door and our two lady friends.''

Jack felt a burst of warmth for his old friend. "I really do owe you for this, Abe.''

"I know. So start paying me back by hanging up.''

"Unfortunately, I'm not finished asking favors yet. I got a big one coming up.''

"*Nu?*''

"I need some equipment: incendiary bombs with timers and incendiary bullets along with an AR to shoot them.''

The Yiddishisms disappeared; Abe was abruptly a businessman. "I don't have them in stock, but I can get them. When do you need them?''

"Tonight.''

"Seriously—when?''

"Tonight. An hour ago.''

Abe whistled. "That's going to be tough. Important?''

"Very.''

"I'll have to call in some markers on this. Especially at this hour.''

"Make it worth their while," Jack told him. "The sky's the limit.''

"Okay. But I'll have to leave and make the pickups myself. These boys don't deal with anybody they don't know.''

Jack didn't like the idea of leaving Gia and Vicky without a guard. But since there was no way for Kusum to find them, a guard was really superfluous.

"Okay. You've got your truck, right?''

"Right.''

"Then make your calls, make the pickups, and I'll meet you at the store. Call me when you get there.''

Jack hung up and settled back in his chair. It was comfortably dark here in the front room with only a little indirect light spilling from the kitchen area. He felt his muscles loosen up and relax into the familiar depressions of the chair. He was tired. The last few days had been wearing. When was the last time he had had a good night's sleep? Saturday? Here it was Wednesday morning.

He jumped at the sudden jangle of the phone and picked it up before it finished the first ring.

"Hello?''

A few heartbeats of silence on the other end of the line, and then a click.

Puzzled and uneasy, Jack hung up. A wrong number? Or Kusum

304

checking up on his whereabouts?

He listened for stirrings from the bedroom where he had left Kolabati, but none came. The ring had been too brief to wake her.

He made his body relax again. He found himself anticipating with a certain relish what was to come. Mr. Kusum Bahkti was in for a little surprise tonight, yes sir. Repairman Jack was going to make things hot for him and his rakoshi. Crazy Kusum would regret the day he tried to hurt Vicky Westphalen. Because Vicky had a friend. And that friend was mad. Madder'n hell.

Jack's eyelids slipped closed. He fought to open them but then gave up. Abe would call when everything was ready. Abe would come through. Abe could get anything, even at this hour. Jack had time for a few winks.

The last thing he remembered before sleep claimed him was the hate-filled eyes of the Mother rakosh as she watched him from the floor of the hold after he had seared the face of one of her children. Jack shuddered and slipped into sleep.

18.

Kusum swung the rented yellow van into Sutton Square and pulled all the way to the end. Bullwhip in hand, he got out immediately and stood by the door, scanning the street. All was quiet, but who could say for how long? There wouldn't be much time here. This was an insular neighborhood. His van would draw immediate attention should some insomniac glance out a window and spot it.

This should have been the Mother's job, but she could not be in two places at once. He had given her the sweaty shirt Jack had left on the ship so that she could identify her target by scent, and had dropped her off outside Jack's apartment building only a few moments ago.

He smiled. Oh, if only he could be there to see Jack's expression when the Mother confronted him! He would not recognize her at first—Kusum had seen to that—but he was certain Jack's heart would stop when he saw the surprise Kusum had prepared for him. And if shock didn't stop his heart, the Mother would. A fitting and honorable end to a man who had become too much of a liability to be allowed to live.

Kusum drew his thoughts back to Sutton Square. The last Westphalen was asleep within meters of where he stood. He removed his necklace and placed it on the front seat of the van, then walked back to the rear doors. A young rakosh, nearly full-grown, leaped out. Kusum brandished the whip but did not crack it—the noise would be too loud.

This rakosh was the Mother's first born, the toughest and most experienced of all the younglings, its lower lip deformed by scars from one of many battles with its siblings. It had hunted with her in London and here in New York. Kusum probably could have let it loose from the ship and trusted it to find the Scent and bring back the child on its own, but he didn't want to take any chances tonight. There must be no mishaps tonight.

The rakosh looked at Kusum, then looked past him, across the river. Kusum gestured with his whip toward the house where the Westphalen child was staying.

"There!" he said in Bengali. "There!"

With seeming reluctance the creature moved in the direction of the house. Kusum saw it enter the alley on the west side, no doubt to climb the wall in shadow and pluck the child from its bed. He was about to step back to the front of the van and retrieve his necklace when he heard a clatter from the side of the house. Alarmed, he ran to the alley, cursing under his breath all the way. These younglings were so damned clumsy! The only one he could really depend upon was the Mother.

He found the rakosh pawing through a garbage can. It had a dark vinyl bag torn open and was pulling something out. Fury surged through Kusum. He should have known he couldn't trust a youngling! Here it was rummaging in garbage when it should be following the Scent up the wall. He unfurled his whip, ready to strike . . .

The young rakosh held something out to him: half of an orange. Kusum snatched it up and held it under his nose. It was one of those he had injected with the elixir and hidden in the playhouse last night after locking Kolabati in the pilot's quarters. The rakosh came up with another half.

Kusum pressed both together. They fit perfectly. The orange had been sliced open but had not been eaten. He looked at the rakosh and it was now holding a handful of chocolates.

Enraged, Kusum hurled the orange halves against the wall. *Jack!* It could be no one else! Curse that man!

He strode around to the rear of the townhouse and up to the back door. The rakosh followed him part way and then stood and stared

THE TOMB

across the East River.

"Here!" Kusum said impatiently, indicating the door.

He stepped back as the rakosh came up the steps and slammed one of its massive three-fingered hands against the door. With a loud crack of splintering wood, the door flew open. Kusum stepped in with the rakosh close behind. He wasn't worried about awakening anyone in the house. If Jack had discovered the treated orange, it was certain he had spirited everyone away.

Kusum stood in the dark kitchen, the young rakosh a looming shadow beside him. Yes ... the house was empty. No need to search it.

A thought struck him with the force of a blow.

No!

Uncontrollable tremors shook his body. It was not anger that Jack had been one step ahead of him all day, but fear. Fear so deep and penetrating that it almost overwhelmed him. He rushed to the front door and ran out to the street.

Jack had hidden the last Westphalen from him—and at this very moment Jack's life was being torn from him by the Mother rakosh! The only man who could tell him where to find the child had been silenced forever! How would Kusum find her in a city of eight million? He would never fulfill the vow! All because of Jack!

May you be reincarnated as a jackal!

He opened the rear door of the van for the rakosh but it wouldn't enter. It persisted in staring across the East River. It would take a few steps toward the river and then come back, repeating the process over and over.

"In!" Kusum said. He was in a black mood and had no patience for any quirks in this rakosh. But despite his urgings, the creature would not obey. The youngling was normally so eager to please, yet now it acted as if it had the Scent and wanted to be off on the hunt.

And then it occurred to him—he had doctored two oranges, and they had only found one. Had the Westphalen child consumed the first before the second was found out?

Possible. His spirits lifted perceptively. Quite possible.

And what could be more natural than to remove the child entirely from the island of Manhattan? What was that borough across the river—Queens? It didn't matter how many people lived there; if the child had consumed even a tiny amount of the elixir, the rakosh would find her.

THE TOMB

Perhaps all was not lost!

Kusum gestured toward the river with his coiled bullwhip. The young rakosh leaped to the top of the waist-high retaining wall at the end of the street and down to the sunken brick plaza a dozen feet below it. From there it was two steps and a flying leap over the wrought iron railing to the East River running silently below.

Kusum stood and watched it sail into the darkness, his despair dissipating with each passing second. This rakosh was an experienced hunter and seemed to know where it was going. Perhaps there was still hope of sailing tonight.

After the sound of a splash far below, he turned and climbed into the cab of the van. Yes—his mind was set. He would operate under the assumption that the youngling would bring back the Westphalen girl. He would prepare the ship for sea. Perhaps he would even cast off and sail down river to New York Bay. He had no fear of losing the Mother and the youngling that had just leaped into the river. Rakoshi had an uncanny homing instinct that led them to their nest no matter where it was.

How fortunate he had dosed two oranges instead of one. As he refastened the necklace at his throat, he realized that the hand of Kali was evident here.

All doubt and despair melted away in a sudden blast of triumph. The Goddess was at his side, guiding him! He could not fail!

Repairman Jack was not to have the last laugh after all.

19.

Jack awakened with a start. There was an instant of disorientation before he realized he was not in his bed but in a chair in the front room. His hand automatically went to the .357 in his lap. There was a rachety click as he cocked the hammer.

He listened. Something had awakened him. What? The faint light seeping in from the kitchen area was enough to confirm that the front room was empty.

He got up and checked the TV room, then looked in on Kolabati. She was still asleep. All quiet on the western front.

A noise made him whirl. It had come from the other side of the door—the creak of a board. Jack went to the door and pressed his ear against it. Silence. A hint of an odor was present at the edges of the door. Not the necrotic stink of a rakosh, but a sickly sweet smell like an old lady's gardenia perfume.

His heart thumping, Jack unlocked the door and pulled it open in a single motion as he jumped back and took his firing stance: legs spread, the revolver in both hands, left supporting right, both arms fully extended.

The light in the hall was meager at best but brighter than where Jack stood. Anyone attempting to enter the apartment would be silhouetted in the doorway. Nothing moved. All he saw was the banister and balusters that ran along the stairwell outside his apartment door. Jack held his position as the gardenia odor wafted into the room like a cloud from an overgrown hothouse—syrupy and flowery, with a hint of rottenness beneath.

Keeping his arms locked straight out in a triangle with the .357 at the apex, he moved to the door, weaving back and forth to give himself angled views of the hallway to the left and right. What he could see was clear.

He leaped out into the hall and spun in the air, landing with his back against the banister, his arms down, the pistol held before his crotch, ready to be raised right or left as his head snapped back and forth.

Hall to the right and left: clear.

An instant later he was moving again, spinning to his right, slamming his back against the wall next to his door, his eyes darting to the right to the staircase up to the fourth floor: clear.

The landing to his left going down: cl—

No! Someone there, sitting on the shadowed landing. His pistol snapped up, steady in his hands as he took a better look—a woman, barely visible, in a long dress, long sloppy hair, floppy hat, slumped posture, looking depressed. The hat and the hair obscured her face.

Jack's pulse started to slow but he kept the .357 trained on her. What the hell was she doing here? And what had she done—spilled a bottle of perfume all over herself?

"Something wrong, lady?" he said.

She moved, shifting her body and turning to look at him. The movement made Jack realize that this was one hell of a big lady. And then it was all clear to him. It was Kusum's touch: Jack had disguised himself as an old woman when he had worked for Kusum, and now ... he didn't even have to see the malevolent yellow eyes glowering at him from under the hat and wig to know that he had spoken to the Mother rakosh.

"Ho-ly *shit!*"

309

THE TOMB

In a single, swift, fluid motion accompanied by her hiss of rage and the tearing of the fabric of her dress, the Mother rakosh reared up to her full height and flowed toward him, her fangs glinting, her talons extended, triumph gleaming in her eyes.

Jack's tongue stuck to the roof of his suddenly dry mouth, but he stood his ground. With a methodical coolness that amazed even him, he aimed the first round at the upper left corner of the Mother's chest. The silenced Ruger jumped in his hands, rubbing against his wounded palm, making a muted *phut* when he pulled the trigger. The bullet jolted her—Jack could imagine the lead projectile breaking up into countless tiny pieces of shrapnel and tearing in all directions through her tissues—but her momentum carried her forward. He wasn't sure where her heart would be so he placed three more rounds at the corners of an imaginary square in relation to the first, now oozing a stream of very dark blood . . .

The Mother stiffened and lurched as each slug cut into her, finally coming to a staggering halt a few feet in front of him. Jack watched her in amazement. The very fact that she was still standing was testimony to an incredible vitality—she should have gone down with the first shot. But Jack was confident: She was dead on her feet. He knew all about the unparalleled stopping power of those hollow points. The hydrostatic shock and vascular collapse caused by just one properly placed round was enough to stop a charging bull. The Mother rakosh had taken four.

Jack cocked the Ruger and hesitated. He wanted to put an end to this, yet he always liked to save one bullet if he could—emptying a weapon made it useless. In this case he would make an exception. He took careful aim and pumped the last round dead center into the Mother's chest.

She spread her arms and lurched back against the newel post at the head of the stairs, cracking it with her weight. The hat and wig slipped from her head but she didn't topple over. Instead, she made a half turn and slumped over the banister. Jack waited for her final collapse.

And waited.

The Mother did not collapse. She took a few deep gasps, then straightened up and faced him, her eyes as bright as ever. Jack stood rooted to the floor, watching her. It was impossible! She was dead! Dead five times over! He had seen the holes in her chest, the black blood! There should be nothing but jelly inside her now!

With a loud, drawn-out hiss, she lunged toward him. By pure reflex

310

rather than conscious effort, Jack dodged away. Where to go? He didn't want to get trapped in his apartment, and the way down to the street was blocked. The roof was his only option.

He was already on the stairs taking them two at once by the time he made the decision. His pistol was no good—not even worth reloading. Kolabati's words came back to him: *fire and iron . . . fire and iron . . .* Without slowing or breaking stride, he bent and laid the .357 on one of the steps as he passed, glancing behind him as he did. The Mother rakosh was a flight behind, gliding up the stairs after him, the remains of her dress hanging in tatters from her neck and arms. The contrast of her smooth, utterly silent ascent to his pounding climb was almost as unnerving as the murderous look in her eyes.

The roof was three flights above his apartment. Two more to go. Jack increased his effort to the limit and managed to widen the gap between himself and the Mother. But only briefly. Instead of weakening, the Mother seemed to gain strength and speed with the exertion. By the time Jack reached the final steps up to the roof, she had closed to within half a flight.

Jack didn't bother with the latch on the roof door. It had never worked well anyway and fumbling with it would only lose him precious seconds. He rammed it with his shoulder, burst through, and hit the roof on the run.

The Manhattan skyline soared around him. From its star-filled height the setting moon etched the details of the roof like a high-contrast black and white photo—pale white light on upper surfaces, inky shadows below. Vents, chimneys, aerials, storage sheds, the garden, the flagpole, the emergency generator—a familiar obstacle course. Perhaps that familiarity could be worked to his advantage. He knew he could not outrun the Mother.

Perhaps—just perhaps—he could outmaneuver her.

Jack had decided on his course of action during his first few running strides across the roof. He dodged around two of the chimneys, ran diagonally across an open area to the edge of the roof, and then turned to wait, making sure he was easily visible from the door. He didn't want the Mother to lose too much of her momentum looking for him.

It was only a second before she appeared. She spotted him immediately and charged in his direction, a moon-limned shadow readying for the kill. Neil the anarchist's flagpole blocked her path— she took a passing sidearm swipe at it and shattered the shaft so that it

311

swung crazily in the air and toppled to the roof. She came to the generator next—and leaped over it!

And then there was nothing between Jack and the Mother rakosh. She lowered into a crouch and hurtled toward him. Sweating, trembling, Jack kept his eyes on the taloned hands aiming for his throat, ready to tear him to pieces. He was sure there were worse ways to die, but at this moment he could not think of one. His thoughts were fixed on what he had to do to survive this encounter—and the knowledge that what he planned might prove just as fatal as standing here and waiting for those talons to reach him.

He had pressed the backs of his knees against the upper edge of the low, foot-wide parapet that ran all along the rim of the roof. As soon as the Mother had appeared he had assumed a kneeling position atop the parapet. And now as she charged him, he straightened up with his knees balanced on the outermost edge of the parapet, his feet poised over the empty alley five stories below, his hands hanging loosely at his sides. The rough concrete dug into his kneecaps but he ignored the pain. He had to concentrate completely on what he was about to do.

The Mother became a black juggernaut, gaining momentum at an astonishing rate as she crossed the final thirty feet separating them. Jack did not move. It strained his will to the limits to kneel there and wait as certain death rushed toward him. Tension gathered in his throat until he thought he would choke. All his instincts screamed for flight. But he had to hold his place until the right instant. Making his move too soon would be as deadly as not moving at all.

And so he waited until the outstretched talons were within five feet of him—then leaned back and allowed his knees to slip off the edge of the parapet. As he fell toward the floor of the alley, he grabbed the edge of the parapet, hoping he had not dropped too soon, praying his grip would hold.

As the front of his body slammed against the brick sidewall of the alley, Jack sensed furious motion above him. The Mother rakosh's claws had sunk into empty air instead of his flesh, and the momentum she had built up was carrying her over the edge and into the beginning of a long fall to the ground. Out of the corner of his eye he saw a huge shadow sail over and behind him, saw frantically windmilling arms and legs. Then came a blow to the rear of his left shoulder and a searing, tearing sensation across his back that made him cry out.

The blow jerked Jack's left hand free of the roof edge and he was

THE TOMB

left hanging by his right. Gasping with pain and clawing desperately for a new grip on the parapet, he could not resist a quick look down to see the plummeting form of the Mother rakosh impact with the floor of the alley. He found exquisite satisfaction in the faint, dull thud that rose from below. He didn't care how tough she was, that fall broke her neck and most of the rest of the bones in her body.

Fighting the agony that stabbed through his left shoulder blade every time he raised his arm, Jack inched his left hand back up to the top of the parapet, secured the purchase of both his hands, then slowly, painfully, pulled himself back up to the roof.

He lay stretched out atop the parapet, breathing hard, waiting for the fire on his back to go out. In her wild flailings to save herself from falling, one of the Mother's talons—whether on a hand or a foot, Jack couldn't say—must have caught his back and torn through his shirt and his skin. His shirt felt warm and sticky against his back. He gently reached around and touched his rib cage. It was wet. He held his hand up before his face—it glistened darkly in the moonlight.

Wearily, he raised himself up to a sitting position with his legs straddling the parapet. He took one last look down into the alley, wondering if he could see the Mother. All was dark. He went to swing his outer leg over onto the roof and stopped—

Something was moving down there. A darker blot moved within the shadows of the alley.

He held his breath. Had someone heard the thump of the Mother's fall and come to investigate? He hoped so. He hoped that was all it was.

More movement . . .   along the wall . . . moving upward . . . and a scraping sound, like claws on brick . . .

Something was climbing the wall toward him. He didn't need a flashlight to know what it was.

The Mother was returning!

It wasn't possible—but it was happening!

Groaning with disbelief and dismay, he swung his legs onto the roof and staggered away from the edge. What was he going to do? There was no use running—despite the lead he had, the Mother would surely catch up with him.

Fire and iron . . . fire and iron . . . the words burned across his brain as he raced around the roof in a futile search for something to defend himself with. There was no iron up here! Everything was aluminum, tin, plastic, wood! If only he could find a crowbar or even a

313

piece of rusted iron railing—something, anything to swing at her head as she poked it up over the edge!

There was nothing. The only thing that even remotely resembled a weapon was the broken remnant of the flagpole. It wasn't iron and it wasn't fire . . . but with its sharp, splintered lower-end, it might serve as a twelve-foot spear. He picked it up by its top end—there was a ball at the tip—and hefted it. It wobbled like a vaulting pole and the oscillations caused waves of pain in his back. It was heavy, it was crude, it was unwieldy, but it was all he had.

Jack put it down and loped over to the edge of the roof. The Mother was no more than a dozen feet below him and climbing fast.

It's not fair! He thought as he ran back to where the pole lay. He had as good as killed her twice in ten minutes, yet here he was hurt and bleeding and she was climbing a brick wall as if nothing had happened to her.

He picked up the pole by the balled end and levered it to a horizontal position by using his left arm as a fulcrum. Groaning with the pain, he pointed the splintered end toward the spot where he expected the Mother to appear and began to run. His left arm began to lose strength as he ran. The point sank toward the roof surface but he clenched his teeth an forced it upward.

Have to keep it up . . . go for the throat . . .

Again, he knew timing would be critical: if the Mother gained the roof too soon, she would dodge him; too late and he would miss her completely.

He saw one three-fingered hand slip over the edge of the parapet, then another. He adjusted his direction to the area above and between those hands.

"Come on!" he screamed at her as he increased his speed. "Keep coming!"

His voice sounded hysterical but he couldn't let that bother him now. He had to keep that goddamned point up and ram it right through her—

Her head appeared and then she was pulling herself up onto the parapet. Too fast! She was too fast! He couldn't control the wavering point, couldn't lift it high enough! He was going to miss his target!

With a cry of rage and desperation, Jack put every pound of his body and every remaining ounce of strength left to him behind a final thrust against the balled end of the pole. Despite all his effort, the point never reached the level of the Mother's throat. Instead, it rammed into her chest with a force that nearly dislocated Jack's right shoulder. But Jack didn't let up—with his eyes squeezed shut he followed through with barely a break in his stride, keeping all his weight behind the makeshift spear. There was a moment of resistence to the spear's path, followed by a sensation of breaking free, then it was yanked out of his hands and he fell to his knees.

When he looked up, his eyes were level with the top of the parapet. His heart nearly stopped when he saw that the Mother was still there—

No ... wait ... she was on the other side of the parapet. But that couldn't be! She'd have to be standing in mid-air! Jack forced himself to his feet and all was made clear.

The miniature flagpole had pierced the Mother rakosh through the center of her chest. The sharpened end of the pole had exited through her back and come to rest on the parapet of the neighboring building across the alley; the balled end lay directly in front of Jack.

He had her! Finally, he had her!

But the Mother wasn't dead. She twisted on her skewer and hissed and slashed her talons at Jack in futile rage as he stood and panted a mere six feet from her. She could not reach him. After his relief and awe faded, Jack's first impulse was to push his end of the pole off the edge and let her fall to the ground again, but he checked himself. He had the Mother rakosh where he wanted her—neutralized. He could leave her there until he found a way to deal with her. Meanwhile, she was no danger to him or anyone else.

And then she began to move toward him.

Jack took a quick, faltering step back and almost fell. She was still coming for him! His jaw dropped as he watched her reach forward with both hands and grip the pole that skewered her, then pull herself forward, pushing the pole through her chest to bring herself closer and closer to Jack.

Jack nearly went mad then. How could he fight a creature that didn't feel pain? That wouldn't die? He began swearing, cursing incoherently. He ran around the roof picking up pebbles, bits of litter, an aluminum can, hurling them at her. Why not? They were as effective as anything else he had done to her. When he came to the emergency generator, he picked up one of the two-gallon metal cans of diesel oil and went to hurl that at her—

—and stopped.

Oil. *Fire!* He finally had a weapon—if it was not too late! The

THE TOMB

Mother had pulled herself almost to within reach of the roof edge. He twisted at the metal cap, but it wouldn't budge—it was rusted shut. In desperation he slammed the edge of the cap twice against the generator and tried again. Pain shot through the earlier wound in his palm, but he kept up the pressure. Finally it came loose and he was up and scrambling across the roof, unscrewing the cap as he moved, thanking Con Ed for the blackout in the summer of '77—for if there hadn't been a blackout, the tenants wouldn't have chipped in for an emergency generator, and Jack would have been completely defenseless now.

Oil sloshed over his bandaged hand as the cap came off. Jack didn't hesitate. He stood up on the parapet and splashed the oil over the slowly advancing rakosh. She hissed furiously and slashed at him but Jack remained just out of reach. By the time the can was empty, the air around them reeked of diesel fuel. The Mother pulled herself closer and Jack had to jump back to the roof to avoid her talons.

He wiped his hands on his shirt and reached into his pocket for the Cricket. He experienced an instant of panic when he thought his pocket was empty, and then his fingers closed on the lighter. He held it up and thumbed the little lever, praying the oil on his hand hadn't got to the flint. It sparked, the flame shot up—and Jack smiled. For the first time since the Mother had shaken off the damage of five hollow-point rounds in the chest, Jack thought he might survive the night.

He thrust the lighter forward but the Mother saw the flame and ripped the air with her talons. He felt the breeze as they passed within inches of his face. She would not let him near her! What good was the oil if he couldn't toss the lighter at her and expect an explosion of flame. Diesel fuel needed more than that to start it.

Then he noticed that the pole was slick with the oil. He crouched next to the parapet and reached up to the ball at the end of the pole. The Mother's talon's raked by, millimeters away from his hair, but he steeled himself to hold his position as he played the flame of the Cricket against the oil on the ball. For the longest time, nothing happened.

And then it caught. He watched raptly as a smoky-yellow flame—one of the loveliest sights he had ever seen—grew and spread across the ball. From there it crept along the upper surface of the pole, straight toward the Mother. She tried to back away but was caught. The flames leaped onto her chest and fanned out over her torso. Within seconds she was completely engulfed.

Weak with relief, Jack watched with horrid fascination as the Mother's movements became spasmodic, wild, frenzied. He lost sight of her amid the flames and black smoke that poured skyward from her burning body. He heard sobbing—was it her? No . . . it was his own voice. Reaction to the pain and the terror and the exertion was setting in. Was it over? Was it finally over?

He steadied himself and watched her burn. He could find no pity for her. She was the most murderous engine of destruction ever imagined. A killing machine that would go on—

A low moan rose from within the conflagration. He thought he heard something that sounded like "*Spa fon!*" Then came the word, "*Kaka-ji!*"

Your Kaka-ji *is next,* Jack thought.

And then she was still. As her flaming body slumped forward, the pole cracked and broke. The Mother rakosh spun to the floor of the alley trailing smoke and flame behind her like the loser in an aerial dogfight. And this time when she hit the ground she stayed there. Jack watched for a long time. The flames lit the beach scene painted on the alley's opposite wall, giving it a sunset look.

The Mother rakosh continued to burn. And she didn't move. He watched and watched until he was sure she would never move again.

20.

Jack locked his apartment door and sank to the floor behind it, reveling in the air-conditioned coolness. He had stumbled down from the roof in a daze, but had remembered to pick up his empty Ruger on the way. He was weak. Every cell in his body cried out in pain and fatigue. He needed rest, and he probably needed a doctor for his lacerated back. But there was no time for any of that. He had to finish Kusum off tonight.

He pulled himself to his feet and went to the bedroom. Kolabati was still asleep. Next stop was the phone. He didn't know if Abe had called while he was up on the roof. He doubted it; the prolonged ringing would have awakened Kolabati. He dialed the number of the shop.

After three rings there came a cautious, "Yes?"

"It's me, Abe."

"Who else could it be at this hour?"

"Did you get everything?"

"Just got in the door. No, I didn't get everything. Got the timed incendiary bombs—a crate of twelve—but couldn't get hold of any incendiary bullets before tomorrow noon. Is that soon enough?"

"No," Jack said, bitterly disappointed. He had to move now.

"I got something you might use as a substitute, though."

"What?"

"Come down and see."

"Be there in a few minutes."

Jack hung up and gingerly peeled the torn, blood-soaked shirt from his back. The pain there had subsided to a dull, aching throb. He blinked when he saw the liverish clots clinging to the fabric. He had lost more blood than he had thought.

He got a towel from the bathroom and gently held it against the wound. It stung, but the pain was bearable. When he checked the towel half a minute later, there was blood on it, but very little of it fresh.

Jack knew he should shower and clean out the wound but was afraid he'd start it bleeding again. He resisted the temptation to examine his back in the bathroom mirror—it might hurt worse if he knew how bad it looked. Instead, he wrapped all his remaining gauze around his upper chest and over his left shoulder.

He went back to the bedroom for a fresh shirt and for something else: He knelt next to the bed, gently unclasped Kolabati's necklace and removed it. She stirred, moaned softly, then was quiet. Jack tiptoed out of the room and closed the door behind him.

In the living room he clasped the iron necklace around his throat. It gave off an unpleasant, tingling sensation that spread along his skin from head to toe. He didn't relish wearing it, nor borrowing it from Kolabati without her knowledge, but she had refused to remove it in the ship, and if he was going back there he wanted every edge he could get.

He slipped into the fresh shirt as he dialed the number of Abe's daughter's apartment. He was going to have to be out of touch with Gia for a while and knew his mind would rest easier after confirming that everything was cool in Queens.

After half a dozen rings, Gia picked up. Her voice was tentative.

"Hello?"

Jack paused for an instant at the sound of her voice. After what he had been through in the past few hours, he wanted nothing more than to call it quits for the night, hop over to Queens and spend the rest of the time until morning with his arms around Gia. Nothing more would be needed tonight—just holding her.

"Sorry to wake you," he said. "I'm going out for a few hours and wanted to make sure everything is okay."

"Everything's fine," she said hoarsely.

"Vicky?"

"I just left her side to answer the phone. She's fine. And I'm just reading this note from Abe explaining that he had to go out and not to worry. What's going on?"

"Crazy stuff."

"That's not an answer. I need answers, Jack. This whole thing scares me."

"I know. All I can say right now is it has to do with the Westphalens." He didn't want to say any more.

"But why is Vicky ... oh."

"Right. She's a Westphalen. Someday when we have lots of time, I'll explain it to you."

"When will it all end?"

"Tonight, if things go right."

"Dangerous?"

"Naw. Routine stuff." He didn't want to add to her worries.

"Jack ..." she paused and he thought he detected a quaver in her voice. "Be careful, Jack."

She would never know how much those words meant to him.

"Always careful. I like my body in one piece. See you later."

He didn't hang up. Instead he depressed the plunger for a few seconds, then released it. After checking for the dial tone, he stuffed the receiver under the seat cushion of his chair. It would start howling in a few minutes, but no one would hear that ... and no one could call here and awaken Kolabati. With luck, he could take care of Kusum, get back here and replace the necklace without her ever knowing he had taken it. And with considerably more luck, she might not ever know for sure that he had anything to do with the firey explosion that took her brother and his rakoshi to a watery grave.

He picked up his variable frequency beeper and hurried down to the street, intending to head immediately for the Isher Sports Shop. But as he passed the alley, he paused. He had no time to spare, yet he could not resist entering it to see the remains of the Mother rakosh. A jolt of panic shot through him when he saw no corpse in the alley.

319

THE TOMB

Then he came upon the smoldering pile of ashes. The fire had completely consumed the Mother, leaving only her fangs and talons. He picked up a few of each—they were still hot—and shoved them in his pocket. There might come a day when he would want to prove to himself that he had really faced something called a rakosh.

21.

Gia cradled the phone and thought about what Jack had said about all this being over tonight.

She fervently hoped so. If only Jack weren't so evasive about everything. What was he hiding? Was there something he was afraid to tell her? God, she hated this! She wanted to be home in her own little apartment in her own bed with Vicky down the hall in hers.

Gia started back for the bedroom and then stopped. She was wide awake. No use trying to go back to sleep just yet. She pulled the bedroom door closed, then searched through the kitchen for something to drink. The liberal amounts of MSG routinely used in Chinese cooking never failed to make her thirsty. When she came across the box of tea bags she grabbed them. With the kettle on to boil, she spun the television dial looking for something to watch. Nothing but old movies . . .

The kettle started to boil. Gia made a cup of tea and sugared it, filled a tall glass with ice, and poured the tea over the ice. There: iced tea. Needed some lemon, but it would do.

As she approached the couch with her drink she caught an odor— something rotten. Just a whiff and it was gone. There was an odd familiarity about it. If she could catch it again, she was sure she could identify it. She waited but it didn't return.

Gia turned her attention to the televsion. *Citizen Kane* was on. She hadn't seen that one in ages. It made her think of Jack . . . how he'd go on and on about Wells's use of light and shadow throughout the film. He could be a real pain when you just wanted to sit and watch the movie.

She sat down and sipped her tea.

22.

Vicky shot up to a sitting position in bed.

"Mommy?" she called softly.

THE TOMB

She trembled with fear. She was alone. And there was an awful, pukey smell She glanced at the window. Something was there ... outside the window. The screen had been pulled out. That's what had awakened her.

A hand—or something that looked like a hand but really wasn't—slipped over the window sill. Then another. The dark shadow of a head rose into view and two glowing yellow eyes trapped her and pinned her where she sat in mute horror. The thing crawled over the ledge and flowed into the room like a snake.

Vicky opened her mouth to scream out her horror but something moist and hard and stinking jammed against her face, cutting off her voice. It was a hand, but like no hand she had ever imagined. There only seemed to be three fingers—three *huge* fingers—and the taste of the palm against her lips brought what was left of her Chinese dinner boiling to the back of her throat.

As she fought to get free, she caught a fleeting close-up glimpse of what held her—the smooth, blunt-snouted face, the fangs showing above the scarred lower lip, the glowing yellow eyes. It was *every* fear of what's in the closet or what's in that shadowed corner, *every* bad dream, *every* night horror rolled into one.

Vicky became delerious with panic. Tears of fear and revulsion streamed down her face. She had to get away! She kicked and twisted convulsively, clawed with her fingernails—nothing she did seemed to matter in the slightest. She was lifted like a toy and carried to the window—

—*and out!* They were twelve floors up! *Mommy!* They were going to fall!

But they didn't fall. Using its free hand and its clawed feet, the monster crawled down the wall like a spider. Then it was running along the ground, through parks, down alleys, across streets. The grip across her mouth loosened but Vicky was clutched so tightly against the monster's flank that she couldn't scream—she could barely breathe.

"Please don't hurt me!" she whispered into the night. "Please don't hurt me!"

Vicky didn't know where they were or in what direction they were travelling. Her mind could barely function through the haze of terror that enveloped it. But soon she heard the lapping sound of water, smelled the river. The monster leaped, they seemed to fly for an instant, and then water closed over them. She couldn't swim!

THE TOMB

Vicky screamed as they plunged beneath the waves and gulped a mouthful of foul, brackish water. She broke the surface choking and retching. Her throat was locked—there was air all around her but she couldn't breathe! Finally, when she thought she was going to die, her windpipe opened and air rushed into her lungs.

She opened her eyes. The monster had slung her onto its back and was now cutting through the water. She clung to the slick, slimy skin of its shoulders. Her pink nightie was plastered to her goose-fleshed skin, her hair hung in her eyes. She was cold, wet, and miserable with terror. She wanted to jump off and get away from the monster, but she knew she'd go down under that water and never come back up.

Why was this happening to her? She'd been good. Why did this monster want her?

Maybe it was a good monster, like in that book she had, *Where the Wild Things Are.* It hadn't hurt her. Maybe it was taking her someplace to show her something.

She looked around and recognized the Manhattan skyline off to her right, but there was something between them and Manhattan. Dimly she remembered the island—Roosevelt Island—that sat in the river at the end of Aunt Nellie's and Grace's street.

Were they going to swim around it and go back to Manhattan? Was the monster going to take her back to Aunt Nellie's?

No. They passed the end of the island, but the monster didn't turn toward Manhattan. It kept swimming in the same direction down river. Vicky shivered and began to cry.

23.

Gia's chin dropped forward onto her chest and she awoke with a start. She was only half an hour into the movie and already she was nodding off. She wasn't nearly as wide awake as she had thought. She flicked it off and went back to the bedroom.

Fear hit her like a knife between the ribs as soon as she opened the door. The room was filled with a rotten odor. Now she recognized it—the same odor that had been in Nellie's room the night she disappeared. Her gaze shot to the bed and her heart stopped when she saw it was flat—no familiar little lump of curled-up child under the covers.

"Vicky?" Her voice cracked as she said the name and turned on the light. She has to be here!

THE TOMB

Without waiting for an answer, Gia rushed to the bed and pulled the covers down.

"Vicky?" Her voice was almost a whimper. *She's here—she has to be!*

She ran to the closet and fell to her knees, checking the floor with her hands. Only Vicky's Ms. Jelliroll Carry Case was there. Next she crawled over to the bed and looked under it. Vicky wasn't there, either.

But something else was—a small dark lump. Gia reached in and grabbed it. She thought she would be sick when she recognized the feel of a recently-peeled and partially-eaten orange.

An orange! Jack's words flooded back to her: "Do you want Vicky to end up like Grace and Nellie? Gone without a trace?" He had said there was something in the orange—but he had thrown it away! So how had Vicky got hold of this one? . . .

Unless there had been more than one orange in the playhouse! *This is a nightmare! This isn't really happening!*

Gia ran through the rest of the apartment, opening every door, every closet, every cabinet. Vicky was gone! She hurried back to the bedroom and went to the window. The screen was missing. She hadn't noticed that before. Fighting back a scream as visions of a child's body smashed against the pavement flashed before her eyes, she held her breath and looked down. The parking lot was directly below, well-lit by mercury vapor lamps. There was no sign of Vicky.

Gia didn't know whether to be relieved or not. All she knew right now was that her child was missing and she needed help. She ran for the phone, ready to dial the 911 emergency police number, then stopped. The police would certainly be more concerned about a missing child than about two old ladies who had disappeared, but would they accomplish anything more? Gia doubted it. There was only one number to call that would do her any good: Jack's.

Jack will know what to do. Jack will help.

She forced her shaking index finger to punch in the numbers and got a busy signal. She hung up and dialed again. Still busy. She didn't have time to wait! She dialed the operator and told her it was an emergency and she had to break in on the line. She was put on hold for half a minute that seemed like an hour, then the operator was back on, telling her that the line wasn't busy—the phone had been left off the hook.

Gia slammed the receiver down. What was she going to do? She

323

was frantic. What was wrong at Jack's? Had he left the phone off the hook or had it been knocked off?

She ran back to the bedroom and jammed her legs into a pair of jeans and pulled on a blouse without removing her pajamas. She had to find Jack. If he wasn't at his apartment, maybe he was at Abe's store—she was pretty sure she remembered where that was. She hoped she could remember. Her thoughts were so jumbled. All she could think of was Vicky.

Vicky, Vicky, where are you?

But how to get to Jack's ... that was the problem. Finding a cab would be virtually impossible at this hour, and the subway, even if she could find a stop nearby, could be deadly to a woman alone.

The Honda keys she had seen earlier! Where had they been? She had been cleaning in the kitchen ...

She ran over to the flatware drawer and pulled it open. There they were. She snatched them up and ran out into the hall. She checked the apartment number on the door: 1203. Now if only the car was here. The elevator took her straight down to the first floor and she hurried out into the parking lot. On the way in this afternoon she had seen numbers on the asphalt by each parking space.

Please let it be here! she said to God, to fate, to whatever was in charge of human events. *Is anybody in charge?* asked a small voice in the back of her mind.

She followed the numbers from the 800s up to the 1100s, and there up ahead, crouched as a laboratory mouse waiting timidly for the next injection, sat a white Honda Civic.

Please be 1203! Please!

It had to be.

It was.

Almost giddy with relief, she unlocked the door and slid into the driver's seat. The standard shift on the floor gave her a moment's pause, but she had driven her father's old Ford pickup enough miles in Iowa as a teen-ager. She hoped it was something you never forgot, such as riding a bike.

The engine refused to start until she found the manual choke, then it sputtered to life. She stalled twice backing out of the parking space, but once she got it rolling forward, she had little trouble.

She didn't know Queens but knew the general direction she wanted to go. She worked her way toward the East River until she saw a To Manhattan sign and followed the arrow. When the

THE TOMB

Queensboro Bridge loomed into view, she slammed the gas pedal to the floor. She had been driving tentatively until now, reining her emotions, clutching the wheel with white-knuckled intensity, wary of missing a crucial turn. But with her destination in sight, she began to cry.

24.

Abe's dark blue panel truck was parked outside the Isher Sports Shop. The iron gate had been rolled back. At Jack's knock, the door opened immediately. Abe's white shirt was wrinkled and his jowls were stubbly. For the first time in Jack's memory, he wasn't wearing his black tie.

"What?" he said, scrutinizing Jack. "You run into trouble since you left me at the apartment?"

"What makes you ask?"

"Bandage on your hand and you're walking funny."

"Had a lengthy and strenuous argument with a very disagreeable lady." He rotated his left shoulder gingerly; it was nowhere near as still and painful as it had been back at the apartment.

"Lady?"

"It's stretching the definition, but yeah—lady."

Abe led Jack toward the rear of the darkened store. The lights were on in the basement, as was the neon sign. Abe hefted a wooden crate two-feet long and a foot wide and deep. The top had already been pried open and he lifted it off.

"Here are the bombs. Twelve of them, magnesium compound, all with twenty-four-hour timers."

Jack nodded. "Fine. But I really needed the incendiary bullets. Otherwise I may never get a chance to set these."

Abe shook his head. "I don't know what you think you're going up against, but here's the best I could do."

He pulled a cloth off a card table to reveal a circular, donut-shaped metal tank with a second tank, canteen-sized, set in its middle; both were attached by a short hose to what looked like a two-handed ray gun.

Jack was baffled. "What the hell—?"

"It's a No. 5 Mk-1 flamethrower, affectionately known as the Lifebuoy. I don't know if it'll suit your purposes. I mean, it hasn't got much range and—"

THE TOMB

"It's great!" Jack said. He grabbed Abe's hand and pumped it. "Abe, you're beautiful! It's perfect!"

Elated, Jack ran his hands over the tanks. It *was* perfect. Why hadn't he thought of it? How many times had he seen *Them*?

"How does it work?"

"This is a World War II model—the best I could do on such short notice. It's got CO_2 at 2000 pounds per square inch in the little spherical tank, and eighteen liters of napalm in the big lifebuoy-shaped one—hence the name; a discharge tube with igniters at the end and an adjustable nozzle. Range is up to ninety feet. You open the tanks, point the tube, pull the trigger in the rear grip, and foom!"

"Any helpful hints?"

"Yeah. Always check your nozzle adjustment before your first discharge. It's like a firehose and will tend to rise during a prolonged tight stream. Otherwise, think of it as spitting: Don't do it into the wind or where you live."

"Sounds easy enough. Help me get into the harness."

The tanks were heavier than Jack would have wished, but did not cause the anticipated burst of pain from the left side of his back; only a dull ache. As Jack adjusted the straps to a comfortable fit, Abe looked at his neck questioningly.

"Since when the jewelry, Jack?"

"Since tonight . . . for good luck."

"Strange looking thing. Iron, isn't it? And those stones . . . almost look like—"

"Two eyes? I know."

"And the inscription looks like Sanskrit. Is it?"

Jack shrugged, uncomfortable. He didn't like the necklace and knew nothing about its origins.

"Could be. I don't know. A friend . . . lent it to me for the night. Do you know what the inscriptions say?"

Abe shook his head. "I've seen Sanskrit before, but if my life depended on it I couldn't translate a single word." He looked closer. "Come to think of it, that's not really Sanskrit. Where was it made?"

"India."

"Really? Then it's probably Vedic, one of the Proto-Aryan languages that was a precursor of Sanskrit." Abe tossed off the information in a casual tone, then turned away and busied himself with gently tapping the nails halfway back into the corners of the crate of incendiary bombs.

THE TOMB

Jack didn't know if he was being put-on or not, but he didn't want to rob Abe of his moment. "How the hell do you know all that?"

"You think I majored in guns in college? I have a B.A. from Columbia in languages."

"And this is inscribed in Vedic, huh? Is that supposed to mean something?"

"It means it's old, Jack ... O-L-D."

Jack fingered the iron links around his neck. "I figured that."

Abe finished tapping down the crate top, then turned to Jack.

"You know I never ask, Jack, but this time I've got to: What are you up to? You could raze a couple of city blocks with what you've got here."

Jack didn't know what to say. How could he tell anyone, even his best friend, about the rakoshi and how the necklace he was wearing made him invisible to those rakoshi?

"Why don't you drive me down to the docks and maybe you'll see."

"It's a deal."

Abe groaned under the weight of the case of incendiary bombs while Jack, still in harness with the flamethrower, maneuvered his way up the steps to the ground floor. After Abe had deposited the crate in the rear of the panel truck, he motioned Jack out to the street. Jack darted out from the store doorway and through the rear doors of the truck. Abe pulled the iron gate closed in front of his shop and hopped into the driver's seat.

"Where to?"

"Take West End down to Fifty-seventh and turn right. Find a dark spot under the highway, and we'll go on foot from there."

As Abe put the truck into gear, Jack considered his options. Since climbing a rope with a flamethrower on his back and a crate of bombs under his arm was out of the question, he would have to go up the gangplank—his variable frequency beeper would bring it down. Events could go two ways after that: if he were able to get aboard undiscovered, he could set his bombs and run; if discovered, he would have to bring the flamethrower into service and play it by ear. If there was any chance to do it safely, he would let Abe get a look at a rakosh. Seeing would be believing—any other means of explaining what dwelled in Kusum's ship would be futile.

Either way, he would see to it that no rakoshi were left alive in New York by sunrise. And if Kusum cared to interfere, Jack was quite

327

willing to help his *atman* on its way to its next incarnation.

The truck stopped.

"We're here," Abe said. "What now?"

Jack gingerly lowered himself to the street through the rear door and walked up beside Abe's window. He pointed to the darkness north of Pier 97.

"Wait here while I go aboard. I shouldn't be long."

Abe glanced through the window, then back at him, a puzzled expression on his round face. "Aboard what?"

"There's a ship there. You just can't see it from here."

Abe shook his head. "I don't think there's anything there but water."

Jack squinted into the dark. It was there, wasn't it? With a mixture of amazement, bafflement, and relief growing within him, he sprinted down to the edge of the dock—the *empty* dock!

"It's gone!" he shouted as he ran back to the truck. "It's gone!"

He realized he must have looked like a crazy man, jumping up and down and laughing with a flamethrower strapped to his back, but Jack didn't care.

He had won! He had defeated the Mother rakosh and Kusum had sailed back to India without Vicky and without Kolabati! Triumph soared through him.

I've won!

25.

Gia ran up the steps of the five-story brownstone and stepped into the vestibule inside the front door. She pulled on the handle of the inner door just in case the latch hadn't caught. The door wouldn't move. Out of habit she reached into her purse for the keys and then remembered she had sent them back to Jack months ago.

She went to the callboard and pressed the button next to 3, the one with the hand-printed slip of paper that said Pinocchio Productions. When the door did not buzz open in response, she rang again, and kept on ringing, holding the button in until her thumb ached. Still no responding buzzer.

Gia went back out to the sidewalk and looked up to the front windows of Jack's apartment. They were dark, although there seemed to be a light on in the kitchen. Suddenly she saw movement at the window, a shadow looking down at her. Jack!

THE TOMB

She ran back up to ring the 3 button again, but the buzzer started to sound as soon as she stepped into the vestibule. She pushed through the inner door and ran up the stairs.

As she approached the third floor, she found a long brown wig and a flowery, broad-brimmed hat on the stairs. A sickeningly sweet perfume hung in the air. The newel post on the landing was cracked almost in two. There were torn pieces of dress fabric strewn all about the hall and splotches of thick black fluid on the floor outside Jack's apartment.

What happened here?

Something about the splotches made her skin crawl. She stepped around them carefully, not wanting to touch one, even with her shoe. Controlling her unease, she knocked on Jack's door.

The door opened immediately, startling her. Whoever was there must have been waiting for her knock. But the door had swung inward only three inches and stopped. She could see the vague shape of a head looking out at her, but the dim light from the hall was at the wrong angle to reveal the face.

"Jack?" Gia said. She was plainly frightened now. Everything was wrong here.

"He's not here," said a hoarse, cracked, whispery voice.

"Where is he?"

"I don't know. Will you look for him?"

"Yes . . . yes." The question was unexpected. "I need him right away."

"Find Jack! Find him and bring him back! *Bring him back!*"

The door slammed closed as Gia stumbled away, propelled by the sense of desperate urgency that had filled that voice.

What was happening here? Why was there some strange shadowy person in Jack's apartment instead of Jack? There was no time for mysteries—Vicky was missing and Jack could find her! Gia held on to that thought. It was all that kept her from going insane. Even so, the sense of nightmare unreality that had come over her after finding Vicky gone gripped her again. The walls wavered around her as she played along with the bad dream . . .

. . . *down the stairs, through the doors, down to the street to where the Honda sits double parked, start it up, drive to where you think—hope! Abe's shop is . . . tears on your face . . .*

Oh, Vicky, how am I ever going to find you? I'll die without you!

. . . *drive past darkened brownstones and storefronts until a dark blue panel truck pulls into the curb to the left just ahead and Jack gets out of the passenger side* . . .

Jack!

Gia was suddenly back in the real world. She slammed on the brakes. Even as the Honda was skidding to a stalled stop, she was out of the door and running to him, crying his name.

"Jack!"

He turned and Gia saw his face go white at the sight of her. He ran forward.

"Oh, no! Where's Vicky?"

He knew! Her expression, her very presence here must have told him. Gia could hold back the fear and grief no longer. She began sobbing as she collapsed into his arms.

"She's gone!"

"God! When? How long?" She thought he was going to cry. His arms tightened around her until her ribs threatened to break.

"An hour . . . no more than an hour and a half."

"But how?"

"I don't know! All I found was an orange under her bed, like the one—"

"No!" Jack's anguished shout was a physical pain in her ear, then he spun away from her, walking a step or two in one direction, then in another, his arms swinging at the air like a windup toy out of control. "He's got Vicky! He's got Vicky!"

"It's all my fault, Jack. If I'd stayed with her instead of watching that stupid movie, Vicky would be all right now."

Jack suddenly stopped moving. His arms lay quiet against his sides.

"No," he said in a voice that chilled her with its flat, iron tone. "You couldn't have changed the outcome. You'd only be dead." He turned to Abe. "I'll need to borrow your truck, Abe, and I'll also need an inflatable raft with oars. And the highest power field glasses you can find. Got them?"

"Right in the shop." He also was looking at Jack strangely.

"Would you put them in the back of the truck as quick as you can?"

"Sure."

Gia stared at Jack as Abe bustled away toward the front of his store. His abrupt change from near hysteria to this cold dispassionate creature before her was almost as terrifying as Vicky's disappearance.

THE TOMB

"What are you going to do?"

"I'm going to get her back. And then I'm going to see to it that she is never bothered again."

Gia stepped back. For as Jack spoke, he had turned toward her and looked past her, looked downtown as if seeing through all the buildings between him and whoever was in his thoughts. She let out a small cry when she saw his expression.

She was looking at murder. It was as if Death itself had taken human form. That look on Jack's face—she turned away. She couldn't bear it. More rage and fury than any man was meant to hold were concentrated in his eyes. She could almost imagine someone's heart stopping just from looking into those eyes.

Abe slammed the rear doors of his truck and handed Jack a black leather case. "Here are the binocs. The raft's loaded."

The look in Jack's eyes receded. Thank God! She never wanted to see that look again. He slung the binoculars around his neck. "You two wait here while—"

"I'm going with you!" Gia said. She wasn't staying behind while he went to find Vicky.

"And what?" Abe said. "I should stay behind while you two run off with my truck?"

Jack didn't even bother to argue. "Get in, then. But I'm driving."

And drive he did—like a madman: east to Central Park West, down to Broadway, and then along Broadway for a steeplechase ride downtown. Gia was squeezed between Jack and Abe, one hand braced against the dashboard in case they had to stop short, the other against the roof of the truck's cab to keep from bumping her head as they pitched and rolled over the hillocks and potholes in the pavement—New York City streets were no smoother than the rutted dirt roads she used to drive in Iowa.

"Where are we going?" she cried.

"To meet a ship."

"Jack, I'm so frightened. Don't play games with me. What's this have to do with Vicky?"

Jack looked at her hesitantly, then past her to Abe. "You'll both think I'm crazy. I don't need that now."

"Try me," she said. She had to know. What could be crazier than what had already happened tonight?

"All right. But just listen without interrupting me, okay?" He glanced at her and she nodded. His hesitancy was unnerving. He took a deep breath. "Here goes . . ."

26.

Vicky is dead!

As Jack drove and told Abe and Gia his story, that inescapable fact stabbed at his mind. But he kept his eyes fixed on the road and held himself away from the agony of grief that threatened to overwhelm him at any moment.

Grief and rage. They mixed and swirled within him. He wanted to pull over to the curb and bury his face in his arms and weep like a baby. He wanted to ram his fist through the windshield again and again.

Vicky! He was never going to see her again, never do the orange mouth gag, never paint up his hand like Moony for her, never—

Stop it!

He had to stay in control, had to look strong. For Gia's sake. If anyone else had told him that Vicky was missing, he might have gone berserk. But he had remained calm for Gia. He couldn't let her guess what he knew. She wouldn't believe him anyway. Who would? He'd have to break it to her slowly . . . in stages . . . tell her about what he had seen, what he had learned in the past week.

Jack drove relentlessly through the near-empty streets, slowing but never stopping for red lights. It was 2:00 A.M. on a Wednesday morning and there was still traffic about, but not enough to matter. He was headed downtown . . . all the way downtown.

His instincts insisted that Kusum would not leave without the Mother rakosh. He would not want to wait too far from Manhattan. To sail on, even at bottom speed, would mean outdistancing the Mother and leaving her behind. According to Kolabati, the Mother was the key to controlling the nest. So Kusum would wait. But Kusum didn't know that the Mother wasn't coming. Jack was coming instead.

He spoke as calmly as he could as he raced through Times Square, past Union Square, past City Hall, past Trinity Church, ever southward, all the while telling them about an Indian man named Kusum—the one Gia had met at the U.K. reception—whose ancestors were murdered by a Westphalen well over a century ago. This Kusum had come to New York with a ship full of seven- and eight-foot creatures called rakoshi whom he sent out to capture the last members of the Westphalen family.

There was silence in the cab of the panel truck when he finished his story. He glanced over to Gia and Abe. Both were staring at him, their expressions alarmed, their eyes wary.

"I don't blame you," he said. "That's just the way I'd look at somebody who told me what I just told you. But I've been in that ship. I've seen. I'm stuck with it."

Still they said nothing.

And I didn't even tell them about the necklace.

"It's true, damn it!" he shouted. He pulled the Mother's scorched fangs and talons from his pocket and pressed them into Gia's hand.

"Here's all that's left of one."

Gia passed them over to Abe without even looking at them. "Why shouldn't I believe you? Vicky was taken through a window twelve stories up!" She clutched at Jack's arm. "But what does he want with them?"

Jack swallowed spasmodically, unable to speak for a moment. *Vicky's dead!* How could he possibly tell her that?

"I—I don't know," he said finally, his vast experience as a liar standing him in good stead. "But I'm going to find out."

And then there was no more island left—they were at Battery Park, the southern tip of Manhattan. Jack sped along the west side of the park and screeched to the right around a curve at its end. Without slowing, he plowed through a cyclone gate and hurtled across the sand toward the water.

"My truck!" Abe yelled.

"Sorry! I'll get it fixed for you."

Gia let out a yelp as Jack swerved to a stop in the sand. He leaped out and ran to the bulkhead.

Upper New York Bay spread out before him. A gentle breeze fanned his face. Due south, directly ahead, lay the trees and buildings of Governor's Island. To the left, across the mouth of the East River, sat Brooklyn. And far off to the right toward New Jersey, on her own island, stood Lady Liberty with her blazing torch held high. The bay was deserted—no pleasure boats, no Staten Island Ferries, no Circle Line cruisers. Nothing but a dark wasteland of water. Jack fumbled the binoculars out of the case slung around his neck and scanned the bay.

He's out there—he's got to be!

Yet the surface of the bay was lifeless—no movement, no sound but the lapping of the water against the bulkhead. His hands began to tremble as he raked the glasses back and forth over the water.

He's here! He can't get away!

And then he found a ship—directly between him and Governor's Island. On previous passes he had confused its running lights with the lights on the buildings behind it. But this time he caught the glint of the setting moon off its aft superstructure. An adjustment of the glasses brought the long deck into focus. When he saw the single kingpost and its four cranes amidships, he was sure he had her.

"That's it!" he shouted and handed the glasses to Gia. She took them from him with a bewildered look on her face.

He ran to the back of the truck and dragged out the raft. Abe helped him unbox it and activate the CO_2 cartridges. As the flat oval of yellow rubber began to inflate and take shape, Jack slipped into the harness of the flamethrower. His back bothered him hardly at all. He carried the box of incendiary bombs to the bulkhead and checked to make sure he had his variable frequency beeper. He noticed Gia watching him intently.

"Are you okay, Jack?"

In her eyes he thought he detected a hint of the warm feelings she once had for him, but there was doubt there, too.

Here it comes. She means, *"Are you all right in the head?"*

"No, I'm not okay. I won't be okay until I'm through with what I've got to do out there on that ship."

"Are you sure about this? Is Vicky really out there?"

Yes. She's out there. But she's dead. Eaten by—Jack fought the urge to burst out crying.

"Positive."

"Then let's call the Coast Guard or—"

"No!" He couldn't allow that! This was his fight and he was going to do it his way! Like lightning looking for a ground, the rage, the grief, the hatred balled up inside him had to find a target. If he didn't settle this personally with Kusum, it would destroy him. "Don't call anyone. Kusum has diplomatic immunity. Nobody who plays by the rules can get to him. Just leave this to me!"

Gia shrank from him and he realized he was shouting. Abe was standing by the truck with the oars in his hands, staring at him. He must sound crazy. He was close to the edge . . . so close to the edge . . . had to hold on just a little longer . . .

He pulled the now-inflated boat to the edge and pushed it over the side into the water. He sat on the bulkhead and held the boat in position with his feet while he lowered the crate of incendiary bombs onto it. Abe brought the oars over and handed them to him. Jack settled himself into the boat and looked up at his best friend and the woman he loved.

"I want to come with you!" Gia said.

Jack shook his head. That was impossible.

"She's my daughter—I have the right!"

He pushed away from the bulkhead. Leaving the land was like cutting a bond with Gia and Abe. He felt very alone at that moment.

"See you soon," was all he could say.

He began to row out into the bay, keeping his eyes fixed on Gia, only occasionally glancing over his shoulder to make sure he stayed on course toward the black hull of Kusum's ship. The thought that he might be going to his death occurred to him, but he let it pass. He would not admit the possibility of defeat until he had done what he had to do. He would set the bombs first, leaving enough time to find Kusum and settle up personally. He did not want Kusum to die in the blind, indiscriminate, anonymous fury of an incendiary explosion. Kusum must know the agent of his death ... and *why*.

And then what would Jack do? How could he go back to Gia and say those words: *Vicky is dead.* How? Almost better to be demolished with the boat.

The pace of his oars increased as he let the rage mushroom out, smothering his grief, his concern for Gia, consuming him, taking him over. The universe constricted, focused down to this small patch of water, where the only inhabitants were Kusum, his rakoshi, and Jack.

27.

"I'm so scared!" Gia said as she watched Jack and his rubber boat melt into the darkness. She was cold despite the warmth of the night.

"So am I," Abe said, throwing a heavy arm over her trembling shoulders.

"Can this be true? I mean, Vicky is missing and I'm standing here watching Jack row out to a boat to take her back from an Indian madman and a bunch of monsters from Indian folk tales." Her words began to break around sobs that she could not control. "My God, Abe! This can't really be happening!"

Abe tightened his arm around her, but she took scant comfort from the gesture. "It is, kid. It is. But as to what's in that ship, who can say? And that's what's got me shook. Either Jack has gone stark raving mad—and comforting it's not to think of a man that lethal being insane—or he's mentally sound and there actually are such things as the monsters he described. I don't know which frightens me more."

Gia said nothing. She was too occupied with the fear that clawed ferociously at the walls of her brain; fear that she would never see Vicky again. She fought that fear, knowing if she let it through and truly faced the possibility that Vicky might be gone forever, she would die.

"But I'll tell you this," Abe went on. "If your daughter is out there, and if it's humanly possibly to bring her back, Jack will do it. Perhaps he's the only man alive who can."

If that was supposed to comfort Gia, it failed.

28.

Vicky sat alone in the dark, shivering in her torn, wet nightie. It was cold in here. The floor was slimy against her bare feet and the air stank so bad it made her want to throw up. She was utterly miserable. She had never liked to be alone in the dark, but this time alone was better than with one of those monsters.

She had just about cried herself out since her arrival on the ship. There weren't any more tears left. Hope had grown within her when the monster had climbed up the ship's anchor chain, carrying her with it. It hadn't hurt her yet—maybe it just wanted to show her the boat.

Once on the deck, the monster did something strange: it took her to the back of the boat and held her up in the air in front of a bunch of windows high above her there. She had a feeling somebody was looking down at her from behind the windows but she couldn't see anyone. The monster held her up for a long time, then tucked her under its arm and carried her through a door and down flights of metal steps.

As they moved deeper and deeper into the ship, the hope that had sprouted began to wither and die, replaced by despair that slowly turned to horror as the rotten smell of the monster filled the air. But it wasn't coming from this monster. It was coming from beyond the open metal door they were heading for. Vicky began to kick and scream and fight to get free as they moved closer to it, for there were rustling and scraping and grunting sounds coming from the darkness beyond that door. The monster didn't seem to notice her struggles. It stepped through the opening and the stench enveloped her.

The door clanged behind them and locked. There must have been someone or something standing in the shadows behind it as they had passed. And then the monsters were all around her, huge dark forms pressing toward her, reaching for her, baring their teeth, hissing. Vicky's screams faded away, dying in her throat as an explosion of terror stole her voice. They were going to eat her—she could tell!

But the one who carried her wouldn't let the others touch her. It snapped and clawed at them until they finally backed away, but not before her nightie had been torn and her skin scratched in a couple of places. She was carried a ways down a short corridor and then dropped in a small room without any furniture. The door was closed and she had been left alone in the dark, huddling and shivering in the farthest corner.

"I want to go home!" she moaned to no one.

There was movement outside the door, and the things out there seemed to go away. At least she couldn't hear them fighting and hissing and scraping against the door anymore. After awhile she heard another sound, like a chant, but she couldn't make out the words. And then there was more movement out in the corridor.

The door opened. Whimpering with helpless terror, Vicky tried to press herself farther into the unyielding angles of the corner. There was a click and light suddenly filled the room, blazing from the ceiling, blinding her. She hadn't even looked for a light switch. As her eyes adjusted to the glare, she made out a form standing in the doorway. Not a monster—smaller and lighter than a monster. Then her vision cleared.

It was a man! He had a beard and was dressed funny—and she noticed that he only had one arm—but he was a man, not a monster! And he was smiling!

Crying with joy, Vicky jumped up and ran to him.

She was saved!

29.

The child rushed up to him and grabbed his wrist with both of her little hands. She looked up into his eyes.

"You're gonna save me, aren't you, mister? We gotta get out of

337

here! It's full of monsters!''

Kusum was filled with self-loathing as he looked down at her.

This child, this tiny innocent with her salty-wet stringy hair and torn night dress, her wide blue eyes, her eager hopeful face looking to him for rescue—how could he feed her to the rakoshi?

It was too much to ask.

Must she die, too, Goddess?

No answer was forthcoming, for none was necessary. Kusum knew the answer—it was engraved on his soul. The vow would remain unfulfilled as long as a single Westphalen lived. Once the child was gone, he would be one step closer to purifying his karma.

But she's just a child!

Perhaps he should wait. The Mother was not back yet and it was important that she be a part of the ceremony. It disturbed him that she hadn't returned. The only explanation was that she'd had difficulty locating Jack. Kusum could wait for her . . .

No—he had already delayed well over an hour. The rakoshi were assembled and waiting. The ceremony must begin.

Just a child!

Stilling the voice that cried out inside him, Kusum straightened up and smiled once again at the little girl.

"Come with me," he said, lifting her in his arm and carrying her out into the corridor.

He would see that she died quickly and painlessly. He could do that much.

30.

Jack let his raft butt softly against the hull of the ship as he ran through the various frequencies on his beeper. Finally there came a click and a hum from above. The gangway began to lower itself toward him. Jack maneuvered the raft under it, and as soon as it finished its descent, reached up and placed the crate of bombs on the bottom step. With a thin nylon cord between his teeth, he climbed up after it, then tied the raft to the gangway.

He stood and watched the gunwale directly above him, his flame-thrower held at ready. If Kusum had seen the gangway go down, he'd be on his way over to investigate. But no one appeared.

Good. So far, surprise was on his side. He carried the crate to the top of the gangway and crouched there to survey the deck: deserted.

THE TOMB

To his left the entire aft superstructure was dark except for the running lights. Kusum could be standing unseen in the shadows behind the blank windows of the bridge at this very moment. Jack would be exposing himself to discovery by crossing the deck, but it was a risk he had to take. The aft compartments were the most critical areas of the ship. The engines were there, as were the fuel tanks. He wanted to be sure those areas were set for destruction before he moved into the more dangerous cargo holds—where the rakoshi lived.

He hesitated. This was idiocy. This was comic book stuff. What if the rakoshi caught him before he set the bombs? That would let Kusum off free with his boat and his monsters. The sane thing to do was what Gia had said back on shore: Call in the Coast Guard. Or the Harbor Patrol.

But Jack simply could not bring himself to do that. This was between Kusum and him. He could not allow outsiders into the fray. It might seem like madness to everyone else, but there was no other way for him. Gia wouldn't understand it; neither would Abe. He could think of only one other person who would comprehend why it had to be this way. And that, for Jack, was the most frightening part of this whole thing.

Only Kusum Bahkti, the man he had come to destroy, would understand.

Now or never, he told himself as he clipped four bombs to his belt. He stepped onto the deck and sprinted along the starboard gunwale until he reached the superstructure. He had been this route on his first trip aboard the ship. He knew the way and headed directly below.

The engine room was hot and noisy, the big twin diesels idling. Their basso hum vibrated the fillings in his teeth. Jack set the timers on the bombs for 3:45 A.M.—that would give him a little over an hour to do his job and get away. He was familiar with the timers and had confidence in them, yet as he armed each one, he found himself holding his breath and turning his face away. A ridiculous gesture—if the bomb went off in his hands, the heat and force of the blast would incinerate him before he knew it—yet he continued to turn his head.

He placed the first two at the base of each engine. Two more were attached to the fuel tanks. When those four went, the entire stern of the freighter would be a memory. He stopped by the hatch that had taken him into the corridor that led to the rakoshi. That was where Vicky had died. A heaviness settled in his chest. It was still hard to

339

believe she was gone. He pressed his ear against the metal and thought he heard the *Kaka-ji* chant. Visions of what he had seen Monday night—those monsters holding up pieces of torn flesh—swept through his mind, leaving barely-controllable fury in their wake. It was all he could do to restrain himself from starting up his flamethrower and running into the hold, dowsing anything that moved with napalm.

But no ... he might not last a minute doing that. There was no room for emotion here. He had to lock away his feelings and be cool ... *cold*. He had to follow his plan. Had to do this right. Had to make sure not a single rakosh—or its master—escaped alive.

He headed back up toward fresh air and returned to the gangplank. Sure now that Kusum was in the main hold, doing whatever he did with the rakoshi, Jack hefted the somewhat lighter bomb crate onto his shoulder and made no attempt to hide as he strode toward the bow. When he reached the hatch over the forward hold, he lifted the entry port and peered below.

The odor rose and rammed into his nostrils, but he controlled his gag reflex and looked below.

This hold was identical to the other in size and design except that the elevator platform waiting a half-dozen feet below him was in the forward rather than the aft corner. He could hear noises like a litany drifting from the aft hold. In the dim light he saw that the floor of this hold was littered with an incredible amount of debris, but there were no rakoshi down there, neither walking about nor laying on the floor.

He had the forward hold entirely to himself.

Jack lowered himself through the opening. It was a tight squeeze with the flamethrower on his back, and for one awful moment he thought he was trapped in the opening, unable to move up or down, helplessly wedged in place until Kusum found him or the bombs went off. But he pulled free, slipped through, and hauled his bomb crate after him.

Once again he checked the floor of the hold. Finding no sign of rakoshi lurking about, he started the elevator down. It was like a descent into hell. The noise from the other hold grew steadily louder. He could sense an excitement, a hunger in the gutteral noises the rakoshi were making. Whatever ceremony was going on must be reaching its climax. And after it was over they'd probably start returning to this hold. Jack wanted to have his bombs set and be on his way before then. But just in case they came in while he was still here . . . he reached back and opened the valves on his tanks. There was a brief, faint hiss as the carbon dioxide propelled the napalm into the line, then all was silent. He attached three bombs to his belt and waited.

When the platform stopped, Jack stepped off and looked around. The floor here was a mess. Like a garbage dump. There would be no problem finding hiding places for the rest of his bombs among the debris. He wanted to create enough of an inferno in here to spread to the aft hold, trapping all the rakoshi there between the forward and stern explosions.

He stifled a cough. The odor here was worse than anything he had encountered before, even in the other hold. He tried mouth breathing, but the stench laid on his tongue. What made it so bad here? He looked down before taking his first step and saw that the floor was cluttered with the broken remains of countless rakoshi eggs. And among the shell fragments were bones and hair and shreds of clothing. His foot was against what he thought was an unhatched egg; he rolled it over with the tip of his sneaker and found himself staring into the empty eye sockets of a human skull.

Repulsed, he stared around him. He was not alone here.

There were immature rakoshi of varying sizes all about, most of them reclining on the floor, asleep. One near him was awake and active—leisurely teething on a human rib. He hadn't noticed them on the way down because they were so small.

. . . *Kusum's grandchildren* . . .

They seemed to be as unaware of him now as their parents in the other hold had been last night.

Stepping carefully, he made his way toward the opposite corner. There he set and armed a bomb and shoved it beneath a pile of bones and shell fragments. Moving as swiftly and as carefully as possible, he picked his way toward the middle of the stern wall of the hold. He was halfway there when he heard a squeal and felt a sudden, knifing, tearing pain in his left calf. He spun and looked down, reflexively reaching toward the pain. Something was biting him—it had attached itself to his leg like a leech. He pulled at it but succeeded only in making the pain worse. Gritting his teeth, he tore it loose amid a blaze of incredible pain: a walnut-size piece of his leg had come away with it.

He was holding a squirming, writhing, fifteen-inch rakosh around the waist. He must have kicked it or accidentally stepped on it as he

341

THE TOMB

was passing and it had lashed out with its teeth. His pants leg was torn and soaked with blood from where the thing had taken a bite out of him. He held it at arm's length while it kicked and clawed with its tiny talons, its little yellow eyes blazing fury at him. It held a piece of bloody flesh—Jack's flesh—in its mouth. Before his eyes, the miniature horror stuffed the piece of his leg down its throat, then shrieked and snapped at his fingers.

Gagging with revulsion, he hurled the squealing creature across the room. It landed in the debris on the floor among the other sleeping members of its kind.

But they weren't sleeping now. The baby rakosh's screeching had awakened others in the vicinity. As a wave spreading from a stone dropped in a still pool, the creatures began to rustle about him, the stirrings of one disturbing those around it, and so on.

Within minutes Jack found himself facing a sea of immature rakoshi. They couldn't see him, but the little one's alarm had alerted them to the presence of an intruder among them ... an edible intruder. The rakoshi began milling about, searching. They moved toward where they had heard the sound—toward Jack. There must have been a hundred of them converging in his direction. Sooner or later they would stumble upon him. The second bomb was in his hand. He quickly armed it and slid it across the floor toward the wall of the hold, hoping the noise would distract them and give him time to get the flamethrower's discharge tube into position.

It didn't work. One of the smaller rakoshi blundered against his leg and squealed its discovery before biting into him. The rest took up the cry and surged toward him like a foul wave. They leaped at him, their razor-sharp teeth sinking into his thighs, his back, his flanks and arms, ripping, tearing at his flesh. He stumbled backwards, losing his balance, and as he began to go down beneath the furious onslaught he saw a full-grown rakosh, probably alerted by the cries of the young, enter the hold through the starboard passage and race toward him.

He was falling!

Once he was down on the floor he knew he'd be ripped to pieces in seconds. Fighting panic, he twisted around and pulled the discharge tube from under his arm. As he landed on his knees he pointed it away from him, found the rear grip, and pulled the trigger.

The world seemed to explode as a sheet of yellow flame fanned out from him. He twisted left, then right, spraying flaming napalm in a circle. Suddenly he was alone in that circle. He released the trigger.

342

THE TOMB

He had forgotten to check the nozzle adjustment. Instead of a stream of flame, he had released a wide spray. No matter—it had been disturbingly effective. The rakoshi attacking him had either fled screaming or been immolated; those out of range howled and scattered in all directions. The adult had caught the spray over the entire front of its body. A living mass of flame, it lunged away and fled back into the connecting passage, the little ones running before it.

Groaning with the pain from countless lacerations, ignoring the blood that seeped from them, Jack struggled to his feet. He had no choice but to follow. The alarm had been raised. Ready or not, it was time to face Kusum.

31.

Kusum quelled his frustration. The Ceremony of Offering was not going well. It was taking twice as long as usual. He needed the Mother here to lead her younglings.

Where *was* she?

The Westphalen child was quiet, her upper arm trapped in the grip of his right hand, her big, frightened, questioning eyes staring up at him. He could not meet the gaze of those eyes for long—they looked to him for succor and he had nothing to offer but death. She didn't know what was going on between him and the rakoshi, did not comprehend the meaning of the ceremony in which the one about to die was offered up in the name of Kali on behalf of the beloved Ajit and Rupobati, dead since the last century.

Tonight was an especially important ceremony, for it was to be the last of its kind—forever. There would be no more Westphalens after tonight. Ajit and Rupobati would finally be avenged.

As the ceremony finally approached its climax, Kusum sensed a disturbance in the forward hold—the nursery, as it were—off to his right. He was glad to see one of the female rakoshi turn and go down the passage. He hadn't wanted to interrupt the nearly stagnant flow of the ceremony at this point to send one of them to investigate.

He tightened his grip on the child's arm as he raised his voice for the final invocation. It was almost over . . . almost over at last . . .

Suddenly the eyes of the rakoshi were no longer on him. They began to hiss and roar as their attention was drawn to his right. Kusum glanced over and watched in shock as a screaming horde of immature rakoshi poured into the hold from the nursery, followed by a fully-grown rakosh, its body completely aflame. It tumbled in and collapsed on the floor near the elevator platform.

And behind it, striding down the dark passage like the avatar of a vengeful god, came Jack.

Kusum felt his world constrict around him, closing in on his throat, choking off his air.

Jack ... here ... alive! Impossible!

That could only mean that the Mother was dead! But how? How could a single puny human defeat the Mother? And how had Jack found him here? What sort of a man was this?

Or was he a man at all? He was more like an irresistible preternatural force. It was as if the gods had sent him to test Kusum.

The child began struggling in his grasp, screaming, "Jack! Jack!"

32.

Jack froze in disbelief at the sound of that familiar little voice crying his name. And then he saw her.

"Vicky!"

She was alive! Still alive! Jack felt tears pushing at his eyes. For a second he could see only Vicky, then he saw that Kusum held her by the arm. As Jack moved forward, Kusum pulled the squirming child in front of him as a shield.

"Stay calm, Vicks!" he called to her. "I'll get you home soon."

And he would. He swore to the god he had long ago ceased to believe in that he would see Vicky to safety. If she had stayed alive this long, he would take her the rest of the way. If he couldn't fix this, then all his years as Repairman Jack had been for nothing. There was no client here—this was for himself.

Jack glanced into the hold. The crowded rakoshi were oblivious to him; their only concern was the burning rakosh on the floor and their master on the platform. Jack returned his attention to Vicky. As he stepped out of the passage, he failed to notice a rakosh pressed against the wall to his right until he brushed by him. The creature hissed and flailed out wildly with its talons. Jack ducked and fired the flamethrower in a wide arc, catching the outflung arm of the attacking rakosh and moving the stream out into the crowd.

Chaos was the result. The rakoshi panicked, clawing at each other to escape the fire and avoid those who were burning from it.

Jack heard Kusum's voice shouting, "Stop it! Stop it or I'll wring

THE TOMB

her neck!"

He looked up and saw Kusum with his hand around Vicky's throat. Vicky's face reddened and her eyes widened as he lifted her half a foot off the ground to demonstrate.

Jack released the trigger of the flamethrower. He now had a wide area of floor clear to him. Only one rakosh—one with a scarred and distorted lower lip—stayed near the platform. Black smoke rose from the prone forms of a dozen or so burning rakoshi. The air was getting thick.

"Treat her well," Jack said in a tight voice as he backed against the wall. "She's all that's keeping you alive right now."

"What is she to you?"

"I want her safe."

"She is not of your flesh. She is just another member of a society that would exterminate you if it knew you existed, that rejects what you value most. And even this little one here will want you locked away once she is grown. We should not be at war, you and I. We are brothers, voluntary outcasts from the worlds in which we live. We are—"

"Cut the bullshit!" Jack said. "She's mine. I want her!"

Kusum glowered at him. "How did you escape the Mother?"

"I didn't escape her. She's dead. As a matter of fact, I have a couple of her teeth in my pocket. Want them?"

Kusum's face darkened. "Impossible! She—" His voice broke off as he stared at Jack. "That necklace!"

"Your sister's."

"You've killed her, then," he said in a suddenly hushed voice.

"No. She's fine."

"She would never surrender it willingly!"

"She's asleep—doesn't know that I borrowed it for a while."

Kusum barked out a laugh. "So! My whore of a sister will finally reap the rewards of her karma! And how fitting that you should be the instrument of her reckoning!"

Thinking Kusum was distracted, Jack took a step forward. The Indian immediately tightened his grip on Vicky's throat. Through the tangle of her wet stringy hair, Jack saw her eyes wince shut in pain.

"No closer!"

The rakoshi stirred and edged nearer the platform at the sound of Kusum's raised voice.

Jack stepped back. "Sooner or later you're going to lose, Kusum.

345

THE TOMB

Give her up now."

"Why should I lose? I have but to point out your location to the rakoshi and tell them that there stands the slayer of the Mother. The necklace would not protect you then. And though your flamethrower might kill dozens of them, in their frenzy for revenge they would tear you to pieces."

Jack pointed to the bomb slung from his belt. "But what would you do about these?"

Kusum's brow furrowed. "What are you talking about?"

"Incendiary devices. I've planted them all over the ship. All timed to go off at 3:45." He looked at his watch. "It's 3:00 now. Only forty-five minutes to go. How will you ever find them in time?"

"The child will die, too."

Jack saw Vicky's already terrified face blanch as she listened to them. She had to hear—there was no way of shielding her from the truth.

"Better that way than by what you've got planned for her."

Kusum shrugged. "My rakoshi and I will merely swim ashore. Perhaps the child's mother waits there. They ought to find her tasty."

Jack masked his horror at the thought of Gia facing a horde of rakoshi emerging from the bay.

"That won't save your ship. And it will leave your rakoshi without a home and out of your control."

"So," Kusum said after a pause. "A stalemate."

"Right. But if you let the kid go, I'll show you where the bombs are. Then I'll take her home while you take off for India." He didn't want to let Kusum go—he had a score to settle with the Indian—but it was a price he was willing to pay to get Vicky back.

Kusum shook his head. "She's a Westphalen . . . the last surviving Westphalen . . . and I cannot—"

"You're wrong!" Jack cried, grasping at a thread of hope. "She's not the last. Her father is in England! He's . . ."

Kusum shook his head again. "I took care of him last year during my stay at the Consulate in London."

Jack saw Vicky stiffen as her eyes widened.

"My daddy!"

"Hush, child," Kusum said in an incongruously gentle tone. "He was not worthy of a single tear." Then he raised his voice. "So it's still a stalemate, Repairman Jack. But perhaps there is a way we can settle this honorably."

THE TOMB

"Honorably?" Jack felt his rage swell. "How much honor can I expect from a fallen ..."—What was the word Kolabati had used?— "... a fallen *Brachmachari*?"

"She told you of *that*?" Kusum said, his face darkening "Did she also tell you who it was who seduced me into breaking my vow of chastity? Did she say who it was I bedded during those years when I polluted my karma to an almost irredeemable level? No—of course she wouldn't. It was Kolabati herself—my own sister!"

Jack was stunned. "You're lying!"

"Would that I were," he said with a far away look in his eyes. "It seemed so right at the time. After nearly a century of living, my sister seemed to be the only person on earth worth knowing ... certainly the only one left with whom I had anything in common."

"You're crazier than I thought you were!" Jack said.

Kusum smiled sadly. "Ah! Something else my dear sister neglected to mention. She probably told you our parents were killed in 1948 in a train wreck during the chaos following the end of British colonial rule. It's a good story—we cooked it up together. But it's a lie. I was born in 1846. Yes, I said *1846*. Bati was born in 1850. Our parents, whose names adorn the stern of this ship, were killed by Sir Albert Westphalen and his men when they raided the temple of Kali in the hills of northwestern Bengal in 1857. I nearly killed Westphalen then myself, but he was bigger and stronger than the puny twelve-year old boy I was, and nearly severed my left arm from my body. Only the necklace saved me."

Jack's mouth had gone dry while Kusum spoke. The man spoke his madness so casually, so matter-of-factly, with the utter conviction of truth. No doubt because he believed it was truth. What an intricate web of madness he had woven for himself.

"The necklace?" Jack said.

He had to keep him talking. Perhaps he would find an opening, a chance to get Vicky free of his grasp. But he had to keep the rakoshi in mind, too—they kept drawing closer by imperceptible degrees.

"It does more than hide one from rakoshi. It heals ... and preserves. It slows aging. It does not make one invulnerable— Westphalen's men put bullets through my parents' hearts while they were wearing their necklaces and left them just as dead as they would have been without them. But the necklace I wear, the one I removed from my father's corpse after I vowed to avenge him, helped mend my wound. I lost my arm, true, but without the aid of the necklace I

347

would have died. Look at your own wounds. You've been injured before, I am sure. Do they hurt as much as you would expect? Do they bleed as much as they should?"

Warily, Jack glanced down at his arms and legs. They were bloody and they hurt—but nowhere near as much as they should have. And then he remembered how his back and left shoulder had started feeling better soon after he had put on the necklace. He hadn't made the connection until now.

"You now wear one of the two existing necklaces of the Keepers of the Rakoshi. While you wear it, it heals you and slows your aging to a crawl. But take it off, and all those years come tumbling back upon you."

Jack leaped upon an inconsistency. "You said 'two existing necklaces.' What about your grandmother's? The one I returned?"

Kusum laughed. "Haven't you guessed yet? There *is* no grandmother! That was Kolabati herself! *She* was the assault victim! She had been following me to learn where I went at night and got—How do you Americans so eloquently put it?—'Rolled.' She 'got rolled' in the process. That old woman you saw in the hospital was Kolabati, dying of old age without her necklace. Once it was replaced about her neck, she quickly returned to the same state of youth she was when the necklace was stolen from her." He laughed again. "Even as we speak, she grows older and uglier and more feeble by the minute!"

Jack's mind whirled. He tried to ignore what he had been told. It couldn't be true. Kusum was simply trying to distract him, confuse him, and he couldn't allow that. He had to concentrate on Vicky and on getting her to safety. She was looking at him with those big blue eyes of hers, begging him to get her out of here.

"You're only wasting time, Kusum. Those bombs go off in twenty-five minutes."

"True," the Indian said. "And I too grow older with every minute."

Jack noticed then that Kusum's throat was bare. He did look considerably older than Jack remembered him. "Your necklace? . . ."

"I take it off when I address them," he said, gesturing to the rakoshi. "Otherwise they wouldn't be able to see their master."

"You mean 'father,' don't you? Kolabati told me what *Kaka-ji* means."

Kusum's gaze faltered, and for an instant Jack thought this might be his chance. But then it leveled at him again. "What one had once thought unspeakable becomes a duty when the Goddess commands."

"Give me the child!" Jack shouted. This was getting him nowhere. And time was passing on those bomb timers. He could almost hear them ticking away.

"You'll have to earn her, Repairman Jack. A trial by combat ... hand-to-hand combat. I shall prove to you that a rapidly-aging, one-armed Bengali is more than a match for a two-armed American."

Jack stared at him in mute disbelief.

"I'm quite serious," Kusum continued. "You've defiled my sister, invaded my ship, killed my rakoshi. I demand a contest. No weapons—man to man. With the child as prize."

Trial by combat! It was insane! This man was living in the dark ages. How could Jack face Kusum and risk losing the contest—he remembered what one of the Indian's kicks had done to the door in the pilot's quarters—when Vicky's life rode on the outcome? And yet how could he refuse? At least Vicky had a chance if he accepted Kusum's challenge. Jack saw no hope at all for her if he refused.

"You're no match for me," he told Kusum. "It wouldn't be fair. And besides, we don't have time."

"The fairness is my concern. And do not worry about the time—it will be a brief contest. Do you accept?"

Jack studied him. Kusum was very confident—sure, no doubt, that Jack was ignorant of the fact that he fought *savate*-style. He probably figured a kick to the solar plexus, a kick to the face, and it would be all over. Jack could take advantage of that overconfidence.

"Let me get this straight: If I win, Vicky and I can leave unmolested. And if I lose? . . ."

"If you lose, you agree to disarm all the bombs you have set and leave the child with me."

Insane ... yet as much as he loathed to admit it, the idea of hand-to-hand combat with Kusum held a certain perverse appeal. Jack could not still the thrill of anticipation that leaped through him. He wanted to get his hands on this man, wanted to hurt him, damage him. A bullet, a flamethrower, even a knife—all were much too impersonal to repay Kusum for the horrors he had put Vicky through.

"All right," he said in as close to a normal voice as he could manage. "But how do I know you won't sic your pets on me if I win—or as soon as I take this off?" he said, pointing to the flamethrower tanks on his back.

"That would be dishonorable," Kusum said with a frown. "You insult me by even suggesting it. But to ease your suspicions, we will fight on this platform after it has been raised beyond the reach of the rakoshi."

Jack could think of no more objections. He lowered the discharge tube and stepped toward the platform.

Kusum smiled the smile of a cat who has just seen a mouse walk into its dinner dish.

"Vicky stays on the platform with us, right?" Jack said, loosening the straps on his harness.

"Of course. And to show my good will, I'll even let her hold onto my necklace during the contest." He shifted his grip from Vicky's throat to her arm. "It's there on the floor, child. Pick it up."

Hesitantly, Vicky stretched out and picked up the necklace. She held it as if it were a snake.

"I don't want this!" she wailed.

"Just hold onto it, Vicks," Jack told her. "It'll protect you."

Kusum started to pull her back toward him. As he went to return his grip from her arm to her throat, Vicky moved—without warning she cried out and lunged away from him. Kusum snatched for her but she had fear and desperation as allies. Five frantic steps, a flying leap, and she crashed against Jack's chest, clutching at him, screaming:

"Don't let him get me, Jack! Don't let him! Don't let him!"

Got her!

Jack's vision blurred and his voice became lost in the surge of emotion that filled him as he held Vicky's trembling little body against him. He couldn't think—so he reacted. In a single move he raised the discharge tube with his right hand and swung his left arm around behind Vicky to grasp the forward grip, holding her to him while he steadied the tube. He pointed it directly at Kusum.

"Give her back!" Kusum shouted, rushing to the edge of the platform. His sudden movement and raised voice caused the rakoshi to shift, murmur, and edge forward. "She's mine!"

"No way," Jack said softly, finding his voice again as he squeezed Vicky closer. "You're safe, Vicks."

He had her now and no one was going to take her away. No one. He began to back toward the forward hold.

"Stay where you are!" Kusum roared. Spittle flecked his lips—he was so enraged he was actually beginning to foam at the mouth.

THE TOMB

"One more step and I'll tell them where you are. As I said before, they'll tear you to pieces. Now—come up here and face me as we agreed."

Jack shook his head. "I had nothing to lose then. Now I've got Vicky." Agreement or not, he was not going to let her go.

"Have you no honor? You agreed!"

"I lied," Jack said, and pulled the trigger.

The stream of napalm hit Kusum squarely in the chest, spreading over him, engulfing him in flame. He released a long, high, hoarse scream and reached his arm out toward Jack and Vicky as his firey body went rigid. Twisting, writhing convulsively, his features masked in flame, he stumbled forward off the platform, still reaching for them, his obsession with ending the Westphalen line driving him on even in the midst of his death agony. Jack held Vicky's face into his shoulder so she would not see, and was about to give Kusum another blast when he veered off to the side, spinning and whirling in a flaming dance, finally falling dead in front of his rakoshi horde, burning . . . burning . . .

The rakoshi went mad.

If Jack had looked upon the hold as a suburb of hell before, it became one of the inner circles upon the death of the *Kaka-ji*. The rakoshi exploded into frenzied movement, leaping into the air, clawing, tearing at each other. They could not find Jack and Vicky, so they turned on each other. It was as if all of hell's demons had decided to riot. All except one—

The rakosh with the scarred lip remained aloof from the carnage; it stared in their direction as if sensing their presence there, even though it could not see them.

As the struggles of the creatures brought groups of them near, Jack began retreating down the passageway through which he had come, back to the forward hold. A trio of rakoshi, locked in combat, black blood gushing from their wounds, blundered into the passage. Jack sprayed them with the flamethrower, sending them reeling away, then turned and ran.

Before entering the forward hold, he directed a tight stream of flaming napalm ahead of him—first high to drive away any rakoshi that might be lurking outside the end of the passage, then low along the floor to clear the small ones from his path. Putting his head down he charged through the hold along the flaming strip, feeling like a jet cruising along an illuminated runway. At its end he leaped up on the platform and stabbed the Up button.

As the elevator began to rise, Jack tried to put Vicky down on the planking but she wouldn't let go. Her hands were locked onto the fabric of his shirt in a death grip. He was weak and exhausted, but he would carry her the rest of the way if that was what she needed. With his free hand he reached into the crate and armed and set the rest of the bombs for 3:45—less than twenty minutes away.

Rakoshi began to pour into the forward hold through both the port and starboard entries. When they saw the platform rising, they charged it.

"They're coming for me, Jack!" Vicky screamed. "Don't let them get me!"

"Everything's okay, Vicks," he said as soothingly as he could.

He sent out a firey stream that caught a dozen of the creatures in the front rank, and kept the rest of them at bay with well-placed bursts of flame.

When the elevator platform was finally out of range of a rakosh's leap, Jack allowed himself to relax. He dropped to his knees and waited for the platform to reach the top.

Suddenly a rakosh broke free from the crowd and hurtled forward. Startled, Jack rose up and pointed the discharge tube in its direction.

"That's the one that brought me here!" Vicky cried.

Jack recognized the rakosh: It was Scar-lip, making a last ditch effort to get at Vicky. Jack's finger tightened on the trigger, then he saw that it was going to fall short. Its talons narrowly missed the platform but must have caught onto the undercarriage, for the elevator lurched and screeched on its tracks, then continued to rise. Jack didn't know if the rakosh was clinging to the undercarriage or whether it had fallen off into the elevator well below. He wasn't about to peer over the edge to find out—he might lose his face if the rakosh was hanging there.

He carried Vicky to the rear corner of the platform and waited there with the discharge tube trained on the edge of the platform. If the rakosh showed its face he'd burn its head off.

But it didn't appear. And when the elevator stopped at the top of its track, Jack pulled Vicky's hands free to allow her to go up the ladder ahead of him. As they separated, something fell out of the folds of her damp nightgown—Kusum's necklace.

"Here, Vicks," he said, reaching to clasp it around her neck. "Wear this. It'll—"

THE TOMB

"No!" she cried in a shrill voice, pushing his hands away. "I don't like it."

"Please, Vicks. Look—I'm wearing one"

"No!"

She started up the ladder. Jack stuffed the necklace into his pocket and watched her go, continually glancing toward the edge of the platform. The poor kid was frightened of everything now—almost as frightened of the necklace as she was of the rakoshi. He wondered if she'd ever get over this.

Jack waited until Vicky had climbed through the little entry hatch, then he followed, keeping his eyes on the edge of the platform until he reached the top of the ladder. Quickly, almost frantically, he squeezed through into the salty night air.

Vicky grabbed his hand. "Where do we go now, Jack? I can't swim!"

"You don't have to, Vicks," he whispered. Why am I whispering? "I brought us a boat!"

He led her by the hand along the starboard gunwale to the gangway. When she saw the rubber raft below, she needed no further guidance—she let go of his hand and hurried down the steps. Jack glanced back over the deck and froze. He had caught a blur of movement out of the corner of his eye—a shadow had moved near the kingpost standing between the two holds. Or had it? His nerves were frayed to the breaking point. He was ready to see a rakosh .n every shadow.

He followed Vicky down the steps. When he reached bottom, he turned and sprayed the gangway with flame from the halfway point to the top, then arced the stream over the gunwale onto the deck. He kept the flame flowing, swinging it back and forth until the discharge tube coughed and jerked in his hands. The flame sputtered and died. The napalm tank was empty. Only carbon dioxide hissed through the tube. He finished loosening the harness, a job he had begun in the aft hold, and shrugged off the tanks and their appendages, dropping them on the last step of the burning gangway. Better to let it go up with the ship then be found floating in the bay. Then he untied the nylon hawser and pushed off.

Made it!

A wonderful feeling—he and Vicky were alive and off the freighter. And only moments ago he had been ready to give up hope. But they weren't safe yet. They had to be far from the ship, preferably on shore, when those bombs went off.

The oars were still in their locks. Jack grabbed them and began to row, watching the freighter recede into the dark. Manhattan was behind him, drawing nearer with every stroke. Gia and Abe would not be visible for a while yet. Vicky crouched in the stern of the raft, her head swiveling between the freighter and land. It was going to be so good to reunite her with Gia.

Jack rowed harder. The effort caused him pain, but surprisingly little. He should have been in agony from the deep wound behind his left shoulder, from the innumerable lacerations all over his body, and from the avulsions where the skin had simply been torn away by the teeth of the savage little rakoshi. He felt weak from fatigue and blood loss, but he should have lost more—he should have been in near shock from the blood he had lost. The necklace truly seemed to have healing powers.

But could it really keep you young? And let you grow old if it were removed? That could be why Kolabati had refused to lend it to him when they were trapped in the pilot's cabin earlier tonight. Was it possible that Kolabati was slowly turning into an old hag back in his apartment right now? He remembered how Ron Daniels, the mugger, had sworn he hadn't rolled an old lady the night before. Perhaps that explained much of Kolabati's passion for him: It wasn't her grandmother's necklace he had returned—it was Kolabati's! It seemed too incredible to believe ... but he'd said that before.

They were halfway to shore. He took a hand off an oar to reach up and touch the necklace. It might not be a bad thing to keep around. You never knew when you might—

There was a splash over by the freighter.

"What was that?" Jack asked Vicky. "Did you see anything?"

He could see her shake her head in the darkness. "Maybe it was a fish."

"Maybe." Jack didn't know of any fish in Upper New York Bay big enough to make a splash like that. Maybe the flamethrower had fallen off the gangway. That would explain the splash nicely. But try as he might, Jack could not entirely buy that.

A cold clump of dread sprang up between his shoulders and began to spread.

He rowed even harder.

THE TOMB

33.

Gia couldn't keep her hands still. They seemed to move of their own accord, clasping together and unclasping, clenching and unclenching, running over her face, hugging her, climbing in and out of her pockets. She was certain she would go stark raving mad if something didn't happen soon. Jack had been gone forever. How long did they expect her to stand around and do nothing while Vicky was missing?

She had worn a path in the sand along the bulkhead from pacing up and down; now she just stood and stared out at the freighter. It had been a shadow all along, but a few moments ago it had begun to burn—or at least part of it had. A line of flame had zig-zagged along the hull from the deck level almost down to the water. Abe had said it looked like Jack's flamethrower at work, but he didn't know what he was up to. Through the binoculars it looked like a burning gangway and the best he could guess was that Jack was in effect burning a bridge behind him.

And so she waited, more anxious that ever, waiting to see if Jack was bringing back her Vicky. Suddenly she saw it—a spot of yellow on the surface, the rhythmic glint of oars moving in and out of the water.

"Jack!" she called, knowing her voice probably wouldn't carry the distance but unable to contain herself any longer. "Did you find her?"

And then it came, that dear squeaky little voice she loved so: "Mommy! Mommy!"

Joy and relief exploded within her. She burst into tears and stepped to the edge of the bulkhead, ready to leap in. But Abe grabbed her.

"You'll only slow them up," he said, pulling her back. "He's got her, and he'll get here faster if you stay where you are."

Gia could barely control herself. Hearing Vicky's voice was not enough. She had to hold her little girl and touch her and hug her before she could truly believe she had her back. But Abe was right—she had to wait where she was.

Movement of Abe's arm across his face drew her attention away from the water for an instant. He was wiping tears away. Gia threw an arm around his waist and hugged him.

"Just the wind," he said, sniffing. "My eyes have always been sensitive to it.''

Gia nodded and returned her attention to the water. It was as smooth as glass. Not the slightest breeze. The raft was making good speed.

Hurry, Jack . . . I want my Vicky back!

In moments the raft was close enough for her to see Vicky crouched on the far side of Jack, smiling, waving over his shoulder as he rowed, and then the raft was nosing against the bulkhead and Jack was handing Vicky up to her.

Gia clasped Vicky against her. She was real! Yes, it was Vicky, truly Vicky! Euphoric with relief, she spun her around and around, kissing her, squeezing, promising never to let her go ever again.

"I can't breathe, mommy!"

Gia loosened her grip a fraction, but could not let go. Not yet.

Vicky started blabbering in her ear. "A monster stole me from the bedroom, mom! It jumped in the river with me and . . .''

Vicky's words faded away. A monster . . . then Jack wasn't crazy. She looked over to where he stood on the bulkhead next to Abe, smiling at her and Vicky when he wasn't glancing over his shoulder at the water. He looked awful—torn clothes, blood all over him. But he looked proud, too.

"I'll never forget this, Jack,'' she said, her heart ready to burst with gratitude.

"I didn't do it just for you,'' he replied, and glanced back at the water again. What was he looking for? "You're not the only one who loves her, you know.''

"I know.''

He seemed ill at ease. He glanced at his watch.

"Let's get out here, okay? I don't want to be caught standing around when that ship goes up. I want to be in the truck and ready to roll.''

"Goes up?'' Gia didn't understand.

"*Kabloom!* I placed a dozen incendiary bombs throughout the ship—set to go in about five minutes. Take Vicks up to the truck and we'll be right there.'' He and Abe started pulling the raft out of the water.

Gia was opening the door to the panel truck when she heard a loud splash and shouting behind her. She glanced up over the hood and froze in horror at the sight of a dark, dripping, glistening form rising out of the bay. It leaped up on the bulkhead, knocking into Jack and sending him sprawling head first into the sand—it was as if it hadn't even known Jack was there. She heard Abe shout "Good Lord!" as he lifted the raft and shoved it at the creature, but a single swipe of its talons ripped it open. The raft deflated with a whoosh, leaving Abe holding forty pounds of yellow vinyl.

It was one of those rakoshi Jack had told them about. It had to be—there could be no other explanation.

Vicky screamed and buried her face in Gia's neck. "That's the monster that took me, mommy! Don't let it get me!"

The thing was moving toward Abe, towering over him. Abe hurled what was left of the raft at it and backed away. Seemingly from nowhere, a pistol appeared in his hand and he began firing, the noise from the pistol sounding more like pops than shots. Abe fired six times at point blank range, backpedaling all the time. He might as well have been firing blanks for all the notice the thing took of the bullets. Gia gasped as she saw Abe's foot catch on the edge of the bulkhead. He flung out his arms, waving them for balance, looking like an overfed goose trying to fly, and then he fell into the water, disappearing from sight.

The rakosh lost interest in him immediately and turned toward Gia and Vicky. With uncanny accuracy, its eyes focused on them. It rushed forward.

"It's coming for me again, mommy!"

Behind the rakosh, Gia had an instant's view of Jack rolling over and pushing himself to his knees. He was shaking his head and looking around as if unsure of where he was. Then she pushed Vicky into the cab of the truck and climbed in after her. She crawled over to the driver's seat and started the engine, but before she could put it into gear, the rakosh reached the truck.

Gia's screams joined Vicky's as it drove its talons through the metal of the hood and pulled itself up in front of the windshield. In pure desperation she threw the truck into reverse and floored the accelerator. Amid plumes of flying sand, the truck lurched backward, nearly dislodging the rakosh . . .

. . . but not quite. It regained its balance and smashed one of its hands through the windshield, reaching for Vicky through the cascade of bright fragments. Gia lunged to her right to cover Vicky's body with her own. The truck stalled and lurched to a stop. She waited for the talons to tear into her back, but the pain never came. Instead she heard a sound, a cry that was human and yet unlike any sound she had ever heard or wanted to hear from a human throat.

She looked up. The rakosh was still on the hood of the truck, but it was no longer reaching for Vicky. It had withdrawn its hand from the cab and was now trying to dislodge the apparition that clung to its back.

It was Jack. And it was from *his* wide-open mouth that that sound originated. She caught a glimpse of his face above and behind the rakosh's head—so distorted by fury as to verge on the maniacal. She could see the cords standing out in his neck as he reached around the rakosh and clawed at its eyes. The creature twisted back and forth but could not dislodge Jack. Finally it reached back and tore him free, blindly slashing at his chest as it hurled him out of its field of vision.

"Jack!" Gia cried, feeling his pain, realizing that in a few heartbeats she would know it herself, first hand. There was no hope, no way of stopping this thing.

But maybe she could outrun it. She twisted the door handle and crawled out, pulling Vicky after her. The rakosh saw her and climbed up on the roof of the truck. With Vicky clinging to her, Gia began to run, her shoes slipping, dragging, filling with sand. She glanced over her shoulder as she kicked them off and saw the rakosh crouch to leap at her.

And then night turned to day.

The flash preceded the thunder of the explosion. The poised rakosh was silhouetted in the white light that blotted out the stars. Then came the blast. The rakosh turned around and Gia knew she had been given a chance. She ran on.

34.

The pain was three glowing, red-hot irons laid across his chest.

Jack had rolled onto his side and was pushing himself up to a sitting position on the sand when the first explosion came. He saw the rakosh turn toward the flash from the ship, saw Gia start to run.

The stern of the freighter had dissolved into a ball of orange flame as the fuel tanks exploded, quickly followed by a white-hot flash from the forward section—the remaining incendiary bombs going off all at once. Smoke, fire, and debris hurtled skyward from the cracked and listing hull of what had once been the *Ajit-Rupobati*. Jack knew nothing could survive that inferno. Nothing!

The rakoshi were gone, extinct but for one. And that one threatened two of the beings Jack valued most in this world. He had gone berserk when he had seen it reaching through the windshield of the truck for Vicky. It must have been following a command given to it earlier tonight to bring in the one who had drunk the elixir. Vicky was that one—the rakoshi elixir that had been in the orange was still in her system and this rakosh was taking its mission very seriously. Despite the death of its *Kaka-ji,* despite the absence of the Mother, it intended to return Vicky to the freighter.

Splashing noises to his left . . . down by the bulkhead Jack saw Abe pulling himself out of the water and onto the sand. Abe's face was white as he stared up at the rakosh atop the truck. He was seeing something that had no right to exist and he looked dazed. He would be no help.

Gia could not outrun the rakosh, especially not with Vicky in her arms. Jack had to do something—but what? Never before had he felt so helpless, so impotent! He had always been able to make a difference, but not now. He was spent. He knew of no way to stop that thing standing atop Abe's truck. In a moment it would turn and run after Gia . . . and there was nothing he could do about it.

He rose to his knees and groaned with the pain of his latest wounds. Three deep lacerations ran diagonally across his chest and upper abdomen from where the rakosh had slashed him with its talons. The torn front of his shirt was soaked with blood. With a desperate surge of effort, he gained his feet, ready to place himself between Gia and the rakosh. He knew he couldn't stop it, but maybe he could slow it down.

The rakosh leaped off the truck . . . but not after Gia and Vicky, and not toward Abe. It ran to the bulkhead and stood there staring out at the flaming wreckage of its nest. Shards of metal and flaming wood began to pepper the surface of the bay as they returned from the sky, hissing and steaming as they splashed into the water.

As Jack watched, it threw back its head and let loose an unearthly howl, so lost and mournful that Jack almost felt sorry for it. Its family, its world had gone up with the freighter. All points of reference, all that was meaningful in its life—gone. It howled once more, then dove into the water. Powerful strokes propelled it out into the bay, directly toward the pool of flaming oil. Like a loyal Indian wife throwing herself on her husband's funeral pyre, it headed toward Kusum's sunken iron tomb.

Gia had turned and was hurrying toward him with Vicky in her arms. Abe, too, wet and dripping, was walking his way.

359

THE TOMB

"My grandmother used to try to scare me with stories of dybbuks," Abe said breathlessly. "Now I've seen one."

"Are the monsters gone?" Vicky kept saying, her head continually rotating back and forth as she stared into the long shadows thrown by the fire on the bay. "Are the monsters really gone?"

"Is it over?" Gia asked.

"I think so. I hope so." He had been facing away from her. He turned as he answered and she gasped when she saw his front.

"Jack! Your chest!"

He pulled the shreds of his shirt closed over his ripped flesh. The bleeding had stopped and the pain was receding ... due to the necklace, he guessed.

"It's all right. Scratches. Look a lot worse than they are." He heard sirens begin to wail. "If we don't pack this stuff up and get out of here soon, we're going to have to answer a lot of questions."

Together, he and Abe dragged the slashed and deflated raft to the truck and threw it into the back, then they framed Gia and Vicky in the front seat, but this time Abe took the wheel. He knocked out the remains of the shattered windshield with the flat of his palm and started the engine. The sand was packed around the rear wheels but Abe skillfully rocked it out and drove through the gate Jack had rammed open earlier.

"A miracle if we make it uptown without getting pulled over for this windshield."

"Blame it on vandals," Jack told him. He turned to Vicky who lay curled up against her mother, and ran his forefinger along her arm.

"You're safe now, Vicks"

"Yes, she is," Gia said with a small smile as she laid her cheek against the top of Vicky's head. "Thank you, Jack."

Jack saw that the child was sleeping. "It's what I do."

Gia said nothing. Instead, she slipped her free hand into his. Jack looked into her eyes and saw there was no longer any fear there. It was a look he had longed to see. The sight of Vicky sleeping peacefully made all the pain and horror worthwhile; the look in Gia's eyes was a bonus.

She leaned her head back and closed those eyes. "Is it really over?"

"For you, it is. For me ... there's one loose end left."

"The woman," Gia said. It wasn't a question.

Jack nodded, thinking about Kolabati sitting in his apartment, and

360

about what might be happening to her. He reached across Gia to get Abe's attention.

"Drop me off at my place first, will you, Abe? Then take Gia home."

"You can't take care of those wounds by yourself!" she said. "You need a doctor."

"Doctors ask too many questions."

"Then come home with me. Let me clean you up."

"It's a deal. I'll be over as soon as I finish at my place."

Gia's eyes narrowed. "What's so important that you have to see her so soon?"

"I've got some personal property of hers"—he tapped the necklace around his throat—"that has to be returned."

"Can't it wait?"

"Afraid not. I borrowed it without telling her, and I've been told she really needs it."

Gia said nothing.

"I'll be over as soon as I can."

By way of reply, Gia turned her face into the wind coming through the glassless front of the truck and stared stonily ahead.

Jack sighed. How could he explain to her that 'the woman' might be aging years by the hour, might be a drooling senile wreck by now? How could he convince Gia when he couldn't quite convince himself?

The rest of the trip passed in silence. Abe wended his way over to Hudson Street, turned uptown to Eighth Avenue which took him to Central Park West. They saw a few police cars, but none were close enough to notice the missing windshield.

"Thanks for everything, Abe," Jack said as the truck pulled up in front of the brownstone.

"Want me to wait?"

"This may take a while. Thanks again. I'll settle up with you in the morning."

"I'll have the bill ready."

Jack kissed the sleeping Vicky on the head and slid out of the seat. He was stiff and sore.

"Are you coming over?" Gia asked, finally looking at him.

"As soon as I can," he said, glad the invitation was still open. "If you still want me to."

"I want you to."

THE TOMB

"Then I'll be there. Within an hour. I promise."

"You'll be okay?"

He was grateful for her worried expression.

"Sure."

He slammed the door and watched them drive off. Then he began the long climb up to the third floor. When he reached his door, key in hand, he hesitated. A chill crept over him. What was on the other side? What he wanted to find was an empty front room and a young Kolabati asleep in his bed. He would deposit both necklaces on the night stand where she would find them in the morning, then he would leave for Gia's place. That would be the easy way. Kolabati would know her brother was dead without his actually having to tell her. Hopefully, she would be gone when he got back.

Let's make this easy, he thought. *Let something be easy tonight!*

He opened the door and stepped into the front room. It was dark. Even the kitchen light was out. The only illumination was the weak glow leaking down the hall from his bedroom. All he could hear was breathing—rapid, ragged, rattley. It came from the couch. He stepped toward it.

"Kolabati?"

There came a gasp, a cough, and a groan. Someone rose from the couch. Framed in the light from the hall was a wizened, spindly figure with high thin shoulders and kyphotic spine. It stepped toward him. Jack sensed rather than saw an outstretched hand.

"Give it to me!" The voice was little more than a faint rasp, a snake sliding through dry straw. "Give it back to me!"

But the cadence and pronunciation were unmistakable—it was Kolabati.

Jack tried to speak and found his throat locked. With shaking hands he reached around to the back of his neck and removed the necklace. He then pulled Kusum's from his pocket.

"Returning it with interest," he managed to say as he dropped both necklaces into the extended palm, avoiding contact with the skin.

Kolabati either did not realize or did not care that she now possessed both necklaces. She made a slow, tottering turn and hobbled off toward the bedroom. For an instant she was caught in the light from the hall. Jack turned away at the sight of her shrunken body, her stooped shoulders and arthritic joints. Kolabati was an ancient hag. She turned the corner and Jack was alone in the room.

362

THE TOMB

A great lethargy seeped over him. He went over to the chair by the front window that looked out onto the street and sat down.

It's over. Finally over.

Kusum was gone. The rakoshi were gone. Vicky was home safe. Kolabati was turning young again in the bedroom. He found himself possessed by an insistent urge to sneak down the hall and find out what was happening to Kolabati . . . to watch her actually grow young. Maybe then he could believe in magic.

Magic . . . after all he had seen, all he had been through, he still found it difficult to believe in magic. Magic didn't make sense. Magic didn't follow the rules. Magic . . .

What was the use? He couldn't explain the necklaces or the rakoshi. Call them unknowns. Leave it at that.

But still—to actually watch it happening . . .

He went to stand up and found he couldn't. He was too weak. He slumped back and closed his eyes. Sleepy . . .

A sound behind him startled him to alertness. He opened his eyes and realized that he must have dozed off. The hazy skim-milk light of predawn filled the sky. He must have been out for at least an hour. Someone was approaching from the rear. Jack tried to turn to see who it was but found he could only move his head. His shoulders were fixed to the wing back of the chair . . . so weak . . .

"Jack?" It was Kolabati's voice—the Kolabati he knew. The young Kolabati. "Jack, are you all right?"

"Fine," he said. Even his voice was weak.

She came around the chair and looked down at him. Her necklace was back on around her neck. She hadn't got all the way back to the thirty-year old he had known, but she was close. He put her age at somewhere around forty-five now.

"No, you're not! There's blood all over the chair and the floor!"

"I'll be okay."

"Here." She produced the second necklace—Kusum's. "Let me put this on you."

"No!" He didn't want anything to do with Kusum's necklace. Or hers.

"Don't be an idiot! It will strengthen you until you can get to a hospital. All your wounds started bleeding again as soon as you took it off."

She reached to place it around his neck but he twisted his head to block her.

363

THE TOMB

"Don't want it!"

"You're going to die without it, Jack!"

"I'll be fine. I'll heal up—without magic. So please go. Just go."

Her eyes looked sad. "You mean that?"

He nodded.

"We could each have our own necklace. We could have long lives, the two of us. We wouldn't be immortal, but we could live on and on. No sickness, little pain—"

You're a cold one, Kolabati.

Not a thought for her brother—Is he dead? How did he die? Jack could not help but remember how she had told him to get hold of Kusum's necklace and bring it back, saying that without it he would lose control of the rakoshi. That had been the truth in a way—Kusum would no longer have control of the rakoshi because he would die without the necklace. When he contrasted that against Kusum's frantic efforts to find her necklace after she had been mugged, Kolabati came up short. She did not know a debt when she incurred one. She spoke of honor but she had none. Mad as he had been, Kusum was ten times the human being she was.

But he couldn't explain all this to her now. He didn't have the strength. And she probably wouldn't understand anyway.

"Please go."

She snatched the necklace away and held it up. "Very well! I thought you were a man worthy of this, a man willing to stretch his life to the limit and live it to the fullest, but I see I was wrong! So sit there in your pool of blood and fade away if that's what you wish! I have no use for your kind! I never have! I wash my hands of you!"

She tucked the extra necklace into a fold in her sari and strode by him. He heard the apartment door slam and knew he was alone.

Hell hath no fury . . .

Jack tried to straighten himself in the chair. The attempt flashed pain through every inch of his body; the minor effort left his heart pounding and his breath rasping.

Am I dying?

That thought would have brought on a panic response at any other time, but at the moment his brain seemed as unresponsive as his body. Why hadn't he accepted Kolabati's help, even for a short while? Why had he refused? Some sort of grand gesture? What was he trying to prove, sitting here and oozing blood, ruining the carpet as well as the chair? He wasn't thinking clearly.

THE TOMB

It was cold in here—a clammy cold that sank to the bones. He ignored it and thought about the night. He had done good work tonight . . . probably saved the entire subcontinent of India from a nightmare. Not that he cared much about India. Gia and Vicky were the ones that mattered. He had—

The phone rang.

There was no possibility of his answering it.

Who was it—Gia? Maybe. Maybe she was wondering where he was. He hoped so. Maybe she'd come looking for him. Maybe she'd even get here in time. Again, he hoped so. He didn't want to die. He wanted to spend a lot of time with Gia and Vicky. And he wanted to remember tonight. He had made a difference tonight. He had been the deciding factor. He could be proud of that. Even dad would be proud . . . if only he could tell him.

He closed his eyes—it was getting to be too much of an effort to keep them open—and waited.

THIS BOOK
was designed by Stuart David Schiff
typeset, printed, & bound by Montrose Publishing Company
in an edition of 2500 copies,
276 of which are signed by the author and designer.